Maggie McKinnon

Beatrice Smith Samples

PUBLISH
AMERICA

PublishAmerica
Baltimore

ISBN: 1-4241-8077-5
PUBLISHED BY PUBLISHAMERICA, LLLP
www.publishamerica.com
Baltimore

Printed in the United States of America

To my son, Stephen Samples,
and the Pruitts: my son-in-law, Darrell; daughter, Vicki;
grandchildren, Joshua and Michelle—
—the lights of my life.

From the Author

Maggie McKinnon is a novel, a work of fiction. Any resemblance of the characters to any persons either living or dead is purely coincidental.

The towns of Rhyersville and Johnson's Corners are fictitious, and are representative of towns in the Blue Ridge Mountains of North Georgia in the 1800's. The town of Cumming is a historical place. The plantation, Cottonwood, is fictitious, as are Black Haw Mountain and Eagle Mountain.

The song, *Gin a Body Meet a Body/Comin' Thru Th' Rye*, was written in the eighteenth century, by Robert Burns (1759-1796).

The song *Aunt Dinah's Quilting Party* was written mid-nineteenth century, by Stephen Foster (1826-1864).

The song *Amazing Grace* was written in the eighteenth century by John Newton, a slave trader turned Church of England minister, (1725-1807).

All Scripture is from the King James Version of the Holy Bible.

They are all in the public domain.

Are not two sparrows
sold for a farthing?
And not one of them
falls to the ground
without your Father.

Matthew 10:29

Chapter 1

"The war is over! General Lee has surrendered—at the courthouse in Appomattox!"

The words floated through a fog of pain and fatigue. Pain—from the rifle ball lodged in his left leg. Fatigue—from short rations and filthy, cramped living conditions in the Union prison at Front Royal—in the green, fog shrouded mountains of Virginia.

"What's this they're saying? Are they saying the war is over?"

The men around him mumble and shuffle about in their paper-thin shoes, their clothes dirt-smeared and in shreds, glassy-eyed, pale and slack-jawed, all the blood drained from their dirty, bearded faces. There'd been no baths or shaves, little water to drink, just a few rotten scraps of food—for how many weeks now? How long had he been in this filthy Yankee prison? What day was it? He wasn't sure, but he thought the month was April—April, 1865.

Like dark ghosts of their former selves, the men wag their heads as if finding it entirely incomprehensible—that after four years of heart-breaking, gut-wrenching bloody combat—the War between the North and the South was finally over—

"They've signed a treaty!" someone was shouting! "Near Appomattox!"

Early in the day, the rain clouds had begun to gather. High up over the northern tip of the Blue Ridge Mountain range, slowly the clouds grew thicker. In late afternoon they started to rumble southward.

The storm scudded along. Thunder shook the ridges. Jagged bolts of lightening split the black clouds, and then shot into the earth below. The rain roared across the ridges of North Carolina, Tennessee, into northern Georgia. The sheets of rain battered the mountains, inundating the farms nestled below, strewn along the rich valleys like hastily dropped scraps of brightly-colored patchwork.

The rain drenched the thick forests, and filled the mountain creeks to overflowing. In the fertile valleys, the land thirstily drank in the moisture, soaking Indian corn and upland cotton, oat, wheat and barley seeds—inert, and lifeless laying in dry furrows, waiting for the spring rains.

John McKinnon stirred uneasily, shifted his lanky form forward in the hand-carved rocker, hunching his shoulders and gazing into the cavernous depths of the mud-and-rock fireplace. He ran a deeply tanned hand over an angular, clean-shaven face. Like a dog shaking off fleas, he wagged his head. *Over a year* since the war ended! It's spring, 1866, he chided himself. *Leave it be—*

—You're safe now, safe at home in the valley.

On the mantel a tall kerosene lamp glowed, throwing long shadows over the square-log interior of the front room. A spring-wound clock beside the lamp chimed the hour.

A log in the fireplace shifted sending showers of red-hot sparks billowing up. Most of them died harmlessly on the stone hearth. John started to rise. A stab of pain in his left leg brought him up short. The ball from a Yankee Enfield rifle, still there, after all this time. Too close to a major artery to risk surgery, the doctors had said. He pulled himself erect, pushing down the pain—must be going to rain. With a slight limp, John McKinnon moved to the thick-paned window beside the fireplace, and stood attempting to look out. His head felt groggy. With a slight jolt of shock John realized he must have dozed off. How could he, at a time like *this*!

His first child was about to be born—!

No—not his first child—his *third*—but this would be the first child he had watched grow—prior to the delivery, the *first*—!

Of course he'd fallen asleep, he reasoned—he'd just had *the dream* again. He glanced toward the worn yellow-pine stairway leading to the second story. John sighed. Then he turned and gazed out the window. He'd been asleep all right! It was already raining cats and dogs out there. He's relieved, about the rain, and more than a little pleased. The downpour is a soft, steady rain. It wouldn't run off taking precious topsoil along with it, but it would soak into the freshly plowed fields. John fervently hoped this would be a good year for the McKinnons—the *first* crop since he came home from the War. Maybe this year the upland cotton would grow thick with bolls—and no yellow leaf. And the Indian corn would be laden with ears—free of worms.

He was not exactly a praying man, not since the War. But, "Thank you, God, for the rain!" John whispered.

And thank God for the farm! John peered out through the thick glass pane. The clock on the mantel chimed five o'clock. Still dark outside, so he couldn't actually see anything, but in his mind, he saw that across the road lay the pasture, then the creek. And beyond the creek, stretched his fields. John had sixty acres all told—twenty in improved land (cropland), and forty in unimproved (forest and pastureland.) Not a great deal, but it had served the McKinnons for three generations.

- - - - - - - - - -

Shawn Ian McKinnon, a tall, lank young Scotsman of eighteen, with a shock of dark hair and golden hazel eyes, arrived in the port of Charleston, South Carolina, in the fall of 1826. Shawn had a rucksack with a change of clothes in it, a worn Bible, and a small hoard of money—and a strong determination to make a good life for himself in America. He'd heard about the fine farmland in the interior, soil rich and black and deep as your knee— and free for the taking. He'd heard about the forests—tall and green and endless—where the sun never hit the forest floor.

By some odd twist of fate (but Shawn was a Christian man and didn't believe in fate) before *The Last Farewell* docked in Charleston, Shawn found himself attached to a young Irish lass—named Katherine Ann McCoullough. Katherine Ann's parents had both come down with the fever not long after the worm-eaten ship sailed, and Katherine Ann was alone, with no kin, no plans, headed for a strange, foreign land.

To compound her problems, the other passengers aboard *The Last Farewell* had decided Katherine Ann McCoullough was cursed.

When the corpses of her parents were swallowed, one right after the other, by the rolling dark swells of the Atlantic, Katherine Ann screwed up her face and shook both her hands toward heaven. In a loud, piercing shriek, Katherine Ann let out a hair-raising string of wails.

After that, no one would come near Katherine Ann. Forsaking nourishment and sleep, refusing to stay below with the other women, Katherine roamed the decks like a lost soul. She grew pale and thin. By day, the winds off the sea made her red-blond hair stand out from her head, and her clothes swirl about her eerily. At night, she walked through the fog that drifted over the decks, like some pale ghost, making the rigging of the sails sough and groan—and even the hardened sailors' hearts failed them.

But Shawn McKinnon was not a superstitious man. Shawn felt that with all the goodness of God he felt welling up inside him, no spell or curse could touch him. To Shawn, Katherine Ann McCoullough was simply a lost waif, crying out for consolation.

His heart breaking, Shawn approached her one night, amidst the creaking of the rigging, the curling of the cold, drifting fog. He reached out and took one of her cold, thin hands. As if in a dream, Katherine Ann turned to gaze at him. Even in the pale light of the distant moon, Shawn could see pain deep in the blue eyes. Shawn drew her into his arms, and began to croon softly, as if soothing a frightened child.

> *Gin a body meet a body*
> *Comin' Thru th' Rye*
> *Gin a body kiss a body*
> *Need a body cry*
> *Ilka Lassie has her laddie*
> *Nane, they say, hae I*
> *Yet a' th' lads they smile at me*
> *When Comin' thru th' rye*

As soon as *The Last Farewell* docked in Charleston, Shawn and Katherine Ann disembarked, and went in search of a Protestant minister. In a small church, in the Parish of St. Michael, they sealed their nuptials.

Shawn and Katherine Ann pooled their meager funds, searched over Charleston and found a pair of skinny oxen no one else would buy—but which Shawn felt with fair treatment and proper feed, he could put to good use. Shawn had a way with animals. He also bought a rickety wagon with a bow frame and graying, mildewed cover with only one hole in it.

Since Shawn and Katherine Ann would be traveling in Indian Territory, from an ironmonger on the edge of town, Shawn purchased a musket—and some powder and shot. He also bought some tools he knew he would need— a hammer, an axe and an adz, a shovel, and a plow and hoe. The ironmonger also sold Shawn a big box of rusted iron tools for one dollar. What some of them were, Shaw had no idea. And afterwards, he wondered if the odd tools were a blessing from God—or if the ironmonger just wanted Shawn to haul off his scrap-iron.

With what little remained of their precious money, Shawn purchased a sack of dried beans, some flour, two tin cups, forks and plates and a battered pewter washpan.

Katherine Ann brought to the marriage what little money her parents left, their and her clothes, two woolen blankets, a black iron Dutch oven—all packed away in a huge brown leather trunk. When Shawn saw the trunk, he wagged his head in stunned amazement.

"*Kathering Ann!* 'Ee expec' mee ta' tak' tha' thin' along?"

"If ye be takin' me, Shawn McKinnon—*ye be takin'* me trunk!"

With a rough map given them by the ironmonger, Shawn headed his team of oxen towards the uplands. Having been warned to avoid the Military Road recently built by the Federal Government to funnel troops through the Cherokee Indian Territory, Shawn followed what appeared to be the most traveled civilian road. But rains had washed out deep ruts, and there was a toll of one dollar for a wagon and team crossing a river by ferry. So Shawn took the back roads, sending his team of oxen splashing through the shallowest fords of rivers and creeks, with Katherine Ann hanging on for dear life.

An axle broke, and the right front wheel cast a spoke, and the weather turned bad making roads impassable. So Shawn and Katherine were forced to winter near an Indian Village named *Tomatly*, in the mountains of North Carolina, on a river called the *Little Tennessee*. Mostly, the Indians of *Tomatly* fed them through the winter. The Cherokee women taught Katherine how to gather ginseng for medicine, and how to dig the roots of the sassafras tree for healing tea. They also taught her what berries were edible, and what other barks and herbs were useful remedies for the body.

With the coming of spring, Katherine Ann informed Shawn that they were going to have a child. Shawn looked towards the cloud-shrouded mountains to the north. They made his heart pound. They reminded him so much of Scotland—except that these were covered with dense timber. He was searching for a secluded valley where he could settle and rear a family, somewhere in these mountains.

But the higher they climbed, the more anxious Katherine Ann became. As the rickety covered wagon perilously ascended immense mountain scarps that seemed to reach to the sky, she clung to the high wagon seat, twisting her hands and anxiously peering down into vast canyons and bottomless gorges choked with dense growth. Silently she prayed, *God have mercy!* And she gritted her teeth.

Late one evening as they stood outside the wagon and gazed over the smoky ridges that reached into the clouds and seemed to go on forever—like a dark rolling ocean with no end—Katherine Ann turned to Shawn. She leaned against him, clinging to him like a frightened child, chewing her lips.

"Just ye *look* at it, Shawn!" she muttered. "*All* those mighty mountains, with scarce 'ary a road or a trail or any folk to be found! We 'ave a *child* coming! I'm afraid we'll become *lost*, and starve—and our bones will be stripped by the buzzards!"

"Kathering Ann," Shawn chided his young wife, holding her close, "where's 'eer faith? Hae 'ee na read that part of the Book that says:

> *"Are not two sparrows sold for a farthing? And not one of them falls to the ground without your Father?"*

"I *try* to have faith, Shawn, aye, I do," Katherine Ann whispered, her lips trembling, "but when night's coming on—and I look out over these prodigious mountains, my heart fails—!"

"I didn't marry 'ee to mak' 'ee unhappy, Kathering. Tomorrow, we'll leave these smoky mountains, if tha's wha' 'ee wan's." Shawn pulled her close, whispering, "Anyhow, God has already tol' me ta go. I wan' a real home. I will'na ha' nae chil' o' mine born in a makeshift camp in th' middle o' nowhere."

"But, Shawn? *Where* can we go?" Katherine Ann sighed, her blue eyes large in a pale, thin face, her belly already swollen beneath her thin dress.

"We'll head south. God has tol' me, Kathering, that we'll *find* a home, somewhere in these mountains. We'll find a place that's not been claimed. And I'll build 'eee a fine cabin against th' wind and th' cold, wher' ee'll feel safe."

"Can we *do* that, Shawn McKinnon? *All* this is yet *Cherokee* Country."

"I dunne' see why not! Look at all th' farms we saw on our way upcountry. You think, Kathering Ann, any o' them men paid for tha' lan'?"

Shawn and Katherine drifted southward, down scarps and over ridges, through narrow gaps scarcely wide enough to accommodate a lone rider, much less a covered wagon. They passed through Indian villages with odd names neither of them could remember. Camping here and there, they lived on game, wild greens and berries, corn the Indians gave them—and odd jobs that Shawn picked up or small trades he made with the few wagons they met.

Shawn could shoe a horse, as well as repair a cart or wagon. He could mend harness and rigging. He even traded off some of the spurious iron tools the ironmonger had gotten off on him. Things for which he though they'd never have any earthly use.

Finally Shawn entered through a tall gap in the mountains, and was told he had left the state of Tennessee and was back in North Carolina. The mountains were still prodigious, and prodigious were the snows that sometimes fell in winter, Shawn was told.

In the summer of 1827, to her great relief and immeasurable joy, Katherine Ann gave birth to a healthy baby boy. Shawn waited until he felt she was able to travel. Then he announced one afternoon:

"Pack up 'eer things, Kathering Ann. These high mountains don't offer much in the way of suitable farmlan'. God has tol' me not to stay here, but to go farther south, where the snow doesn't lie deep, or the winters get as cold. We won' stop, until we've foun' our valley."

With a sinking heart, Katherine Ann clung nervously to the high wagon seat, clutching to her breast little Thomas Shawn McKinnon. Katherine Ann had begun to fear that the constant travel would never cease. She began to entertain grave doubts—that the Almighty *really* talked to Shawn Ian McKinnon.

There followed more weeks of travel. Slowly the tallest mountains fell behind them. They stopped so that Shawn could mend a wheel on a passing wagon.

"What be this place called? 'Ereee we still in North Carolina?"

"Nope. Just a few miles back, when you drove through that gap," the leather-faced traveler drawled, "you crossed into a part of th' Cherokee Territory called *Georgia.*"

That afternoon, Shawn drove his thin, half-spavined team of oxen into a lovely valley that stretched for miles along the edge of a creek twenty feet wide. The mountains were still beautiful here, but not that high. The creek ran clear as crystal, from a spring higher up in the Blue Ridges.

The valley stretched before them most of the afternoon. It stood knee-deep in grass. Here and there stood the remnants of Indian dwellings—their cane summer houses, as well as clay-domed winter houses.

Abandoned fields lay alongside the creek, where Indians had grown their tobacco, corn, beans and pumpkins. A few nubbins of corn still clung stubbornly to dry stalks. Here and there lay a half-rotten pumpkin. Beans dried, their shells popping open. Such a fine valley! Shawn wondered why the Indians abandoned it. He wondered if it was because of some sickness—

But in the past months, the farther north and west they had traveled, Shawn noticed that many Indian villages had been left with empty houses and deserted fields. Some of the Cherokee had abandoned their communal villages, and had set up individual farms, many of which appeared as prosperous as any English farms. The largest, most impressive of these, Shawn was informed, belonged to the mixed-blood Cherokees—those who had intermarried with the whites.

Shawn moved Katherine Ann and their infant son into one of the abandoned Indian houses in the broad, beautiful valley. He fortified the little cane hut with stout poles and pine branches, and daubed the cane and poles with thick, red river clay, to shut out the cold of the coming winter.

Shawn became so pressed in keeping body and soul together with what he could grow off the few seeds he gleaned from the Indian fields—a handful here and there to eat—and a handful to plant—and with what game he could snare and shoot, that the abandoned Indian summer house was their only shelter for several years.

The *voice* kept telling Shawn, *"This is still Indian Territory, don't get too attached to any particular spot. Don't sink your roots too deep. Yet—"*

Then word came over the mountains—gold had been discovered, in a place to the southwest they called *Dahlonega*. Men flocked into the region of the gold strike.

Meanwhile, Shawn was informed that the State of Georgia had laid claim to all Cherokee land within its borders. They passed a law that every white man who wished to remain in Indian Territory must sign a pledge swearing allegiance to the State of Georgia. If he refused, he must leave the territory, or he would be thrown into jail.

Shawn McKinnon signed.

Then Shawn heard that all the Cherokees were being rounded up, like cattle, and herded into corrals—to be sent west of the Mississippi River; that is, all those who had not escaped into the remote fastness of the high mountains to the north.

The Cherokee Nation valiantly resisted this illegal seizure of vast lands guaranteed to them forever by Federal treaty. Some of the more educated mixed-blood chiefs contested the matter—carrying their case to the United States Supreme Court.

Of course, as everyone had expected, the State of Georgia won. Now, within that vast territory they had occupied for more than a thousand years, there remained only scattered pockets of Cherokee families—those who could prove they had some legal claim to the land by intermarriage with whites, those who had fled and disappeared into the smoky ridges of the inaccessible mountains to the north, where troops found it impossible to rout them out.

When Shawn McKinnon heard this disturbing news, he gazed around at the little Indian dwelling that had sheltered him and his family. He thought of all the Cherokees who had given him handouts over the past few years. He thought of the Indian corn and beans he and his little family had subsisted on. A great sadness overwhelmed him.

But this soon passed.

In the year 1832, news came over the hills that the Cherokee Territory was to be surveyed, and parceled out in forty, sixty, and one-hundred-sixty-acre lots. Some of these, those within the vicinity of the gold strike, were to be termed *Gold Lots*.

A land lottery would be held. To enter the lottery, a man must have been a resident of the State of Georgia for at least four years.

By some great stroke of fortune—or as Shawn put it, by the Mighty Grace of God—Shawn just met this requirement.

Shawn McKinnon declared to Katherine Ann that it was due solely to the hand of God that he drew a plot in the very valley where they had fortified the Indian summer house. The plot Shawn drew in the lottery was a little farther on up the valley, but that was fine with Shawn. Now he would have *free and clear title* to *his* land.

Shawn drove his team into his own valley. They lived in the big sheet-covered wagon, mended many times, sleeping beneath the curving bows, until the cabin was well roofed with split-oak shingles.

Sleeping snugly between his father and mother lay little Thomas Shawn McKinnon, born in the summer of 1827.

By the time Thomas was six years old, Shawn had cleared enough rich land along the river and the creek to plant several acres of Indian corn, and some tobacco and pumpkins and beans. He had felled enough giant timbers to construct a large two-room cabin of square-hewn logs. He also erected a big, stout barn, a row of chicken coops—and an outhouse, decently placed so it would not be seen from his new road coming through the low gap in the mountains and leading into his farmyard. He built a little oak-shingled house over the spring back of the cabin, so Katherine Ann could keep her milk and butter cold and safe from critters. He even built a few bee gums—into which Katherine Ann lured a hive of wild bees that produced wax for candles and sweet honey for the table.

A few days before they moved into the new cabin, Shawn did what he thought was possibly the dumbest thing he had ever done in his life. He bartered away a good skinning knife for a fiddle and a bow from a passing trader down at the crossroads where the new man, Johnson, was operating a ferry across the river.

What on earth did he need with a bow and a fiddle, out here in the middle of nowhere—in the wilderness of the North Georgia Mountains? He needed that about as much as he needed to grow a pair of horns!

In fact, Shawn was soon to learn the horns might have come in handier. He couldn't learn to play even the simplest tune, not even *Comin' thru' th' Rye,* a song his Pa had taught him when he was no taller than a sprig of straw, a song he had known by heart since he was two years old—on that stupid fiddle.

When he had the cabin finished, Shawn brought in their meager belongings—the straw-stuffed mattress, the bed frame he had fashioned from logs and strung with deer-hide thongs, and the puncheon table and benches.

And, of course, there was Katherine Ann's big brown leather trunk.

The trunk rested its great bulk against the wall, not far from the fireplace, where Shawn had put the heavy iron hook for Katherine Ann to hang her cooking pots on.

Shawn took the useless fiddle and hung the offensive instrument on the front-room wall, off to one side in the shadows, where he wouldn't have to look at it so much, and be reminded of his stupidity and folly. Think of all the other things they needed—more than they needed that stupid fiddle. But Kathrine seemed to enjoy gazing at it of a long winter's night. Her father, she told Shawn, had played the fiddle gloriously. She would take it down now and again, dust it and rub its fine finish. And she would absently draw a small finger along the strings. Shawn wondered if it made her think of being in Ireland—with her Pa and Ma still alive.

The fiddle hung there, on its two pine pegs, the wood darkening slightly, gathering dust, for, after moving into the cabin, there was so much to be done in the valley, that Katherine Ann clean forgot to dust the fiddle.

One day as Shawn walked up on the front porch and knocked the field mud off his boots, he heard a queer whining and scraping noise from inside. It sounded something like an angry cat makes when it's cornered. Shawn panicked. A panther had gotten into the house! Before he could unlatch the door and thrust it open, the sound leveled out. Suddenly it became a soft, quivering, lilting thing that made his hair stand on end. It was that beautiful.

His ruddy face filled with wonder, Shawn ran a tanned hand through his long mop of dark curly hair and stepped inside, not knowing what to expect.

On the floor of the front room, the firelight flickering off the fiddle and its tiny player, sat little Thomas—

—His face like that of an angel, his hair still light, like his mother's, the bow hovering light as a dove's wing, wielded by that tiny hand.

"See, Shawn?" Kathrine announced proudly, sitting atop her big brown trunk, a dressed deer hide for a cushion, her face wreathed in a big smile:

"*See! Tha's* why God had 'eee buy th' fiddle."

Chapter 2

He planned on rearing a big family, so Thomas Shawn McKinnon added a second story to the square-hewn log house that his Pa, Shawn, had built.

Thomas had married a wife named Mary Margaret O'Hirlahy, from over the ridges, in Lumpkin County—where Thomas had gone one fall to look over the gold fields he'd heard his father talk about.

But Thomas hadn't liked the gold fields. By the year 1842, the Cherokee tribe of Indians was long gone. And by 1843, most of the gold—first discovered in 1828, and the reason the Indians were all ordered out—had all but been worked out of the mountains. Small pockets were left here and there. But there was not enough for Thomas to get excited about.

After the surveying of the Territory for the land lottery, the Territory had been divided into ten or so counties. Other changes had come. To the west, they had begun building something—with huge oak timbers resting atop beds of thick gravel, and with massive iron rails spiked on—called the *Western and Atlantic Railroad*. Thomas heard that giant, wheeled carriages linked together would use it. It ran through a town called *Chattanooga* up on the Tennessee River, to a place somewhere on down on the Chattahoochee River—which soon came to be called *Terminus*. Thomas thought that was sure a queer name for a town.

By 1844, Thomas' attention turned elsewhere. Mary Margaret was expecting their first child.

In the summer of 1845, John Thomas McKinnon was born.

The fall of 1847, roughly two years later, came little Kathleen Ann. And Thomas heard that the thriving town down on the Chattahoochee called Terminus had been re-named. Now, it was called *Marthasville*.

John Thomas flourished. Kathleen Ann took sick of some unknown aliment and died when she was two. Probably the same type of fever, Thomas supposed, that had taken his Pa, Shawn, three years earlier.

His heart heavy as lead in his chest, Thomas Shawn McKinnon told Mary Margaret, "Well, she's gone. Our little wee one is gone."

He knocked together a little hand-hewn pine-plank casket and carried it up the hill on his shoulder, his farm shovel in his free hand.

It was a long way to anything that resembled a proper burial ground. So when Shawn had died, Thomas walked the little mountain back of the house, searching for a proper burying spot. Someplace where Pa could rest, his face toward the rising sun—from where the great trumpet would one day be sounded and the dead in Christ would rise. Here, Shawn McKinnon could rest, and just turn his head a little sideways, and see spread out below him, the breadth and width of the valley he searched so long to find.

Thomas had found a little flat sort of plateau, atop the first mountain rise back of the cabin. Here he and Mary Margaret had laid Shawn to rest. And not long afterwards, Katherine Ann followed. She died of a broken heart, Mary Margaret told Thomas—she had no desire to live, without Shawn.

Now, here little Kathleen could turn her head from the rising sun, and look down on the valley below—where lay the farmstead of her Papa and Mama, passed from Grandpapa and Grandmamma. So, Thomas brought the little pine casket he had built—still smelling of fresh resin—up the side of the mountain, into the shade of the sweetgum grove.

Mary Margaret spoke a few words from the Bible old Shawn had hauled all the way over from Scotland—which Thomas could not read, there being no schools and not much of anything else in the Cherokee Territory when Ma and Pa settled here. And though his Ma, Kathrine Ann, could read, she never took the bother to teach Thomas.

But Mary Margaret could read, so Shawn's Bible became hers.

Thomas and Mary Margaret clasped hands. Together, they sang an old hymn. Then Thomas threw in the dirt.

The grave looked so small. And it looked so barren, where she lay, that Thomas wondered if anybody would ever know that his sweet little baby girl lay here on the side of this mountain.

Standing there the day he buried his only baby daughter, tears blurring his vision, Thomas looked at the tall rocks he had stood on end at the head and foot of both Pa's and Ma's graves. He swore to himself that the first good crop he brought in, he'd go somewhere to a stone mason—and buy carved headstones for his family. After all, Thomas told Mary Margaret, sitting on the front porch that night, a person went through so much, just to get through this life, that a person's final resting place should be permanently marked— to at least show that he'd been here. Shawn and Katherine deserved that, he said.

To say nothing of sweet, sweet Kathleen. Mary Margaret agreed.

The years came and went. Not much changed in the mountains. Except that more and more folks came in every year, settling in the river valleys— where the remnants of the Cherokee villages still stood. But still the mountains were so vast, the valleys so numerous, folks were pretty widely scattered. But despite that, little towns sprang up—here and there—in the valleys.

A little community grew up, down by what was called Johnson's Corners—where the ferry crossed the river. It was ten miles or more away from Thomas' and Mary Margaret's place.

Then a man named Rhyer bought a place a few miles up the river—no more than three or four miles up the valley. He built a little store. Not as big as the General Store down at Johnson's Corners, where the ferry ran.

But the fellow down at Johnson's Corners built a water-powered grist mill—for grinding Indian corn and wheat and oats, and such. It was something, to see that giant water wheel spill its sparking load!

Then somebody started calling the place with the small store *Rhyersville*. The Rhyer family offered to donate a few acres for the building of a school not too far from the little store—if enough men in the immediate vicinity would donate labor and a few logs, in order to raise one.

The little school was built in the middle of a field that Mr. Rhyer no longer cultivated—since opening his store. He also handled mail service. There was a stagecoach that came through about twice a month, going on down to Johnson's Ferry. And where it went to from there, Thomas had no idea. Probably on down country, to that place they called Marthasville for a while, but now, he had heard, was called *Atlanta*.

A few of the families put their heads together. They decided that since they already had the little log cabin for a school—why not let it double as a church, now and again, on a Sunday? That is, if they could get some itinerant Baptist preacher to visit the place occasionally.

But Thomas soon learned that not many children attended the school. And on some Sundays when the circuit preacher was supposed to stand, he didn't even put in an appearance. So attendance was sort of haphazard and erratic. And the school charged tuition. So that left a lot of the mountain folk completely out.

Not that they didn't desire that their growing families be good, educated Christians, they just simply had not the time, the energy, or the money to afford it.

Impassible roads when the rains came, and still few if any bridges—to say nothing of fewer paying passengers—soon led to the demise of the stagecoach line.

But mail routes by horseback were established.

And a tiny Post Office rose beside the little store and the little school/ church at Rhyersville.

They were good years, mostly, for Thomas and Mary Margaret McKinnon. The cows dropped down strong calves. Crops filled the furrows of the growing plots beyond the trees and the creek.

John Thomas grew tall and strong.

Almost as soon as he could stand, John pointed to the fiddle Shawn had bought. Thomas had taken the fiddle out of the shadows, but since his father died, he could seldom bear to play it. He came in to lunch one day, and found the boy toddling about on fat little legs, the old wood fiddle literally dragging the puncheon floor from one hand, the horsehair bow from the other.

"Hey! Hey, there, fella! That's no way to handle a fine instrument. Now, let your Pa show you a little thing or two—"

Patiently Thomas tuned the instrument. Between the two of them, on rainy days and Sunday afternoons, Shawn's fiddle took on new life—

Comin' Thru' th' Rye, Green Grow the Rushes, Lock Lomond, Aunt Dinah's Quiltin' Party—

—And some tunes Thomas picked up and had no earthly idea what their names were, where they had originated, or whether they just flew out of his head.

Sometimes Thomas would take his fiddle along, when he went down to the mill at Johnson's Corners. And as the men sat around waiting for their grain to be ground, they would strike up this tune and that, sometimes lounging about in the sun on the front porch or steps of the General Store, sometimes sitting in the back, on sacks of Indian corn or wheat. Two or three of them had fiddles, two had banjos. One had a harpsichord, and another had a French harp.

As John grew, he took to riding along with Pa, down to Johnson's Corners. When they struck up the music, Thomas would hand his son the fiddle, and John began playing more and more. Soon, every free minute was spent tuning and fiddling, until John Thomas was the best fiddler in the county.

"I wish Pa could come back—and hear his grandson sawing on that old fiddle of his, just once," Thomas said to Mary Margaret one Sunday afternoon. They were resting on the wide front porch Thomas had added to the place, in the two rockers he had carved from seasoned maple, and bottomed with split oak. Young John sat on the steps, playing away.

"Why, Thomas McKinnon," Mary Margaret teased. "You bein' such a fine Christian man—and your Pa, Shawn, bein' even a finer one—you know good and well your Pa can hear John Thomas—clear as a bell, even way up in God's heaven!"

It was the fall of the year 1860.

"The boy likes the fiddle so well, I believe I'll just *give* it to him. And then …one day soon…John'll get the land," Thomas told Mary Margaret one day as he stood gazing out the front door. A slight rain had begun to fall—over the tall oaks in the front yard, on the fields by the creek, down the road through the gap.

"Thomas Shawn McKinnon!" Mary Margaret fairly yelled at him. She stood speechless—behind him, in the shadows of the front room. Young John was sitting on the old brown leather trunk, across the room, with the fiddle.

The fire crackled. John looked up, saw his father turn, his dark eyes sadly gazing at his wife.

Mary Margaret had gone white as ashes.

"What a strange thing to say, Thomas," she moistened dry lip, "and you just now in the prime of your life."

"You know what I mean, Mary Margaret!" Thomas' voice sounded angry. His gold-flecked brown eyes urging her to understand, he said, "All this past year, you've heard the talk. You know what's buildin' over th' mountains. There's a *war* comin.' All th' men down at the store and mill say so. It's somethin' about this *slavery* thing—"

"Well, Thomas…I mean…well!" Mary Margaret floundered about, searching for words. "That won't affect *us*. How many people do *we* know who have *slaves?* Nobody we ever heard of—except for one or two over in the next county, maybe!"

"Makes no never mind, Mary Margaret," Thomas insisted, "whether there be slaves in this part of the mountains or not—if a war breaks out, you think them Northern soldiers are going to stop to find out the difference between them that's got—and them that's not got—slaves? When they come down that road a shootin'—they're goin' ta shoot *anythin'* that moves—and that includes *us and ours.* That is, if we don't stop 'em, and don't ever let 'em get this far."

"Thomas!"

"War's comin', Mary Margaret. And it'll sweep th' whole country like wildfire."

"You hush, now Thomas," Mary Margaret ordered, "and come on in the house. I'll warm up the leftover beans and corn pone for supper. John Thomas, you go on and draw up the buttermilk from the well. And while you're at it, pull an onion and pick a tomato or two from the garden."

Mary Margaret never forgot that fine spring day. The day they heard the news—

—The first shots of the war they were calling a *Civil War*, were fired, at a fort called Sumter, down in South Carolina.

Then, it was on a dry day in July, when Thomas mentioned the War again. Mary Margaret knew Thomas had been to some sort of muster, two or three times, down at the little schoolhouse.

But, still, she never expected to hear it—that July afternoon.

"Well, it's here, Mary Margaret. Come the twenty-first of the month, I'll be goin'."

"Nooooo, Thomasss!!!"

"Now, hear me out, woman!" Thomas lifted one brown hand to silence his wife's keening wail. "You know sometimes things just have to be done. And this is one of 'em. But, before I go marchin' off to this war, there's somethin' I have to do. I promised myself that I'd put proper markers on Pa's and Ma's graves. And I want one for little Kathleen. Time's passed, and money's been scarce, but before I march away to this war—from which I might not come back—I want to keep that promise. Now, I know money's tight, but it might mean a lot to John, here, and his children."

"Well, Thomas," Mary Margaret smiled as she fought back the tears, "we've got plenty to take care of that." When she said it, Mary Margaret knew it was a lie. But Thomas was talking about marching off to war *and not coming back*!

23

John McKinnon, just sixteen years old, helped his father load the heavy hunks of granite onto the one-horse farm sled, and together they pushed and pulled and urged the horse, dragging the heavy headstones up the slope back of the house.

The headstones in place, Thomas took a long look at the three graves, then out across the valley that spread before him, so beautiful in the July sun. The Indian corn was high in the fields beyond the pasture. He had walked the fields this morning. Upland cotton was greening up with plump bolls, down by the creek.

The bottomland was lush with peas—and with oats needed for the table and for feed for the stock. In the pasture, tall rye grew for grazing.

He had hoped to spend his remaining years, here in McKinnon Valley.

The next morning—after a breakfast that neither of the three of them touched—Mary Margaret rose from the table. Brushing away her tears with the tail of her apron, she tried to busy herself with packing Thomas a big lunch. He'd scarcely touched his biscuit, or ham and eggs.

Tears in her eyes so hot she could scarcely see, she determined she would *not* let Thomas see her cry. She took the sack lunch out onto the porch, and stood waiting. In her mind, she could see Thomas, taking down Shawn's old musket from its pegs over the fireplace, just above the ancient blunderbuss. There had never seemed much need to invest in newer firearms, just for shooting an occasional wild turkey, raccoon, hawk, or some marauding wildlife. They'd never been in a *War*—

There was so much pain, so much sorrow in Mary Margaret's eyes, when she turned to him that hot July day to hand him his lunch, that Thomas almost changed his mind about going. Maybe they could go up in the mountains and hide—

But the Yankees were coming—and there was no getting around it.

"Has it really come to this?" Mary Margaret sighed, blue eyes brimming, choking back her tears.

Thomas reached out, and barely touched her hand. He feared that if he took her in his arms, he might not go.

"Goodbye, Mary Margaret," he said.

Slamming his sweat-stained hat down hard on his head, Thomas stepped off the porch.

Shawn's ancient, half-rusty musket slung over one shoulder, his powder bag strung on a stout deer-hide thong over the other, and in his pocket a tin box filled with lead shot, Thomas McKinnon marched down the road.

Margaret watched as Thomas disappeared through the gap. Not a breath of air stirred down from the mountains. She felt as if she might choke, standing here on the porch. She sighed, wiped her eyes on her apron tail, and went back into the kitchen.

She received a sketchy letter from Thomas, written for him by some soldier completely unknown to Mary Margaret. Thomas had found out, when he met the other men at the schoolhouse, that he wouldn't need the weapon or ammunition, and had left them at the Rhyersville Store, he wrote, for Mary Margaret to pick up.

He had been taken to a place called Norcross, Georgia. On the eleventh day of August, he was mustered into Company H, of the Flint Hill Greys. Then from there, the company was sent immediately, by rail, to a place called Stone Mountain.

Thomas was furnished with an Enfield musket, a bayonet, leather slings and bayonet scabbard, leather belt and a cartridge box. The letter went on to say that Thomas was doing mighty fine, for he had also been furnished with a mess-kit, a blanket roll and twelve pounds of straw—for his bed on the ground.

His company would be given a few weeks of military training. By early October, they would be considered trained soldiers, ready for combat—and shipped out, to Yorktown, Virginia.

Mary Margaret never heard from him again.

Then, not long after Thomas had gone, after she had gone to the store and picked up the musket and the powder and shot, and she had just about gotten to where she didn't cry all day, could kind of sleep part of the night—

—Here stood John Thomas McKinnon—sixteen years old—staring at her with his boyish, tanned face, declaring in a choked whisper:

"*I can't stay at home, Mama*, not with Papa gone off to fight the War. I'd feel like a coward and a shirker."

"But, John," Mary Margaret protested, "you're just a boy!"

"I'm going off to war, Mama. And then I'll be coming back home. I want something to fight for—and something to come back home to."

"John! You're just *sixteen*!"

"I intend on marryin' Callie Sue Perkins. From over near Johnson's Corners? I've been walkin' out with her—now and again."

"John, you haven't—?"

"'Course not, Mama." Then all in a rush: "Callie Sue's a good Christian girl. The only girl I'll ever want. Grandpa Shawn married Katherine Ann when she was just fourteen. I love Callie, and she loves me. And if I'm old enough to go to war, I'm old enough to marry. And I'm marrying Callie Sue Perkins."

John Thomas and Callie Sue had a week, before John took the old musket down and the powder horn and the shot.

"You go on and take it," Mary Margaret insisted, "just in case they run out and you don't get a weapon to defend yourself with!"

"I'll take it," John told his mother, "if that will satisfy you, Mama. But, I'll probably just leave it down at the Rhyersville Store, the way Pa did."

Mary Margaret grabbed her son, even if he was sixteen. She clutched him so tightly John laughed:

"If you don't let go of me, Mama, I'll not live to see the fightin'. You'll just choke me to death here on th' front steps."

Reluctantly, Mary Margaret released her grip. Then she backed away.

Wiping her face with her apron tail, she smiled at her only son and asked, "Where's Callie, isn't she coming down to see you off?"

"Callie's feeling poorly, Mama. She says she can't bear to watch me walk down that road."

"All right, John." Mary Margaret put her right hand against her young son's chest, and pushed him gently toward the door—

"—You go on, John Thomas, if you feel that's God's callin' on your life."

"What about you, Ma? And Callie? Who'll look after y'all?"

"Ever since Shawn and Katherine Ann set foot in this valley, John Thomas, God's been here, too. Besides, Son, scarcely 'ary a soul knows or cares about this valley—'ceptin God and us. Who's gonna bother us, way over here? You go on, now, and we'll be just fine—just fine. I'll look after Callie. And the Good Lord will take care of us both."

John Thomas hesitated on the front doorsteps. He reached up and gave Mama a quick hug. Then, "You'll probably get the gun back, Mama. I'll no doubt be issued one, just like Pa. And that'll be a good thing. You might need to slaughter a hog, or kill a wild turkey." He thought but didn't say—there might be bears and panthers comin' round—

—And Yankees.

Mary Margaret did the very best she could, to take care of all three of them, for scarcely had John been gone a month, than Mary Margaret knew that her son John Thomas was going to be a father.

Almost nine months to the day that John marched away, his first daughter was born.

Callie Sue McKinnon deferred to her mother-in-law, who had been so wonderful to her. She let Mary Margaret name the little girl.

"She'll be little Nellie, like from the song John loves to sing, and play on the fiddle so much. And Sue—after yourself."

"You mean—?"

Mary Margaret sang a couple of bars—

> *And 'twas from Aunt Dinah's quiltin' party ...*
> *I was seeing Nellie home ...*

A few months after John's first child was born, his mother, Mary Margaret came down with a fever. She soon slept by her only daughter, Little Kathleen, in a corner of the graveyard—not far from where Shawn and Katherine Ann lay.

———

John McKinnon would walk up there sometimes, his bad leg slowing his progress up the steep slope. He would look at the McKinnon family grave plot and wonder where, exactly, *did* his father's bones lay—somewhere in Virginia—where the dirty Yankees had shot him dead.

But, then, maybe there had been time and opportunity—for the men of Company H to bury his body?

John knew there had been no time or thought for burial in that nightmarish bloodletting disaster they had called *The War Between the States*. His father wasn't the only Rebel whose bones lay bleaching in some forgotten pile of mosses and lichens. He would glance down the hill, see the house, the barn and outbuildings, the little dirt road winding up the slight hill—and on through the gap—

How well John recalled that day. The day he had finally come marching home—

Callie had been in the barnyard, pouring what meager feed she had left into the cow trough.

She patted the cow absently, thinking how thin she was getting. Soon be no milk, if she didn't get more feed.

Callie looked up. There was some stranger coming through the gap. He moved very slowly, as if walking with a very painful limp. He leaned heavily on a stick he seemed to be using for a crutch. Matted dark hair and scraggly beard hid most of his face.

Then as he moved slowly, painfully closer, Callie thought maybe she should reach for the loaded musket she always kept handy, since that night the Yankees came—

But he didn't seem to pose much of a threat, as he progressed painfully down the slope from the gap. She could make out the tatters and rags hanging off his gaunt frame.

He seemed to struggle so, as if each step might well be his last. He stopped two or three times, to catch his breath. Callie was afraid the young stranger would expire, right there in her road. *Oh, God! Please*, she prayed, *I don't want to have to bury him!*

He stumbled, and it looked as if he was about to collapse. He made a feeble attempt to stand, lifting his right hand, waving it in some sort of greeting. Callie lifted her hand, shading her eyes, to get a better look at the ragged skeleton that had once been a man.

Moving closer, now, he began to sing in a strained voice:

> *If a body, meet a body...*
> *Comin' thru th' rye...*
> *If a body, kiss a body...*
> *Need a body cry...*

"*John!*

The milk pail banging against her thigh, Callie was hurtling herself forward—through the barnyard gate, through the thin fall sunlight streaming through the trees.

They had had one night—he had stolen away from his company when they were moving across a ridge up in Tennessee—since John had marched away—four long years ago.

"How close am I, to home?" John had kept wondering, as they had marched that day. It was rumored the Yanks might make a push south, in a desperate attempt to break the supply lines—the railroad—

I won't be gone long—John had told himself—just long enough to see Callie. He couldn't even recall afterwards, how long he had been away—exactly how he had gotten away with it. He could have been shot. Going AWOL. But the world was so crazy. The Company so frazzled and disorganized, no one seemed to notice when John returned, that he had been missing.

"John!" She was crying, hanging on to him, and burying her face in the sweet stink of him.

"The war's over, they said," John whispered hoarsely into her hair. "They all went crazy. They piled onto every wagon or cart, every freight car—anything heading south. But there wasn't room, for half the men. All headed in the same direction—"

"Oh, no, John! You had to *walk* home?" Callie gasped.

"It was either that—or stay in Virginia."

Callie released him, seized with horror.

"Sorry it took me so long." John grinned at her through his dirty beard, "Guess you thought I wasn't coming back—I kinda lost track of time—

"—Didn't know where I was, half the time. What month is it?"

"It's *July!* Oh, Thank God, John! Just Thank God! You made it back home!" Callie heard herself blubbering on.

"Yeah," John rasped. "So many of them didn't. Pa fell somewhere—in Virginia, I heard. Never could learn exactly where."

"John! Don't talk about that now. You're *half-dead!* Let's get you into the house! Get some hot food into you—"

Callie had talked on. But John hadn't listened.

Four long years of blood and starvation and suffering—

But when he had entered the gap and walked down the road, having no idea what he would find—there stood the log house—not burned down by the Yankees! Then Callie, out at the barnyard doing the milking, had seen him—their place, she said, hadn't been confiscated by the Federals!

John had Callie in his arms, crushing her to his chest as best he could, with her laughing and crying and spilling warm milk all over them both. Then she was insisting he go into the house. She'd get some food into him. She'd clean him up.

His mind was going around and around today over the same thoughts.

"No, honey," John remembered whispering into her hair that smelled of hay and warm milk, "all that can wait. For now, Callie, let me just hold on to you—"

All those years without her sweetness against him, he had barely been able to stand—

—Callie was saying, "Some folk can scarcely keep body and soul together. Borrowing from Peter to pay Paul. Hand to mouth existence. No meal in the meal chest. No meat in the saltbox. No horse to pull the wagon—if the Yankees didn't take the wagon along behind them. Which most likely they did—steal the wagon. The War left us much better off than most, John, you're home! And we still have the house, and the land. We didn't get our salt allotment, though, the way soldiers' families were supposed to—"

When he entered the house that day, Katherine Ann's heavy, iron Dutch oven that Shawn had hauled all over the mountains from Charleston still sat on the hearth beside the fireplace.

Callie dragged John into the kitchen, sat him down at the old oak table, and shoved food in front of him. She talked and laughed. Suddenly she stopped, buried her face in her apron, and just sobbed uncontrollably.

John, too weak to rise, said softly, "Callie! Don't, honey! I'm all right! It's all right now! I'm home."

"I'm almost afraid—to look at you, John McKinnon!" Callie had sobbed so he could scarcely make out her words, "I'm afraid—you'll just up—and disappear—the way you have on so many nights when I reached for you—!"

A little girl appeared in the kitchen doorway. Her hair was gold-blond, her skin creamy pink. She had the most beautiful blue-green eyes.

"Come, here, precious. Com'on, Nellie Sue. This is your Daddy! Daddy's come home from the War!"

The child looked so strange, standing in the door in her little white dress. Like a dream from another world. John had gotten his mother's letters, then Callie's when she was able to write. Callie had a hard pregnancy. Then the baby was born—a little girl—with hair and skin like Grandma Katherine's—

Suddenly there was a sharp insistent cry from somewhere up the stairs.

"What—?" John stared at Callie dumbly. "Yes, John," Callie laughed at him, such pure joy in her eyes.

Callie raced upstairs, and returned carrying a wiggling, protesting child—a girl—in her arms. She started to hand the child to John, but knew instantly his frail frame could not bear even Barbara Jo's slight weight.

"Remember the night you showed up, in '63, banging on the door in the middle of the night? I thought for sure we were about to be set upon by a band of thieving Yankees!" Callie broke off short, staring at John.

He looked as if he was about to faint.

"Anyhow, Mr. John McKinnon," she hurried on, "meet your youngest daughter, Barbara Jo!"

John scarcely saw the child.

"The Yankees were here!" the little blond girl spoke up.

John had forgotten all about her. He realized with a shock that his oldest daughter was speaking to him—for the first time in his life—

"We heard a racket out in the barn. Mama looked out the window, with me right behind her, and we could see them, plain as day. They stole nearly all the chickens. Then they took the horse. But Mama went out after them—and got him back."

"Callie?"

"It wasn't nearly as bad as it sounds, John." Callie laughed, nervously swiveling her gaze from his face to the baby in her arms. Then she looked up. "It was nothing really, John. They snatched some of the chickens from their roost, and then led the horse from the stable. They went on down across the yard, into the pasture, across the creek, where they made camp." She paused. John was staring at her as if he was about to swoon.

"We could see their fires burning from here," the little blond girl piped up, "and then Mama says, 'Them thieves are not takin' my horse—not with me with spring plowin' ta do—'

"—She snatched her shawl off the wall, and out the door she flew!"

The little blond girl seemed to have finished her story.

John was afraid to speak, for fear his heart would fail him.

"I just walked into the edge of the woods, into the fringe of light comin' from their campfires. There must have been about two dozen of them—no more than that." Callie gave a quick, dismissive wag of her head, as if two dozen well armed Yankee soldiers were nothing to give account to—

"TWO DOZEN?" John gasped, then he lost his voice.

"No more than that," Callie replied quietly. "I saw the horse, tied to a young oak tree, but I knew I'd have to make myself known, otherwise, if they heard someone sneaking about, they'd most likely shoot me. So I just called to them from the shadows—

"'—Hallow! Hallow th' Camp!' Most of them scrambled to their feet. Dirty, hadn't had a bath for a long time, I could tell. They all looked at me— then they all looked at each other.

"'Gentlemen,' I said, 'I've come for my horse—the one you just stole from my barn! I'm takin' him back! I've got two little girls waitin' in that house, and I won't see them starve! And without this horse, they surely will!' I never looked back. I just took the horse and walked on home."

"ARRRRRGGGGGGGHHHHHHH!!!!!" John screeched, just before he fainted.

Chapter 3

The trees on the mountain behind the house turned to fiery balls of orange. The grasses down in the pasture lost some of their green. The days became shorter. The nights longer. John grew a bit more used to sleeping on a feather mattress, and to eating three times a day—although Callie apologized profusely at each meal for setting before a husband just returned from the War such poor and sorry fare.

"Callie," he said to her one day, taking her pretty face between his two painfully thin hands, "this food is just fine. You wouldn't believe, Callie, how many times I dreamed of just this—sitting at my own table, with you bustling about behind me. A good fire in the cookstove. Coffee brewing, even if it is *parched-acorn coffee*. Food steaming—no mind if it's wild greens. No mind at all, Callie. Just sit your pretty little self down here beside me, and let me look at you."

The days and nights passed. Fall came. John put on a little weight. His bones no longer protruded through his skin. His wound seemed to improve. Then winter was coming on, and with scarcely any food left, he built rabbit boxes, snared birds, trapped turtles and squirrels. He even began to think of hitching up the horse and doing a little plowing for a winter garden.

"No," Callie insisted, "not yet, John. I'll scratch in the few turnip seeds I've got left. I'll rob the bee gums, then go up on the mountains, dig some sassafras roots for tea. Look for nuts and acorns and honey locust pods. You just listen out for the girls. They're down for their nap." John didn't tell Callie, but he'd much rather have been plowing.

On his better days, John would take the little trail that led east from his place, and walk the half-mile or so down to the river. He'd hang a cane pole with a worm on it, off the grassy bank where he and Thomas had sat so many afternoons fishing. John didn't think he'd ever been happier. Nobody knows, he would say to himself, how much his home means to him, a sound roof over his head and food in his belly every day, even wild greens and acorn dumplings, until he loses it all.

Some days, John would just sit on the front porch, and watch the birds sail out over the barn, then on over the pasture and down the creek.

The Yankee thieves had missed a few chickens—three hens and one rooster. One day one of the precious hens went missing, and John went searching for her.

"I found that hen, Callie," he said as he entered the kitchen door. "She's built herself a nest—way up under the front porch—hidin' away her eggs and *settin'* on 'em. You want me to break up her nest and roust her out? We need th' eggs."

"Leave that settin' hen be, John! When th' eggs hatch, and th' biddies grow—if we can find somethin' to feed 'em—we'll soon having frying chickens again!"

Most days Callie bustled about with the little girl always at her heels, or hanging onto her dress tail. The little child would gaze at John, her eyes wide—at first with fright—a bit later on, with pure curiosity. But she seldom said a word. As she sat on the floor playing, she would look up at John when he rose to knock the ashes from his pipe into the fireplace. She'd look as if she wanted to say something, but was waiting expectantly for John to speak first.

But John didn't speak. He could find *nothing* to say to the child. She was beautiful. And she was *his*. He knew this very well. But she didn't *seem* like his—she didn't *look* like his—she didn't *feel* like his.

Maybe, he told himself, it was because he never *saw* Callie while she was carrying little Nellie Sue—wasn't that what they had named her?

As the days passed, John worried and chewed over this—that he felt little or no connection to the little blond girl playing about at his feet—in his house—that he felt so numb and distant from her. He could never even bring himself to pick her up, hold her on his lap, like he recalled Thomas had done with him. And the second child, the one Callie had named Barbara Jo, she was just beginning to stand and walk on her own without falling over her own feet.

John would watch her sometimes, still crawling as often as walking. He would feel a sharp stab of guilt. She seemed even more distant to him than the other child. He hadn't even known a thing about her—until he came walking home. Or had he received a letter from Callie telling him he had another child? Everything had been so blurred and blood-smeared those last two years. Scant rest. Scant food, just enough to keep body and soul together. Maybe he did know about the child.

John was aware that Callie watched him—with the children. This heightened his sense of guilt and unease. What did Callie expect him to say …to the little blond girl …or the one toddling about his feet? When John looked at them, they only served to remind him how much this War had taken out of his life. He left home, in '61, a boy of sixteen. He returned, in '65, an old man of twenty.

But, he told himself, he shouldn't grumble. Be thankful he was alive, in a fine, snug farmhouse, with a wife who loved him—and two healthy baby girls.

Now, they were sitting on the floor just in front of him. The little blond one, named Nellie Sue, smiled at him suddenly—and John thought he heard the angels singing. That's how sweet she looked, her hair like a halo about the little head, the firelight behind her, like a sweet apparition a man would die to claim for his own.

And sitting beside her, leaning forward now to pick up a stuffed rag doll Callie had made, the child they had named Barbara Jo. Her hair was just beginning to grow a bit. It was straight—but fine. She wasn't as pretty as the other one, but, then, what were looks? She didn't have the angelic glow of the little blond. Her eyes were more demanding, John thought, than trusting. Or loving. She kept staring at him, making John grow terribly uncomfortable. *What did the child expect of him?* He'd been home now for several weeks, and he still didn't even *know* her! She could have belonged to any man on earth!

NO! John, you know that's not true. She's yours, John, she's yours.

As winter drew on, John's health slowly improved. Somehow, they had food on the table—a few dried beans, and, a real treat for John, an occasional yam or Irish potato Callie had dug up in the fall. And dried apples and peaches Callie had scrounged from the orchard before the hog that Callie had turned loose on the mountain to forage for himself, got them. John watched the hog closely, waiting for cold, hog-killing weather to arrive, so all that meat wouldn't spoil. He could almost taste fresh ham and sausage. But a few weeks back, before hog-killing weather came—the hog had simply disappeared.

And John wondered who got him—stray Yankees troops still occupying the state? Or a band of rogue Rebels—come home to nothing—and starving after the War?

As John grew stronger, he scoured the mountains for fallen logs. He still couldn't chop down a tree, but he could break apart the fallen logs with his axe.

He would walk about the front of the house—then around back. He would go out and inspect the barn, the corncrib, and the smokehouse—the saltbox empty now of hams and middlings. But he'd soon take care of that. And then John wondered how on earth he was going to buy a pig to raise—when he had not one cent to his name, nothing to barter, and was near starvation? And should he be able to plow and plant by the time spring came, how could he put in crops—without one cotton or corn seed—or a pound of fertilizer or side dressing? He began to pray in earnest, that by February, he'd be strong enough to begin breaking ground for spring planting.

Somehow, he'd have to come up with some fertilizer and seed. He might have to take out a loan—until he could get the farm up and going again.

It was cold, when John stepped off the low porch. He could hear Callie inside, cleaning up after breakfast. Several years before the war, Thomas had bartered a fine hog, for Mary Margaret a huge iron cookstove. Now, banging about the big cookstove, Callie was talking to the little girls in a low, lilting voice, with such love in her voice it made John's eyes tear up and a great lump rise in his throat. It shot him through with guilt. Why couldn't *he* do that? Why couldn't *he* pick them up, and cuddle them, and talk to them? John sighed to himself—in time, maybe the healing would come. Today, just go on up and see about your Grandpa's and Grandma's graves—and little Kathleen's—and Mama's.

As John climbed, his left leg, bothering him today, began to throb painfully, and several times he was forced to sit down and rest beside the path. Although it was cold, sweat popped out on his forehead. His bad leg began to tremble, shaky as mush. He'd never in his life imagined he could be in such sorry shape.

Finally, he reached the little plateau. He could see that most of the leaves had fallen. The graves were completely covered. Weeds grew almost up to his shoulder. His first thought was why did Callie let this place get in such poor shape?

Immediately, John chided himself. The woman had kept the farm going. Had looked after—then buried—John's mother, Mary Margaret. Had birthed and cared for two little babies! Had even brazenly snatched her horse back from a pack of thieving *Yankees*! How much did he expect from one pretty little blond-haired woman?

Contrite, stricken to his soul—John leaned against a sweetgum tree, and struggled to pray. This wasn't at all easy.

How many prayers? He couldn't count how many prayers he had sent heavenward—in all those awful years, on those cruel, desperate marches of death. How many had he whispered at night, as he lay in the darkness, the rain, the mud, and the blood?

How many, as he had watched …as men were blown apart …

But that was all in the past. Surely, he could forgive God—if God could forgive him.

"We'll make a mutual pact!" John shouted to a vast blue sky dotted with puffs of white.

John pulled some of the tallest weeds, so that he could at least read the names on the granite markers:

Shawn McKinnon	Katherine Ann McKinnon	Kathleen McKinnon
Born 1808	Born 1812	Born 1847
Died 1844	Died 1845	Died 1849

Beside Kathleen, John saw a grave with no marker, just rocks at the head and the foot. He knew this was his mother's. Due to what men called the *Civil War,* John thought angrily, Mary Margaret would forever lie alone. When he was able, he could at least get her a headstone.

John often wondered where that name came from. What on earth was *'civil'* about that war?

John made his way slowly back down towards the house.

Once he reached level ground, his leg didn't ache that much.

———————

A few fish on his string, John entered the kitchen, washed his hands at the washstand beside the stove. He was glad that Pa had dug a well close to the house, so the womenfolk no longer had to fetch water—and their milk and butter—from the spring house up on the hill, overgrown now with wild muscadine and honeysuckle vines.

Callie came up behind him, her arms encircling his waist.

"John Thomas McKinnon," Callie whispered, "how would you feel if I told you—you're going to be a father, again?"

John didn't even bother to dry his hands. He just turned around, took Callie in his arms, and whispered softly into her hair:

"When?"

"Come spring, John. Come the time of spring, the baby will be here."

From that day forward, John's step seemed lighter. The awful dreams came less often.

He immediately began carving a new cradle. He was having a baby! He would *feel* it, moving beneath the touch of his fingers! *His* baby!

Only Callie had been here for the growing and birthing of the other two, but this time—this time—

—*This child would be his!*

John closed his eyes, and leaned back in the hand-carved rocker. Now, Callie's time had finally come.

He had kept his quiet vigil, through most of the night. He'd heard nothing but an occasional moan, throughout the long night. He had received no word from upstairs. How long had it been—since he'd ridden over to the Thomas place and fetched Lizzie Thomas? Hours and hours! John attempted to pray.

He got up from the rocker, walked over, lifted the latch, and opened the front door.

The rain had stopped. The air rushed in, cool against his face, crisp and clean, carrying the scent of the mountains, of wet grasses and trees and fields.

John sighed, and stepped out onto the front porch, down the front steps and around the side of the house, where a little lean-to sheltered the stacked firewood from the rain. Light had begun to break over the mountains to the east. Balancing a load of dry oak logs on his arms, John stepped back inside. He threw a couple of logs on the fire. It began to crackle and leap and roar. He'd better not put on any more wood for a while.

He heard steps on the stairway. It was the little girl, Nellie Sue. Her blond hair hanging about her in glossy waves, she clutched her rag doll, fear in her eyes—that had gotten even greener since John came home.

"What on earth are you doing up, sugar? It's way too early for you. You go on now, go on back up to bed."

"Is Mama all right? Is Mama going to be all right?" Nellie Sue mumbled anxiously, a hand half covering her mouth.

"Sure, honey, sure. Your Mama's going to be just fine. Now! Shoo!"

John watched until the little blond girl disappeared at the top of the stair landing. Then, John turned and paced nervously back and forth, from the fireplace to the front door.

More steps. This time, it was Mrs. Thomas—!

"Well, John!" Lizzie Thomas' voice boomed cheerily as she made her way slowly down the steep stairway, balancing her considerable bulk carefully on each narrow tread.

"You've done it again! You've gone and got yourself another beautiful baby girl!" Her round face bathed in sweat, Mrs. Thomas smiled broadly as she progressed slowly downward. But before she reached the foot of the stairs, John was yelling at the top of his lungs.

"Callie! Callie, honey!"

John pushed his way past Mrs. Thomas, went tearing up the stairs—despite his bad leg—taking them two at a time. At the landing, he turned, yelling joyously down to Mrs. Thomas.

"God Bless you, Mrs. Thomas! We're sure much obliged to you. I'd pay you, but I don't have any cash money. But I'll be sending you ...*somethin'*, the next time I go huntin', and come back with a fine fat bird or possum. You can make stew or dumplin's. Or I could come over and chop some wood—!"

"That'll be fine, John, whatever—"

John didn't hear the rest.

He burst into their bedroom, much too wildly, too fast he told himself. But he couldn't contain himself.

"John!" Callie looked up and smiled at him.

"Callie! You all right?"

"Good grief, John," Callie laughed, "is the house on fire?"

"No'm," John teased her, pushing one strand of blond hair off her wet forehead. "But my heart sure is. Where's my baby girl?"

"Let me see ...she's around here some place. Oh! Here she is! Hiding herself beneath the corner of this pink blanket! Come on out, sweetie, and meet—"

John didn't hear any of the rest.

When the corner of that little pink blanket lifted—

Ahhhhhh! And there she was!

"Oh ...my ...Callie! Oh ...my!" was all John could manage to stammer.

"Isn't she beautiful, John?"

"Oh ...my ...Callie!"

"You want to hold her?"

"I ...don't know about that, Callie. I never held a new-born baby before."

"Here." Callie thrust the tiny bundle towards him.

John reached out his rough, work-hardened brown hands. And Callie laid the baby gently in his arms.

Her eyes were closed. Her skin was perfect. The little mouth, perfect—one tiny hand curled beneath an exquisite chin. The other little fist curling and uncurling like a tiny bud. How beautiful she was! Like a lovely rose! Then she opened her eyes, and looked at him.

She stared at John for a minute.

And in that one instant, John felt that the girl child they would call 'Maggie' truly knew who he was. Then she uncurled one perfect little hand, and curled it about her Papa's warm finger.

"This is your Papa, sugar," John nuzzled the little forehead, planting the lightest of kisses. "And you're my *only baby girl*!"

"What're we going to name her, John?" Callie asked, determined that she'd ignore John's last remark. Callie put it down to the excitement of the moment.

"I don't know, Callie. But, then, you did name the other two—so this one's mine. How about ...Margaret ...for my mother ...and Ann ...for Grandma Katherine—?

"—Well, how about that! World!—here's little Margaret Ann McKinnon!" John laughed.

Then he began waltzing around the bedroom, spinning the tiny infant around in his arms.

"John McKinnon!" Callie laughed. "She's too young to go dancin'!"

Chapter 4

John stepped into the coolness of the shade of the front porch. He took off his sweat-stained hat and fanned himself with it before turning to go in. When he opened the front door, there stood beautiful little Maggie.

"Hello, baby girl," John laughed down at her, with a sweeping bow, his hat in his hand as if greeting a queen.

"I'm not a baby, Papa," she informed him sternly, stomping one tiny foot. "You know I'm not a baby anymore. I'll be *three* tomorrow."

With a delighted laugh, John swooped his beautiful little daughter into his arms, smelling the sweet scent of her, feeling the warmth of her little body. How he loved this child! "Little lady, you won't be three until day *after* tomorrow." With that he began whirling Maggie about in a waltzing dance that carried the two of them circling crazily through the kitchen door and what Callie thought was dangerously close to the hot cookstove.

"Put the child down, John!" Callie ordered, "Come, sit down and eat your supper! I've about got everything on the table."

"I'm not hungry! My arms are too full of happiness for me to be hungry!" John whirled the two of them on about the little kitchen as best he could, maneuvering by the oak eating table with its two benches, the meal chest, and the big black iron cookstove, and then past the walnut pie safe crafted by his father.

"Not hungry!" Maggie echoed her father's happy delirium.

"John! *Do* mind where you're stepping. Put the child down and come and eat!"

John plopped Maggie down on the oak bench beside a solemn-faced Barbara Jo. Nellie Sue was sitting silently beyond her.

Taking a seat opposite the girls, John reached a brown hand into his denim jumper pocket, and pulled out a small carved object.

"Look, Maggie," he smiled, and held it forward to his youngest child. "It's *just* for you."

A worried frown creasing her brow, Callie looked across the table, at the two other girls. Nellie Sue sat watching her father with a sweet, open gaze. Barbara Jo's little hands had come up to cover her mouth. Her light blue eyes pulled into a squint; her little mouth opened. She looked as if she was about to burst into sobs.

"What is it, Papa?" Maggie asked, turning the wooden object over in her tiny hands.

"Why, it's a painted Indian chief, Maggie, can't you see his eyes, see there—and a beautiful feather in his hair?"

"Don't you have something for *me*, Papa?" Barbara Jo took her hands from her mouth, gazed at her father, tears now flooding the blue eyes. "Don't you have *anything* for me?"

"Why ...sure ...honey ..." John hesitated uncomfortably. Who would ever have dreamed that at her age his second daughter would have wanted a carved wooden toy? John reached into his pocket again, making a great pretense of searching for something.

"Ah! Here it is!" He drew out his bent tobacco can, unsnapped the lid with a little flip of one finger, dumped the remaining tobacco into his jumper pocket, and with a pleased flourish, slid the battered tobacco can across the table toward Barbara Jo. "Here! You can fill it with all your peculiar treasures, little stones, seeds—and such."

Barbara Jo's little face crumpled into a pale lump. She took one small hand, and gave the tobacco can a swat, sending it clattering to the floor. She began to weep hysterically. The weeping grew quickly into long, loud wails.

"*John!*" Callie cried.

John could only stare at Barbara Jo helplessly.

"Papa!" little Maggie said suddenly, "Play us something on your fiddle!"

"That's it!" John cried in relief, "Some music to cheer us all up!"

He leapt up, got his fiddle down from its peg in the front room by the door, and began to draw the horsehair bow across the strings of the fiddle. Barbara Jo's wails grew even louder. The fiddle not having the desired effect, John halted his playing, and burst into song:

In the sky ...the bright stars glittered...
On th' banks, the pale moon shone...
And t'was from Aunt Dinnah's quilting Party...
I...was...seeeinnnggg...
Nellie...home...

Barbara Jo's mournful howls drowned out the singing. John threw the fiddle back up under his neck, and began to saw the horsehair bow across the strings again. Maggie clapped and giggled with glee. She thought it was all great fun.

The lilting strains of the fiddle flew about the kitchen, mingling with Barbara Jo's mournful wails that had risen now to ear-piercing heights.

"*John!*" Callie leapt to her feet, shouting above the din, "*Sit down! And eat your supper*!

"—And *Barbara Jo! Hush that!* You're five years old! *You're not a baby!*"

With a sheepish grin, John laid the fiddle aside, pushed back his dark mop of hair, gave Maggie their secret wink, and took his place at the table.

"*Now!*" Callie announced as sternly as she could manage, "*We will say Grace.*"

As they lay in bed that night, Callie pretending to read her Bible, John's arm about her waist as he slumped low into his feather pillow, Callie began slowly:

"John, I don't quite know how to say this ...but I feel I must speak to you."

"About what, Callie?" John murmured his eyes already shut.

"About how you spoil Margaret Ann."

"Not really, Callie. It's just that she's so special. She's such a beautiful child. She holds my heart in her hands—"

"That's just the problem, John. You have only one heart—but you have *three* daughters."

"You talkin' about th' other girls?" John mumbled.

"They have *names,* John."

"Sure," John muttered, "names ..."

Callie snapped her Bible shut.

"Get up, John," she ordered, "and blow out the lamp."

The next day when John came in, he knocked field dirt from his plow boots, strode onto the back porch, sloshing cold well water over his sweaty face and neck, and smoothing down his hair. He wanted to look especially nice for his women.

Last night, he realized through a sleepy fog, Callie was trying to tell him something. Did that foolish woman think he loved his child more than her? Today, he'd freshen up a bit, go and sit with her on the other end of the porch, where Callie and the older girls now sat, stringing beans.

"Well!" John walked up in his wool socks and work clothes, his handsome, tanned face beaming, "How are all my womenfolk?"

"What's up with you, John?' Callie asked warily. "You need somethin'?"

"Do I have to need somethin' in order to knock off a bit early, just to come in and sit a minute with my beautiful ladies, and drink a cool cup of well-water?"

"John," Callie asked quizzically, "is something wrong?"

"No. I just wanted to spend a part of this afternoon with my girls. Honey," John said to Nellie Sue, "go fetch me a cool cup of water." Then turning to Barbara Jo, "And why don't you go help your sister?"

"Since when, John McKinnon, does a seven year old child need help in fetching one dipper of water?"

"Callie," John sat down, stretching his left leg stiffly out before him, "nice day isn't it?"

"Fine day," Callie nodded.

"Might rain."

"It could."

"Saw clouds gathering over the south fields."

"Many clouds?"

"More than a few. Oh, thanks, girls! And look, here comes *my little Maggie*! Come on out here, *sugar*, and sit on Papa's good knee. Give Papa a *big hug and a kiss*—

"Now the thing is, Callie …I just wanted you to know, each and every one of you…wellllll…you know how I feel about all of you—

"—And that's what I wanted to say."

John beamed at Callie, well pleased with himself. Callie looked at Maggie, sitting on her Papa's good knee, John's eyes glued to the top of that dark curly head.

"Is that it, John?" Callie paused, her blond brows raised, her blue eyes boring into him, "That's *all* you have to say?"

"Why, yes, Callie, except—" frantically John searched his mind…to pin down Callie's meaning. She was, apparently *waiting*…for him to say *something else*, but he was *at a total loss as to what*—!

Callie gave a little miffed tilt of her chin.

Her eyes never leaving his face, Callie rose slowly from her straight-backed chair—

—And carried the green beans into the kitchen.

"Girls," John said, thoughtfully, rising to his feet, "you all just stay out here for a few minutes. I need to speak to your Mama."

John entered the kitchen. Callie turned her back to him. He walked up behind her.

"Callie? Callie, look at me."

Slowly Callie dropped the dipper back into the water bucket, and turned to face him.

John put his hands, one on either side of that pretty face, "Callie, honey, you know, don't you, that I love you more than my own life." It was not a question.

"Oh, John," Callie leaned into him.

John gathered her in his arms.

He bent his head. His mouth against her ear, he whispered softly, as he began to dance her around the room in a slow, rhythmic waltz:

If a body,
Meet a body,
Comin' thru th' rye
If a body
Kiss a body
Need a body cry
Ev'ry lassie
Has her laddie
Nane, they say, hae I
Yet a' the lads they smile at me
When comin' thru th' rye…

John released Callie, and turned to see three heads, one right behind the other, in the kitchen door.

"Com'on in, girls!" John bent and opened his arms.

The three girls flew toward Papa.

John gathered his girls and Callie to him.

And in a whirling mass of arms and legs, the five of them went whirling about the kitchen table.

Chapter 5

"I'm going to th' store, to get some ammunition for my rifle, and a bit of pipe tobacco," John announced that Saturday morning. "Anythin' you need, now's th' time to sing out."

"Some kerosene for the lamps, John," Callie said matter-of-factly, "and some matches for lightin' lamps and fires."

"Anythin' else?" John mused, "Long way to th' General Store. Not a trip I'll be makin' anytime soon."

"Oh, I don't know," Callie frowned. "If you had said somethin' yesterday—"

"Well, yesterday I wasn't out of pipe tobacco. Why don't you come along, get away for a spell? Trip will do you good."

"And bring all the girls? How long you going to be?"

"Got to get some Indian corn ground, meal chest's almost empty. Might take most of the day, there, doing th' business, then back. Could pack a lunch?"

"I don't know, John …"

"Oh, come on. How about it, *Maggie m' darlin'*? Want to go to the mill and store *with your Papa?*"

"Oh! We're all going to the mill and store! Not to the little store we always go to, but the big store?" Maggie asked.

"Yeah, sugar. This is a different store. Not in Rhyersville, where we usually go, but on down at Johnson's Corners, where th' ferry waits to carry folks across th' river. And my little *Maggie* loves to watch th' ferry, so I know *she* wants to go."

"I don't know," Callie hedged.

Maggie was five now. And John liked having her along. It improved his image. What other dirt farmer in the valley had such a strikingly beautiful child, with her peach-perfect skin, protected by the sunbonnets with their great flopping brims Callie sewed for her? And, often, if yard goods allowed, in matching colors and patterns with her little dresses that Callie would whip up out of a few scraps of calico or gingham. Her hair swung down her back in dark, lustrous waves. She was tall, too, at age five, tall, and smart for her age. And she swung her hair just so, carried herself with grace, with long, purposeful strides—as if she was always certain *where* she was going, and exactly *what* to do when she got there.

"*Maggie!*" John lifted her, and carried her to the wagon.

"Well," Callie muttered to herself, gathering the other two girls' bonnets and shawls, "no need to help *Maggie.* I can see that John has already taken care of that!"

And John had her seated on his lap, in the wagon.

"What can we buy at the store, Papa?"

"Not much, sugar. Papa doesn't have a lot of money—just a lot of love for *Maggie McKinnon.*"

"Oh, Papa, stop your teasing. I'm too big for that, now. I mean candy. Can we have at least *one* piece of candy?"

"Okay," John grinned, "I think we can afford at least one piece of candy."

"Yes, John," Callie called out a bit too loudly, "a piece for *each of your girls! Right?*"

"Sure, Callie. Sure thing!" John tried to keep his voice cheerful. But it riled John a bit. Did Callie feel she had to *give him purchasing instructions,* as if he was a snot-nosed child?

"Don't I always get somethin' for *all* my girls?"

"I'd be afraid to say," Callie replied rather coolly.

John tried not to notice.

Callie then turned to the two girls in the back of the wagon, "Well, better decide now what you want, girls."

"*I* want a licorice stick!" Barbara Jo sang out, her narrow face beaming.

"Well!" Callie smiled at her second daughter, "won't that be a treat.

"And how about you, Nellie Sue? What kind of candy would *you* like?"

"I don't know, Mama," Nellie Sue smiled, "peppermint, I guess."

The wagon clattered and rattled on. Maggie grew sleepy. She enjoyed riding through the sunlit countryside, the greening woods and fields rolling slowly past, the sound of the wagon wheels on the dirt road—like a song Papa plays on his fiddle. And Papa—leaning against the strength of his chest, feeling the strong rhythm of his heart …kaathump …kaathump …

"Are we there yet?"

"Almost, sugar," John smiled down at the little face, so sweet beneath the ruffled brim of the blue sunbonnet.

"Here we are!" Maggie announced to one and all. Papa lifted her down from the seat. Then he unloaded his sacks of Indian corn—some to be ground for corn meal, the remainder to be bartered for supplies.

Callie interjected, "We'd best go over there in the shade of that tree, and eat our lunch!"

After lunch, holding Papa's hand, Maggie followed him up the weathered, gray-oak steps of Johnson' Corners General Store and Mill.

They made quite a sight—the tall, darkly handsome man, the strikingly beautiful child, dressed in a new blue dress and bonnet.

Then, on the top step, Maggie stopped dead still, tugging at Papa's hand. "What is it, Maggie?"

"There, Papa! *Look there! See* that! Isn't she *beautiful?* Oh! *Isn't she?"* Maggie began jumping up and down.

"Maggie," John squeezed the little hand, "be still, honey."

Oh, please, God! John felt sick, as he whispered a prayer, *Please! Let me get her that doll! Just this one thing! She gets so little—*

Then cold reality kicked in. "No, sugar. Not for us. Too expensive. It's not Christmas. Or your birthday, anyhow. Maybe someday—"

"But, Papa …somebody *else* will get her!" Maggie pulled her face into a frowning pout.

John knelt carefully down on his bad leg, patiently explaining, "I know that, *sweetheart*." He frowned sorrowfully. "That's just the way things are sometimes. We can't *get* everything we want."

"Why *not?*"

"Because, Maggie," Callie cut in, "we don't have enough money. Tell the child, John. And quit beating about the bush. Just tell her the *truth*."

"Mama's right, sugar. Probably not even for Christmas—"

But Maggie appeared not to hear. She ran over, demanding of the proprietor of the mill and store, "How much is that? That *doll* in the window? The *pretty* one with the *painted* face and *hands, and the pink* bonnet and coat?"

"That? Oh, she's not for sale, little Miss. She belongs to the ladies of the Shiloh Baptist Church. I'm just holding her for them, for the drawin'."

"What's a drawin'?"

"Maggie!" Callie ordered sternly, "Come away! Leave the man alone!"

"But, Mama, *I want to know*. What's a drawin'?"

"Why, the church ladies sell these here tickets, raffle tickets they're called, and whoever's name is drawn …well, he—or she—gets to keep the little doll."

"Papa! Papa! *I want to buy a ticket!*"

"No, Maggie, no, sweetie," John's voice felt strained and forced. "How much …*are* th' tickets, Calvin?"

"*John*," Callie gave John's elbow a warning jab, "there's no *money* for a *raffle ticket!*"

Ignoring Callie, "How much?" John asked again,

"Ten cents."

"That's *just* about what we had allowed for the candy, Maggie. But, see, here's the thing …if we buy the *raffle ticket*, there's *no money* left for the *candy*."

"Papa! *I want the ticket! I* want the doll!"

"You might get the ticket, sugar, and still not get the doll."

"*John!*" Callie hissed at him, "Candy's only *a penny a stick!*"

"We'll take one," Callie heard him say.

Callie reached down, snatched Nellie Sue by one hand, and Barbara Jo by the other. She marched out the door, and sat herself and the two girls down on the bottom step.

John and Maggie walked to the back door of the store, to watch the water spilling over the giant wheel, turning the mill, grinding the corn. John was so caught up in listening to the roar of the water, showing Maggie the whirring gears that he hadn't noticed when Callie flounced out the door. Then Maggie and John moved on, John pointing out this and that to Maggie. Most of which she had no interest in whatsoever.

John took his sweet time, sauntered about, and made his few purchases. He looked about, searching for Callie and the girls. Then he saw Callie's back. She was sitting outside, on the store steps! She must be tired, he thought. The two older girls were sitting with her, leaning inwards, like two bent trees. Sort of a sad spectacle, John thought with a little smile. Nellie Sue's hair shone golden-blond in the sun. And Barbara Jo's light-brown tresses looked almost pretty, with the sunlight falling on her hair. Callie was talking to the girls, so low John couldn't hear what was being said. He stepped to the door, to call to them.

"Hey, what are you all doin' out there? Why don't y'all come on in?"

No response. Nothing. Callie didn't even look at him.

"Callie? Honey?"

She didn't move a muscle, or make a reply. Must not have heard him, John reasoned. He shrugged, called a bit louder. "Callie? Soon be time to go home. Don't you three want to com'on in th' store, and look around?"

No reply.

Strange, the way the three of them were huddled together on the steps—

"—Callie, honey?" Louder this time, "Look! They're bringing out the big earthen pitcher, with the raffle tickets in it—!"

Did Callie's back stiffened—or did he imagine it?

We won't win, anyhow, John thought dismally. Hard lesson for Maggie, but she has to learn.

"Callie? Honey, come on in, now! They're drawing the ticket—"

"The winner is—

"John McKinnon!"

With a loud whoop, Calvin Johnson waved the tiny stub of brown paper aloft.

"What?" John was beside himself with disbelief. "I never won the first thing—in my whole life! *Princess*! Little *Maggie*, we won!"

He snatched Maggie up and whirled her about the store, singing: "We won, *princess*, little *Maggie*, we won!"

"We won, Papa? *I get the doll!*"

"Did you hear that, Callie? Girls? *Our little Maggie* won! They're bringin' the doll out of the window!"

John loaded his supplies.

Callie sat on the steps.

She didn't offer to help with the loading, even the light things, the way she always did.

She didn't even *look* at him as he passed her, carrying the purchases.

"Ready, hon?" John turned to help Callie into the high wagon seat.

Her pretty face set as stone, Callie pulled away from him, and clambered up by herself.

She sat white-faced and silent, not even so much as glancing at John as he helped the girls into the back, then climbed up beside Maggie and Callie.

"Uppppp, thereee! Getttyyy upppp!" John made a clicking sound with his tongue, and started the horse off at a slow trot.

Between him and Callie, Maggie cuddled her new doll.

"What can I name her, Papa?" She looked up at John, such happiness on her face. John felt his throat tighten.

"I don't know, sugar. What do you think, Callie?"

No reply.

"How's about-uuuhhmmmm ...Katie, for Great-grandma Katherine Ann?" John offered with a big smile, determined nothing would spoil this special moment for Maggie.

"Katie! I love you, Katie! You're so pretty! Isn't she pretty, Mama?" Maggie sang happily.

Callie did not even glance at the doll, said not a word.

In the back of the wagon, Nellie Sue and Barbara Jo glanced apprehensively at one another.

John thought the chill in the air was so thick you could safely have slaughtered a hog—with no fear of losing your meat.

They're all tired. So am I, John reflected, glancing over at Callie, a feeling of unease stealing over him. This was so out of character for Callie.

"You all right, hon?"

She looked as if she was carved of ice.

"Callie?" he ventured, beginning to get the notion that something *really* was out of joint here. Usually John had no problem teasing Callie out of any mood.

John reached out, touched her hand. She shifted farther away on the wagon seat.

John turned from the store yard, into the rutted red dirt road that ran on up to Rhyersville. He drove very slowly, as if waiting for some calamity to fall upon him.

"John," Callie said, as soon as they got out of sight of the store.

Then Callie turned on him, and swatted him on the arm with her small reticule.

"Callie! What was that for?"

"John McKinnon, *you've finally done it.*" She shook her head so hard one of her blond plaits came loose.

"Done what?" John asked, a sick feeling stealing over him. Was she jealous of Maggie's new doll?

"John!" Callie paused as if to catch her breath. She spoke very deliberately, as if she had to choose each word very carefully, as if she was addressing a two-year-old—or an idiot:

"Of all the insane, lopsided, pig-headed, half-brained things you've *ever* done! What about *th' candy—John!?* What about *your promise—John!?* You do have *two other children!"* Her voice rose to a piercing shriek.

John was almost afraid to look at her. What was that, *tears* in her blue eyes? Callie never cried.

"What, Callie?" John wagged his head innocently, turning out the palms of his hands.

"John McKinnon! You know what!!! You spent the candy money on that— that—raffle ticket—"

Callie spat out each word, and it whipped through the air.

John felt confused.

His mind wasn't working.

What had he done?

He must have done something *awful*—

—To upset her like this.

What did she just say, the *raffle* ticket?

"The *raffle* ticket?" John asked incredulously.

She was upset because he bought the raffle ticket?

"But ...Callie. It was so *cheap*! Only ten cents! We were going to spend the *money* on candy, anyhow—which they would have just popped into their mouths—gone in an instant! Look *how happy Maggie is*!" Maggie, fast asleep in Papa's lap, missed all this. "I could never have bought her a doll like *that*! *That* doll ...*for ten cents?* And th' money went to th' church—"

"John McKinnon, this has nothing to do with the *church*! Sometimes you are as dense as an iron stob! Stop the wagon!"

"Callie?"

"What about Nellie Sue and Barbara Jo?"

"The girls?"

"They have *names* John!"

The two girls drew their heads down, huddled together miserably in the back of the wagon, as their mother's voice rose to a higher and higher pitch.

"What's wrong with Mama?" Barbara Jo whispered to Nellie Sue.

"Shush!" Nellie Sue hissed with a warning frown.

"They didn't get any candy!" Callie shouted.

"Candy?" they heard Papa ask unbelievingly.

"All this big *hoop-te-doop* over a few lumps of *candy*? But, they're big girls!"

"*Stop!!!!——the!!!!——-wagon!!!!*"

"But …Callie, we're still *five miles from home—!*" His tanned face stubbornly set, John drove on.

Callie seemed incapable of speech. She stared at him, her light blue eyes blazing with anger, her slight chest heaving beneath the print cotton fabric of her best dress.

Finally, she hissed from between gritted teeth:

"John McKinnon, if you don't *stop* this wagon, I may say something *God will not soon forgive me for!*"

In amazement, John looked at her.

"Whoaaaa!" John slowed the mule to a complete halt.

Callie fairly leapt down from the high wagon seat. From beneath the brim of her sunbonnet, John could see the tears pooling in her eyes. Her cheeks were flushed red as raspberries. Without so much as a glance in his direction, she drew her shawl about her shoulders, and walked stiffly down the road. One blond plait dangling from beneath her bonnet.

"Callie—!" John gave the reins a tiny slap, just enough to get the horse started at a slow walk, and, seated on the high wagon seat, peered worriedly down at her from time to time, his handsome face creased with astonishment.

They met a wagon. Israel Clements nodded at John. His bushy brows shot up, his eyes widened, taking in the slender form stalking doggedly along in front of the horse, her blond hair awry, the horse's nose almost touching the crown of her bonnet.

John flushed red with embarrassment. He tipped the brim of his hat to Doreen Clements, who stared openly, her mouth gaped wide enough to catch any low-flying bird that happened by.

John groaned. Another wagon was coming towards them. Mrs. Paula Sterns could not stare hard enough. As their rig drew near, she swiveled her head around, and kept staring after they had met and passed, until John wondered if she was going to wring her neck off. A little smile touched Jules Stern's mouth, as he gave John a knowing little wave with one hand.

John called to Callie, "Now just look at that! Look what you're doing—

"Folks will be talking—

"—It will be *all over the community*—

"—The McKinnons are havin' trouble—"

Usually that would get her. Callie was very big on maintaining a good standing in the community.

Nothing.

Every fifteen or twenty minutes or so:

"Callie? *Get* back in the wagon.

"Get back in the wagon, Callie, and we'll talk about this.

"I know I must have done something.

"Something ...just awful.

"And, *whatever* it was—

"—I'm sorry.

"Callie? *Real, real,* sorry.

"Honey?"

Thus they made their strange journey home. The girls in the back, turned forward now, watching their mother as she strode angrily along, the horse practically on her heels, until they reached their own dooryard.

Once in the yard, they watched as Mama stalked up the front steps, her single plait swinging, through the front room, up the stairs—

—Leaving John and the girls to unload the wagon.

She did not appear again—until it was time to fix their supper.

Chapter 6

After the strange episode about the candy, John tried to be much more circumspect in his spending—and in his attention to Margaret Ann. He still could not for the life of him figure out exactly what he did, to set Callie off on such a tangent. But whatever it was, he certainly didn't want to repeat it.

After the incident about the doll and the candy, John felt as if he was walking a tightrope.

He took to speaking to *all* the girls, or none of them. He tried his dead level best not to favor Maggie above the older girls. But he found this hard to do.

All those years …he hadn't even known them.

Sometimes John would turn away, when Maggie asked to be picked up, pretending he didn't know she was there—

—For fear that if he showed Maggie too much attention, Callie would be offended.

He felt the need to somehow impress upon Callie …just what an impartial, responsible father he truly was.

He took to speaking to Maggie in a deep, stern voice, a voice—he hoped— that showed no partiality—nor brooked the slightest disobedience.

On the first occasion John tried this particular tactic, Maggie gazed up at him with wide eyes. She cocked her pretty little head to the side. Was this a new game Papa was playing?

She looked so cute. Her eyes so wide and wise for her age, so blue-blue …*so* beautiful. But, no! He could not give in to that winsome little charmer! Complete, absolute *sternness*—that was the name of *this* game.

And a game it became—with Maggie soon catching on, she was such a brilliant little thing.

"*Yessss, Papaaa!*" she soon learned to reply, and she did so in her lowest, slowest voice. Just like *Papa* used. This so amazed and startled John the first time she tried it, that he burst out laughing. Then Callie gave him an icy glare, and John quickly straightened his face.

The longer this continued the more Maggie delighted in it. She would purposefully do some *little* something, sure to raise Mama's ire, sure to bring that *lowwwww* voice out of Papa.

Then, John took up the game—

And they began to play it in earnest.

John would chase her about the house, when Callie wasn't in the room, and chide her, in his deepest, most authoritative, sternest voice.

And Maggie, her little face wrinkled in deep contrition, would reply in a low, strange drawl from somewhere deep in her chest:

"Noooooo, Paaapaaa. Maggie…McKinnon…will…not…do…that …again. Nooooo…Maggie…McKinnon…will…not…do…that…"

They were playing this game today, John in his rocker on the front porch, Maggie hanging over the arm of his chair, intoning solemnly, "NOOOOOO, Maggie McKinnon! You will not do *that* againnnn!!"

Very unexpectedly, the front door swung open.

Mama stepped out.

John wiped the silly grin from his face with a tanned hand, and snapped instantly erect. Sober as a parson, he nodded his head, like the fellow-conspirator he was—alerting Maggie that just to their right—they had company.

Maggie immediately straightened her face, turned to smile sweetly at her Mama.

Sober faced, Callie walked to her usual rocker, and seated herself, laying her sewing in her lap. Slowly, she began to rock, and sew. Sew, and rock.

John arched his brows, shot a warning glance at Maggie.

He settled back a bit uneasily in his rocker, put a hand on Maggie's little arm, "Sugar, you go on and play now," he whispered, giving Maggie a sly little wink.

"No, Papa." Maggie said, pouting charmingly, "I want to talk *to you.*"

"I thought, *John,*" Callie said, in an icy voice, "I *thought* you had told Maggie to go and play."

OH, NO! Callie had heard!

But John felt he couldn't just *dismiss* Maggie so abruptly.

"Okay, sweetie, we'll talk—for just a minute." Suddenly John was feeling reckless and brave. "What do you want to talk about? Haven't we talked about everythin' under the sky, Maggie m'love?"

"Papa …let's …talk …about …what's a Re-bu-lu-tion?"

"A what?"

"I think, John," Callie said quietly, "Maggie means a 'Revolution.' Is that right, Maggie?"

"Yes, Papa. Nellie Sue's studying it in school. But when she told me about it, she didn't tell it so good. What's a Reb—a—lut—ion?"

"It's a …sort …of …fight."

"A little fight—like me and Barbara Jo have? Or a big fight?"

"Well …Maggie …"

"Tell her the truth, John. It's a *war*, Maggie." Callie's voice sounded very matter-of-fact, as if a *War* was a very *ordinary* thing.

"Nellie Sue said it was a big war. Why did they fight such a big war?"

"Because the King wanted them to pay tax on tea, and stuff," John replied absently. "But they just …dumped all the tea into the Boston Harbor …then they went to war."

"Why'd they do that?" Maggie screwed up her face with curiosity, one small hand tucked beneath her chin as she leaned on the arm of Papa's rocker. "Didn't they like tea? I like tea, when Mama let's me have it."

"We don't get it that often ourselves," Callie remarked dryly, never slowing her rhythmic rocking. "The only tea we get—is sassafras."

"Me and Barbs fight," Maggie surmised quietly. "But I don't think we'd go to war—not over a bunch of tea."

"There was a little more to it than that," John said, leaning forward so he could tap his pipe against the front porch post. John then leaned thoughtfully back. "Who knows why men go to war, sugar—?" He paused, reflecting on the bloody conflict he had endured—

—The floodgates opened. It all came streaming through his mind—

The bloodied, mangled bodies, strewn about the ground, like carelessly flung sticks of wood—

—Lying in the creeks and rivers until they ran red—

—Beneath the trees—

—In the cornfields—huge pools of blood seeping into the corn rows—

—From Georgia into Tennessee and North Carolina—into the valleys of Virginia—

Suddenly John felt cold and sick.

"Men fight wars for all sorts of reasons, Maggie," Callie said calmly.

Callie could see little beads of sweat on John's tanned face. He looked awful, as if he was about to be sick.

"War's a very bad thing, Maggie," Callie said hastily. "Let's not talk about it anymore."

John put a hand to his mouth. He felt so sick to his stomach—

He hoped Maggie wouldn't go on, and on …about the blood, the bodies flying apart …Suddenly his leg began to ache. He felt as if he might retch.

He heard Maggie asking something. And Callie giving a reply.

John said, in a low, slow voice, "Go on, Maggie, go on and play with your sisters."

"Is war that bad, Papa? As bad as Mama says?"

"Is there any other kind, Maggie?"

"I don't know, Papa. I've never seen a war."

"And, pray God," John said, feeling the bile rise in his throat, "pray God you never will!" John touched the tip of one finger to Maggie's smooth cheek, her eyes so innocent, so trusting. The world was such a hard and cruel place, sometimes. What would become of this child? What would become of any of them?

John looked out over the yard, the older girls at play, Callie sitting quietly with her mending. Maggie her usual inquisitive self, suddenly spinning about in circles now, just in front of him, just for the fun of it.

Why was he suddenly gripped with this *sick, cold panic?*

"You've seen a War, haven't you, Papa? And it hurt your leg?"

"Yes, sugar. I've seen all the war I ever want to see. Now, go and play."

John felt as if he had to get up, and move around. Get some air. Do something to stifle the awful fear that was clawing at his innards, washing over him in waves. He couldn't recall feeling this terrible—since Front Royal—

Maggie could see that Papa was tired, and didn't want to play their game anymore, or talk to her any more. She quickly turned her attention to Nellie Sue, just bounding up on the front porch, whirling about the porch post. Maggie flew away:

"You can't catch me! Catch me if you can! Catch me if you can! I dare yoooou…!"

Then something went terribly wrong. Maggie was never quite sure what happened that sunny autumn afternoon—

She just recalled how that suddenly Nellie Sue was bounding off the porch after her, laughing, blond hair flying, crying: "I'll get you—Maggie McKinnon—I'll get you!"

Then Nellie Sue was lying in the yard, her right leg twisted way up, almost out of sight, beneath her body—

"*Papa!*" It was Papa, Maggie recalled, that Nellie Sue called.

John was up, out of his rocker—

—"*Nellie! No! Oh, no—!*"

Lunging up, John hurled his tall frame awkwardly off the front porch, and stumbled forward. His face cotton-white, his eyes wide with fear, he bent over Nellie, brushing the gold-blond hair from her forehead, grasping her hand.

Callie was sobbing in shock and disbelief: "John! *Do something!* Take her inside!"

"No, Callie, don't you touch her! We can't move her. Just keep her still—real still—as comfortable as you can. I'll go saddle the horse, be faster, ride for the doctor! Barbara Jo, honey, quit crying, now, help your Mama. Go get some cold wet cloths. Try to keep her face wet and cool. I'll be back, Callie, honey, just as soon as I can."

Nellie Sue sat propped up in bed. The leg was broken in two places, the kneecap knocked out of place. But hopefully, now, all had been put right.

But Nellie Sue would be abed for weeks.

Maggie flitted and fluttered about the room—determined to make amends for her terrible sin.

It was Maggie's fault, she felt, that Nellie was hurt. Maggie had dared her.

"It's not your fault, Maggie," John said, kneeling before Maggie, laying a finger alongside Maggie's beautiful face. "It's just not your fault—and you can't *make* it be by saying so! So, you just forget about it, you hear? It was an accident—pure and simple."

"That's right, Maggie," Callie looked at them across Nellie Sue's bed. Maggie standing there, pale-faced, John's arm around her shoulders—"You go on now, and leave Nellie Sue alone. She had a bad accident, and that's the end of it. Once it's spilled," Callie said, "you can't put the milk back in the pitcher."

But Maggie had been praying very hard lately.

She felt that her sins were many. And varied.

She knew that Papa spoiled her.

She knew that Mama disapproved.

But Maggie was uncertain as to what to do about it.

And this thing about Nellie …Nellie getting hurt—

Then Nellie Sue's condition began to improve.

Four weeks—and she was out of bed, walking about the upstairs.

Eight weeks—and Papa picked her up and brought her downstairs—to sit at the table and have supper with them.

Maggie watched Nellie Sue closely. She was very careful not to *do* or *say* anything that might upset her.

Or hurt her.

When Nellie Sue got hurt, Maggie promised herself, she would turn over a new leaf—

She promised God that she wouldn't issue *dares* to people.

She promised God that she wouldn't mention *war* to Papa. Mama told her it might make Papa sick.

And she promised herself she wouldn't *pester* people, asking so many questions. This last promise, Maggie made to *herself,* and *not* to God—for she was certain, even as she made it, that it was *the one* that was sure to be broken.

Chapter 7

"What's the matter with my girl?" John noticed that Maggie seemed too quiet the past few days, too subdued, to be Maggie. No flying about the house. No constant babble of questions.

"What's wrong, sugar?" John asked. She was seated across the breakfast table from him, fiddling with her food.

"It's.... Katie...Papa. I went and hurt Nellie. Now I ruined Katie, too." Her lower lip began to tremble. Her blue eyes were downcast.

"Maggie. Come on now, lift your chin and look at me. Now, good. You just listen to me, baby girl, and you listen real good. What happened to your sister was an accident—nothin' more. You understand me? No more of this moping and moaning. Nellie Sue's better ...Nellie Sue's just fine. Now, what is it you did to Katie?"

"She got left outside, by the feed trough, last Monday," Maggie whispered. "And her little head ...and ...her ...little ...hands ...they got all doughy. And she ...fell apart."

"Doughy?"

"It rained, John. Monday night," Callie said.

"I don't understand how such a thing could have happened," John said slowly. "You always sleep with Katie. You didn't miss her?"

"It rained way before dark, remember, John? By the time Maggie missed the doll—it was too late."

"I don't understand," John repeated carefully, his baffled gaze passing from Maggie, to the faces around the table. Callie, who, eyes on her plate, kept quietly eating. Nellie Sue, she smiled at him so innocently. Barbara Jo, she never looked up from her food.

John decided to let the matter drop for the moment. But something seemed highly out of kilter here.

After supper, while Callie was cleaning up the kitchen, John, as usual, stepped out onto the front porch, sat down on the steps, and lit his pipe.

After a while, as she usually did, Callie came out, wiping the sweat from her face with her apron, to join him. She sat down in one of the two porch rockers, fanning herself with her damp apron tail.

"Get everything all cleaned up?" John asked.

"Sure did."

"Girls all bedded down?"

"Uh-huh."

"Kinda sad, huh, for Maggie? She's been lookin' about like she's going to cry all day. Funny, the way I haven't heard about Katie, until now. Had to pick it out of her. Not like Maggie."

"What, John? What on earth are you running on about? That doll?"

"Yeah, Callie. That doll. Maggie's favorite toy. Practically her only toy. Peculiar, she should leave it down by the feed trough, like that. You didn't see it? With you right there? Milking the cow?"

"No, John. I didn't see it. If I had, I'd have brought it on to the house."

"Odd. That you didn't see it."

"If you have something to say, John—exactly what *is* it you're trying to say? You think I deliberately walked off and left Maggie's doll for it to get ruined?"

"I don't know, Callie. You're always saying she has to learn responsibility."

"Well, I don't think I would teach it to her by letting her doll get soaked by rain."

"It's just not like Maggie ...to go off and leave Katie—"

"John! I declare! How you do latch onto things and then chew on them like a hungry hound! It was just a *doll*. And Maggie's just a child! Even Maggie's not always perfect!"

"I didn't say I expected Maggie to be perfect, Callie. I just meant to say—"

"Well, tell me, John? What is it you meant to say?"

"It's just that ...if somebody was mean and hateful enough to put that doll out there ...knowing it was going to rain—"

"John McKinnon! I can't believe my own ears! Is that what this is all about? Just who do you suspect, in this heinous crime? Maggie is a child! She carelessly left her only doll out in the rain! It got ruined! And that's the end of it!"

Callie leapt up out of her chair, sending the rocker banging against the square logs of the house.

John heard the loud bang of the front door.

But, somehow, John couldn't just let it go like that. If someone had done this on purpose, punishment should be meted out. He needed to get to the truth of this.

"Maggie?" John called the next morning, picking up his hat just after breakfast. "You know it's Saturday, don't you?"

"Sure, Papa."

"Why don't we two just make our way down to the river, and see if the water has cleared up ...and the fish are running."

"Mama? Can I? Can I?"

"Whatever your father says, Maggie. Fine with me. Fine with me."

"Go on, young lady, now you heard what your Mama said. Go on and put on your oldest shoes—and your raggedest dress."

Maggie glanced up at her mother. But Callie seemed not to hear. She was bustling about the kitchen, her back to them.

"Oh, anybody else——want to come along?" John offered magnanimously from the front door.

"Little late for that, isn't it John?" Callie called out from the kitchen. "Don't you go worrying yourselves about us. We girls will find something to occupy ourselves on a fine Saturday mornin'."

"Is Mama mad at us, Papa?" Maggie asked as they made their way through the tall grass in the pasture. They took off their shoes, waded the creek, then decided to walk on barefoot—as they might decide to wade in the river, once they'd reached it.

John didn't answer. They walked on. The walking was easy here. Once past the creek, the grassland gave way to deep stands of hardwoods—huge water oaks, red oaks, hickory nut trees forming the top canopy, with underneath, the flowering dogwoods, the sweetgums, the honey locust trees. The chinquapins.

The floor of the woods was smooth, spread with a deep carpet of leaves from over the years. Here, Maggie knew, the cow and the horse would come in out of the sun on hot summer days, and stand, and sometimes the milk cow would lie down, in the deep shade.

"Not far, we'll come to the river soon, now," John said.

"I know, Papa. I've been this way at least a million times."

"Really?" John stopped and gazed down at her in mock surprise, "That many times, huh?"

"Oh, Papa, you know what I mean. You're just trying to get me to forget that Mama's mad at us. Why, Papa? Why is Mama mad at us?"

"You never mind about your Mama," John took Maggie's small hand in his and squeezed it tightly. Then he knelt as best he could with his bad knee. Maggie's beautiful little face between his hands, he looked straight into those blue-blue eyes, so dark with concern right now.

"You listen to me, Margaret Ann McKinnon," John said, his lean face marked with laugh lines and deeply tanned from all the hours spent in the sun. "Just you listen to me and don't you ever forget it. Your Mama's a *grand* lady. Your Mama loves you *very* much. But your Mama, sometimes she gets these—*bees* inside her bonnet."

"How do the bees get in there?"

"I haven't exactly figured that out—yet. Exactly how the bees get in there—but she loves you very much."

"I know that, Papa."

"Well, that's just what I wanted to say. You see, Maggie," John hesitated, wanting the child to truly understand, "your mama's like a fine dollop of fresh butter."

"Butter—Papa?"

"You know, Maggie, how butter's so pur'ty to look at. And when it's cold, it's so hard. But once you touch it—beneath the warmth of your touch, it gets all sweet and soft—you see what I'm saying, Maggie?"

"You're saying you like to hug and kiss Mama. And she likes to hug and kiss you back—when you do. And then that makes her not be so mad."

"That's—about the long and short of it."

Maggie smiled at John, the sweetest smile ever God put on the face of a child.

She threw her arms about his neck, squeezing him tightly. And despite his bad leg, John picked the child up, and carried her on down to the river, where he plunked her down, ordering:

"Now you remember the rules—don't step over the sandbars—over into the deep water. Watch out for snakes, and the like, in the shallows—"

"Papa, you talk like I'm a *baby*."

"Well, you'll always be *my* baby. Here, let me put a bit of bait on that cane pole of yours."

They sat quietly, John contemplating the murmur of the water, the blueness of the sky. The companionship of his youngest child.

"You know, Maggie, the Cherokees used to do just what you and me are doing today. Right here. In this very river."

"They did?"

"But sometimes, they would catch fish in a different way."

"How, Papa?"

"Well, the grown folk would weave a bunch of wild vines and deerskin thongs together and take poles, and such, and make a kind of big "V" in the river. Then little children would all race upstream, and take limbs and branches, and such, and beat up the water."

"Why'd they do that?"

"To drive th' fish into their weirs. They'd have enough fish to eat, and some to hang over th' fire and smoke for winter.

"They lived here, remember how I told you? Had little summer houses all up and down th' valley. Little winter houses, too. Remember, how I told you Grandpa Shawn and Katherine Ann lived in a little Indian house, when first they came to this valley?"

"Why'd they have two houses?"

"It was too hard, when winter swept down off those mountains," John gestured broadly, "to keep th' summer houses warm—just made of river cane. Lots of cracks between the canes. So, they fixed them some little clay-capped houses, with hide doors, and a fire inside, and a little smoke-hole. Snug as could be. And you see, way down yonder? Not far, and you know where th' *big mound* rises up out of th' fields? You know, where I never plow or plant. Well, Maggie, that's where they had their seat of government—their Council House. And some of them may be buried in that mound."

"But, they're all gone. Where'd they all go, Papa?"

"Government marched them all out of their villages, at gunpoint, and over the mountains and plains, and all the way clear to the Oklahoma Territory."

"Is the Goverrr...ment bad, Papa?"

"I guess it's no worse than the rest of us. They do some good things—some bad."

"Are they still there, Papa?"

"Yeah, sugar, they are...out on the Oklahoma plains...except for those that escaped the soldiers ...and hid out in the high mountains."

"Why'd the Government do that, Papa?"

"Because of the gold, Maggie. Some men found gold, you know you heard all about it …over in Dahlonega. They still wrestle a bit of gold out of those hills about Dahlonega. But the big veins petered out within a few years after the Indians were all hauled off."

"It's sad, isn't it, Papa?"

"Yeah, sugar, sometimes life is sad. It's always sad—when folks do other folks wrong."

"Even Indians?"

"Well, Maggie, folks are folks. The Indians …they're folks just like us.

"You see this skin, Maggie? Well's it's just like a suit of clothes. No matter what color it is, take it off, and we all pretty much bleed alike underneath.

"But we didn't come down to the river to talk about the bad things of life. We'll just talk about the good parts—like today—you and me—sittin' here in the sun on this riverbank, wiggling our toes in the water. We've come a'fishin'—and not worried if we even catch a thing."

"If we don't care if we catch anything, why'd we even come?"

"I just wanted to spend a little time alone with you. To see how you were getting on …without Katie." John looked down at Maggie. Tears pooled in her blue eyes.

"I'm all right, Papa. Mama says you just have to stick your chin out, and march on, even when things happen you don't like. I'm so sorry, Papa."

"I didn't ask you about Katie to make you apologize, Maggie. I just want to find the truth about what happened to her. You recall taking her out to the barnyard, then running off to play, and leaving Katie there by the feed trough?"

"I must have Papa. Nobody played with Katie but me. Barbara Jo didn't even like her. She told me one day, 'That doll of yours, with her bright, painted face and eyes! She looks reee-diculous. She looks just like a Jezebel.' You know, Papa? The bad lady in the Bible? You think Katie looked like Jezebel, and that's why God rained all over her?"

"No, Maggie. And I'm sure your sister didn't mean what she said. But, you don't recall putting the doll down—there by the trough, and leaving her there?"

"I don't remember it, but it *had* to be me, Papa. I just don't know what's wrong with me!"

"Nothing, sugar—nothing in the whole wide world is wrong with you, Margaret Ann McKinnon. Race you to the house, to see if Mama's got any lunch ready!"

John didn't know anything else to do, but put Katie to a final rest, although he was certain that beautiful doll and her mysterious demise would haunt him until his dying day. The way they had gotten Katie—

So, after lunch, John raised himself up from the table and said, "Think I'll go for a little walk. Up on the mountain. You got the final remains of Katie, Maggie?"

"Yes, Papa, in a cardboard box, beneath my bed."

"Well, why don't we do the decent thing, and take her on up on the mountain, and put her to rest with the others."

"Oh, Papa! That's a grand idea! Let me just fetch her—"

"John!" Callie sighed, pouring up a kettle full of dishwater to heat, "You're goin' to walk all the way up that mountain—to give that melted doll a funeral? You'd think for all the world that thing was a real person!"

"Well, for Maggie, Callie, I suppose she sort of was."

"Well, John, it looks to me like you'd be tired, and want to go sit on the porch a spell, and rest a bit, it being Saturday. A man who's been followin' a mule and a plow, and plantin' all week, a body needs to just sit himself down and recuperate, every now and then. And let his soul take its ease."

Callie set the black iron kettle on the iron stove with a little bang.

"What makes you think my soul's not at ease, Callie?" John asked, coming up behind her, as she stood waiting for the water to heat. He put his arms around her waist, and pulled her back against him. "I know tonight's Saturday night, honey. I'll try not to tire myself out too much—"

"Oh! You—! Go on, John McKinnon! Get out of here, before I take my broom to you!" Callie turned and gave him a little shove, "You do beat all I ever saw!"

"Yes, Ma'am!" John grinned at her, gave her a little swat on the bottom, set his hat on his head at a rakish angle, and, humming softly, stepped out the back door to get his shovel from the barn. Maggie was anxiously waiting with her little shoebox and its soggy contents.

"You think we should sing a hymn, or somethin'?" John asked Maggie as they marched up the hill.

"Yes, Papa," Maggie said solemnly. "And you can, maybe, say a few words of comfort—over Katie."

"I don't know about that, sugar. I'm no preacher man. But, how's about if you recite a verse or so of the Scriptures Mama's been teaching you?"

Maggie stood tenderly holding her soggy box.

John dug out a fairly deep little hole, lined it with a soft carpet of leaves and straw.

Maggie bent and gently laid the wet little box on the warm leaves.

John watched, scratched his head, "You think we should have brought the fiddle? I should have thought of that. A little music to see Katie to rest?"

"You want me to go fetch it, Papa?"

"Up to you, Maggie."

Maggie was soon back, the fiddle carried carefully in her right hand, the bow clasped in her left.

As solemnly as if he was playing a requiem for a king or president, John placed the tip of the fiddle beneath his chin, lifted the horsehair bow, and began to play.

Callie could hear the strains of music, beautiful, soul stirring, drifting over the mountains, and down the valley. She muttered wonderingly, *"That John McKinnon! Playing a funeral dirge for a doll!"*

"That was beautiful, Papa," Maggie breathed when John lowered the instrument and gazed down at her. "I'll never forget this day, as long as I live."

"Nor I, sugar. Now, you go right ahead, and say your Scripture."

"All I can think of right now, Papa, is what Mama said about the sparrows. I know Katie wasn't a person like us, but surely she was worth as much as a sparrow—if they were bought two for a penny. And Katie cost you a whole ten cents."

"I'm sure she was worth much more. Now, say your Scripture."

"Not one sparrow ...

Falls to the ground ...

But your ...Heavenly Father sees it ...

And they cost ...two for a penny."

"That's close enough, Maggie. Now, you think we're about finished here?"

"Yes, Papa."

"Then, why don't you run on down and see if your Mama might need any help, and I'll just...clean up...a little...about this place."

John watched Maggie almost running down the hill, her long wavy black hair flying out behind her, her sunbonnet off and flying with it. He thought she flew like one of God's sparrows—free now.

Very solemnly, very slowly, John threw dirt over the little box, and then he placed a fair-sized rock at either end. He had placed the little "grave" off to one side, in a private place back in the trees. "We don't need to put her so close to the others," he had told Maggie.

"She wasn't that old, Maggie. And she might appreciate the quiet."

John was sure that soon the leaves would fall, the seasons pass, and Maggie would forget all about Katie.

Maggie burst into the kitchen. "Papa said I should hurry on back, Mama. He said that you might need me."

"Got everything taken care of, up there, did you, the two of you?"

"Yes, Mama. It's all over."

"Well! Good! Seems like your Papa knowed the exact dose of medicine that was needed."

"We didn't have any medicine up there, Mama. We just buried Katie."

"It was just a ...well, never mind Maggie—

"Nellie Sue," Callie ordered, "you pour the dishwater into that slop bucket, and go on down and pour it in to the pigs."

"Yes, Mama."

"And you, Barbara Jo, you go on out and draw us up a fresh bucket of water."

"Why do I have to do that? I always have to go out and draw up the water. That's much more work than slopping the pigs. And what's Maggie goin' to do?"

"She'll do whatever I tell her to ...just like you, young lady, now scoot!

"Well, Maggie. You and Papa have a good time, down at the river this mornin'? Don't seem to have caught a single fish."

"Fish weren't biting, Mama," Maggie said. "Anyhow, we didn't really go to fish."

"Well, so if the fish weren't biting, and you didn't go to fish ...what did you and Papa do?"

"Mostly talked."

"Oh? What about? Not that your Papa's not given to idle chatter from time to time."

"This wasn't idle chatter, Mama. This was *real* serious stuff."

"Oh? What exactly did you and Papa talk about?"

"He told me all about the Cherokee Indians. How they used to live in this very valley. Fished from that very river where we were sitting. They even made these fish net things ...out of leather thongs and wild grape vines ...to trap fish in a certain season, and hang them on poles over fires, and smoke them and dry them ...to eat during *cold* winter ...just like we do things ...you know—hams …and peas and beans and apples. Then the white men found gold. And the soldiers all marched the poor Indians to a place called Okle—homee. Then he told me about how the Indians all had two houses apiece—one for summer and one winter. One made of cane …the other of clay, and such, with a little hide door. And how—"

"That's okay, Maggie," Callie sighed, wiping her face with her apron tail, "Why don't you go on out and help Barbara Jo draw up another bucket of fresh water, for the wash shelf on the back porch? Your Papa'll be back down from that graveyard in a little while, and he might want to wash up. How I do wish he'd stay off that mountain! All that fretting and frowning and worrying—it's not going to bring your Grandpa Thomas Shawn McKinnon back home to his final resting place!"

Chapter 8

The three girls were playing tag, out in the front yard, beneath the huge oaks. They had become tired and sweaty, and had gone to sit down on the edge of the porch for a few minutes, to catch their breath.

Three pairs of bare feet dangled over the edge of the oak planks. Nellie Sue was the only one whose feet actually reached to the sandy yard. Nellie stretched out her legs, sinking bare toes into the white sand. Last nights rain had left the sand a bit damp. Her footprints showed plainly in the wet surface.

"Look at that!" Nellie cried, "See how big my feet are getting?"
Barbara Jo slipped off the porch, and planted her two feet beside Nellie's.

"Look," Barbara Jo bragged, "mine are almost as long as yours, Nellie."

Maggie slid forward on the porch, straining to reach the wet sand with her small feet. Just then, she felt something cold and wet against the back of one leg.

Giving a little squeal, Maggie yanked her bare feet onto the porch.

"Something tried to bite me!" she yelled.

"Did not!" Barbara Jo jeered. "You're just a little ol' scairdy cat! Scairdy Cat! Scairdy Cat!"

"Well, if you're so brave," Maggie challenged, "you just get down there and look, and see what's underneath this porch!"

"There's nothing underneath this porch," Barbara Jo hooted.

"Prove it!" Maggie shouted.

"All right, I will." Barbara Jo did not slide off the edge of the porch, but she stood up and walked down the steps. Reaching the sandy yard, she glanced at her sisters, and then she took a step towards the edge of the porch. Lifting her chin and shaking her hair, she gave them a brave smile, and bent low, to peer underneath.

Giving a piercing scream, Barbara Jo leapt back, and fled up the steps, squealing, "Mammmmaaa!"

"Well!" Nellie said nervously, "I wonder …what she saw under there?"

"Why don't you look?" Maggie suggested quietly.

"No!" Nellie refused. "Why should I be the one to look? It was your idea."

"All right," Maggie announced dramatically, "I will!"

She moved slowly towards the steps. Then descended them, one at a time.

Reaching the yard, she glanced at Nellie Sue, sitting on the porch, legs drawn safely up beneath her, naked feet tucked tightly beneath her long skirt.

"Go on!" Nellie urged.

Just as Maggie bent to peer beneath the porch, the front door swung open, and Callie stepped out.

"What's going on out here?" Callie demanded, "Your sister just told me—"

Cutting off Callie's words, a creature came bounding out from beneath the porch, flew at Maggie, and sent her toppling backwards into the sand.

Callie gave a piercing scream.

Maggie gave a series of frightened little yelps, as she rolled backwards, a thick ball of fur astride her chest—

—Happily licking her face.

"It's a dog!" Maggie declared gleefully. "It's a little dog, Mama! Isn't he beautiful?"

Barbara Jo said snidely, "You can't even see his eyes, for all that hair hanging about his face. He looks just like a bundle of old dirty rags."

"That's what I'll name him!" Maggie gave a joyful little squeal. *"Rags!* Come here, Rags!"

"Now, just a minute," Callie's stern voice cut off Maggie's gleeful calls.

"We don't know a thing about this dog. He may have some terrible disease. He probably belongs to some farmer near here. He's just lost, and looking for something to eat."

"Then let's feed him," Maggie smiled.

"No." Callie wagged her head vigorously. "Once you feed an animal, he expects to be fed again, in the same place, and we'll never get rid of him. Just go back in the house, and leave him alone. He'll soon get the idea there's nothin' here for him. He'll get real hungry and go home. You hear me, Maggie? You come away from that dog, and go on in the house. You, too, girls. Now scoot!"

"You think Rags is still out there?" Maggie whispered to Nellie Sue that evening as they lay in bed.

"How should I know? I can't see through walls." Nellie murmured sleepily. "Besides, what does it matter if he is? You can't play with him. And you can't feed him. Mama and Papa both said so."

"Well, good night," Maggie said sweetly.

"Do you really mean that?" Nellie Sue sat up in bed and gazed at her sister in the thin light. "I never did know you to give up *that* easily."

"I don't know what you're talkin' about," Maggie sighed innocently.

"I mean—don't you go gettin' yourself up in th' night, and sneakin' out and feedin' him—and playin' with that dog."

Every morning, Rags was waiting at the back porch steps, when John stepped outside. This morning, John knew that Callie was watching him from the kitchen.

"Well, *hellow* there, little fella'. I figured you'd be long gone by this time. You still here? Where do you live? You think anybody's missin' you by now? Why don't you just skeedadle it on home, now?"

"John?" Callie called from the kitchen door, "You out there talkin' to that dog? I thought you warned the girls not to do that. Now, here you are, a grown man—"

"It's not a panther or a bear, Callie. He's just a little dog, not much bigger than a—"

"John, I thought we discussed this, the afternoon the dog showed up. We decided that he definitely had to go. He's just something else to be fed and to be looked after."

"He might keep th' mice out of the barn," John offered.

"He might—and he might not!" Callie snapped. "He'd be always underfoot."

"He'd be lots of company for Maggie. She did find him, after all, and she just lost Katie Ann—"

"All right, John! All right! I don't know why I even *try* to reason with you about these things. Have you and Maggie been feedin' and pettin' this little animal?"

"Why, Callie! What *ever* gave you such a fool notion?"

"I just can't imagine, John. Can you?"

"Com'on, Rags!" Maggie ordered sternly, as she walked down the back doorsteps and out into the yard. "It's our turn to gather the eggs, remember, I told you? Now, you just stay behind me, and don't scare the chickens too much, and don't bark at the pigs or the cow. And if you see any rats or mice, you go right after them. This is a farm, and we all have to swing our weight. That's what Papa and Mama said. So if you intend to stay around the McKinnon farm, Rags, you have to swing your weight! Do you understand? This afternoon, I'll pick up some sticks and things, and we'll start letting you practice on fetching. So if a rat or mouse darts out of the hay, or out of the corncrib, you can get right on it. Then Mama will be proud of you, and there won't be any question—what are you doing—wandering off over there? Didn't I tell you what we had to do today? Now, keep your head about you."

John watched from the edge of the porch, as the pair made their way slowly towards the chicken coops, Rags trotting obediently along at Maggie's heels, gazing up at her with worshipful brown eyes, as if he was indeed soaking up every wise and wonderful word of his mistress' instructions. John smiled, and went back into the house.

A few months later, Callie remarked dryly, "I wonder what kind of dog *is* that? He sure keeps growin' and growin'. Table scraps go mostly to the hogs. Now, we're forced to share our food with that calf-like creature."

"He is big, that's for sure," John agreed, "but if you'll notice, Callie, there's not been hardly any rats about the hayloft. No egg has gone missing. Nothing trying ta' dig up th'—"

"All right, John, you've made your point. But I still say, that is some big dog. I wonder—"

"What does it matter, Callie, what kind of dog Rags is? Rags is pullin' his weight, and Maggie loves him. That's all that matters."

"Yes, John," Callie smiled sweetly, "That's really all that matters."

Maggie banged the back door shut. The empty water bucket in her hand, she was headed for the well curb. But just as she stepped out onto the back porch, Maggie noticed a strange dog. He gazed at her with glassy eyes. White foam dribbled from his mouth in little flecks.

"Hey, there," Maggie called softly. "What th' matter with you, doggie? You sick? You want me to draw you up a cool drink of water?"

"Maggie? Who you talking to out there? Is Rags sick?" Callie called.

"No, Mama, this is a different dog. He looks like he might be—"

"*JOHN!*"

"What is it, Callie? What's happened?"

"There's a dog…in the back yard …Maggie thinks he's…sick!"

"Where is Maggie?"

"She's…out there…she went to get a bucket of—"

In a flash, John was in the front room, snatching down the blunderbuss. He might only get one shot. He couldn't afford to miss.

The gun in his hand, he sprinted for the back door. John flung it open—to see Maggie by the well curb, Rags, teeth bared, ears laid back—between Maggie and the strange dog. The dog was not far from the back porch steps.

"Oh, my! John—!" Callie was on the verge of tears.

"You just stay inside, Callie. Don't you come out, no matter what happens, you hear me?"

Maggie stood beside the well curb, looking frightened and confused.

"Pa?" she called, "I think somethin's—"

"Be real quiet, Maggie, and just stay where you are. I'm going to try to get off a shot—"

Not waiting another moment, John crept along the porch, looking for a clear shot at the strange dog, which he immediately recognized as rabid.

Before John could get his shot in, the thing he had feared happened. Rags sprang for the throat of the mad-dog. There was an instant yelping and whirling of furry bodies, thrashing about between Maggie and the porch.

"Get around behind the well curb, Maggie!" John ordered. "And crouch down real low!"

Maggie hesitated.

"Do it now!"

John knew that he had no choice. He'd have to shoot both dogs. The blunderbuss gave a belching roar, sending shock waves through John's right shoulder. He hadn't missed. The mad-dog gave a terrified howl, and lay sprawled in the yard. Rags, blood spattered, his throat torn, stood guard over him.

"Maggie!" John yelled, "You can come on in the house now!"

"John!" Callie whispered, standing now at his elbow.

"I know, Callie. I know. Just get Maggie on in the house."

"Come on in here with me, Maggie," Callie called. "Forget the water for now. I need you to help me in the front room."

Her face pale with fright, Maggie scooted up on the back porch.

"But, Mama, Rags has been hurt. He's been hurt real bad. I need to—"

"It's okay, Maggie, your Papa will…take care of Rags."

"What do you mean, Mama!? You don't mean—?"

"You're right, Maggie. Rags *has* been hurt. Hurt *real* bad. He can't ...ever get well again."

"No, Mama! Let me go! I have to doctor him—"

The boom of the blunderbuss echoed through the kitchen.

"Noooooooooo!" Maggie jerked away from Callie and went flying out the back door, shrieking:

"Nooooooooooo! Noooooooooooooooo!"

"Get inside, Maggie!" John ordered.

"Nooooooooooo!" Maggie screamed.

She fled past John before he could catch her, and past the two still, bloody forms sprawled between the well curb and the back porch. She ran up the little slope to the outhouse. Darting inside, she banged the door shut, latching it from inside.

"John, how long do you think Maggie's going to stay in there? You'd think sooner or later the unpleasant odor would drive her out," Callie worried, as she gazed out the back door toward the outhouse. "Why don't you—"

"All right, Callie, I'll see if I can talk to her."

"Maggie? You all right in there? You didn't have any breakfast. Or any lunch. You gettin' hungry in there? Not much in there, to whet your appetite—"

"That's not funny, Papa!"

"It wasn't meant to be, sugar. I just want you to come on out of there, and talk to me about this thing."

"You didn't have to kill Rags, Papa. You didn't have to—"

"Yes, I did, Maggie. If I hadn't killed Rags, he would have turned all wild-eyed and mean, foaming at th' mouth—just like th' mad-dog. Then he would have been spreading that horrible rabies—all over the community."

"We could have doctored him!"

"Maggie, I sure do hate talkin' thru' th' outhouse door. Why don't you come on out of there, so we can speak face to face, like civilized people?"

"Go away, Papa!"

"Look, Maggie, there's no amount of doctorin' will cure rabies. It kills *everythin'* it touches. That's why, when an animal comes in contact with another animal with th' same disease—"

"We could have doctored him!" Maggie screamed.

"All right, Maggie. I'm just goin' on down to the house now. And *whenever* you feel like it, you can come on out. And we can talk about this some more. I'm going now ..."

"John, it's gettin' dark out there!"

"I know it, Callie."

"Well, supper's soon goin' to be on the table, and I'm not goin' to sit down to eat one bite—until that child is safe and sound in this house. Do you hear me?"

"If I bring her in now, Callie, and she's been out there in that outhouse all day, you may not want Maggie at the supper table."

"Well, we can give her a bath. Nellie Sue, you go out and fetch in a tub. Barbara Jo, you head on out to the well, and draw up a few buckets of water. I'll put on th' kettle, and go on up and fetch her a nice change of clean clothes. I declare! This is the *craziest* house on Earth!"

"Maggie?" John called through the oak planks of the outhouse door. "Mama says you have got to come on in the house. *Now!* And your Mama, she means *business*, young lady. Now you just come on out of there, no argument about it, or I'm going to get my axe and chop th' latch off this ... well, helllow, sugar. You have a good day ...in there?"

"Good as any, I suppose," Maggie answered, her chin quivering.

"Oh, sugar," John reached for her, picked her up in his arms and held her tight—despite the offensive odor. This was Maggie. "Your Papa would rather have done anything in this world, than shoot your Rags. But, sometimes, Maggie, life doesn't give us any *choice*."

"I know, Papa, it's just that ...why does life have to hurt so much?"

"Maybe that's what keeps us strong, Maggie, pushing back with all our might, against that tide that's always threatening to just swallow us all up."

"Well, Maggie," Callie scolded, "I must say! You have given this entire family quite a day—"

"Let's just leave it at that, shall we, Callie? And if you don't mind, tonight, I'd like to say Grace."

"Well...John..."

"Dear Lord, we thank you for keeping us all safe through this day. Watching out for us every minute, just like *You* do the sparrows. We know that when *You* send bad things our way, Lord, it's most likely just *Your* way of keeping us on our toes, wakin' us up by shoutin': '*Look up!—Look up here, at ME.*' And, well, I guess that's about all I want to say, Lord, except ...much obliged...for sending Rags to save Maggie's life. Amen"

Without a word, Callie slipped from her chair, and walked out of the kitchen, onto the back porch. The moon hung high up on the mountain ridges, like the most beautiful thing Callie had ever seen. She fought to keep the tears at bay. Callie was not a whiner, or a crier. But tonight—

"Sweetheart?" John came out and stood beside her. They stood silently for a few moments, not touching.

"Isn't that a lovely moon, John?" Callie sighed.

"Oh. Yeah. Sure," John replied. "Lovely."

"John, there's just something I want you to hear. Something I should have said, a long time ago."

"What's …that …Callie?" John steeled himself, having not the faintest idea what was coming.

"I just want to say, 'I'm much obliged to you, God, for sending John Thomas McKinnon, to marry that silly little blond that talks too much. I don't know what on earth she would have done without him …'"

"You're right, Callie," John said.

Callie turned and looked up at him.

"That there *is* about the *pur'tiest* moon I ever did see. Let's you and me just forget about supper …and go for a little walk in the moonlight…"

Chapter 9

The berries hung heavy on wild blackberry, huckleberry and dewberry vines. Apples ripened in the orchard back of the house. Peaches and cherries were ready to preserve and dry. Green beans grew plump in Callie's kitchen garden. All this was to be gathered, and stored for winter.

And in the fields beyond the pasture and the creek, cotton bolls were bursting with fluffy white. Ears of Indian corn slowly matured, their sweet grains bursting with white corn milk, down in the river bottoms.

Early each morning, as soon as breakfast was cleared away, Callie and the girls donned their oldest, most worn dresses, most faded, floppy-brimmed sunbonnets, stocking gloves (stockings with the toes cut out to allow free motion of the finger tips to grip the fibers) and headed for the cotton fields.

Callie always carried along a basket of food, which would be voraciously consumed when the sun stood high overhead. She also carried along an empty pitcher and dipper. Water they would scoop up from the nearby creek or spring.

Maggie always enjoyed the days in the fields. The girls would pick cotton for a while, until their hands and backs got a little tired, and then they'd be tossing empty cotton bolls across the rows at one another. Then they'd be hiding in the tallest cotton stalks, playing tag, and hide-and-go-seek.

"John McKinnon!" Callie would call every now and again, when all this dilly-dallying was going on, "Do you see what your daughters are doing?"

John would stand, gaze out over the cotton rows, at his three beautiful nymphs, sporting through the green, glistening rows, "Yeah, Callie. I sure see. And, personally, I never *ever* saw anything come near to how pretty them three are."

At the end of a day of picking, Callie and the girls would be resting at the edge of the field, on the leaf-strewn grass beneath the tallest trees.

John would be busy loading the farm sled he had brought down from the barn early that morning, leaving the horse tied to a tree in the shade at the end of the field, where he could graze.

"I do believe—!" Callie observed, "That Papa of yours, girls …that man can pick more cotton in a single day than any man I ever did see!"

"How much does he pick, Mama?" Maggie asked.

"Way more than two hundred pounds…maybe two seventy-five…most probably…three hundred."

"How much do you pick, Mama?" Maggie persisted.

"Me? Well, now, compared to your Papa, I'd be almost ashamed to say."

"How much, Mama?" Maggie insisted.

"Maybe a hundred fifty pounds on a good day. A hundred seventy-five would be pushing it."

"How about us, Mama? How much do we pick?"

"Well, Maggie, given all the giggling and cavorting amongst the stalks, I'd be afraid to hazard a guess."

"Well, we can settle this," Maggie announced, getting up and walking off.

"Papa? How much cotton do your girls pick? Nellie Sue, Barbara Jo and me?"

"Hummmm. Right off hand, I'd be afraid to stick my neck out on that question. Maybe when we get the sled back to the barn and unhitch the horse, we could just get out the steelyards—and find out. We might even have ourselves a cotton-pickin' contest."

Maggie and the girls hurried up to the barn. The three of them were waiting in the huge entrance when Papa and Mama came up with the horse and the sled.

"C'mon, Papa," Maggie was urging him. "Come on and weigh our picksacks. I know exactly which one is mine!"

"We do, too," Nellie Sue and Barbara Jo chimed in, "let's weigh them!"

"Okay," said John. "And let's say …the winner …that is to say, the one who picked the most cotton …therefore, her sack weighs the most …gets …"

"*Gets what, Papa?*" all three girls chorused.

"She gets out of washing the dishes, slopping the pigs, drawing the water—so, then, *who's going to do all that*?" John asked, as if highly puzzled.

"*The losers!*" they all chimed.

"Let me get the steelyards, and hang them on the big iron hook up there on that beam." Papa fetched the steelyards, an iron contraption with a big teardrop-shaped iron ball that swung from a notched scale.

"What's that, Papa, beside the steelyards?" Maggie pointed.

"Oh, that's a cooling board, sugar, that your Grandpa Thomas built for his Pa, Shawn, to rest on and cool after his passing, before he was dressed for burial."

John hurried on, wanting to change the subject. He didn't want to think about the board for cooling corpses. He snatched the three small picksacks off the sled, "Remember now, winners *never* boast...and losers *never* whine!"

Maggie seemed to have forgotten the board. "Go on, Papa! Weigh them!"

"Whose shall we start with?"

"Nellie's! She's the oldest!" Maggie jumped up and down in excitement.

"Okay, here we go...Nellie Sue McKinnon picked...ninety-three pounds of cotton! Let's all give Nellie Sue a *big hand*!"

"You're just stalling, Papa!"

"Okay. Let me see. Who is next? Oh? Yes...that would be Barbara Jo. Barbara Jo McKinnon...has picked...thirty...pounds."

"*Only thirty?*" Barbara Jo whined.

"And....Maggie..."

"*Margaret Ann*," Maggie yelled.

"And Margaret Ann McKinnon...has...picked...*forty*...pounds!"

"No way!" Barbara Jo yelled angrily. "No way, did Maggie pick more than me! I'm way older than she is ...and I worked way harder!"

"Sorry, Barbs," John wagged his head. These steelyards are the government approved tool for weighing cotton...all over the—"

"I don't care! It...just...isn't fair."

"Barbara Jo!" Callie ordered, "Did you vote to weigh th' picksacks?"

"Yes, Mama."

"Then you and Maggie go on and start your chores. Nellie Sue, you can just go and sit out on the porch, and take your ease. When you're through with your chores, girls, you two can come on in the kitchen, and help me get supper started. Is that understood?"

"Yes, Mama."

"Sure, Mama," Maggie added cheerfully, "I didn't expect to win. I don't even care if Nellie Sue gets to sit out on the porch. Sitting on the porch can be *migh—ty* boring sometimes. I'd much rather go lean over the well curb, and see if it's still light enough for me to see my reflection down there. And the pigs are growing so much. They're fun to watch, snorting and rutting each other from the trough. You want me and Barbs to pull them some extra weeds, down along the pasture fence? Some mighty fat weeds growing there—"

"Maggie!" Barbara Jo cried, stunned. "You're going to make this thing worse that it already is! I'm tired from all that cotton pickin' …and you want to add extra chores…you want to *go pulling weeds for the pigs?*"

"It's all right, Barbs," Nellie Sue smiled, walking over towards the woodpile and the chop block, "I don't mind one bit helping out. I'll chop up some kindling and bring in the wood. You and Maggie can do—"

"Bringing in the wood…that's the *easiest* part," Barbara Jo whined.

"Okay, then," Nellie Sue said slowly, "I'll draw the water and—"

"I *always* draw the water," Barbara Jo interjected.

"Okay, Barbs, come on, and we'll work this thing out. How about if—"

"What do you want me to do, Mama?" Maggie asked, looking up at Mama a bit confused.

"Just go along with the others," Callie said tiredly. "I'm sure—among the three of you—it will all come out fine. Just see to it that everything's done."

Maggie ran off, her dark hair flying.

"Okay!" she yelled, "here's what we're going to do. Nellie Sue will chop the kindling, just like she offered. 'Cause *she's* the winner, and *she* gets first choice. Then Barbara Jo, because you whine so, and we are tired of hearing it, you do whatever you want to choose—and whatever's left, I'll do the rest!"

John laughed to himself. What a trio! Then, even the moment the laughter rose in his throat, it died there. Was Nellie Sue walking with a limp? But she had done so well, since that awful spill she took off the front porch. So well, in fact, that the rest of the family had almost forgotten the entire incident. But, yes, she was definitely limping. "Nellie Sue, honey?" John called to her.

Nellie Sue turned, and John recalled the first time he ever laid eyes on the child. How he had thought she didn't look quite real, with her long blond hair, fair skin, and light blue eyes. Now, John thought, she hasn't changed a bit. She's just taller, filled out. Nellie Sue's almost a woman. What is she now? She must be going on fifteen. She still looks like an angel.

"Come over here, Nellie Sue. I want to talk to you for a minute."

"Yes, Papa?" Nellie Sue hesitated. "But, we have all the chores to do. Can it wait?"

"No, honey," John said slowly, "I don't think this can wait. You see the thing is…" he began, laying a hand on her slender shoulder as she approached, sweeping a strand of the long blond hair with one of his fingers, "…the thing is…we don't need to let these girls get *away* with this."

"What, Papa?"

"You and I know good and well that you won that cotton-pickin' contest, fair and square—and by a *whoppin'* margin."

"That's all right, Papa, I really don't mind—"

"Well, I'm the Papa. And *I* mind. Now, you just go on over yonder, and sit your pretty little self down on that front porch. Put your feet up on a stool or chair—and you just rest, now, you hear me? This is your Papa, speaking to you?"

"Sure, Papa," Nellie Sue laughed, "but...Maggie's expecting me."

"You go on, now, and never mind. I'll speak to Maggie."

Maggie would recall for years to come, how Papa approached her, all quiet like, as she was loading her arms with split wood for the cookstove. He stood watching her for a moment, then he spoke, all choked and strained.

"Maggie? Your sister, Nellie Sue, has gone to rest on the porch, just like she was supposed to, you see—"

"That's fine, Papa," Maggie flashed John a sweet smile. "She was the winner."

"Well, the thing is Maggie, Nellie Sue really wanted to get in the wood, but I wouldn't let her."

"Why not, Papa?"

"Because ...Nellie Sue's not doing as well as we all thought she was. I don't know how long this has been going on ...but I just noticed ...that Nellie Sue's begun to limp, again."

"Is Nellie Sue sick, Papa?"

"I don't know, sugar. I'm just goin' to go on in th' house, now, and talk to your Mama. See if we can sort this thing out."

"I don't think it's anything to be worried about John. Nellie Sue's been limping...off and on...sometimes worse than others...ever since the accident."

"Well, Callie...you never called it to my attention!"

"Nellie Sue's your daughter, John. Why should I have to call it to your attention?"

"It's just...that...we need to take her to see th' doctor. This might be something serious."

"I don't think so, John. She's been in the cotton field all day. All of us are tired to the bone—except perhaps for Maggie, who never runs down. Nellie Sue will be just fine come mornin'. You'll see."

"Be that as it may, Callie, I don't want Nellie Sue goin' to the field *anymore*! Not for pickin' cotton or pullin' corn, or diggin' up groundnuts—

you understand? If she feels like piddlin' about in th' garden or th' house, then good. But no more going to th' fields."

"Of course, John, whatever you say. But, it *is* harvest time, and there's so much work to do—and if Nellie Sue's feelin' better tomorrow—"

"I know how much work there is, Callie. And from now on, I intend personally to do Nellie Sue's share of the field work. I can stay a bit later, after you and the other girls come to the house. And if Nellie Sue's feelin' better, tomorrow, well, good and fine for that—but she's to stay in the house or th' garden."

"Of course, John. Whatever you say."

"Look, Papa!" Nellie Sue cried cheerily, gliding ever so gracefully down the stairs the following morning.

"Well, just look at you, sweet thing! And don't you look so beautiful. Papa's angel! Come on down, honey, and give your old Papa a kiss. My! My! It just breaks my heart!"

"What, Papa?" Nellie Sue's lovely face was suddenly stricken.

"Why, at how many young fellas I'm goin' to have to run off this place with my shovel or a hoe handle, or maybe even that old blunderbuss of your Grandpa Thomas'."

"Oh, Papa! I love you so much!"

"Me, too, sugar, the same for you. Now, you just go on and find yourself something restful to do today."

"But, Papa, there's—"

"You won that cotton-picking contest…and I, the Papa of this place, hereby extend the benefits of the winner…indefinitely! I saw you limping yesterday, Nellie, and don't you go tryin' to hide it from me, any more, you hear. Nor from your Mama. How bad is it?"

"Is that what this is all about? It's not …too bad, Papa. Sometimes, the knee swells up, but then it goes back down again."

"Well. We'll just see how a while off that leg does you, you hear me? Don't you have some good books you can read, or somethin'? Seems like I recall you like to read, honey?"

"Not many books, Papa. They're—"

"Then we'll just send your sisters scoutin' the neighbors. See what we can scare up."

"Well, what did you find?" Papa asked Maggie, as they sat on the front steps, a cool evening breeze bathing their faces, fireflies flickering, and night sounds bouncing off the sky.

"Not much, Papa," Maggie said. "Nobody in this whole valley can afford books. But, there's an old house. I bet that old house is just full of books. I heard they have a *library*...and a *music* room, a room just for music."

"What old house, Maggie? I never heard of any such place around here?"

"I heard this talk about it, at school, Papa. Big house, over the other side of the mountain."

John stared at Maggie for a moment. Then he realized the house she meant.

"That's private property, Maggie," John warned. "Nobody's been living at that place, as far as I know, for nigh onto ten or twelve years now...since sometime during the war. And that's just a rumor. It's a long way over there. And none of our affair. No matter if there's a *hundred* books in that house, it's of no use to us."

"But, couldn't we just check it out Papa? If we could find the people who own the place...for such a good cause, they might lend—"

"Maggie, now your hear me and hear me good. Nellie Sue seems fully recovered...from whatever afflicted her the other day. All she needed was a little rest and recuperation. I just want her, from now on, to take it a bit easier. You see that you girls do your share of the chores, and hers, too, for a while. Now, I want you to promise me that you won't do anything foolish...like trying to contact the owners of Cottonwood."

"*Cottonwood?*"

"Yes, Maggie, that's what I hear the old plantation is called."

"Do they have lots of *cottonwoods*, Papa?"

"I haven't the slightest idea, Maggie. Who knows why names like that catch on? Could be two, could be two dozen over there. But that's neither here nor there. *No* trying to contact the owners of Cottonwood!"

"What were their names, Papa? The owners of Cottonwood—"

"I don't know...something like Hunston, or Houston—no you don't young lady—! You're not gettin' another word about that place out of me!"

Chapter 10

With their empty berry buckets, the three girls came walking up the road. "When are we going to find the blackberry patch? I thought it was closer than this. Why are we going this way? It's hot out here."

"Stop being such a cry-baby, Barbs," Maggie ordered. Adjusting her huge sunbonnet with her free hand, her empty berry bucket in the other, she stepped smartly along as if she was bound for a party. "We'll be there soon."

"Where, exactly, Maggie?" Nellie Sue asked wearily. Her knee had begun to throb. "Where is this lovely blackberry patch?"

"I don't think there *is* a blackberry patch. We're *lost*! I'm going to tell *Mama*!" Barbara Jo exclaimed. "It seems we've walked for miles! We left early this morning! The sun is getting so hot! Look at all the dust on my dress! This road is all rutted and full of gullies. I don't think *anybody* has been this way forever! Not one sign of a wagon track!"

From beneath the brim of her floppy sunbonnet, she tried to glimpse the sky, to see how the sun stood, to see what time of day it might be. Her hair clung to her head in damp tendrils. In exasperation, Barbara Jo came to a complete halt. She stood stubbornly in the middle of the road, a deep frown on her narrow face, lips protruding in a pout, refusing to budge another step.

"Stop whining, Barbara Jo!" Maggie ordered again. "It's right around here somewhere. Right around this bend. Oh! Look there! Oh, my!" she cried innocently, "Look at that old house!"

It was a *big* house. A huge veranda ran the entire length of the front, and above that a second veranda of equal length and grandeur spanned the upper story. Giant columns rose, supporting the verandas. Roses, now gone wild, twined about the columns. Above the upper veranda, the white oak shingles of the roof had weathered to a silvery gray.

At either end of the big house and along the back, rose several tall chimneys. Just a piece to the side of the house, there was the kitchen, connected to the main structure by a narrow dog run. The floor of the dog run was cobbled with river rock. The run was sheltered by a roof of silvery oak shingles that matched the roof on the main house. Beside the kitchen, there stood a carriage house with great double doors. Several hundred feet behind the house, across the valley and in the shadow of the mountain ridge, loomed a great barn. Several outbuildings clustered around it—a granary, a smithy, and a smokehouse.

Off to one side, beneath the giant oaks that shaded the southern end of the property, stood a little row of sturdily built cabins.

The three girls halted dead still in the narrow dirt road. Solemnly they stared at the house, none of them speaking.

"It sure is a big house, isn't it?" Maggie finally whispered. "Is it what they call in the story books a *castle*?"

"No. At least I don't think so," Nellie Sue replied. She had not been informed about the book hunt. "But then, I haven't read all that many story books. Books are so expensive. I don't know a soul that has one in their house, except for their Bibles."

"Miss Stillwell has some, under her desk at school," Maggie spoke so softly Nellie Sue had to strain to catch the words, "She let me look at one, once. It had all sorts of pictures in it ...of a place with big buildings and streets with rocks laid all over them."

"Cobblestones," Nellie Sue said absently. "Did it have any castles?"

"I don't think they were castles. Just big houses. Like this one. And look! It has verandas running all across the front of the lower floor and all across the front of the upstairs, too. It's a plantation house, *'Cottonwood'*...just like ...just like he said."

"Just like *who* said?" Nellie asked quickly.

As if she didn't hear, Maggie hurried on. "And no one lives here. They haven't for a long time. I wonder why they built it, if they didn't want to live here?"

"Who told you all this?" Nellie Sue asked. "I never even so much as *heard* of this place. How would I know why they don't live here, Maggie? You'll have to ask Mama."

"Because it's haunted, that's why," Barbara Jo stated importantly. "I've heard about this place. That's why the yard's all grown up and nobody comes here anymore. It's *haunted*, because some woman died in there. Her ghost still lives in the upstairs hall."

"That's silly," Nellie Sue laughed uneasily.

"I'll say!" Maggie put in, forcing her voice to a normal level. "Mama says there's no such thing as ghosts—except the Holy Ghost of God. He's the only one that's real. All the rest are just make-believe. And *He's* not scary at all."

"There are, too, such things as ghosts," Barbara Jo countered. "I've heard that sometimes she appears in the upper windows, moving from window to window, wailing and moaning as she goes."

"Where did you hear that?" Maggie asked, a little put out that apparently Barbara Jo knew more about this place than she did.

"I heard about it at school. From someone who ought to know. The place *is* haunted."

"That's silly," was all Maggie could think to say, echoing Nellie Sue's words of a few moments ago.

Nothing more was said for several minutes, as the three girls all turned their attention to the great house. A breeze had begun to stir down from the mountains, causing the giant trees at either side of the property to sway softly. The front yard bristled with weeds and wild flowers. Clumps of broomsedge had grown up in the curved graveled drive that circled in a half moon, and led up to the carriage house doors on the south side.

"What are those, I wonder?" Maggie pointed to the row of little cabins south of the main house.

"That must be the slaves' cabins. They must have had slaves here ...before the war," Nellie Sue gazed at the little shacks, a small frown wrinkling her pretty brow. "Oh, I remember now. This must be the old *Hurston* place. I've heard Papa speak about it. That's why Papa went to fight the War."

"Because this is the old Hurston place?" Maggie asked incredulously.

"No, Maggie! Because this place, and other fine plantations like it, had slaves." Nellie Sue explained patiently.

"That's not much reason to fight a whole war," Maggie surmised thoughtfully.

"I don't know. You know Papa doesn't like talking about the war. So don't you go pestering him about it. Nor about this place," Nellie Sue ordered.

"Oh, don't you go worrying yourself about that, Nellie Sue," Maggie said a bit too innocently. "I don't pester Papa! And certainly, not about this place. Might just be a good idea...if we *all* promise here and now, *none* of us will pester Papa about this place, all right? All right, Barbara Jo, do you promise? None of us will say *one word* about this place. *Not one word*!"

"You're the one's always pestering Papa!" Barbara Jo stated defiantly, "You pester *everybody* that will listen to you. Always asking all those stupid questions!"

"Well," Maggie asserted stoutly, "how else do you get smart and learn anything if you don't ask? Do you solemnly promise?"

"You're not all that smart. You just *think* you're smart!" Barbara Jo countered.

"I never said I was smarter than anybody else," Maggie denied angrily. "Now, do you promise—"

"Hush, you two. Stop your arguing. We need to get on; it's getting late. If we're going to pick any berries…is that why we came all the way over here?" Nellie Sue turned on Maggie, "Is this great long walk about picking wild berries, or about an old haunted plantation house? We need to get enough berries at least to make a pie."

"It's not haunted," Maggie replied meekly, her eyes asking her big sister for understanding and forgiveness. "Honest, Nellie, I just wanted to see it for myself. I'd heard about it …don't you want to see it?"

"So, all right, we've seen it. Now, we best be getting on."

"Did you see that?" Barbara Jo gasped, a hand flying to her mouth.

"What?" the two other girls asked.

"Something *moved*! There's someone at that upstairs window!"

"No, there's not. It's only your imagination." As Maggie said this, she wondered if a ghost *did* inhabit the once-fine plantation house. "Nobody else had slaves in the valley," she murmured, "why did this place have slaves?"

"There *is* someone there!" Barbara Jo cried in a tiny voice, all but jumping up and down in fright, her empty berry bucket jangling against her thin leg.

"Hush, Barbara Jo!" Maggie ordered. "You're scaring Nellie."

"Nellie Sue's not the scared one!" Barbara Jo narrowed her light blue eyes and glared at Maggie defiantly. "You're the scared one. Too scared to go up and knock on the door, to see if there *is* anyone inside."

"If there *is* a ghost in there," Nellie Sue's voice sounded a bit shaky, "do you think she's going to open the door and politely invite us in?"

"Well, maybe she's out riding in her fine carriage," Barbara Jo shrugged thin shoulders.

"Fine carriage?" Maggie asked.

"Yes," Barbara Jo replied importantly. "Didn't you know? They say she takes it out occasionally, a fine black carriage drawn by midnight-black horses."

"All right. That settles it. I'm going to walk right up to that door, and give a loud knock." True to her word, immediately Maggie marched off—through the broomsedge and the beggar lice and the cockleburs. Just as she reached the front door, and tried to catch a glimpse inside by leaning towards one of the tall windows beside the door—

—A great jangling and rattling rolled out of the carriage house! The huge double doors burst open. Out plunged two midnight-black horses, heads up, nostrils flared, drawing a grand black carriage that flew like the wind.

"*Maggie!*" Nellie Sue yelled.

But Maggie had already reached the road by the time the warning was out of Nellie Sue's mouth.

Whirling about, the three girls fled down the dirt road, their bonnets and skirts flying.

William Bartram Hurston stood gazing out the upstairs window. He had seen the three girls, sauntering up the road, their lard-buckets swinging in their hands. He supposed those were meant to be their berry-picking buckets. But they seemed to be pretty light, empty, as they came jauntily swinging them along. How long since he'd seen anybody walking up that road? One of the little girls, a truly beautiful child, from what William could make out from this distance, was gesturing and talking, attempting, it seemed, to convince her companions of something. He drew his eyes away from the window and from the girls.

How long since he'd been back to Cottonwood? Not since his daughter, Ellie, had gone off with that Yankee!

When William carried his only daughter to Philadelphia with him on a business trip, shortly before the War Between the States broke out, Ellie had met Robert Japheth Logan.

William Hurston had been conducting business with Robert Logan's father for some years past, and had always found Paulus Lee Logan to be a man of highest intellect and integrity. But on this particular trip, it soon became apparent to William that he and his old friend held widely differing views concerning certain affairs—the affairs that were drawing their respective states into a bloody conflict.

The old friends had parted in a huff, and William had ordered Ellie not to see—or be in contact with—young Robert Logan.

That very night, Ellie disappeared from the hotel where they were staying.

The next day, William Bartram Hurston received a message—

—Ellie and Robert Logan were married.

William left a curt reply for Ellie, at the Logan residence.

She had made her choice. She had disobeyed and disgraced him, had turned her back on him and on their home. She was no longer his daughter.

William returned home, broken hearted.

After several weeks, William finally received a letter—which he promptly consigned to the fire. As far as he was concerned, Eleanor, his beautiful Eleanor, was dead.

She wrote three additional letters. Each letter, William burned immediately upon arrival. Then he was told by a friend who made a furtive business trip to Philadelphia, that he had seen Ellie. He said she had married into a fine family. She had a little boy—whom they had named *William Bartram Logan*.

William had replied angrily to his friend, "There is no such thing, as a *fine Yankee family*!"

"But William, what about the boy?"

"As for the boy," William had replied angrily, "I'll not share my name— even if it *is* only my given name—*with a bloody Yankee*! *No matter his relationship!*"

The next letter that arrived, William—seeing how it tore the heart out of the girl's mother—copied the return address onto a fine white envelope, and wrote a cryptic note with his own hand:

My Dear Young Woman,

> *In the future, please refrain from writing to this place of residence, claiming to be the daughter of the house. I have no daughter. My only daughter is dead.*

No more letters arrived, from that fine street in Philadelphia.

His wife never forgave him. She died of a broken heart—the year the war began.

William buried her in the family plot, in the willow trees at the foot of the mountain. Then he freed all the Negroes.

Then he left Cottonwood. He couldn't bear the empty rooms. He moved to Charleston, where he felt he might do something to support the war effort. He was not young enough to take up arms, but he had a good deal of money, and a good head on his shoulders.

He purchased two fast sloops, the *Midnight* and the *Raven*, that sailed up and down the coast, undetected, and during the siege of the Charleston Harbor, ran the blockade swiftly and silently, transporting supplies and ammunition all up and down the Rebel lines. Several bloody assaults were made upon Charleston, but the city withstood them all—until Sherman made his march through the interior of the south. In January of 1865, the Confederate Army was evacuated from Charleston. But William did not come home to Cottonwood. He couldn't bear the thought of the big empty house.

William Bartram Hurston, had, during these hectic years, kept track of Ellie, through his friend who visited Philadelphia. But he made no attempt to contact her.

Now, the war had been over for several years. William felt old. Drained. Alone. He had divested himself of all his interests in Charleston. He had returned home to Cottonwood, more than comfortably well off.

Now, before he died, he wanted to see his daughter. His grandson. Now, here it was the Year of Our Lord, 1875, ten years, since the War ended—

—And William Bartram Hurston had never seen his only grandchild.

He sat down at his writing desk and penned a short note. Not really a letter. No apologies—far too late for that—just:

> *"I am an old man, now, Eleanor. Too old to journey all the way to Philadelphia. But I am still your father. And before I make that final crossing to meet my Maker—may He in His eternal mercies forgive me for all my sins and shortcomings—I have but one wish. To see my grandson."*

> *Your Father,*
> *William Bartram Hurston*

Across the front of a fine envelope, he wrote in an angular hand the address he had saved all these years—in Philadelphia.

Then William Hurston drew a large hand across his brow, sat back in his plush chair, laid down the pearl-handled writing pen near the ivory inkwell. Then, slowly he rose:

"Jacob?" he called as he made his way slowly down the great winding staircase to the first floor.

As he reached the bottom step, William hesitated. A great lump filled his throat, threatening to choke off his breath. There it sat! Like a great lump of guilt—there against the far wall in the corner of the front parlor. He had it moved off to one side, away from the big window that let in the light that used to fall across her face, her hair, her gown, as she sat there, playing so beautifully. His Ellie! His only child! What great plans he had for her! Marriage into some fine Southern Methodist family—but there it sat. And every time he descended the stairs, he felt as if it was mocking him.

Why didn't he get rid of that pipe organ? It was a costly instrument, a grand instrument, brought over the mountains at great bother and expense.

But the very sight of it had become repulsive to William. It had become a thorn in William's flesh.

He'd sell the thing …no …give it to some good charity.

"Jacob?" William called again, tearing his gaze from the fancy pipe organ, and looking to the high arch at the side of the parlor.

Jacob came trotting.

As his frail form reached the great arch leading into the grand dining room, Jacob slowed, his head bowed respectfully,

He was the last of the Negroes that used to work the fields and clean the house and cook fine meals—at Cottonwood.

When his wife had passed, and William had freed all the Negroes before leaving for Charleston, Jacob had looked at his Master that day, cocked his head to one side and sadly surmised:

"Massa William, where Jacob gwin' to go? Jacob's got nuthin'. Jacob's got nobody. Jacob's got no place to go. If it be all right with you, Massa William, I goes with you, to this new house you done bought, over in that place called Charles Town."

Jacob moved slowly into the room. He was still strong, at fifty—or was it sixty years of age? Few of the Negroes knew when they had been born into this world. But all the Negroes at Cottonwood were in fine health when they were freed. William Hurston had always seen to it that every soul at Cottonwood was well treated.

"I'd like you to hitch up the carriage, Jacob, and take a letter into town." He held out the envelope and Jacob took it.

Then William checked out the front window. They were still there, gazing at the house, arguing.

Then one of them, apparently the youngest, turned and set her gaze on the house. With determined little steps, she started toward the house.

William watched the child, making small progress across the front yard choked with cockleburs and beggar lice and thorn bushes. Then, to his amazement, he saw that apparently her intention was to come right up to the door. Should William open the door himself, and invite the three of them in for tea and biscuits?

Probably not. If that big front door flew open, it would probably scare the child to death. From her determined approach, she had no idea that a soul was inside—watching her.

She reached the front veranda. She mounted the broad steps, and turned towards the very window where William was so delightedly peering out.

Oh, my, she would catch him spying on them!

William ducked into the shadows, behind the heavy velvet curtains flanking the front windows. Still the child came on.

Then, there she stood, her small face so close to the window that the brim of her bonnet pressed against the glass. William could see little puffy fogs of breath on the pane. William's heart almost ceased beating. He blinked his eyes. Was she a vision? Or was she *real*? He'd never seen such a beautiful little face.

Had Eleanor come back in the guise of a child, to haunt him?

Then she was gone.

When Jacob led the pair of matched blacks up from the stables and into the big carriage house through the back, and hitched them up to the carriage, they pranced and pawed the graveled dirt floor before the closed front carriage doors. Impatient to be out for a run, it was all Jacob could do to hold them. It took him some time to find the harness and get them all hitched up. Seemed to Jacob it took about forever. So when they were all hitched up, and when Jacob swung open the double carriage doors and leapt onto the front seat, out they burst, and went thundering through the doors and down the weed-choked drive.

Old Jacob smiled to himself, as he saw two slender figures go tearing down the road, bonnets flying, at the sight of the stallions and rig. And behind them, several steps back, a third little figure was lifting up her feet and putting them down with amazing alacrity. In less than a minute, she had caught them.

"Them little gurls!" Jacob laughed to himself and slapped a bony knee, "They's must'a thought they wuz seein' a ghost!"

———————

"Well?" Callie inquired, fixing her eyes sternly on her three daughters, seated across from her at the battered oak table, "*Where was* it you girls were supposed to be today?"

"Picking blackberries," Maggie replied in a small, pert voice, staring fixedly down at the peas and turnip greens in her plate. Nellie Sue and Barbara Jo said not a word.

"Well," Callie said again, slowly stirring the food about on her plate, "wild blackberries must not be in season ...eh? ...seeing that not one of you has the first blackberry? And I couldn't help but notice Maggie's skirt tail. While you two girls remain apparently unscathed, Maggie's skirt tail is about hidden from sight—by cockleburs, beggar lice, briar limbs, puffs of broomsedge—"

"It was *all her fault!*" Barbara Jo accused. Her thin face flushed, she was anxious to absolve herself of any blame. "Maggie took us all the way over on the far side of the mountain, just to see that old house, and then...it was *way* too late to look for blackberries ...so we came back home. And *I* didn't promise!"

"Maggie?" Callie asked, voice low, still stirring her food, her face set and calm, "Do you have something to add to what your sister has just told us?"

"It *wasn't* my fault, Mama. I heard ...about this old plantation house ...over there on the other side of Black Haw Mountain. These people ...just ...kept *telling* me about it ...and *telling* me about it ...and I just *had* to see it for myself. Nellie Sue said they had slaves. Did they have slaves, Mama?"

"Did *who* have slaves, Margaret Ann? Good grief! You must have gone all the way over to the old *Hurston* place. If *that's* where you went, then yes, Margaret Ann, they did own slaves." Callie paused, sighing. What did she say now? Some sort of discipline seemed in order. What was she to *do* with this child! "Do you realize how far it *is* over to the Hurston plantation? No wonder it was all but *dark* when the three of you came straggling into the yard! And your Papa worked all day in the fields, and then he had to come in and do your chores! And, do you realize that *bears* also go hunting for berries in the mountains? Do you realize ...?"

"But we didn't have slaves, did we Mama, before the War? We didn't have slaves?"

"No, Maggie. We didn't have slaves."

"What happened to them?"

"To whom, Maggie?"

"To the slaves? And the people?"

Callie glanced at John, who had remained strangely silent during this entire conversation.

John cleared his throat and fixed Maggie with a strange, knowing stare, "Are you interested in particular ...in the colored folk, and their condition, Maggie? Or in the white folk that *own* that place?"

"Oh, both, Papa!" Maggie answered sweetly, one little hand propped underneath her chin, as if she were all ears. "I want ...to hear about *all* of it! About *everything*! Where did they go? After the War? Where did the gentleman and the lady go? Did they have any children? If they did have children, did they have girls or boys? Or did they have some of both ...and what were their names?"

John propped his elbows on the table, one on either side of his plate, and fixed his youngest daughter with a stare. The kerosene lamp cast small shadows over the table, over the bowls of food and over Maggie's lovely face, framed by dark tresses of hair that fell below her shoulders. She's growing up, John thought with a sudden pain in his chest. Maggie was ...she was ...nine years old this past spring!

"You want to know all that, Maggie? And just why, if I may ask? You wouldn't be thinkin' of ...say ...trying to get in touch with any of these folks?"

"John!" Callie suddenly broke into soft laughter, "Even for *Maggie*, don't you think such a thing would be a bit far fetched?"

"Well, Callie, I just don't know, now. A person walks clear across to the other side of the mountain, over a road that's not been used for who knows how long. And she takes along her two sisters, one of whom has not too long past been ...sort of ...off her feet, shall we say. And I don't see that anything might be too far fetched for such a person."

"You've got it all wrong, Papa!" Maggie quickly defended herself.

"Oh?"

"The reason I went over there, Papa ...well ...it was because *I care so much*!"

"And just what ...or who ...*is it* that you *care for* so much, Maggie?"

"Just everybody, Papa. Because I care, Papa! I care so much about ...people. What they do and where they live and what happens to them ...and why ...and how they fare ...and if they have good books to read ..."

"Books?" Callie couldn't restrain her laughter. "What on earth do *books* have to do with this?"

John ignored Callie. He had his eyes glued to Maggie's face.

"You're telling the truth, aren't you, Maggie? You really do care ...that much?"

"Yes, Papa."

"Well then ..." John paused, aware that Callie was staring at him strangely, trying to figure out what was going on here. But this was between John and Maggie.

"If I tell you what little I know ...what *very* little I know ...will you promise to let the matter drop? And never set foot on that side of Black Haw Mountain, again, Maggie? And ...now ...I *mean* that."

"Yes, Papa. I solemnly promise."

John knew practically nothing about the place or the people. It was seven or eight miles, over steep, winding mountain roads, clean over in the next county. John did not frequent the same mill or store or post office as the folks on that side of the mountain. Near half a day's walk over there. And for three little girls—

"The gentleman of the house." John began, making up the story with whatever came to mind as he went along ...anything to satisfy Maggie. "The gentleman of the house and his son went off to the War. One of the ladies of the house, his son's dear wife, fell ill soon after his departure for the fighting, the summer of '61. She died. The other good woman of the house, his wife, was left alone, except for her young grandson. Not long after the death of the daughter-in-law, the gentleman's son was brought home, grievously wounded. He soon died, too. His mother, heartbroken with grief, took her grandson, all she had left, and moved away. To Charleston, I believe." The only part of the story that John knew for sure was true, was that some person had died in the house. And they might have owned property in Charleston.

"Oh! Papa!" Maggie breathed, "How *sad*! It isn't fair! All that *sadness* to be borne by *one poor woman*! It isn't *fair*!"

Callie had listened to the fantastic, totally fabricated story, immediately recognizing it for what it was. But she said nothing, for she knew less about the place than John did. Which, she now knew, was very little at all.

"As you will learn, Margaret Ann, as you get older," Callie said a bit sternly, "Life is not always fair—not all picking *imaginary* blackberries. Life can give one some *very* hard knocks. It helps if one is fortified by *truth* and a firm faith in God."

"What truth, Mama?"

"The *truth* in general, Maggie. *Always* tell the *truth*, no matter if you know very little …just say you know very little. Or, just say, that *you know nothing at all*. You tell one lie, you soon find yourself forced to tell another …to cover up the first one. And from there, the lies just grow, and grow, until you forget what *is* really true."

John sat silently forking food into his mouth.

"And what about God?" Maggie asked.

"What about God, Margaret Ann?" Callie looked her daughter straight in the eye.

"Doesn't he care?"

"Of course, he cares, Margaret Ann. What a foolish question."

"Then why didn't he help the lady? Does he care about me?"

"Wherever she went …with her grandson," Callie said slowly, not wanting to add to John's lie, "I'm sure God is seeing after both of them. Now, be quiet, and eat your supper."

"You didn't answer my other question, Mama."

"Yes, Margaret Ann, God cares about you, even if you do try a body's soul and patience sometimes to the point of screaming."

"Does it say so in the Bible?"

"What? Maggie? That you try a person's soul and patience? I don't think it does, but if it doesn't, then it surely should. For nothing I know of could be any truer than that."

"That he cares about me?"

"Yes, daughter," Callie couldn't restrain the smile that had begun behind her blue eyes, and now reached the thin lips, "Remember, Maggie, *Are not two sparrows sold for a farthing? And not one of them falls to the ground—*"

"Without your Father," John cut in, smiling, well pleased with himself.

"Well, John, you do surprise a body." Callie raised light brows, and couldn't suppress a little laugh.

"Just because I can't read or write, doesn't mean I'm an altogether ignorant man. I was, you well know, born of a good, solid Scotch-Protestant family."

"You're not ignorant, John McKinnon, you're the smartest man I know," Callie remarked. "And one who can spin a fine yarn …and pull th' wool over a person's eyes …and charm the very *sparrows* out of the trees."

"Where is he now?"

"I do declare, Maggie, *who*?" Callie sighed.

"The little boy? Maybe it wasn't the ghost!" Maggie cried, her beautiful face ringed with damp curls, glowed now with excitement, "Maybe it was the little boy that the grandmother took off. Could that have been him ...all grown up now ...and driving that big black carriage ...that came tearing out of that carriage house ...I wonder where he was going—"

"Margaret Ann McKinnon—!" Callie cried, putting one hand to her breast.

"It might just be the boy, Maggie," John smiled, "Now all growed up. He'd be thirteen or fourteen, now. He may have come home for a visit ...because someone took sick with a fever ...he has come home for a visit ...but he *is* big enough to hitch up the carriage ...and go tearing off to town ..."

"John McKinnon! You're worse than the child!"

"It was him!" Maggie whispered into her milk cup. "He's almost grown up, like me. He's probably two or three years older than me. Maybe more, like Papa said. He would be more ...being born during the War ...and me not 'til the War was over. So he would be a bit older ...quite a bit taller. I wonder what he looks like. Do you think he has dark eyes and hair, Papa? Or blond hair like Nellie Sue's?"

"I think you and me better be quiet, and eat our supper!" John warned her in a loud whisper, "Before your Mama throws both of us out of her kitchen!"

"Are you all right, Nellie?" Maggie asked when the two of them reached the privacy of their bed in the upstairs room they shared with Barbara Jo— who had already fallen fast asleep.

"I'm fine, Maggie. Just a little tired. I suppose it'll be my job—to pick all that *mess* off the tail of your dress tomorrow."

"I wouldn't ask you to do that! Besides, Mama'll probably make me do it. If she remembers."

"Oh, she'll remember all right. I never saw Mama quite as exasperated or upset."

"What's—"

"Go to sleep, Maggie."

But Maggie couldn't go to sleep. She lay still for several minutes, contemplating the mystery of the missing boy. Then she sat up.

"I wonder," Maggie said, as she sat on the foot of the bed, staring into the soft moonlight streaming through the curtains and flooding the little bedroom. "I just wonder—"

"*What*, Maggie?" Nellie Sue asked wearily, as she snuggled beneath the warmth of a handmade quilt, in the semi-darkness almost hiding the iron bedstead against the wall of the room.

"I wonder if it was the boy ...

"I wonder what he looks like ...

"I wonder if he would like me ..."

"Maggie!"

Swooooshhhh!!!

Maggie wasn't sure exactly what it was that Nellie flung at her head, but it barely missed her. Whatever it was, it went sailing right past her ...and out the window ...into the yard far below.

"Well," Maggie muttered, snuggling down beneath the covers, "whatever it was, it will come up missing in the morning. Guess I'll get blamed for that, too."

The two girls came down very early the next morning. The light had just begun to break, lovely red and orange streaks, over the mountains to the east. While Nellie Sue stood watch at the bottom of the stairs, they planned that Maggie would escape outside, retrieve the lost shoe, and be back inside and back upstairs in the bed, before Papa or Mama came down.

But here came Papa. He'd been up much earlier than usual, to make his trip to the outhouse. And on the way back, something in the yard caught his eye.

He met them at the foot of the stairs.

"Morning, girls! My! But you two sure are up early. Somethin' goin' on I should know about?"

"Oh, no, no, Papa. Nellie Sue and I ...we just ...is that Mama I hear in the kitchen?" Maggie changed the subject in mid-sentence, hopefully shifting Papa's attention. "Is Mama sick, or something, that's why the two of you are up so early?"

"Your Mama's not feeling well this mornin'."

They heard the back door bang shut, and heard odd, gurgling sounds from out on the back porch.

"Is Mama truly sick?" Maggie cried, a fit of guilt and remorse seizing her.

"Nothing she won't recover from ...given some time. Now, about when I was out this morning ...looking things over. I happened to find a fine shoe ...just laying in the side yard. Just below you girls' bedroom window. Either of you know anything about a lost shoe? Practically new."

"A shoe, did you say, Papa, how very odd!" Maggie remarked with a slight toss of her pretty head.

"Yes," John mused, taking the shoe out of the pocket of his old denim jumper. "And what's even odder, this particular style and brand of shoe is for sale down at Johnson's Corners Mill and General Store."

Nellie Sue had scooted on into the kitchen, to see about Mama. She hissed into Maggie's ear as she hurried past, *"Do something!"*

Maggie just kept smiling innocently at Papa.

As she entered the kitchen, Nellie Sue gave a little cry.

John whirled away to the kitchen, to see if Callie was all right.

"Callie, honey, you go on upstairs and lay yourself back down."

Barbara Jo heard all the commotion and came down to see what exactly was going on.

"Nellie Sue," Callie said, clutching the edge of the table to steady herself, "you can finish putting the biscuits in the oven—and don't let them burn. Barbara Jo, you can stir up some eggs in the big iron skillet. First put in some butter. There's a pot of hominy grits, already cooked, on the back of the stove. Maggie, you can set th' tab—"

Callie broke off, making a mad rush for the back door.

The three girls stood waiting, their faces pale with worry. They couldn't recall Mama ever starting to cook a meal—and then not finishing it. They figured that the day the last trumpet blew, and the world came to an end, Mama would still be standing at the black iron cookstove.

They stood mute, trying to catch the low words passing between Papa and Mama.

"I'm ...too ...old ..."

"You're not old!"

"I ...can't ...believe ...this ...is happening ..."

"Well, if it happens, it happens."

Then Papa was helping Mama back inside, cleaning her face with what appeared to be the dishcloth, but who cared? Mama was really sick.

Papa helped her up the stairs, holding to both elbows speaking little words of comfort.

"Whatever happens, as you yourself have said all these years, Callie, everything will be all right. You'll be all right. We'll *all* be all right."

Then Papa was coming back down the stairs ...alone.

He sat down at the table, beamed around at the three girls, and announced airily, "Well, ladies, I trust, that among the three of you, you have my breakfast ready?"

Wordlessly, Nellie Sue snatched the biscuits out of the oven ...hardly scorched ...just a little burned on the bottoms.

Barbara Jo ladled a portion of rubbery, over-cooked eggs into their plates—except Mama's. When she reached towards Mama's plate, and looked at Papa questioningly, he just shook his head and smiled, "Later. Mama will eat later."

Papa began to scoop the rubbery eggs into his mustached mouth, while taking appreciative little sips of the coffee Maggie was pouring.

Maggie sat down, stealing a glance at Nellie Sue, as if to say—whew, that was a close one!

But, just then, Papa halted mid-bite with his burned biscuit—

—And pulled the almost-new shoe from his pocket.

"I almost forgot in all the commotion. And I know you girls wouldn't want that to happen." Papa beamed a smile, very broad, around at all of them.

"Is Mama really—" Maggie began.

"Let us just forget your Mama, just for a moment here. Now, you see this shoe? As I've already mentioned, I found it just lying in the side yard ...all wet with mornin' dew ...such a fine shoe."

"Yes," Maggie remarked, her mouth full of grits and eggs.

"Is it, Maggie, by any chance *yours*?"

"Mine, Papa? Don't you think it's a little long for my foot? It's certainly not mine, Papa." And of course Papa knew that.

"Nellie Sue, could this fine shoe by any chance belong to you? You do know how *dear* money is to come by on a mountain farm? I can't believe a responsible person, one with the *first* sensible thought in her head, would just chuck such a fine shoe *out the window! A stray dog could have picked it up!*"

"Ommmmm ummmmm hummmmm."

"Well, that's certainly a dusty answer."

Nellie Sue was kicking Maggie beneath the table—with her foot that had the shoe on it—and smiling at Papa, pointing to her mouth—can't talk! Mouth full!

"We can wait," Papa said patiently, while he was still holding the little slender shoe.

Another kick brought Maggie's head up. Her blue-blue eyes flew wide.

"Papa! Have you ...thought ...about ...this ..."

"Yes, Maggie? Go on."

"What if some ...traveler ...say ...was ...passing by ...in the night ...and just ...dropped her good shoe. Don't you think that might explain it?"

"Your bed's not far from the window, Maggie? Did you see any lady travelers passing by ...while you were looking out the window?"

"I *was* looking out the window, Papa."

"I thought you might have been."

"And ...this ..." Another kick.

"And something went flying past my head. Until this very moment, I couldn't *possibly* guess what it was."

"How big was this thing?" John asked, his lank, tall form leaning suddenly forward—as if this were the most interesting tale he had ever heard.

"How big ...? Not ...too ...big. It couldn't have been a person ...or anything."

"No." John said staring Maggie straight in the eye. "I wouldn't expect so."

"But ...then ...it could have been a mountain fairy! She flew in ...before I went to look out the window. Then ...she flew out past me ...probably startled that I was just sitting there so long."

"That's it?" John raised dark brows. "But ...well, of course!" John smiled, nodding his head. "Now why on earth didn't I think of that—this shoe must surely belong to a beautiful mountain fairy. But—

"—You know, Maggie, I was born on this mountain and except for the years spent away at the war, I've scarcely left it—except to go to the farmers' market one time down in Atlanta. And for the life of me, I can't *ever* recall seeing *one* mountain fairy."

"But you *have* heard tell of them? Didn't you say Great-grandpa Shawn used to see them?'

"Your Great-grandpa Shawn also claimed that God the Almighty spoke *personally* to him." John lifted dark brows, nodded his head wisely, hopefully to accentuate what he felt was the absurdity of such a statement.

"Well," Maggie leaned herself back on the oak-backed bench, her beautiful blue eyes gleaming, "There you have it!"

"Well, Maggie ...yes, I guess I do."

Nellie Sue heaved a great sigh of relief. She couldn't believe her ears, when Maggie piped up:

"Papa? When were you down in Atlanta at the farmers' market? What did you take to sell down there? I don't recall you ever going down there? Did you pack your food to take with you? I bet you did, huh, with everything being so expensive and all? How much would a dozen eggs bring, down in Atlanta? Did Mama go with you? How long did it take you ...coming and going? Several days I bet? Where did you sleep—?"

"In the wagon, Maggie."

Whatever it was that afflicted Mama that morning, it soon passed. And nothing came of it.

Chapter 11

They had gone searching in earnest for blackberries this time. They had their buckets about two-thirds full. Their faces were all scratched from picking in the tallest vines—where Maggie announced only the really *good* berries grew. Their long hair was matted and tangled from vines and briars and brush. Their hands were stained blue-black with berry juice.

"Let's go!" Nellie Sue called from across the patch where they were picking. "I'm getting tired."

"Me, too!" Barbara Jo echoed.

"I'm coming! Wait for me. Don't you dare start back without me!"

"Well, come on then, Maggie!" Nellie Sue shouted.

"Wait—just a minute! I've found something—here in the blackberry vines! It's a baby rabbit! It's *three* baby rabbits!"

"Just leave them alone, Maggie, and come on out. Barbara Jo and I are already out in the road. We're all set to go. Come on!"

Maggie came out. Her berry bucket was hanging over one arm, and her bonnet over the other. And nestled inside her bonnet—still resting in part of their mother's nest—three tiny rabbits.

"Oh! Maggie!" Nellie Sue wailed. "Look what you've gone and done! They scarcely have any fur on them! And their little eyes are not even open yet!"

"I know! Isn't it exciting! I'll take them home. Make them a little bed beside mine. And then, I'll feed them every morning and at dinner time—"

"Maggie!" Nellie Sue said in a tired, strained voice, "You know very well what Mama and Papa have to say about bringing wild things into the house—"

"But, they're so tiny! Not much bigger than—"

"It won't matter, Maggie." Nellie Sue wagged her head. "You know what the rules are. Wild things stay outside—people inside."

"That's a silly rule. Papa—"

"Maggie. That's *Papa's* rule."

"Well, I'll just carry them on to the house, and I'll find some place to put them. Maybe in the barn."

"They'll die, Maggie. Those poor little things—they'll die—without their mother."

"What if she's gone, and doesn't *ever* come back? What if she's been killed by a hunter? Or snared by a rabbit box? What about that, Nellie? Do you think I should just walk off and leave them to the foxes and the hawks? *I don't think so*! How *cruel* can you be, Nellie Sue McKinnon?"

Maggie turned and stomped away, her precious find cradled in her bonnet.

Maggie sneaked them up the stairs, while Papa was out in the barnyard, and Mama was down in the kitchen washing and picking the blackberries the three girls had brought back.

"My! These are fine berries, girls! Where are you? Well, that's strange. Berry pie going into the stove, and suddenly everybody's vanished."

By hook and crook, her two older sisters sworn by a blood oath to silence about the tiny baby rabbits, Maggie somehow managed to smuggle a bit of milk up to them, which she dropped with the end of a straw into each little mouth.

At first the tiny, pink, furless creatures seemed to thrive, wriggling about in the clean straw Maggie had covered them with to keep them warm. She kept the little box she had placed them in well hidden beneath her bed.

One morning Maggie scrambled out of bed after her sisters had already gone downstairs. Anxiously she drew the little box from underneath the bed, and gently raked back the straw.

One of the tiny rabbits lay sprawled on its back. Its legs stuck straight up in the air.

When Maggie picked it up, it was cold and stiff. No tears. A heavy sigh. Nellie Sue had warned her—some of them might die without their mother.

Callie watched, later in the day, as Maggie made her way slowly up the mountain. Callie couldn't decide, just viewing Maggie's back, what exactly Maggie was carrying, but she definitely appeared to have something in her hands.

When this same incident was repeated again several days later, Callie felt she should speak to John. He usually not only knew what Maggie was up to, but nine chances out of ten—he was in on it.

"John? What's going on with Maggie?"

"Like what?"

"She's been making regular trips …up to the graveyard. She hardly ever went up there before, except with you. I just thought you might know …if something is up …with Maggie?"

"Why are you so suspicious minded, Callie? Just because Maggie does something so innocent as to go visit the family graveyard, and here you go and try to make something sinister out of it!"

"I'm not suspicious minded, John. It's just that I know Maggie. And I know you. And if Maggie's going up to that graveyard for no reason at all either you or I can logically think about—then I say *look out*—something's afoot."

Now that he had the box all to himself, Ruffles, the last of the little rabbits, decided to begin to grow.

And grow.

And grow.

Ruffles no longer lay docilely in the little box beneath the bed. Now, his eyes were open. And he saw a bigger world than his little box. He began to sprout fur. And to hop around. Maggie would often find the box empty, and the little rabbit crouched in a corner, or in a shoe.

"You know, don't you, that you can't keep that *big* bunny in this room," Nellie warned her. "Why don't you tell Mama and Papa about Ruffles, and let them help you figure out what to do with him?"

"I know exactly what Mama will say to do with him. That's why I keep him hidden."

"Well, that little trick's not going to work much longer. How long do you think it will be …before he hops out that door and into the hall or onto the landing …and Mama or Papa sees him? I have a bad feeling about this Maggie. I've half a mind to tell Mama—"

"Don't you dare, Nellie. I saved your hide—about throwing that shoe at me. Now you owe me."

"Okay. So, all right. I won't say anything, for now. But you'd sure better keep that door shut. And you'd better get something to put that little fellow in that will keep him safely shut away."

"Like what?"

"How do I know like what? I don't have any wild pet rabbits! Use your head, Maggie, build him a rabbit hutch, or something."

"Oh, Nellie! That's a fine idea! And you can help me. There's scrap lumber in the barn. And some old rusty nails. We'll—"

"I suggested *you* build a hutch. I'm not about to get involved any further in this escapade!"

"Nellie, remember the shoe—"

"Oh, all right. Come on!"

"John, did you see that?"

"What, Callie?"

"The way those two girls came sneaking around the side of the barn. And they stopped at the corner—to look this way and that—then out came Maggie carrying a *crude* looking object. Couldn't really tell what it was. Nellie Sue seemed to be playing guard—"

"Just a game, Callie. You yourself just said they were playing."

"Hmmmmm" Callie looked at John. "I've got a bad feeling. Something *is* going on."

"Don't look at me!" John threw up both hands, as if to ward off evil, snatched an extra buttered biscuit, and bolted for the door.

The hutch, Maggie and Nellie Sue congratulated themselves, worked pretty well—until the bunny grew large enough to *really* hop—against the tin lid.

Then, in the dead of night, there would come this weird thumping noise, reverberating *all* through the house—

THUMPPPPP

THUMPPPPP

THUMPPPPPPPPP

"John? Do you hear that odd noise?"

"Hummmmm? What, Callie?"

"Wake up, John! I think someone's walking on the roof!"

"Go back to sleep, Callie. It's probably the wind."

"John McKinnon, you get *right* up out of this bed! Now you just *listen* to that!"

THUMPPPPP

THUMPPPP

THUMPPPP

THUMPPPP, THUMPPPP, THUMPPPP

"Might be mice in the attic, Callie."

"*Mice in the attic*? Must be pretty big mice!"

"Well, what do *you* think it is?"

"How do I know? That's why I awakened you. Put on your trousers, and go out and look on the roof!"

"It's pitch black out there, Callie. How am I going to look on the roof in the pitch black?"

"John—I can't stand that horrible noise—not one minute longer. If you don't put on your trousers and go—"

"All right, Callie. Okay. I'm going. Back in a minute."

Callie heard the front door bang shut. A few minutes later John was back. And the horrible thumping sound had stopped.

"Well, whatever it was, I guess I scared him away. At least the thumping seems to have stopped. Lay back down, honey. Come here, Callie, lay down beside me—"

THUMPPPP

THUMPPPP

THUMPPPPPPPPPPP

"*John!*"

"Callie. I honestly don't know—I'll light the lantern, and go back outside."

Back inside, then, "John, *why don't you go up into the attic*!?"

"Oh. Yeah. Could be a squirrel, or a raccoon has gnawed a hole and got his self trapped—" THUMPPPP—THMPPPP—THUMPPPP

"*Just go!*"

"Nothing in the attic, honey, Callie, not a single thing I could see. Not even any mouse droppings. Clean as a whistle."

THUMPPPPPPP—THUMPPPPPPPP

"*JOHN! WHAT IS IT?*"

"I can't seem to pinpoint the source of the sound," John mused. "One minute it seems to be coming from up on the roof; the next minute it seems to be coming—

"—From down the hall—"

"You ...don't ...think ...?" Callie gazed at John wide-eyed.

"Maggie!" John was banging on the door. Maggie shoved the little rabbit hutch beneath the quilt stack. Papa already had the door open.

"Maggie?" John stuck his head in the door. "What's going *on* in there?"

"We're trying to sleep, Papa. But it's real hard—with all that bumping going on."

"Okay, sugar, sorry to bother you. You go on back to sleep."

"That was *too* close!" Maggie breathed.

"You're going to really *get* it this time!" Barbara Jo hissed, looking like a ghost in her white mobcap, "Keeping Mama and Papa awake all the entire night. And poor Papa, crawling into the attic and—"

"Hush, Barbara Jo!" Maggie whispered, "you're as deep into this as I am!"

"No! I'm not! And come mornin' I'm just goin' to march right down those stairs, and tell Mama 'bout that horrible wild creature!"

"Remember? Tomorrow's your birthday, Barbs. You go blabbing to Mama, and I'll—"

"You'll what!?"

"I'll not even give you the present I made for you—"

Bleary eyed and foggy brained, the family gathered around the breakfast table as usual. John felt as if he had been hit in the head with a poleax. Whatever that thing was, it had kept up the horrible thumping most all night. It would halt for a minute. But just when you took a breath of relief, it started up again.

Callie was disheveled and cranky. Snapping at John. Barking at the girls.

"John, *must* you sit with both elbows on the table? Girls, you *straighten up*! And why didn't you at least *comb your hair* before you came down!? Honestly! *Look* at the three of you! Like a pack of *gypsies*! What's *wrong* with you? You're all silent as—"

"Maybe, Callie, honey," John sighed, "it's because the poor girls didn't get scarcely a wink of—"

"Well, neither did I, for that matter. But, just for the information of you all, I do *not* intend to go through another night like that. If your Papa has to take this house apart …board …by …board …by …board …I …I'm *not* putting up with another night like that!" Callie banged the coffee pot loudly down on the eye of the iron stove.

"You want me to tear the house apart, Callie? Just to find what's probably some harmless little critter—just trying to make hisself a bed or somethin'?"

John thought for a moment she was going to bang *him* in the head with the hot coffeepot.

By mid-morning, Callie had somewhat revived, the girls were relieved to see. Barbara Jo joined her mother in the kitchen, for the annual ritual each girl enjoyed—baking her own birthday cake—with Mama's aid and directions.

Maggie and Nellie Sue huddled together in their room, trying to decide what to do about the rapidly growing rabbit.

"You've got to get him out of the house, Maggie!"

"But ...where'll I put him?"

"In the barn!"

"Papa will be *sure* to find him in the barn!"

"Better if he finds him there than here! *Anywhere* but in the house! Just go ahead now, while Mama and Barbara Jo are busy with the birthday cake. Just go on, and take his hutch and I'll watch out for you."

"But ...where's Papa? Now?"

"He's on the other side of the house, chopping wood. Now's the time! GO!"

Maggie, the little rabbit hutch clasped in her arms, turned to look at Nellie Sue, "You'd better watch real good."

"*OH, MAGGIE—!*"

"I'm going! I'm going! Open the door for me."

Nellie Sue moved to open the door. The door swung wider than Nellie Sue had expected.

Maggie felt the rabbit hutch being knocked from her arms. The tin lid flew open, and then the rabbit was on the landing—now he was on the stairs—

"Maggie! Get after him!" Nellie Sue hissed.

Maggie took off after the rabbit. The rabbit hopped down, from one step to the next. Each time Maggie grabbed for him, he hopped to the next step. Then he was in the front room. Then he headed for the kitchen—

"*—What—?*" Callie's mouth flew open; her eyes widened in fright—

—Some sort of *wild animal* came hurtling into the kitchen—*onto her feet*!

—Callie flung down the bowl of batter.

—The bowl hit the hard wooden floor and splintered into a million pieces.

—Barbara Jo ran to grab the falling bowl, her birthday cake!

—Seconds after the bowl hit the floor Barbara Jo's right foot hit the puddle of cake batter.

—She hit the floor with a heavy thud—

—Sprawled awkwardly in the mess, she set up a howling wail—

—Callie gazed wildly about her—

—Cake batter covered the floor—

—Barbara Jo sat in the middle of it—howling like a banshee—

—This *crazed creature* kept flinging itself about the kitchen—

—The water bucket flew over—sending a plume of water arcing high into the air—

—Hitting the cookstove pipe—

—The pipe fell with a loud clatter, spewing hot soot and ashes all over the kitchen—

Coming up the back steps, John heard the commotion inside—

—And flung open the kitchen door—

"*—What in th'—!*"

"*John!*" Callie squawked.

"*My ...oh ...my,*" John drawled slowly, "when you girls throw a *party* ...you *really* do things up right!"

Callie, her face and clothes covered with ashes, water and soot, could only gawk at him.

Had she been capable of speech, any words would have been drowned by the continual wails of Barbara Jo—partially sitting, partially reclined—on the kitchen floor, covered with cake batter, water, ashes and soot.

Nellie Sue stood to one side. Dazed and speechless.

Maggie was over in the corner, behind what was left of the black iron cookstove, valiantly attempting to keep hold of a wriggling, water-splashed, batter-and soot-covered creature.

John closed the door, walked to the edge of the back porch, sat down, slowly took out his pipe and lit it.

This might be a *bad* day.

Chapter 12

Margaret Ann woke long before the sun lifted its crimson glow over the mountain ridges. She rose silently out of bed, crept over to the window, and looked down into the yard below. She turned around, gazing at the two lumps, still fast asleep beneath their colorful quilts.

"Wake up! Wake up," she shouted, "this is the day! The day of the Hiawassee Mountain Fair!"

Nellie Sue stuck one pale hand out from beneath the covers and yawned heavily. Her leg throbbed. It had been bothering her more and more lately. But, just for today, she'd keep quiet and try not to worry everyone about it. Lately, Papa had been watching her like a hawk.

Maggie had already flown out of the room and across the little hall and landing that separated the girls' bedroom from that of their parents.

Without so much as a knock on the door, she burst in, "Papa! Mama! Aren't you up yet? There're so many things to do!"

"Go *away*, Margaret Ann," Callie said sleepily.

"Come on in, sugar, and give your Papa a kiss," John smiled at Maggie and held out his arms.

Prettily clad in her newest dress and bonnet of red-plaid gingham trimmed in Mama's white hand-tatted lace, down the stairs Maggie flew. Someone might need her help in getting ready.

All through breakfast, Maggie chatted on; no one seemed to listen. Maggie talked so much, sometimes they just tuned her out.

Then the girls were clearing the table, putting the breakfast things in the dishpan to soak.

Mama gathered up her newest quilt. She would be showing her Dutch Doll in the quilt contest, as well as a lovely lace mantel scarf in the crocheting contest. Into a basket she stuffed apples, left-over biscuits and some pieces of fried chicken.

In a flurry, they were out the door, Papa bringing the wagon around.

Callie climbed onto the high seat beside John. My, didn't her husband look fine and handsome this morning! She gave him a huge smile. John gave her a wink.

The girls piled into the back of the wagon.

"You think we'll be all dusty and dirty from the road, by the time we get there?" Maggie drew her beautiful face into a worried frown.

"All the other folk will be traveling the *same* way, Maggie," Mama assured her. "Over dusty dirt roads. So if we're dirty, then we'll just *all* be dirty together, don't you suppose?"

"Well, I'm going to put this corner of the quilt over me. I don't want to look like some old mud pie when we get there. How far is it, Papa?"

"If you start asking me that now, sugar—and us seven or eight miles off, you'll wear yourself out talking and be plumb out of words—before we ever get there."

"Wouldn't *that be* somethin'!" Callie muttered drolly.

Maggie crawled beneath the corner of the old quilt Callie had spread in the wagon bed, in order to protect her new dress and bonnet from the dust. But within a few minutes, she had tired of that. She scooted out, sat up in the wagon, and announced:

"I know! Let's play a game!"

"What sort of game?" Nellie Sue asked.

"You can't play a game. How'er we goin' to play a game in the back of the wagon?" Barbara Jo hooted. She was already irritated and bored, and the day had scarcely begun.

"Sure, we can!" Maggie cried, "Uh …there must be all sorts of games we can play. We could count the trees …and name all the different kinds. See who can name the most kinds of trees. Or we could look for wild turkey along the roadside …and see how many each person spots. We could count the coveys of quail and—"

"It would be nice," Callie said slowly, "if you could just settle down, Margaret Ann, and pick either one or the other."

"We'll count the trees …" Maggie prattled on.

In the back of the wagon, John heard the happy chirping of the girls. Callie sat quietly beside him. Along the road, aflame in splashes of reds and yellows and oranges, towered thick forests of hickory, chestnut, oak and tulip poplar, wild sumac, locust honey heavy with ripening pods, sycamore shedding its bark—and showing ripples of white along its trunks. Plenty for the girls to count—

The wagon rolled over the rutted red-clay roads, around horseshoe bends, up steep mountain grades. Now and again a slight breeze would come tumbling through the gaps and gorges, pushing its way through the dense trees, ruffling the sunbonnets. In this pleasant way, the hours passed.

Then John announced: "Well, girls, we're here!"

They were out of the wagon in a flash. John hitched his rig to a sapling in a nearby grove with the other wagons and buggies and surreys.

"What will we do first, Papa?" Maggie asked, excitedly tugging one leg of Papa's pants.

"Well, why don't we just sort of give a gander around—and see what all there might be to do."

"Do we get to buy something?" Maggie queried, "Do we have any *money*?"

"A little bit, sugar."

"How much, Papa? How much is a little bit?"

"About …a dollar," John mumbled into his hand. He stroked his mustache, and gazed around. He was ashamed of the amount. He wanted to give his family more—much more. But the south was still going through hard times. Crops weren't bringing that much. He had worked hard and brought in some mighty fine harvests, but still his debts kept mounting. Most of John's purchasing was done by barter. To get the dollar, John had worked almost all night—each night for a week—carving a cradle for a neighbor.

"A whole dollar?" Maggie grinned. "That's the most money I ever had."

"Well, sugar," John rested a tanned hand on Maggie's shoulder. "The whole dollar's not just for you. It's for *all* of us."

"That's all right, Papa. A whole dollar's still a lot of money. What can we buy with it?"

"Well, like I just said—why don't we just look around?"

John reached for Maggie's hand. Callie followed, Nellie Sue and Barbara Jo in tow.

There seemed to be noise from every place Maggie looked. She'd never seen so many people milling about! The ladies all looked so fine, in colorful dresses and bonnets. One or two carried bright little parasols, to protect their complexions from the sun. The men were dressed in their best, some wearing new hats.

There were colorful stands draped with streamers of bright-colored crepe paper, selling candied apples and lemonade, jars of homemade preserves and pickles.

A bit farther on, a large pine-pole pavilion sheltered pigs, cows, sheep and horses.

"What are the animals for?" Maggie asked.

"Well, sugar," John said, "they're here to be …shown off …to see which farmer has raised the finest—"

"Why don't we show off our horse?"

"I …don't think *our* horse, Maggie, would get far in the competition …"

"Why not, Papa?"

"Well …sugar …"

"Because he's not young, anymore. Maggie," Callie said. "He's not prime horseflesh. He's no prize animal to display at a fair."

"Look!" Maggie yelled suddenly.

On a low wooden platform—sat *a grand pipe organ*!

—Beautifully crafted of highly polished cherry wood, and with a round stool to match, it gleamed in the sun, with its intricate carvings—trailing vines with clusters of blossoms. Below the trailing vines, ran a row of knobs—round, black knobs, tipped with red velvet.

"Look, Papa!" Maggie was awestruck, almost afraid to breathe, afraid the grand pipe organ might vanish before her eyes. "Isn't that something?"

"Sure is, baby girl," John sighed, "but that's way, *way* out of our reach. Let's move on."

John tried to pull Maggie away. But she refused to budge. "See there, Papa," John heard her saying, "they're *giving* it away, as a *prize*!"

John turned back.

"Well, I'll just declare! *Grand Prize—for the winner of the log-splitting contest—*

"—But, look, Maggie," John heaved a sigh, "there's an entrance fee. A whole dollar. And that's all we've got to spend …for all of us …for the entire day."

"I *do* so *want* that pipe organ, Papa!" Maggie's blue eyes widened. "I could …"

Callie watched the two of them, her heart sinking—as John paid his entrance fee. As usual, John could deny Maggie nothing that came remotely within his power. She thought of all the things she should say. And, as usual, Callie begin to say them—

"But ...John ...what would we *do* with *that* thing? Nobody can even as much as play a *note* on it. What do we *know* about pipe organs?" J o h n looked at Callie. His tanned face showed little lines at the edges of the eyes, at the corners of the mouth.

"Well, Callie," John drawled, "*I* don't know much about pipe organs, either. But that looks to me to be a mighty fine instrument. I think it's a rare and a beautiful thing. Just think how it would impress all out neighbors? None of them has anything like that in *their* farmhouses. And just think ...if Maggie could learn to play it ...we'd have music ..."

"Most of our neighbors have the good sense not to *want* anything like that in their farmhouses!" Callie argued. "And since when, John McKinnon, have you been so set on *impressing* your neighbors? And do you really *think* for one instant Maggie is going to sit still long enough to ...*to learn to play a pipe organ?*"

"Maggie wants it, Callie." John said slowly.

"Well," Callie sighed, "of course, John ...if Maggie *wants* it ..."

Callie turned away. She didn't want John to see the tears brimming in her eyes. With quick, nervous little flutters of both hands, she ushered the three girls into the shade of a nearby grove. They could stand here and at least be in the shade, while they watched their Papa make a fool of himself—*and lose all their fair money.*

But as Callie watched, she also worried. John was not a boy. She had recently noticed a few gray hairs sprinkled among the dark brown. And he had that bad leg—he had no business over-exerting himself in a *log-splitting contest!*

But, Callie chided herself, standing there in the shade of the fragrant sweetgums—

—John was her husband.

—John was head of the family.

—John worked hard.

She'd make it up to Nellie Sue and Barbara Jo, somehow.

"Come on, girls!" Callie leapt up from her seat in the shady grass, her voice a little too loud and her eyes a bit too bright: "All together now!—Let's give Papa a rousing cheer—!" But Maggie was gone; she would *not* stay put, despite all Callie's protests.

She pushed and shoved her way to the front of the spectators.

Callie held her breath. She was almost afraid to look. Afraid she'd see John Thomas McKinnon drop over dead—so furiously did he attach that stack of oak logs.

He was like a well-oiled machine. There was *nothing* to compare to him. *No one* to compare to him. He moved in strong, rhythmic strokes, his lank frame rising, hauling the heavy axe up over his head plunging it down deep into the tough oak fibers—

Again …and again …and again …

John! Stop! Callie wanted to cry, but her eyes felt dry, hot and scratchy. John McKinnon, she feared, would kill himself, to get Maggie that pipe organ.

During the ride home in the wagon, everyone was strangely subdued.

Callie made simple, short comments. John gave terse, low replies—none of which the girls—bundled in the back of the rolling wagon—could catch.

The massive pipe organ, like something from another world, rode securely lashed to the sideboards.

"*Whatever* on Earth …will we do with the thing …?" Callie wagged her head and muttered beneath her breath.

"We'll put it in the front room, Callie," John replied in a low, slow voice.

"It'll be way, way too big for our house, John. *Way, way*—"

"It'll be just *fine*, Callie," John's voice began to rise, and to take on a tinge of anger.

"It'll *dwarf* everything in the room. Such a thing belongs in a great, *rich man's* house—or in a *fine church* somewhere—"

John stopped the wagon. He turned to look at Callie.

Callie felt a shiver run down her spine, though the day was hot and sweat dampened her upper lip. What she saw in John's eyes—she'd never seen that look in John's eyes—

"*Hauuuuup*," John slapped the horse smartly with the reins, and the wagon began to roll.

Callie never said another word about the grand pipe organ—

—Though she had been right about one thing.

It did dwarf everything else in the front room. It was horribly out of place. But John was also right—Maggie did learn to play the thing.

And today, she had been invited to play during the church service down at the Shiloh Baptist Church.

"You're going to church with us today, aren't you Papa?"

"No," John surmised, looking at Maggie all dressed up in her Sunday finest—a white cotton dress, sprinkled with all colors of bright little floral sprigs. "Don't suppose I will. I have all this ...work to do—"

"*Why*, Papa?" Maggie persisted.

"Why, what, sugar?"

"Why do you hardly ever go to church with us? Don't you believe in God?"

"Of course, I believe in God!" John defended himself smartly. "Don't I even say the blessing sometimes at the supper table?"

"Saying it ...and believing it ...that's two different things, Papa."

"Well, Maggie, look—"

"Why don't you believe, Papa?"

"Didn't I just say I believed, Maggie? I ...mean ...what would you have me *do*, Maggie?"

"I'd have you go to church with us, Papa ...and hear me play the organ."

John would never forget that day; not until he took his final, dying breath. How proud he had been. Walking down the isle of the Shiloh Baptist Church. Callie beside him, in her finest dress and bonnet. The girls walking just in front of them, all in their best. And he, his newest shirt and trousers on, his hair all parted so carefully in the middle, and water-combed down on each side. His moustache all trimmed and smooth—

And when Maggie McKinnon sat down at the church organ and began to play, John felt a soft, sweet peace, like some giant hand came stealing over him, like no peace he'd ever known, not since Appomattox—

"Well, John," a strange voice inside him whispered, "Welcome home!"

Chapter 13

The raven circled over the barn several times, his wings shiny-black and glistening in the morning sun, watching with a wary eye as the three girls played hide-and-go-seek about the corn crib and the chicken coops.

"I wonder what that old raven's doing, flying about over the barn?" Nellie Sue remarked to Maggie. "I bet he's trying to get at some of the corn—through the cracks in the corn crib."

"He'd better watch himself," Barbara Jo surmised wisely, "or Papa will be after him, with the blunderbuss."

"Papa wouldn't shoot that poor helpless raven," Maggie remarked *very* quickly. "That bird's not harming a thing."

"He *might* be harming a thing!" Barbara Jo said, "He might be stealing the corn that Papa worked so hard to raise. And Papa sure wouldn't appreciate *that*!"

"Have you seen him eat a single grain?" Maggie asked. "And anyhow, he's part of God's creation, the same as the sparrows. And if God looks after the sparrows and provides for them—"

"Barbara Jo's right, Maggie," Nellie said slowly nodding her head, "We should shoo him away from the corn crib."

"If he was a sparrow, we wouldn't shoo him away!" Maggie replied angrily. "I don't think we should show favorites—amongst God's creatures! It just wouldn't be fair."

"Sparrows don't eat the corn, Maggie. Anyways, if they do, they're so tiny, they couldn't eat very much," Nellie said, attempting to reason with her youngest sister—which sometimes wasn't that simple. "I wonder why he's hanging about the barn so close. It's almost as if he's watching…expecting…"

"Expecting what?" Barbara Jo asked, all ears now.

"Nothing," Nellie Sue said, giving Maggie a peculiar stare. "We'd better head on to the house. It's about time to do our evening chores. Maggie, why don't you help me bring in the wood?"

Maggie followed along behind Nellie Sue, a few steps back. Then, when Barbara Jo had disappeared inside to fetch the kitchen water bucket, Nellie turned on Maggie, "Have you by any chance been *feeding* that raven?"

"Me?" Maggie asked, blue eyes wide, all innocence. "Why on earth would you think that?"

"Because of the way that bird was hovering about, and circling and circling, as if he expected to be fed, or something. His eyes seemed to be particularly on *you*, Maggie. I thought for a minute there he might actually come down and light on your head or shoulder!"

"Isn't that Mama, calling me?" Maggie flew away.

The following morning, when the girls were out feeding the chickens and gathering the eggs, Nellie Sue again noticed a raven, circling about their heads, lighting now on the limb of an apple tree, then fluttering off to perch almost in reach of their hands, on top of a chicken coop.

"That wouldn't by any chance be a *friend* of yours, would it?" Nellie eyed the raven, and then frowned at Maggie suspiciously.

"What on earth do you mean?" Maggie shrugged one small shoulder, her blue eyes wide.

"He seems to be *following* us," Nellie frowned, "and I was just wondering …I had hoped—that after that *batter* and that *soot* all over the kitchen—that you had learned your lesson."

"You don't see me carrying that raven into the house, do you, Nellie Sue? You don't see me hiding him beneath our bed, or the quilt stack?"

"No, but …oh …I don't know. It's just something about the way he looks. He doesn't look as if he's that *wild*, or frightened of us. He seems …I've never seen a raven fly that close."

"He probably has *very* good eyesight. He probably sees *all* the corn through the cracks of the crib," Maggie suggested. "And you can't blame that on *me!*"

"I know. I'm sorry, Maggie. It's just that …"

"You always think the worst of me! That's what it is, Nellie Sue McKinnon! Everything in the whole wide world that goes wrong …"

"It's not like that at all," Nellie Sue defended hotly, "I just hate to see you always getting yourself into hot water. The last thing we need is for some

raven to take up residence about the place, and just begin to make himself
right at home! Papa and Mama would be furious."

"Humpppppph!" Maggie stomped off in a huff.

Since Nellie Sue made such a fuss about the raven circling about over the
barn and chicken coops, Maggie was very careful, the next time she sneaked
a handful of corn out of a tow sack in the barn, and carried it up the edge of
the mountain, into the heavy stand of low cedars that flanked the old spring
house that Great-grandpa Shawn had built for Katherine Ann to store her
milk and butter in. She was very careful, to make sure no one was in sight, and
that she wasn't followed.

And she hoped that *Blackie* would be equally as careful, and not just come
flying in a bee-line, straight for his usual feeding spot. If he did, he was sure
to give away their secret. Maggie sure didn't want anything bad to happen to
Blackie. She couldn't understand why, but it seemed that everything she
loved—something *bad* happened to it.

And she didn't see the harm in having a pet raven. Ravens were part of
God's creation, just the same as sparrows. And Maggie thought, standing
there, dropping the grains one by one into the cedar straw—watching Blackie
swoop in, cock his head at her, then scoop them up—that she recalled
something in the Bible about ravens. What was it that Mama had read to them
not too long ago? Didn't the ravens actually feed a Man of God? She couldn't
recall exactly who he was. But if ravens *did* feed a Man of God, then they
must not only be part of God's creation, but also some of His *best* workers!
She'd have to try to find out about that—*the ravens of God.*

Mama had fixed her usual excellent supper. Grace had been said, and a
low conversation began between Mama and Papa, about the plans for
Mama's upcoming quilting party.

Mama was smiling and happy, and Papa seemed to be basking in the glow of
her joy. Nothing pleased Papa more, than to see Mama brimming with pleasure.

"I've already got th' quiltin' frames down, out of the hay loft," Papa was
smiling at Mama, "All I need to do now, is take a clean rag, and rub 'em off,
real good, so that none of the ladies gets herself all dirty on anythin' that
might come fallin' off of 'em. I did notice that dirt-daubers had built a nest
along one of the rails. But I feel sure that can be knocked off, with no problem
a'tall. Then I can just swing 'em up, to th' front room ceiling. And I found the
iron pegs for scotching the corners. So, as far as I know, Callie, honey, you
should be all set, soon as I hang 'em up."

"Thank you, John," Callie smiled. And Mama looked so happy that Maggie thought now was a good time to bring up the subject.

"Mama," Maggie said, very seriously, "Are the *ravens* just as important to God—as the *sparrows* are?"

"What, Maggie?" Mama glanced over at Maggie, a little frown creasing her smooth brow.

"I asked if the ravens—"

"I …heard …what you asked, Maggie," Callie frowned, "I just don't understand …why you asked it."

"I was just watching a raven …the other day …and I wondered …if the ravens were as important to God as the sparrows. Didn't you read us a story, from Grandpa Shawn's Bible, about the ravens feeding a Man of God?"

"Well …yes …Maggie, I think we *did* study that particular passage. About how God sent the ravens to feed *Elijah*, when poor Elijah was so depressed and dejected, that he was about ready to give up. And he imagined, wrongfully, of course, that he was the last Man of God on the whole Earth. And he sat himself down beneath some trees by a brook, and waited for death, but God had other plans for Elijah. And, yes, God did send ravens to feed the Man of God."

"Then, if God used ravens, they can't be *all* bad," Maggie asserted.

"Well …Maggie …" Callie said slowly, "Nothing is all bad. Everything that God made has something good about it, I suppose. And God, in his Might and his Majesty, can use anything, to carry out His way and His will. Even the lowly ravens."

"Thank you, Mama," Maggie smiled triumphantly over at Nellie Sue. Nellie Sue wrinkled her nose at Maggie, narrowed her eyes—and stuck out her tongue.

That night when the girls were in bed, Nellie Sue turned on Maggie and demanded.

"What was *that* all about?"

"I don't know what you mean," Maggie replied innocently. "I was just trying to prove to you that ravens are *not* all that bad."

"Well, all I have to say to you Maggie McKinnon is *this*—*you* get yourself into another jam with some of your wild animal friends, and *I* will *not* be there to bail you out! Do I make myself clear? I am not about to get involved in *any more* of your wild pranks or schemes! I will not be helping you build—"

"Nellie Sue!" Maggie declared innocently, "Surely you don't think I intend to bring a *raven* into the house?"

"No, I don't suppose I ...really think ...that .... even *you* would go so far as that. But, Maggie, I know you *so* well, and I *know* something is afoot with you ...and this ...raven ...thing. Though for the life of me, I *cannot* imagine what!"

"Good night, Nellie," Maggie whispered, a smug little smile stretching her mouth, as she snuggled down contentedly beneath the warm covers.

"Good Night!" Nellie Sue snapped.

"I don't know why," Maggie said to Blackie the following morning as they hid themselves in the depths of the little cedar grove, "that Nellie is so *set* against you, Blackie. You're one of the prettiest birds I've ever seen. Just look how your glossy feathers shine in the morning sunlight. And those eyes of yours, why you look as if you know *every* word I'm saying to you. Just you be careful, you hear, and don't come too near the house! Oh, look at you! Aren't you something! That's the very first time you've done that! That's the very first time you've actually *perched* on my shoulder! Tomorrow, I'll bring you some *extra* kernels of dried corn." Then Blackie stuck his yellow-glowing bill into the warmth of Maggie's hair.

A few mornings later, Maggie awoke with a terrible itching on her left leg. She pulled back the cover, to discover two or three spots of poison ivy rash, just above her ankle. Oh, no! She'd have to be sure and not scratch it, or it would spread. And if Mama learned she had it—there weren't that many places where it grew that near the house—and one of the worst was up near the little cedar grove—where she usually fed Blackie!

"What on earth is wrong with you, Maggie? Can't you sit still long enough to eat your breakfast?" Mama asked, gazing at her youngest daughter.

"It's .... nothing, Mama. I'm ...all right," Maggie smiled.

Later in the day, as Maggie helped Papa stack some freshly-split oak logs beneath the little lean-to on the east side of the log house, Papa suddenly asked:

"You don't by any chance have a bit of *poison ivy*—on one of your legs or ankles, do you, Maggie?" Papa ceased his work and stood looking at her so solemnly that Maggie found it impossible to speak. "Seems to me," Papa continued, "I saw a little trail of dried corn kernels, leading up into a certain cedar grove. And seems to me ...I saw a certain *raven,* no doubt *one of the workers of God,* flying straight to a certain cedar grove. It seems to me ...that

I recall a big patch of poison ivy, near the edge of that grove. And if a person wasn't careful, she just might end up with her a good case—"

"Papa, he's not a bad bird! All my rabbits died but one! And I had to release Ruffles—after Barbs' birthday. And Katie Ann got all wet and doughy and fell apart. And Rags ..."

Maggie's voice caught, and she found it impossible to continue.

"I know, sugar," John said softly, "I know. But you just make sure this *raven doesn't end up gettin' into your mama's hair, you hear me?*"

"How would he do that, Papa?" Maggie asked, so innocently.

"I haven't the faintest idea, Maggie, how such a thing could *in any way* happen. But knowing ...what I do, I would ...not at all ...rule out that possibility."

The following morning, Maggie could never find the time to go up to the cedar grove to feed Blackie. By lunchtime, she had forgotten all about the raven. There was simply too much else occupying her mind—

"Girls!" Callie called, "Hurry up! The ladies will be here at two o'clock! Set the teacakes on the rose platter! Get out the real glasses ...for the punch. Get out the saucers, for serving the cakes ...they're just finger cakes ...no need for forks or whatever. Have we forgotten anything? Nellie Sue, wash up those last few dishes. Barbara Jo, you give the kitchen floor a fast sweep."

"What's Maggie going to do?" Barbara Jo asked.

"Maggie's going to ladle the punch into the glasses. Be sure, Maggie, to put the same amount in each glass, and hold the pitcher real steady, so you don't dribble it all over the outsides of the glasses. You know how berry juice can *stain*. And I certainly don't want any stray drops falling onto my new quilt. Now, your Papa's helpin' me let down the quiltin' frames from off the ceiling. When we've got them down, and got the quilt and batting and lining all laced in, I'll give a call and you girls can bring in the kitchen benches and chairs. And we'll place them so all the ladies can reach the quiltin' real easy. And, is that it?"

"What are *we* going to do Mama—Nellie Sue and Barbs and me—while you ladies are doin' your quiltin' and havin' your punch and cakes?" Maggie asked.

"What would you like to do? You want me to try to make a place at the frames for you girls? I don't know how many ladies will accept my invitation, but we might just squeeze you in, if you want to do some quiltin'?"

"No thanks, Mama!" the three girls chorused.

"Then, you just serve the punch, Maggie, on the wooden tray that Grandpa Thomas carved. And Nellie Sue can bring in the teacakes, and Barbara Jo can sweep up the front room, when the party's over, and the quiltin' frames have been rolled back up to the ceiling. You got that, girls?"

"Yes, Mama."

"How about the needles and thread, for the quiltin'?" Nellie Sue asked.

"Well, each lady always brings her favorite needle and thimble, and the hostess supplies spools of thread. So I got the thread the last time we were at the General Store, remember? Now, girls, get at it ...and I'll just see if John's about got the frames let down."

"Can we have some teacakes and punch, Mama?" Maggie called to her mother's departing back.

"When the other ladies are served, if there's any left over after they've gone, you can each have a cup, Maggie, and a cake. But, always remember, guests are *always* served first."

"I sure would like to taste this punch," Maggie mused giving the enticing liquid in the big crock a brisk stir with the water dipper.

"You heard what Mama said," Barbara Jo warned. "No punch, until the ladies of the quiltin' party are served!"

Nellie Sue began rambling in the kitchen cupboard for saucers that weren't too cracked. Barbara Jo began to slowly draw the homemade broomsedge broom across the planks of the kitchen floor, toward the back door. From there the trash would be swept out onto the back porch and flirted into the yard.

Now, Maggie decided, was a good time to sample the punch ...just a taste.

"Seems a bit flat to me," she mused, licking her lips, wrinkling up her pretty nose.

"Maggie! You heard what Mama said!" Nellie Sue hissed a warning. But Maggie had waited until Barbs had swept her remaining trash out the back door, and onto the back porch, before sneaking a sip.

"But, Nellie, I tell you it *needs* something!"

"Well, you *forget* what it needs. It's already got grape juice and some wild muscadine and some fresh dewberry and some sugar."

"I still say it needs something," Maggie asserted.

"Does that look to suit you, Callie, honey?" John beamed at his wife. Callie had been in a good mood lately.

"It looks fine, John! Just fine! I've been to several quiltin' parties, but I've never had one of my own! Thank you, John!" Callie gave John a bright smile, and planted a little kiss on his sun-tanned cheek.

"Anything for my favorite girl!" John grabbed Callie, lifted her feet clean off the floor, swung her wildly around …and gave her a big hug and a resounding smack on the mouth, before putting her down.

"Get on out of here, John Thomas McKinnon! And don't you show your face! Until you're called for supper!

"Girls! Bring in the chairs and benches."

Six rigs of different sizes and descriptions drove into the McKinnon dooryard about two o'clock, Saturday afternoon. Six pretty ladies in their best dresses and bonnets crossed the yard onto the porch, and stepped into the McKinnon's front room.

A fine bouquet of freshly cut blossoms from Mama's flowerbeds out front filled the room with sweet perfume. One of Mama's latest quilts was spread atop Katherine Ann's big brown leather trunk—in case extra seating might be required. The front room rockers had been moved to the front porch, to allow for the lowering of the quilting frames—which now filled the entire center of the front room, and backed up against the grand pipe organ.

Into the quilting frames, Callie had fastened her latest creation—a lovely hand-pieced flower garden, intricately sewn of hundreds of tiny, perfectly cut squares and diamonds of brightly-colored cotton scraps. Piecing the quilt-top had consumed countless hours—rocking in the shade of the front porch in summer—rocking in the warmth of the fireplace in winter.

Exchanging excited greetings, quick hugs, chatting merrily, the ladies all took seats of their choosing. Each took out of her reticule her sewing scissors, her favorite thimble, and quilting needle. The spools of stout cotton thread were passed around; proper lengths were cut—as much as a lady felt she could properly quilt up without her thread binding itself into knots because it was too long.

Each lady sat with her *quilting needle* poised above the quilt at the proper angle, in order to plunge it through quilt-top, batting, and lining. She put her *thimble* on the index finger, to deftly push the butt of the needle through as many stitches as the lady could manage to pick up in one pass, as she wove the tip of her needle in and out with a practiced flair—through *all* the layers. The left hand, she tucked underneath the quilting frames, to hold the multiple layers steady, for firm and ready access of the needle tip.

The party seemed to be progressing amazingly well. Needles were flying in and out, creating lovely shell patterns, all about the edges of the quilt. As the quilting progressed, the lively conversation slackened, each lady busy with her needle. When the first row was done, the iron pins scotching each corner would be removed, each side of the quilt frame would be rolled under, so that another section could be easily reached. The pins would be reinserted. And so on, until the center of the quilt was finished—and the entire quilt had been perfectly stitched in the shell pattern.

A word was spoken now and then—quietly, softly, a polite cough. Nothing else could be heard by the girls in the kitchen.

The girls remained quite as three mice, waiting for the signal to serve the refreshments.

The signal came. Mama excused herself politely from the quilting, stuck her blond head momentarily in the kitchen door, and gave a little nod.

Nellie Sue went in first, the platter of homemade teacakes poised on her left hand, very prettily, just so.

"Oh, and how is Nellie Sue?"

"Isn't she growing up?"

"And very prettily, indeed, I must say!"

"Soon, Callie, John will need a big log to beat the fellows off!"

"Thank you, teacake, Mrs. Haskins? Take two if you want. There's plenty more in the kitchen—"

Maggie came next, bearing the wooden tea tray carved by Grandpa Thomas, with the beautiful grapevine scrolled across its fine maple planes.

She had poured the punch beautifully. Callie noticed with satisfaction that there was not a drop dribbling down the outsides of the glasses to soil the ladies' quilting hands. None spilled onto the tray, either. Callie gave both girls a beaming smile of approval.

The girls withdrew, reappearing a few minutes later …to offer refills of punch …a second or third teacake …as they are rather small …and plenty left in the kitchen.

On her last trip, Nellie Sue returned to the kitchen with only two teacakes remaining on the rose platter.

The big crock was completely emptied of punch.

"Well, they sure liked Mama's teacakes!" Nellie Sue wagged her head. "Only two left. Since I'm the oldest, and I really don't care for them all that much, Maggie, you and Barbara Jo go ahead and help yourselves."

After the refreshments were served, it got real quiet in the front room, an occasional word now and then, a sigh, a quiet, "Ummmmm ummmm." Words so low the girls waiting in the kitchen could not catch them. Maggie began to be bored.

"We can't even sit down. All the benches and chair are in the front room," Barbara Jo complained.

"Well, we can always drag in the log bench, off the back porch," Maggie offered. She was a bit tired herself, from all the work and excitement of getting things ready for Mama's quilting party.

"Nellie Sue," Maggie instructed her sister, "you come hold the door open, and Barbs and I will drag the log bench in."

"I don't know whether that's such a good idea—"

"Why not? Come on!" Maggie said, "Hold the door for us!'

Nellie did as Maggie asked, swinging the back door wide, as the two girls dragged the heavy log bench along the back porch and towards the open door.

Then suddenly there was a flash of black past her face, and Nellie gave a high, piercing shriek—

"Magggggiiiieeee———!"

"What?" Maggie called.

"A big black bird just flew …past me …and into …the …*house!*'

Maggie dropped her end of the log bench with a bang, and went racing into the kitchen.

"Nellie! I don't see any bird!'

"In …there!" Nellie screamed, her face pale with horror, as she pointed towards the front room—

Before she reached the door to the front room, Maggie heard a bevy of shrieks and screams. Opening the door, she was horrified to see that most of the ladies had vacated their seats, and assumed all sorts of odd positions, stunned looks on their faces, their cups of punch waving perilously in the air—

—As they watched the fattest, blackest crow they had ever seen, circling and cawing about their heads.

Then Mrs. Wilkes gave a terrified, trilling scream, as the crow—apparently liking the looks of her dark hair—honed in on her head. She slung down the cup of punch, onto the newly laced quilt, flung up a hand to shield her face, and went screeching about the room.

Callie watched in horror as one lady after another, leapt from her seat, spilling her punch, dodging the crazed bird. Chairs, cups, and cakes were hitting the floor—and her quilt—as the swiftest, blackest bird she had ever seen went sweeping and diving at this head and then that.

The front room had turned into a mad-house! Her *quilt!* Her quilting party had turned into a *rout*! *Where had that bird come from!? How had it gotten into the house!!???*

Maggie had flown away to the barn to get Papa. And just as Callie collected her senses enough to open her mouth and scream:

"*JOHNNNNN—*"

John came bolting in the door—

—The front room was in utter chaos. Mrs. Pratt, leaping from her end of the bench and screeching to the top of her lungs, went crashing around the quilt, Blackie in swift pursuit—dead set on perching on her shoulder.

"*Ladies! Ladies!*" John called, catching Mrs. Pratt in her frantic flight, setting chairs aright and attempting to restore order. "Please," John urged calmly, "take your seats! It's nothing but a *wild bird*, somehow got inta th' house! We'll just lure him out, and you can continue on with your party!

"Maggie," John turned to his youngest daughter, standing at the foot of the stairs, pale and distraught, "Why don't you just …take this handful of corn …and see if you can get the bird …to maybe follow you …up the stairs. Then you can just open all the windows up there, and let the poor thing find his way out. I'll just take my fiddle down, here, and play a couple of hymns, to help the party along. Any of you ladies have any particular song you'd like to hear—?"

Fleeing up the stairs, Blackie hot on her trail, Maggie felt sick and weak in the knees. She led him to her bedroom window, and set him free. Maggie never wept, but now, she laid her head forward on her arms, on the window sill, and burst into sobs. Downstairs, she could hear the haunting strains of Papa's fiddle, then she heard the ladies of Mama's quilting party begin to sing:

Amazing grace, How sweet the sound—

Callie wagged her head in disbelief, as the family sat about the supper table that night.

"I simply cannot for the life of me …imagine what got into that crazy bird! I have *never* in my entire life heard of such a thing! Happening at the very worst time it possibly could."

"Well, now, Callie," John drawled, "the ladies *all* seemed to have a real good time, to me. They were all just laughin' and talkin', as they took their leave. I'll bet that was th' *most* excitin' quiltin' party any of them ladies ever attended. I bet none of them ladies ever had such a surprisin' quiltin' bee in their lives. They'll have somethin' to talk about—for years and years to come."

"I'm sure they *will!*" Callie moaned sorrowfully. "And I'd sure like to know what brought that stupid bird flying into this house!"

"Strange, isn't it," Barbara Jo remarked with narrowed blue eyes, "that a *crow* comes flyin' into the house, just the next day after Maggie was asking about—"

"Mama!" Nellie Sue piped up suddenly, "Isn't it about time to rob the bee gums? I'd sure like to help!"

"Why ...Nellie," Callie beamed at her oldest daughter, "How sweet of you to offer!"

Chapter 14

"Maggie?" John called up the stairs, "I'm going to the Stillwell place now, to see about getting' th' horse. You still want to come along?"

"Yes, Papa! I'll be right down."

"Well, hurry along now. They won't wait on us all day!"

Maggie came bounding down the stairs, out the door and onto the wagon seat before John could get the front door closed.

"You sure are mighty anxious to get goin', I see," John drawled.

"I've never been to a horse farm before, Papa. What kinds of horses do the Stillwells raise?"

"Oh, I don't know. Haven't had to do much horse tradin'. But th' one we've got now's got some years on him. He stepped in a hole th' other day. I don't think he even saw it. I have to be *real* careful, when I drive him, kind of watch the road for him. We may have to put him down."

"What does that mean, Papa?"

"It means, Maggie, he may be near the end of his life."

"He can't get better?"

"No, sugar."

"That's sad, Papa."

"I know, sugar. Nothing lives forever, Maggie. That's just the way things are. And we just have to go on and do the best we can with what we have."

They rode on in silence for a minute. Maggie, watching the horse, "We can't just trade him in, Papa?"

"I don't know, Maggie. We can sure try. Could be that I'm wrong. Mr. Stillwell knows more about horses than I do. He may think the animal's got some good left in him yet. But like any other practical-minded farmer, I can't afford to keep an animal that can't pull his weight, Maggie. Feed costs too much."

Maggie stayed unusually quiet for the remainder of the trip to Stillwell's farm. John knew she was fretting about the idea of the horse meeting his demise. He made up his mind to tell Stillwell to keep the animal, even if he thought he was worthless, just to spare Maggie the trauma of knowing the horse was to be shot in McKinnon Valley.

Before the horse farm itself came into view, Maggie began to catch glimpses of beautiful stallions and mares, grazing in pastureland fenced with split-oak rails, with rich grasses to their knees.

"Look at them, Papa!" Maggie exclaimed, the excitement making her lovely cheeks glow, her eyes take on a deeper blue. "Aren't they grand?"

"They sure are, sugar," John readily concurred, "But I'm afraid those fine animals are not for us. Those look like saddle mounts—not plow horses."

"What's the difference, Papa? Aren't all horses alike?"

"No, Maggie. Horses are bred for all sorts of tasks."

"Like what?"

"Well, there's the work horse—of sturdy stock, for pulling your plow or your wagon.

"Then, there's the saddle mount. A bit taller and leaner, he's mostly for riding around on. But if called upon to do so, he can also pull your wagon or light carriage.

"Then there are horses bred mostly for pulling large carriages …and coaches. A little larger than a saddle mount, but they'll also take a saddle, if the occasions demands it, and let you climb on and ride.

"Then there are the draft horses. Nineteen …sometimes twenty …hands high. They haul *real* heavy loads, like pulling loaded ferries and barges along the rivers and hauling logs to mill, and such."

"What's a *hand*, Papa?"

"A hand? Oh, that's a measure for gauging the height of horses—the span of a man's hand, Maggie." John held up a hand.

They were pulling into the yard of the horse farm, and Maggie grew quiet. Her curious gaze swept the split-pole corral, a gigantic circular affair with a huge barn behind it. Several men stood about the outside of the corral, watching a young boy who appeared to be about Maggie's age, sitting astride a prancing red-gold horse.

"You want to step down, Maggie, or do you just want to wait in the wagon?" John asked, looking up at Maggie with a smile, as if he already knew the answer to that question.

"I want to go over there, and see that boy ride that horse!" Maggie declared.

To Maggie's great embarrassment, John, out of habit, took her by the hand.

That boy is looking at me, Maggie thought, mortified, and he'll think I'm still a baby, and not twelve, going on thirteen!

Gently, for the very first time in her life, Maggie pulled her hand from Papa's.

John looked down at her, and gave her a little smile. He had seen the boy, watching Maggie even before she stepped down from the wagon.

"Well," John drawled, "we're growing up, are we?"

"I don't know what on earth you mean, Papa," Maggie declared, and giving a little flounce of her long dark hair, she skipped ahead of John and ran to climb up on the bottom pole of the split-rail fence.

The boy on the beautiful horse rode slowly past. He smiled at Maggie, and then he turned, and rode straight towards her.

Maggie hung over the fence, meeting his gaze

"Hey, there!" he called, "You here to look at horses?"

"My Papa is. He's over there. John McKinnon," Maggie announced.

"And what's your name? Haven't seen you around these parts. Where you from?" the boy asked.

"Over the other side of Rhyersville."

The boy stepped down off the horse, and led it right up to the split-rail fence. Papa was busy talking with the men, and seemed not to notice.

"You want to ride her? She's gentle enough. Ever been on a horse?"

"Of course," Maggie replied, a bit miffed that he would ask her such a thing, "but …not a horse like that."

"If you'd like to ride, I'll help you mount? I don't think we'll even have to shorten the stirrups. You're about as tall as me."

Maggie noticed that she was, in fact, a bit taller than the boy standing before her, holding the reins of his beautiful horse. "I'd love to. But I don't know if Papa will let me."

"We can always ask him. Mr. McKinnon? Mr. McKinnon? Can she ride my horse?"

John had watched out of the corner of his eye, as the boy approached Maggie. He saw how Maggie talked excitedly to him for a moment, then hung her head.

"I don't know, son," John called in reply. "What does your Pa think about that?"

"All right with me, John. I'm surprised you recognized Alfred. He's growed quite a bit since you last saw him. He's eleven now, going on twelve. She can ride the horse, I guess. She should be safe enough on Dumplin'."

"That's her name?" Maggie piped up, excitement building at the thought of her first ride on a real saddle mount. "Can I, Papa?"

"Okay, sugar. Just remember," John warned, as he watched the lad, Alfred, give Maggie a boost up, "ride her *real* slow, just once around th' corral. And whatever you do, don't nudge her with your knees."

"Okay, Papa," Maggie called, sitting astride the horse, which, since she was just a child, was considered proper.

Alfred stood gazing up at Maggie, then he handed her the reins, and gave her hand a little squeeze. "Just take it nice and easy now. Sit up straight, and relax. Dumpling'll know what to do."

Maggie rode slowly off. Not much different than riding Papa's horse, she thought, except that the ground looked such a long way off.

The horse swung Maggie this way, then that, with every step. Then, half way around the corral, Maggie got the rhythm of the horse's gait. And she began to enjoy the ride.

She made a loop, then rode right past the waiting group of men. Giving them a little wave and a bright smile, she started around the corral again. She tried to recall, exactly what it was that Papa said—*don't* give the horse a nudge with your knees? Or—*give* the horse a nudge with your knees. Maggie moved her knees the slightest bit.

Dumpling shot forward like a startled rabbit. She went loping about the worn tracks of the corral. Then around she came again, gathering speed with each stride—until she was in a full, heart-thumping gallop. Suddenly Dumpling whirled—and headed across the corral—straight for the split-rail fence. Then, her front legs swept up and up—and Dumpling sailed over the fence in one clean sweep.

Behind her, Maggie could hear the excited yelps of Papa and Alfred and all the other men gathered around the corral.

But soon their voices faded, and there was just Maggie, Dumpling thundering along beneath her. The air whipped past Maggie's cheeks. Her bonnet flew off. Her hair streamed out behind her.

Maggie bent low over the horse's neck, and hung on for dear life. Never had she felt such a thrill. The world whirling past her at breakneck speed, she wished the horse would gallop on forever.

But Dumpling seemed to regain her senses. She slowed to a trot, then to a prancing walk. What a grand horse, Maggie thought.

Maggie drew a deep breath. Careful not to nudge the mare with her knees, she pulled lightly on the left rein. Dumpling turned herself about, and began a beautiful, slow trot back to the corral.

Halfway there, Maggie met Papa and Alfred and the other men—some mounted, some afoot—tearing down the road towards her.

She trotted Dumpling up to them, and pulled her to a gentle halt.

"Maggie!" Papa cried, snatching off his hat and waving it about, "Are you all right?"

"Sure, Papa. Can we come back sometime soon? So I can ride Dumpling again?"

"Probably not!" John squawked.

"I could ride out to Rhyersville, out to your place, maybe, sometime, and we could go for a ride." Alfred stared admiringly at Maggie, a silly grin on his freckled face.

"We'll …just have to wait and see …about that." John remarked dryly. This was not at all how he had envisioned Maggie's first visit to the horse farm. "I think we'd better just …take care of our business, and be on our way."

John settled on a fine looking horse. And Maggie agreed he was the pick of the lot.

"Not as big as some of the others," John reflected with a frown. "But he looks sound in the hocks, and his back is straight and he has a good look about his eyes."

"His eyes, Papa?" Maggie asked.

"Sure, Maggie." John replied, "His eyes are steady when he looks at you. He doesn't look as if he'd spook real easy—like if a rabbit darts across the road in front of him, or he comes unexpectedly upon a wash-out in the road."

"He's a tough one. Stepped in a hole a year back, but he recovered," Mr. Stillwell remarked.

"Let's name him *Job*, Papa."

"Why Job, Maggie?" John asked.

"Because he's had such a hard time."

"How old is Job?" John asked Wilfred Stillwell.

"He's comin' up on about four now, I reckon."

"Four?" Maggie gasped. "He's still a baby!"

"You don't count the age of horses like you do people, Maggie." John explained.

"How do you count it?" Maggie asked, feeling hot in the face with embarrassment. She should have *known* that. Why hadn't she ever heard that? Alfred Stillwell was grinning at her as if she was a stupid *child*!

"You count ...about three years for a horse ...to every one year for us."

"Then, Job's about twelve!" Maggie cried excitedly, "He's the same age as me!"

All the men burst out laughing.

Maggie leapt down from the fence, stuck her nose in the air, lifted her skirts, and flounced off to the wagon to wait.

Alfred Stillwell followed Maggie to the wagon.

She refused to look at him.

"I didn't think it was all that funny," he apologized.

"Well, you were sure haw-hawwwing! Just as loud as the rest of them!" Maggie accused, refusing to look at him, her cheeks burning.

"Look," Alfred hung his head, dug the toe of one shoe into the dirt of the yard, said, "I meant what I said, about riding over some time. I'd bring an extra mount for you. A real gentle one. And you could learn to ride, really well."

"I already know how to ride!" Maggie declared angrily.

"Yeah! I know! That was really somethin'!" Alfred grinned up at Maggie. He had blond-red hair and a scattering of light freckles across his nose. His skin was fair as a woman's.

"Well, I might—and I might not—go riding with you. That is, if you were to come over."

John walked up, to find the two of them chatting. Frowning, he mounted the wagon seat. He gave a curt nod to Alfred, and a quick glance at Maggie.

Then John picked up the reins, and drove off.

"What was that boy sayin' to you?" John asked.

"Nothing much, Papa. He just said he was sorry he laughed. He really didn't think it was all that funny. He said he might ride over and bring another horse, so I could learn to ride. That's all."

"Well ...now ...Maggie, that sounds like quite a bit, to me," John said slowly.

"Did you buy the horse?" Maggie asked, wanting to change the subject. "Did you buy Job? Why aren't we driving him home?"

"They'll be bringing him out to our place, sometime in the next week or so, I was told, Maggie. And I can't imagine for the life of me, exactly who that person will be …that brings Job out."

The next Saturday afternoon, Alfred Stillwell knocked on the door of the log house in McKinnon Valley. John opened the door. "Alfred." John said.

"Mr. McKinnon, Pa sent me out with the horse you bought. Said I was to pick up the other one, the one you …wanted him to take." All the while he was talking to John, John noticed that the boy's eyes went past him, and on into the house.

"Was there something else you wanted, Alfred?" John drawled.

"I was just wondering—if Miss Maggie was at home?"

"You mean, Margaret Ann?"

"Yes, sir! I mean Miss Margaret Ann!"

"I think she might be around here …someplace. But, why don't you and me take care of our business, first."

"Yes, sir! Where do you think she might be?"

"Could be," John drawled, "that she's out back, drawing up a bucket of fresh water."

"Oh. Well, then, I'll just go on …and pick up th' other horse. Th' one you're …"

"Yes." John shook his head and led the boy down the steps. John took his new horse, named Job, by the reins. He led him on out to the barn. He took the halter off Job, and put it on the old horse. He gazed at the horse a minute, patted him gently, then turned and handed the reins to the boy.

"It's all right," John told the boy as they walked out of the barn, "if you want to walk around back …see if Margaret Ann's still out at the well shelter."

John watched the boy walk around the corner of the house towards the well, and he felt cold chills traveling up and down his spine. Something was about to die, and it looked like something new was about to be born. Maggie was twelve. And already, a boy liked her.

"You traded that sick, blind horse in, John? Is that what you're saying? Just how much did Mr. Stillwell allow you—on that horse?"

"Well, Callie, it was like this. He didn't allow me one cent. He just agreed ta' pick up the horse."

"Pick it up? You mean to tell me, that you, a *grown man*, left it to that poor man to put down your horse?"

"Well, Callie, Maggie was askin' what was to become of th' old horse …and I hadn't the heart to tell her—"

"John McKinnon! Well, if you don't beat all! When are you going to let that child begin to grow up? Sooner or later, John, Maggie's going to find out—that there's a cold, cruel world out there. And you won't always be there to protect her from it. You want to turn her into a stunted soul, who can't face the realities of life?"

"It wasn't exactly my intention, Callie, to turn Maggie into a stunted soul—when I asked the man to pick up the horse. I just wanted to spare her—"

"Well, you listen to me, John McKinnon! You'd better learn to let that girl *grow up*! Give her a little room to breathe! Don't make each and every decision for her! Don't try to smooth out each and every little bump in the road!"

"You're right, Callie. And from here on, I'll surely try to do that. Oh, by the way, Callie, that young son of Stillwell's—I believe his name's Alfred—he's going to come callin' on Maggie. I believe they're going out ridin' …this comin' Saturday afternoon."

"They're *what*?" Callie screeched. "John! Maggie's *twelve*!"

"Well, Callie, the boy's younger than that—he's eleven. The boy asked if he could come out Saturday and teach Maggie how to ride. And I said, 'Well, Maggie, what do you think about that? You want young Alfred here to come out on Saturday, or not?'"

"John! You left the decision up to *Maggie*?"

"Well, Callie—I mean, I don't want to turn Maggie into some sort of *stunted soul*—"

"John McKinnon—!"

John went on out to the barn, to check on Job.

Callie soon grew accustomed to the sight of Alfred Stillwell riding into the yard of the McKinnon farmstead, a spare mount in tow.

It was John who became concerned, asking Callie one day, "Callie, you did have *that* talk with Maggie, didn't you?"

"What talk do you mean, John?"

"Well, the one about boys and girls. And how they're different."

"Of course, John."

"What did you say to Maggie, Callie?"

"Oh ...I ...don't recall exactly. That was three or fours years ago. She asked where babies came from. And I told her that God gave every man a little sack of seed ...and when the season was right ...he planted them."

"A little sack of seed? Well, Callie, that sure should have set her clear in her thinkin'! Maybe I better just have a little talk with her, myself."

"You do that, John."

"Maggie," John began, clearing his throat loudly, "I just want to talk to you a bit about somethin' that's been on my mind ...lately. It's about that boy."

"You mean Alf?"

"Oh. So, it's 'Alf' now, is it? Well, what I want to tell you, Maggie ...I just wanted to ask you ...did your Mama ever talk to you *about* ..."

"Oh, sure Papa, Mama told me *always* to keep myself covered, and *always* to act like a lady."

"Well, good! And you just always remember ...do *exactly* what your Mama told you to ...and everything will be all right."

"Sure, Papa."

"And, Maggie ...remember to ...see to it ...that Alf always stays on his best behavior."

"Well, did you have your little talk with Maggie?" Callie asked John that night as he climbed into bed beside her.

"I sure did. And I'm certainly glad of it. Now I feel somewhat more relieved, about that boy."

"Well, good, John ...John exactly what did you say ...to Maggie?"

"I told her, Callie, to just see to it that Alf always stayed on his best behavior."

"Well ...John ...that should certainly set her straight in her thinking about—"

John interrupted. "Would you like to blow out the lamp, Callie, or should I?"

"Why don't *you* do it, John?" Callie said very sweetly, "You're so much *better* at these things, than I am."

"Maggie's got a boyfriend! Maggie's got a boyfriend!" Barbara Jo danced around the well curb, her taunting words drifting up into the trees in the back yard.

"I do *not*!" Maggie yelled angrily. "Alf's only a *friend*! *Do you hear me?*"

"Maggie's got a boyfriend! Maggie's got a boyfriend! Maggie's got a—"

"You *stop* that right this minute, Barbara Jo McKinnon, or so help me, I'll—"

"Yeah? You'll *what?*"

Slowly, with her mouth set in a grim line, Maggie bent and picked up a handful of pebbles.

"Just go ahead and *throw* that!" Barbara Jo taunted, "I dare you …dare …you …dare—"

Before Barbara Jo could get the other words out of her mouth, Maggie drew back her hand—and flung the handful of pebbles.

One of them struck Barbara Jo—just above her left eye. A big knot popped out on her forehead.

"Maaaammmmaaaaaaaaaaaa!" Barbara Jo set up a wailing howl.

Callie flew to the back door and flung it open. In an instant, she was down the steps, staring at Barbara Jo's head.

"How on earth did you manage to do that?" Callie demanded.

"Magggiieeee!" Barbara Jo wailed.

"Margaret Ann McKinnon! Did *you* do *that* to your *sister*—?

"JOHN! I think you'd better come on out here!"

"I don't really know what to say to you, Maggie." John wagged his head. "I mean, I know …I've *always* knowed …that you have a …bit of temper. But to go and throw rocks at your sister's head …well, Maggie, I just can't believe it."

"But Papa," Maggie put up a valiant defense. "She was taunting me! She was daring me, with her hollering all over the mountains—that I had a boyfriend!"

"But, Maggie, that's *still* no reason …what I mean to say is …you can't just go throwing things at folks, ever time they say somethin' that don't exactly suit your own personal fancy. Do you see what I'm trying to say here, Maggie? You can't throw things at people! Just because you get mad at them! You could hurt somebody …real bad. That rock could have hit your sister's *eye*, Maggie! Putting out her *sight*! This is serious, this time, Maggie. It's real serious! Can you see that?"

"Yes, Papa."

"Then you go on in the house, and tell your sister you're sorry."

"Do I have to do that, Papa?"

"Yes, Maggie, you do. And that's not all. You're to tell your sister how very sorry you are. Then you're not even to sit down, just go on up to your room. And stay there! Until mornin'!"

"Eat your supper, John," Callie said. "You did the right thing. Maggie has to learn. She can't just go around ...flinging rocks at people. You did the right thing, John."

"If I did the right thing, Callie, why on earth do I feel so *dog-take-it rotten.*"

They rode their mounts down to the river, dismounted, and stood watching the waters roll past.

Alfred Stillwell had been at the McKinnon house almost every Saturday—for the past year. Maggie had gotten accustomed to Alf's being there, each Saturday, with a fine horse for her to ride. They galloped all over the country. They walked in the pasture, and they waded in the creek. They shared books and helped each other with homework. Maggie had come to enjoy Alf's company, the mop of red-gold hair that always hung half in his eyes, his silly, lop-sided grin, his voice that was sometimes up, and sometimes down. His freckled face had become almost as familiar to her as the faces of her two sisters.

As they stood now and watched the river roll past, Alf asked suddenly:

"You want to go swimming?"

"Swimming?" Maggie looked at him as if he had just lost his senses. "It's not that warm. Besides, silly, we're not dressed for swimming."

"We could hang our clothes on the trees, and keep them—"

"*What? Are you crazy?* What on earth has gotten into you, *Alfred Jonas Stillwell! What kind of a girl do you think I am!?*"

Maggie was in his face, backing him slowly down the riverbank.

"Why're you so mad?" Alfred asked. "I didn't mean nothin'!"

"You want to go swimmin', Alfred? Well ...here ...you ...*go!*"

Maggie put both hands against Alf's chest ...and gave him a mighty shove.

"Maggie!" he gasped, as he hit the cold water with a splash—and sank.

"You come on up out of there!" Maggie yelled angrily. Time stood still. "I know you can swim, Alfred Stillwell! You come on up out of that water—!

"Do you hear me! *Alfredddd!!!!*"

Her heart pounding furiously, fully clothed, Maggie leapt into the frigid water. Suddenly something latched onto her legs, pulling her completely under.

Then they were circling about, thrashing their way up.

Alf came up laughing, a hoarse, boyish, innocent laugh. Well pleased with himself.

Maggie floundered away from him and clambered angrily onto the bank, leaving Alf still treading water, laughing to the top of his lungs.

"You! *Youuuu*—-!" Maggie fumed, unable to call to her mind just what vile names she could shout at him—

"—You just take your fine horses, and your sorry, good-for-nothing self—back through the gap—and don't you *ever* ride out this way again!"

"Maggie! I'm sorry! I didn't mean anything! I was only joking. Maggie?"

Alfred's voice echoed behind her, as Maggie stalked off through the trees and towards the house, so angry her lips began to quiver.

Or was it because of the cold drenching in the river?

"Maggie!" Callie shouted, horrified at the sight of her youngest daughter. "You're wet as a drowned rat! What on earth *happened* to you?"

"Nothin', Mama. I just fell in the river. I'm goin' up to change."

"John! You get yourself in here! Our daughter went off with that *boy*!— And she says she *fell in the river!*"

John came bounding up the stairs, two at a time.

"Maggie?" John called at the closed bedroom door. "Your Mama said …are you all right in there, Maggie?

"—Maggie McKinnon! You answer me! You open this door!"

Maggie slowly drew the door open, "What is it, Papa?"

"What is it, Papa?" John repeated her words in an odd voice Maggie had never heard before.

"What it is, Maggie, is that your Mama said you went off with that boy— and came back looking like a drowned gypsy! And I want to know what went on down at that river?"

"I pushed Alf in. He didn't come up. So I jumped in after him."

"You pushed Alfred in the river? Why on earth, Maggie, would you do a fool thing like that?"

"Because …Papa." Maggie looked down at her bare toes. She hadn't had time to put on any dry shoes, when Papa started shouting at the door.

"Because what, Maggie? What happened at th' *river*?"

"Because he said something I didn't like. And it made me mad."

"I thought, Maggie, I had told you about your temper. What on earth did Alfred say, that made you all that mad?"

"He ...he wanted to go swimming."

"And for that you pushed him in the river?"

"I told him we didn't have any ...proper clothes."

"And—?"

"And ...he said we could just hang our clothes on the trees ...and I told him I *was not* that kind of a girl. And some *other* things besides that. Then I pushed him in the river."

"Did Alfred ...say ...or do ...anything else? How did he look?"

"He looked just like he always looks, Papa. He said he didn't mean anything and that he was just joking."

"Well, Maggie ...sometimes boys ...and men ...say things ...*stupid things* ...and they just don't *think*. And then, *afterwards, they're very, very sorry.* He might actually have not meant any harm. But you were right to set him straight ...as to what kind of girl you are. I'm proud of you, Maggie." John gave her a warm hug. "Now you just take your time, and get yourself together, and come on down to supper when you feel like it."

"Okay, Papa," Maggie said very solemnly, "And you won't have to worry about that sorry Alfred Stillwell comin' around this place, anymore."

"Is that so, Maggie? You sent him packin', did you?"

"Papa, I did. And I told him not to show his sorry self in this valley, not *ever* again."

"Well, Maggie, now ...that's a long, long time.

"I know Papa, but I meant every word."

"Well, John? What on earth happened?" Callie asked as John descended the stairs.

"It seems that Alf somehow fell in the river, and Maggie jumped in to pull him out."

"You mean that boy can't *swim?* "

Chapter 15

The beautiful new dress Mama had made for her lay spread on the bed. Disappointment was so real to Maggie that she could almost taste it. *Why* must they miss the Bidwell's corn husking party, just because Papa wasn't able to go? After all, Mama promised they could go, weeks ago, when the Bidwells first invited them. And even if she wasn't fifteen yet, Maggie felt old enough to go without her parents along. She was perfectly capable of managing the horse and wagon.

Rising from the bed where she had been pondering her sad dilemma, Maggie decided to make one final effort to persuade Papa to let them go without him. After all, when would there *ever* be another corn husking party within driving distance of McKinnon Valley!?

Smoothing her dark hair, and putting on her most beguiling smile, Maggie entered her parents' room, where Papa lay propped up in bed. The room smelled strongly of the heavy steamed-onion-and-garlic poultice Papa wore on his chest. And of elderberry tea—and wintergreen rub. Papa had been laid up with a terrible cold for the past few days, and Maggie's entrance was like a burst of sunshine illuminating the dimly lit room.

"Hello, Papa. Feeling better?" Maggie cooed in her sweetest, most innocent voice, making certain she conveyed her deep concern as to the state of Papa's health.

"Why, pumpkin! Hello! Come sit here beside me on the bed," John smiled, patting the brightly-patterned quilt. "How could a fellow not feel better, with such a lovely visitor?"

"Oh, Papa," Maggie murmured, coyly turning her head aside, so that her hair swept her shoulders, just so, "you say the silliest things."

"Well, it's true," John smiled.

Then Maggie was looking John full in the eye, her own blue orbs locking with John's gold-flecked brown ones.

"Papa," she moaned, "if I don't get to go to that party at the Bidwells, I'll just *die*, Papa! I'll just *die! Everybody will be there*! And who knows when we'll *ever* be invited to another party?"

John, patiently, "Maggie, you know *good and well* how your Mama feels about that. Lettin' you girls go off in the dark, all alone. She wouldn't have an easy minute."

"But, Papa, you know I'll drive *real* careful! I promise!" Such an imploring look from those blue-blue eyes! If a man could resist that look, John though, he's made of sterner stuff than me.

"Okay, Maggie," he sighed, wondering how he could go against his better judgment like this. "There'll be a full moon tonight, so you shouldn't have any problem seein' the road. Anyhow, Job could find his way in th' dark. But you'd *better* drive *real* careful. And you'd better be home *early*, you hear me, young lady?" John's dark brows pulled a warning frown.

"Oh, thank you, Papa! I do love you so! And I know that you'll soon be well!"

With that, Maggie floated out of the room, holding the tail of her long calico dress out in a graceful arc.

Down the stairs she swept, taking them two at a time. She simply had to find Nellie Sue and Barbara Jo, and give them the good news!

But, then …there was still Mama to deal with.

"Mama," Maggie said pensively, as she entered the kitchen where Mama was molding up freshly churned butter, "Papa says he doesn't see why we can't go to the Bidwells' corn huskin'. After all, we are *all grown up*, now."

"Margaret Ann," Callie began, eyeing Maggie suspiciously, "are you *certain* your Papa said you could go?"

"Yes, Mama! He just now said that we could go!"

"Well. I suppose any critters you encounter on the way would be more in danger from you—than you from them. All right. But—"

Maggie didn't hear the rest. Her heart was thumping so, she could scarcely breathe.

She was going to the corn huskin'! Parties in Maggie's life were so rare! Since the War, few folks had the means, the energy, or the inclination to entertain.

Maggie made several trips to the well, drawing up bucket after bucket of water, which she heated on the big iron cookstove in the kitchen. Maggie and

Barbara Jo lugged Mama's big oak washtub in from the wash bench out back between the two huge water oaks. The tub filled, Maggie tossed in some crushed rose petals. Then they took turns, climbing into and out of the oak tub, adding kettlefuls of hot water, and finally toweling themselves dry.

Then Maggie was standing before the dresser, closely scrutinizing her reflection in the mirror. Maggie never really gave much thought to her appearance. But tonight was special. Gazing at herself in the mirror, Maggie could see that she really was growing up. She knew she was beautiful. It was very apparent, from the way folks gazed at her. But Maggie took this for granted. Mama said it wasn't how one looked on the outside …but how one looked on the inside …which truly mattered.

But, tonight, Maggie McKinnon wanted to look good on the outside.

Maggie turned from the mirror, and slipped into the new dress Mama had made. Blue cotton flocked with tiny white flowers, it was by far the prettiest Maggie had ever had. And the big blue velvet sash spanning her middle exactly matched her blue eyes, enhancing their color beneath the dark lashes curled upward in a graceful sweep.

She piled her hair atop her head, and then decided against that particular arrangement. Letting it down, she pulled it back with a length of the velvet that matched her sash.

She leaned in close to the mirror. Her skin was fair, and clear. But she felt that her lips and cheeks were in need of a little color.

Stealing to the door, she peeked furtively out …no one in sight. Nellie Sue and Barbara Jo must still be in the kitchen, finishing their baths. She moved back to the dresser, and very quietly slid open the drawer assigned to her. Carefully, she felt beneath her nightgowns and under things, and brought out a brown paper parcel.

Very carefully, she removed the cotton twine, and removed the contents.

Back in the spring, just before Easter, Papa had gone to the General Store and Mill and bought the girls some colored candy eggs, the first Maggie had ever seen. After eating a red one, Maggie had noticed the unnaturally red tint of her lips and fingertips. She had thought at the time that the lip color was rather becoming.

So, without a word of explanation, she had traded Nellie Sue and Barbara Jo—her white and yellow eggs, for two more red ones. These she had squirreled away in the brown paper, and hoarded in her dresser drawer.

Slipping one of the precious eggs from its nest in the paper, Maggie moistened her full lips. Barely touching the red egg to her lips, Maggie transferred the lovely red color to her mouth. Then, regarding herself in the mirror, Maggie daubed a touch of the red onto each cheek. She took a step back, and was quite pleased with the effect.

Hearing footsteps outside the door, Maggie quickly re-wrapped her candy, and crammed it back into the dresser drawer, making an exaggerated pretense of arranging her hair, as Barbara Jo flounced into the room.

"Maggie," Barbara Jo frowned, "have you got a fever?"

"'Course not, silly," Maggie replied tartly. Maggie turned quickly away, to avoid Barbara Jo's penetrating gaze.

"Well ...I don't know ...maybe I should call Mama. Your colorin' sure is high ..." Barbara Jo made every effort to sound genuinely concerned, but she failed to hide the touch of envy in her voice. Maggie looked absolutely radiant.

"Don't be such a busy-body, Barbara Jo," Maggie said, attempting to divert her sister's attention. "I'm just excited about the party. Aren't you?"

"Oh, my, yes! I *do* hope Bob Sorrells is there. I think he's just about the best lookin' thing in these mountains! Do you think Alf might show up? You haven't seen him since—"

"That Alfred Stillwell?" A lift of the chin, and a tart reply, "I don't know. And I don't care."

On the stairs, Maggie met Nellie Sue, fresh from her bath, her blond hair still damp. Nellie Sue had not been feeling well lately. She had been keeping to the house, and had to stay, more and more, off her bad leg.

Maggie gave her a sweet smile, as they met on the stairs. Nellie Sue's gaze followed her younger sister, as she floated past. Then, with the aid of the cane that John has carved for her from a stout oak sapling, Nellie Sue limped on up. At first Nellie Sue had refused to consider attending the corn husking. She had been confined to the house for so long now, she dreaded the thought of going out. It took all of Maggie's considerable charm to persuade her otherwise.

Now, Nellie Sue slowly descended the stairs, a vision of loveliness in her pale green cotton dress, her blond hair laying in a shining cloud about slender shoulders.

Maggie had the horse hitched to the wagon and waiting by the front doorsteps.

Maggie and Barbara Jo pulled Nellie Sue up into the wagon. Then with great fanfare—last minute warnings from Mama, waves from Papa hanging out the upstairs window, giggling and murmuring from the three girls—they were ready. Maggie picked up the reins, and with a deft flick, sent Job trotting gently out of the yard, down the road, and through the gap.

Callie stood and watched the wagon disappear. The sun was setting, painting the western sky with brilliant streaks of red and orange, with scattered here and there a few puffy white clouds against deep blue. Callie heaved a great sigh, whispered a little prayer, and went back into the house.

Maggie had promised to give a ride to the Stenson girls—Sally and Beth. And they, beautifully dressed, were soon clambering aboard, Maggie on the seat, the other four girls sitting on one of Mama's old quilts in the back of the wagon.

An immediate chatter began in the back of the wagon. Soon it rose to a loud din of yapping and laughing. Maggie could scarcely believe her ears. Seated sedately on the seat, driving old Job, Maggie felt far more mature than the other girls, though, in truth, they were all older than she was.

With each passing turn of the wheels, the noise from the back of the wagon rose higher, until the giggling and twittering became a thunderous roar.

The wagon topped a ridge, and started down a long hill. It wasn't yet dark, and Maggie could see the shimmering ripples of the wide creek, murmuring over smoothly worn stones at the bottom of the hill—a creek they must ford.

Listening to the waves of sound rising from behind her, Maggie was suddenly seized with a titillating idea. Wouldn't it shock those clattering females in the wagon box, if she should send Job dashing across the creek, spraying them all with water!

The more she rolled it around in her mind, the more intriguing the thought became. Suddenly, Maggie gave Job a slap on the rump with one rein.

But Maggie was not the only creature to hear the noise coming from the back of the wagon. The crescendo of unfamiliar racket swirling about his head, Job had become more than a little skittish.

When that rein dropped on his rump, Job took off as if shot from a cannon.

Eyes wide, ears laid back, he lunged forward. Maggie felt the violent jolt, and hoped her passengers were still in the wagon box.

The light wagon gained speed at an alarming rate. The wind whipping past her cheeks, her hair standing out behind her head, the wagon flew. Maggie hung on to the reins—and prayed.

In the back of the wagon, all chatter had ceased.

As they clung to the sides of the wagon for their lives, the four girls were all screaming hysterically.

"Please! God!" Maggie prayed.

Maggie could see the fast-approaching creek. For one horrible instant, she was seized with remorse, as she envisioned her four hapless passengers sitting spread-legged in the creek, their fine new dresses drifting out about them in the water—

But ...no ...to keep the dust off their new dresses and high leather shoes, she had put the tailgate up before leaving their dooryard.

"Please, God! Don't let us burst a wheel—when we hit that creek!"

Maggie closed her eyes, and hung on for dear life.

They hit the creek at such a high rate of speed that water came splashing up and over the sideboards. Maggie could hear the sound of the iron rims, crashing over the stones. Then, almost as soon as they were in the creek—they were out—and ascending the steep slope on the other side.

Thankfully, the wagon slowed, as it began the long pull up the hill. Maggie slackened the reins, gulped in a deep breath.

All was quiet in the back of the wagon—except for a few sharp gasps. They were all too stunned to speak. Then they were pulling into the Bidwell's farmyard.

"Margaret Ann McKinnon! Have you lost all your *senses?*" Barbara Jo recovered herself, and screeched at Maggie as she leapt down from the wagon box. "You just wait! You just *wait*—until Papa and Mama find out about this! You'll *never* get to go anywhere again. *Ever!*"

Barbara Jo's new yellow dress was thoroughly damp. Her light brown hair had been considerably sprinkled—

—As had that of the other passengers. But Maggie was so relieved to see that all four wheels of the wagon were still on—and not one of the girls had lost life or limb, that she heaved a great sigh of relief.

"Well," Maggie smiled at them all and wagged her head innocently, "Sorry 'bout that. Job *sure* got excited when he saw that creek!"

"*Job?!!!*" Barbara Jo screeched, "You're going to try to blame this on that poor horse that you drove into that creek like a mad woman?"

Nellie Sue, smoothing down her damp dress, gathering her breath as they helped her alight, said sweetly, "Now, I'm sure it *wasn't* Maggie's fault. You *know* she wouldn't have done anything like that *on purpose.* And since everyone seems to have all their legs and arms ...just a little *wet* here and there ...why don't you just help me down from here. We'll just forget the whole thing, and try to have a good time ...now that we're all here."

With considerable muttering and murmuring, the five girls made their way toward the huge Bidwell barn. Maggie cast a glance back over her shoulder, amazed that *all* the wheels of the wagon *were* actually intact!

Once inside, the awful fording of the creek was quickly forgotten. Bright lanterns swung from the rafters of the big barn. Folks of all ages were congregated inside and outside the huge structure. It was Maggie's first corn husking. She'd never seen so many beautifully dressed people. Most of the older folk gathered about the huge pile of corn at one end of the barn—where they were seated on barrels and kegs, a pile of newly-husked ears of corn slowly rising before them.

All the girls seemed clustered in one corner, surreptitiously eyeing the boys. All the boys seemed clustered in the opposite corner, eyeing the girls.

Long tables laden with food and drink were spread just outside the open barn doors.

Three or four men were clustered together, thumping and plunking, tuning up their banjoes and fiddles. Soon the music swelled, and drifted up into the lantern light, past the hayloft, and out into the star-sprinkled night sky. Laughing couples began to drift into the open area of the barn, and stomp and circle and swirl in time with the music.

The excited talk and laughter rose around Maggie, transporting her into another world. Poor crops and Papa's illness were soon forgotten.

"I hear there's a *new boy* here," Sally Stenson whispered into Maggie's ear.

"Who?" Maggie asked.

"He's not from our school. Or even our county. He's from over in the next county. The grandson of the owner of that old haunted house, remember, the one called *Cottonwood?"*

"He's *here*? *Where is he?"* Maggie gasped excitedly. She would *never* forget the day the three of them walked over to Cottonwood. And that big black carriage came tearing out of the carriage house and down the drive—

"He *was* here, just a minute ago," another girl informed them, "but someone said he just left. I heard that his *grandfather* wasn't able to attend, and insisted he come. Oh! He was *so* handsome! But he didn't know anyone. So I guess he felt a bit out of place."

"I think an old colored man just picked him up," someone murmured.

Maggie's acute disappointment at not meeting the mysterious grandson from Cottonwood was soon forgotten. Almost the minute she entered the door, Maggie was surrounded by a bevy of male admirers, all vying for the privilege of fetching a cup of punch, asking for a dance. One of them was Alfred Stillwell. Maggie let him take her hand, and guide her into the line of dancers.

Maggie McKinnon was far and away the most beautiful, the most vivacious girl at the gathering. Her loveliness was enhanced by a rosy, radiant glow that seemed to emanate from her cheeks and lips. But she gave Alfred only a fleeting smile—and passed on to another partner.

There were so many other boys …and Barbara Jo was pale with envy.

Nellie Sue was indulgently approving, and found herself a seat on a bale of hay to one side, where she could watch the proceedings, safely off her feet. Nellie Sue was enjoying herself thoroughly, a foot keeping time to the music, until she noticed a young man across the cavernous hall of the barn. A tall, slender young man, dressed in a dark suit and snow-white shirt with a little black string tie. He kept staring intently in her direction.

Nellie Sue cast a glance around, to see if perhaps he was staring at someone in her vicinity. But no one was sitting near her. She looked down quickly, to see if something was horribly amiss with her appearance. But the tail of her dress had almost dried, and looked fine for what it had undergone.

The young man was crossing the barn. He was headed in her direction.

Thomas Beyers had stood in the corner, watching as the people gathered. Since he was new in town, he was not acquainted with that many folk, and felt slightly ill at ease. Then he had seen a group of young ladies enter, almost hidden in the press—but one of them, he could see, was a strikingly beautiful blond, in a mint green dress. Suddenly, Thomas forgot his discomfort—

—She had smiled, almost since entering the room. She had not risen to dance, and had refused several invitations to do so.

Thomas Beyers stood before Nellie Sue, smiled, and bowed, and politely introduced himself.

"I'm Thomas Beyers, the new school teacher. I don't believe I've had the pleasure …"

"Nellie Sue McKinnon, Mr. Beyers. We have a farm …over the next ridge."

"Well, Miss McKinnon, could I perhaps fetch you a …a bit of food, or a cup of punch?"

"Maybe …some punch …" Nellie Sue averted her blue-green eyes, and blushed prettily, to the roots of her blond hair, as the young man stood gazing steadily at her. She had never even so much as had a date. They were so isolated on the farm. She had been out and about very little, had not been able to attend school as regularly as Barbara Jo and Maggie.

When he returned with a brimming cup, she lifted her gaze and bestowed upon the young man a dazzling smile. "Thank you, Mr. Beyers."

Holding his punch, Thomas Beyers smiled, struggled to find his voice, asked politely, "May I?" At Nellie Sue's nod, he seated himself beside her and began a low conversation.

"I've noticed …you're …not dancing."

"I'm not able …to dance. I'm …I had an accident …I'm crippled."

"Oh! Please excuse my impertinence!"

"No need to apologize, Mr. Beyers," Nellie Sue said very quietly. "It's a condition I've lived with for some years now. And, mostly, I've become quiet accustomed to it."

"Well …" Mr. Thomas Beyers passed on to other subjects, soon learning to his great delight, that although Miss Nellie Sue McKinnon had missed a great deal of her formal schooling, she loved books.

"Perhaps I could …assist you in furthering your studies. Perhaps I might call on you …at your leisure, of course, and bring along some fine reading materials …that might interest you greatly, Miss McKinnon?"

"I'm sure, Mr. Beyers, that any subject that interests you …would certainly interest me. But …I couldn't possibly ask you to come all the way out to McKinnon Valley …just to bring me a few books."

"Miss McKinnon, I fear you misunderstand. I assure you, the pleasure of seeing you again …would be all mine. I would love to meet your family."

"I'm sure you're already acquainted with my two sisters," Nellie Sue smiled, her head in a whirl—that this handsome young man was engaged in conversation with her. "Barbara Jo …and Margaret Ann McKinnon?"

"Oh, *yes*," Thomas Beyers smiled and ran a hand through his light hair, "Margaret Ann!"

Maggie noticed the young teacher, chatting with Nellie Sue.

Barbara Jo noticed how all the boys continued to buzz about Maggie. How Maggie fairly glowed, her cheeks and lips that amazing rosy hue—

But there was still the matter of the drenching they all received when the wagon plunged into the creek. Just wait until she told Papa and Mama …*that* should take some of the color from Maggie's prettily flushed cheeks!

Maggie, knowing what no doubt lay in store for her once they reached home, drew Barbara Jo aside, and promised to share with her the secret of her heightened coloring—if Barbara Jo swore to keep silent about the creek.

A bargain was reluctantly struck.

The moon cast a shimmering, silvery light over the Blue Ridge Mountains as the girls rode home in near silence, each busy with her own thoughts.

Maggie still floated about the dance floor.

Barbara Jo dreamed of the next gathering, when she would be adorned with a rosy hue that would draw all the boys to her side, like a covey of stunned birds.

Nellie Sue fingered the worn knob of her hickory cane—and wondered wryly if the schoolteacher, Mr. Thomas Beyers, would actually come calling at McKinnon Valley.

Mr. Thomas Beyers did indeed visit the McKinnon farm. So often, in fact, that he soon became a fixture around the place. The log house became piled with books. And Thomas could be seen, shirtsleeves rolled above his elbows, bringing in firewood—

—Or in the back yard, hauling a bucket of water from the cold depths of the well—

—Or tossing forkfuls of hay down to Job or the cow.

Thomas Beyers found no chore about the farm too tiring or demeaning.

He could be found sitting at the kitchen table with the family, most evenings, laughing and talking, his eyes locked with Nellie Sue's, the faces of the two glowing, as they became more and more oblivious to everything and everyone around them. Later of an evening, the two would sit on the front porch, long after darkness descended and John and Callie were ready to put out the lamps and go to bed. John would call out the front door:

"Nellie Sue? Isn't it about time to bid Mr. Beyers a *goodnight*?" John could read all the signs. Despite her handicap, the new school teacher was intoxicated with Nellie Sue McKinnon.

John knew it was just a matter of time.

"Mr. McKinnon?"

"Yes, Thomas?"

"I was just wondering …that is …I've been meaning to speak to you."

"Yes, Thomas?"

"Being a school teacher …well, I don't make a great deal of money."

"You make enough for a decent living, Thomas?"

"Yes, sir."

"Then what is th' problem with that?"

"I wish to ask you for the hand of your daughter, Nellie Sue, in marriage!"

"Well, Thomas! And just how does my daughter, Nellie Sue, feel about this?"

"I think she is of a mind to agree to marry me, if you please, sir?"

"Then I suppose that pretty much settles th' whole matter."

"We have your permission, then, and your blessing?"

"You have both, Mr. Beyers. I only ask one thing of you."

"Yes, sir?"

"I ask that you treat my Nellie Sue like the beautiful angel she is."

"Oh, yes, sir. She certainly is! That is, I certainly will!"

"Then I suppose," John smiled at Thomas, "th' next question is ...when is th' weddin'?"

Soft dusk had fallen. The young couple had gone for a drive down to the bend of the river.

As soon as Thomas Beyers' buggy pulled out of the front yard, Callie heaved an angry sigh.

John waited.

"You should have said *no*, John," Callie finally spoke from her rocker, in the gathering shadows at the far end of the porch.

John could hear the frogs calling from the creek down in the pasture, the crickets in the tall grass out behind the garden, chirping loudly. He leaned forward slightly in his rocker, laid his head on his hands. Sometimes ...life could be so hard.

"John, you know, she's not strong enough to be a wife. There ...there could be a child ...if Nellie Sue marries. John, have you even considered that?"

"Yes, Callie," John raised his head, and finally spoke, "being the father of three, I know a little something about what goes on ...between a man and a woman. This was not a decision I made lightly."

"John, Nellie Sue's—"

John turned to study Callie in the dimming light. "Nellie Sue's nineteen years old. She's a grown woman, Callie ...and before Thomas Beyers came around, she spent 'most every day and every night of her life tied to a chair and a bed. Is that what you want for your daughter, Callie? To live the rest of her life ...here with you and me ...a spinster invalid ...while the other girls go on to take husbands and rear families?"

"John, I'd rather have her ...here ...alive ..."

"That's what *you* want Callie. Did you ever stop to consider what Nellie Sue wants? Maybe Nellie Sue would rather have a few years of happiness— even *one* year of happiness—with a fine young man who can laugh with her, and hold her ...and love her ...than to lay all alone up there in that upstairs room of her Pa's and Ma's house, with a bunch of dry, dusty old books! What sort of life is that?"

"All right, John," Callie said shortly. Then all in a rush, she flung down her needlework, and leapt up, "Just tell me this, John McKinnon," she hissed, "if it was *Maggie* up there in that room—would you let *Maggie* marry that boy?"

John didn't even turn to look at her. His voice came out of the shadows, low and cold, "This was *not* my decision to make. It was *Nellie Sue's*. So, leave it be, Callie! *Just leave it be!*"

Callie bent with a jerk. Snatched up her needlework, and started into the house.

"Well," she said, flipping down the tail of her apron with her free hand, her chin in the air as she reached the door, "I suppose it's about time to fix us all some supper!"

The wedding was on a Saturday afternoon, at the Shiloh Baptist Church in Rhyersville. Thomas Beyers was dressed in a new blue suit and sparkling white shirt. Nellie Sue was wearing the wedding dress Callie had painstakingly, with tears in her eyes, sewn for her daughter. Almost everyone in Rhyersville attended the ceremony, followed by a reception at the home of the new couple, a cottage not far from the new school building that would be constructed over the summer.

The couple settled happily into the vine-draped country cottage near the school.

Throughout the summer, things seemed to be progressing handsomely. Come fall, the new school year began; Maggie and Barbara Jo were the envy of all their classmates. Their teacher was now their brother-in-law.

They could easily drop around for a visit with Nellie Sue on almost any given afternoon, if they kept the visit short and they arrived home in time to do their chores.

Then it became evident that Nellie Sue was pregnant. Both she and Thomas were, of course, elated. But the pregnancy, Dr. Ellis prognosticated, would be a difficult one.

Nellie Sue's knee and leg began to swell. Nothing Dr. Ellis prescribed seemed to be of any effect. Despite her growing difficulties, Nellie Sue's smile remained confident, and her spirit strong. When Maggie dropped by, Nellie Sue would ask her younger sister in, offer her milk and cake. They would talk for hours about the latest book they had read, for Maggie, now that the school teacher was so closely related, found herself privy to almost all the reading materials her bright mind could absorb. She became especially enamored of a book on the subject of *accounting*. She found the columns of assets and liabilities simply fascinating, as well as the aspect of writing bank drafts to transfer funds from one person to another. Since she was so caught up in the book, Thomas Beyers gave it to her.

But as winter passed and Nellie Sue's time drew near, Maggie often cut short her visits, for it became clear that Nellie Sue was in great discomfort a good deal of the time. Dr. Ellis seemed totally unable to hit upon any relief for this distress. None of the emollients applied, or the infusions ingested, seemed of any particular benefit. He told her husband, her father and mother:

"About all a country doctor can do in these situations, is what the patient's family is already doing—watch, and pray."

Barbara Jo had suspended her visits, when Nellie Sue's condition began to worsen.

"I cannot *bear* to see Nellie Sue like that," she whined to Maggie one afternoon. "I can't *bear* to watch what's happening to her."

"You talk as if Nellie Sue was already dead!" Maggie accused.

"Have you really *looked* at her, Maggs?" Barbara Jo asked pointedly, "She looks like a bloated toad frog!"

"Barbs! What a cruel and cold thing to say!" Maggie frowned angrily at her sister, "Nellie Sue will *always* be beautiful! No matter—"

"She's *not* beautiful! Not any more! And we both know that this child will never make it into the world! And Nellie Sue is not long for it, either! I heard Dr. Ellis tell Papa and Mama, her kidneys are failing. And I can't bear …I can't bear to see her …anymore!"

"Look, Maggie," Nellie Sue whispered, ensconced in a large armchair by the front door of the little cottage. "There in the ivy on the garden trellis. It's a little sparrow! The first I've seen this spring! Isn't he a *sight*?"

"You know, Nellie Sue, what Mama says about the sparrows."

"Oh, yes," Nellie Sue sighed, laying a hand on her swollen middle. "Our Father loves us so much. He looks after all his creation, even down to the very tinest of his creatures …"

"Yes," Maggie smiled at her. She thought her sister looked more beautiful than she had ever seen her. Her blue-green eyes were sparkling with love and with life. She seemed full of hope and joy ...and plans for the future.

"You know, Maggie, we've decided on names already—Mary Margaret, if it's a girl, and Thomas Shawn, if it's a boy."

"Mary Margaret Beyers! Or *Thomas Shawn Beyers!* They both sound so lovely, Nellie! I can't *wait* for the wee babe to be born," Maggie took Nellie's swollen hand between her two warm ones and gave it a confident squeeze.

Thomas Beyers came out to tell them about Nellie Sue—and the baby— and to borrow the cooling board.

They were both buried in the casket John nailed together in his barn. The baby, Thomas Shawn Beyers, nestled in his mother's arms. Thomas Beyers had bought a burial plot behind the Shiloh Baptist Church, not that far from his cottage.

John guided old Job into the yard. He sat motionless on the wagon seat. His arms and hands felt like dead sticks; his eyes hot and dry with unshed tears. He felt as if a shovel was lodged in his throat. He didn't think he could climb down, if his life depended on it. Callie got down from the wagon seat. "You coming on in?" she asked in a strange voice that sounded about like John felt. She didn't as much as glance at him.

"Think I'll go ahead ...put the horse and wagon away. Callie?" She had turned her back, had taken a step or two toward the house. She halted. John said in a stilted, choked voice, "You got anything ...you need to say ...to me?"

John felt his body go even more rigid, preparing himself for an onslaught of accusations. Of anger, white-hot and filled with tears and I-told-you-so. He wanted to just go ahead and get it over ...shoot him with both barrels ...lower the cleaver and cut him to the bone. One clean cut, then it would be over, and the healing could begin. Not leave it like this ...like some half-closed, half-open wound, festering between them.

Callie still didn't look at him. "No," she said, flatly, as if this was just an ordinary day, as if they'd just returned from one of their regular trips to the mill or store—and not from their oldest daughter's funeral. "No, nothing, except ...there's some clouds gathering...back of the barn. Could be we're in for a deal of rain." In her black-stuff bonnet and dress, stiff-backed, Callie strode toward the house.

John fed the horse and rubbed him down, put the wagon away. He and Callie had been married now for a good many years. They had always been able to work out their differences. John began plotting in his mind, how to go about healing this present, gaping wound.

And apparently, John was successful, for in a few weeks, Maggie noticed there was a new spring in Papa's step, a new smile on Mama's face.

And Mama's middle began to expand, as Papa and Mama's affection for one another seemed to heighten. Papa always made sure to give Mama a hug and a kiss, each time he got near her. He picked up some of her chores, like milking the cow, and gathering vegetables from the garden.

Even Maggie was not so forward as to ask about such things. And such things were not generally discussed at the family dinner table. But it soon became apparent to Maggie, that Mama was expecting a baby.

"At *her* age?" Barbara Jo scoffed, a scowling frown on her narrow face.

"What has age to do with anything?" Maggie countered. "I'm glad Papa and Mama still love each other! No matter what age they are! And they're not that old!"

Maggie just had to know, so finally she gathered up the courage to speak.

"Mama, I've been watching you …and Papa …and I was just wondering, if you were going to have a baby or somethin'?"

"How would you feel, Maggie, if you weren't the baby any more?"

"Oh, Mama! It would be grand! Just grand! Is it …for real, Mama?"

"Yes, Margaret Ann," Callie smiled at her baby girl, "I would say *this* is for real."

Maggie was so excited she could scarcely contain herself. She flew away, to break the news to Barbara Jo. Barbara Jo wasn't quite as thrilled as her sister.

"Yes. I had suspected as much. Now, I'll be so *loaded* with chores. There'll be no time for anything but *work*!"

But Maggie's joy was not so easily dampened. She met Papa at the door that night, "Oh, Papa! It's so wonderful. About the new little boy!"

"Boy?" John grinned at her, "What makes you think it'll be a boy? Might be another little girl. After all, we do have our record to maintain."

"It'll be a boy!" Maggie nodded her head confidently, "I just know it. And we'll fix up the spare room for him. I could braid one of those soft rag rugs for his floor, like Mrs. Baldwin has in her front room. To keep the room warm for him. And put some pretty curtains on the windows …and …"

John, Callie and Barbara Jo all listened, as Maggie rattled on, all through supper, until Callie wished she could have kept her secret a bit longer. But, oh, how she hoped Maggie was right! How she longed to give John Thomas McKinnon a son!

After supper, John took his fiddle down off its pegs. For the first time in a while, he took it and sat on the front steps, playing softly, until full darkness had fallen. Callie sat silently rocking. Maggie leaned against the warm strength of Papa, and listened.

As Callie grew heavier on her feet, she was confined to the house, and Maggie was up early each morning, doing the milking. Then, day by day, Maggie assumed more and more responsibility for running the household.

Barbara Jo felt she assumed too much responsibility, but Maggie ordered Barbara Jo about with such a complete air of authority, that Barbara Jo did not dare disobey.

The crops were maturing in the fields, and John would need help with getting in the harvest; so Barbara Jo was assigned to look after Mama, and the garden, and the house, while Maggie helped Papa in the fields.

Now, every morning, when it became light enough for them to see, Papa and Maggie were up, getting the milking and the other outside chores done, then they were in the fields. But Barbara Jo felt that with all her extra duties, she needed her rest, so they did not awaken her each morning.

There was cotton to be picked ...and hauled to the gin ...over ten acres of it. And five acres of Indian corn to be gathered ...and the fodder pulled and stacked in the barn for winter feed. Wheat and oats to be scythed and stored, Irish potatoes and yams to be dug and hauled to the root cellar. Peas to be shelled and dried. Groundnuts to be pulled. Apples in the orchard to be gathered, peeled, sliced and sun-dried.

Weeks of mind-boggling, backbreaking work lay ahead.

As the days passed, Maggie lost count of the work that still waited to be done. She tried not to think about it. She lost count of the hours in the day. The days of the week.

The rows and rows of cotton stretched across the valley and up the terraced sides of the gently rolling hills. Maggie's back ached. Despite the protection of her stocking gloves, her hands became scratched and sore from the sharp, prickly bolls, chafed and cracked from continual contact with the dry, fluffy cotton. But still the cotton rows stretched on ...for what seemed to Maggie, into infinity. There was no time for books, or school.

Maggie had no energy for them. All she wanted in the evenings was a warm bath, and her bed.

Thomas Beyers came out every afternoon and on several Saturdays, and made at scything the fields of wheat and oats. They needed the wheat for light bread and biscuit, and the oats for breakfast, and for feed. Thomas Beyers was slightly built, a scholar, not accustomed to farm work, but he soon caught the rhythm of swinging the heavy scythe, and of keeping it sharpened on the grindstone in the smithy attached to the barn. Thomas thrashed out the grain, winnowed away the chaff, and poured the precious kernels into brown tow sacks.

At night, Maggie dreamed of the endless rows of white bolls waiting in the cotton fields. The green stalks with their fine balls of puffy white beckoned her ever onward.

But, load by load, the cotton was hauled to the house, and piled onto the end of the front porch. This was their money crop. This would buy necessities for the coming year. Thomas Beyers hitched up the one-horse wagon, and carried some of the wheat and oats to the mill.

Then, after what seemed an eternity of emptying the prickly bolls and lugging the heavy picksacks, the cotton was all in …the last load ready to be hauled to the gin.

Maggie was never more relieved in her life, than the day she and Papa heaved the last basketful of the cotton into the borrowed two-horse wagon with its side planks up. A two-horse wagonload, Papa said, weighed approximately one thousand to twelve hundred pounds. And after ginning, which removed all the seed, it weighed about four hundred pounds— constituting a bale of cotton. This was the fifth load. She and Papa had picked five or six thousand odd pounds of cotton.

"A yield of a bale to two acres!" Papa bragged, "A fair return, I would say, for a crippled old man and one young girl!"

Maggie was young and strong, and with the cotton in, she felt she had been liberated, and had energy to spare.

When she helped Papa pile on the last load, it was a Saturday. A beautiful fall morning. Even Mama and Barbara Jo were up, excited to see Papa off with this final run to the gin.

He drove down the dirt road and through the gap, whistling a little tune.

Maggie walked indoors, and surveyed the house. Barbara Jo's style of housekeeping, to Maggie's way of thinking, left much to be desired. She determined to clean the entire house.

She put Barbara Jo to washing windows in the downstairs. Maggie set about scrubbing all the floors until they were clean as a pin. She shoveled the ashes from the black iron cookstove, and from the fireplace, and dumped them onto the vegetable garden, for fertilizer. She washed the bed linens, and cleaned the kitchen. She fixed lunch, and ordered Barbara Jo to help her clean out the yards. Piles of dead leaves had drifted dangerously close against the sides of the house.

It was late afternoon, before Maggie found a chance to check on Mama.

Maggie walked into Callie's room, to find her propped up against her feather pillows, a deep frown creasing her brow.

"Hello, Mama." Mama smelled like roses, as Maggie planted a wet kiss on her mother's forehead, smoothed down her covers, and then plunked down beside her on the bed. "Why're you looking so grim?"

"I'm getting a bit worried about your Papa. John should be back by now."

"He's okay, Mama. He'll be along any minute now. Today's the day he'll be gettin' paid. All that figuring and settling up to do. You just lie back, and don't you worry. I'm going down to start supper." At the door, Maggie turned to give Callie a reassuring smile, she said, "We'll eat as soon as Papa get's home."

Callie sank back into her soft pillows with a heavy sigh. Something is wrong, she thought, I can feel it.

The sun had set over an hour ago. The food was getting cold on the back of the stove.

And still John was not home.

A chill seemed to be creeping over the house. Maggie went into the front room, and laid some kindling on the dog irons in the huge river-rock fireplace. She threw on two logs. The fire roared up, flooding the entire room with a warm glow, the familiar smell of burning oak.

Still, Maggie felt oddly chilled. She went into the kitchen, stoked up the fire in the black iron stove, heated up the supper, and insisted that they all go ahead and eat. "Papa will be home soon. No need in our starving ourselves, just because he ran into a little ...problem."

It was pitch dark outside. A slow drizzle began to fall. Soon this changed into a heavy downpour.

No one had mentioned Papa for the last hour or so, as the three of them sat around the fire, watching the flames leaping up, sending shadows dancing into the corners of the room. Maggie's eyes fell on the huge brown leather trunk brought over from Ireland on *The Last Farewell,* by Katherine Ann. Her gaze traveled up the stout walls of logs hewn by the axe of Shawn McKinnon, more than fifty years before. The old fiddle Shawn had bartered his knife for, hung on its wooden pegs over the brown leather trunk. On the stone hearth, the familiar iron Dutch oven, strewn with ashes, blackened by decades of red-hot coals shoveled under and heaped over it.

When the eight-day wind-up clock struck ten, Maggie insisted that Mama go on to bed. Barbara Jo had turned in an hour ago. Callie resisted, but Maggie took her by the arm and guided her firmly to the stairs, up to her room, and tucked her in with a kiss, and soft reassurances.

"Go on to sleep, Mama. Papa'll be in ...any minute. I'll wait up, and heat him up some supper. We'll all have a good laugh about this ...tomorrow."

Maggie sat in the rocker in the front room. The fire crackled. The cold rain drummed incessantly on the roof, never letting up, hour after hour.

Then Maggie would rise and walk to the window, attempting to see out. Her gaze was met with a wall of inky blackness, rain drenching the window panes.

"Where are you, Papa?" Maggie whispered into the darkness, "Where are you!"

She sat back down. Got back up. Threw more logs on the fire. The room was warm, but still Maggie felt cold.

Callie lay in bed, the kerosene lamp casting a pale yellow glow over her blond hair, spread over the feather-stuffed pillow with its embroidered flowers twining about on the snow-white case. Her Bible lay open before her, across the bright quilt top. It was the quilt she had in the frames ...the day of her one and only quilting party. She frowned slightly, fingering the flower garden quilt, recalling how the day had—at the time—seemed a total disaster. That big black crow swooped in, cawing, swirling about all the ladies' heads. The spilled cups of punch. But she could scarcely see *any* of the stains, now. And afterwards, when she met any of the ladies who had attended, they all assured her with bright smiles that it was the most exciting quilting part they had ever attended.

Recalling the happiness engendered by her quilting party, Callie finally drifted off to sleep.

Through the long night, Maggie kept her vigil, never closing her eyes, lest Papa come home, and need her help. Once she covered her head with Papa's blue denim jumper, and dashed out to the lean-to for an armload of wood.

But, mostly, she just sat, and waited.

The clock on the mantel struck five. The rain had slackened. The rooster soon sounded his daily alarm. Light was beginning to show in the eastern sky—

—And Papa was still not home.

Maggie stirred from the rocker, going out for more wood, stoking up the fire. She went into the kitchen, and laid a fire in the cookstove. Anything to take the chill off the house. Anything to keep her mind occupied. Mama and Barbara Jo would need breakfast. The stock needed tending. The chickens must be fed.

Where was he?

Almost unaware of her actions, Maggie fixed some biscuit and scrambled eggs for Mama and Barbara Jo. Some hot coffee with fresh, rich cream.

Upstairs with her tray, she found Mama awake, sitting up, the frown deepening on her smooth brow. Maggie could see that she had been crying.

But Callie pasted on a weak smile, as her youngest daughter entered the room. "You up already?" Callie asked, the smile on her face feeling forced and frozen. Maggie had been working so hard, trying her best to take care of all of them.

Maggie retrieved Shawn's Bible that had fallen to the floor.

"Yes, Mama. I'm going on out to milk the cow. See that the chickens and pigs are fed. Maybe Barbara Jo will be up soon, and draw up some fresh water. We'll heat it up. Then you can have a good warm bath. Might make you feel better."

"Maggie?" Callie gazed at her, her blue-green eyes welling with tears, "Not a word? Not even a word? All night long? You needn't wait on me like this, Maggie. I could have come downstairs."

"No, Mama. No word. Not yet. But ...I'm sure Papa will be home soon. Maybe the darkness and the rain caught him, and he decided to stop over at Trap's in Rhyersville. And I love waiting on you."

"Maybe. Yes. Well. Thank you," Callie smiled. She seemed almost to be talking to herself. She took a long sip of the hot coffee.

Maggie poured the last of the cottonseed meal from last year's crop into the cow's trough. She perched on the milking stool, and quickly filled the large pail. She carried the milk to the kitchen, strained it though a sterile milk cloth, and lowered it very slowly, very carefully, into the cool, damp depths of the well. Then she securely scotched the windless. The remainder of yesterday's sweet milk, which she had just drawn up from the well, she carried into the kitchen, and poured into the brown earthen churn, to work up later for sweet butter.

Maggie went back out to the barnyard, to lead the cow out to pasture to graze on sweet fall grasses.

She fed the pigs and the chickens, and gathered the eggs. She looked at the bee gums, frowned, and wondered if it was time to rob them of their sweet treasure of honey. The bee gums had always been Callie's particular turf. Callie would talk to them and sing softly to them. She could rob them with never one sting. But the bustling, buzzing hives of bees might not accept anyone else stealing their honey. Maggie would think about that later.

Maggie turned now, to look down the narrow dirt road leading past the house, and into the low gap. Nothing.

The rain clouds had all passed, leaving the air clean, the world shiny and fresh, with only tiny puffs of white drifting lazily here and there, far up over the mountains. She could smell the sweet, faint odor of the new-mown straw Thomas Beyers had tossed into the hayloft.

Everything appeared so right. So normal. So perfect.

But something, Maggie knew, was terribly, terribly wrong.

If Papa had not shown up in the next hour or so, Maggie determined to walk toward town, to see what she could learn.

John was immensely relieved, when they loaded the last of the cotton onto the wagon, for the final run to the gin. John hoped to get a much better price for this year's crop. Since the War, prices had been depressed. Many of the farmers had given up cotton, and planted mostly Indian corn. But John had stuck with cotton. Last year had seen an overabundance of rain, and one third of his crop had taken yellow leaf. A disappointing yield. But this year was different.

John jostled down the road, through the gap, the sun warm on his back. Now he might have cash in his pocket—for the first time in years. He would have to pay some on that loan. He'd no choice, that first spring after he came back from the war, but to take out a loan in order to plant his crops. They had *nothing* left. What little corn and potatoes Callie had managed to raise were almost gone. They needed to plant a garden. Flour was totally out of reach, at one hundred dollars a barrel. Sugar and salt were not to be had at any price. For years, Callie had parched acorns, ground them, and called it coffee. Ground and baked them—and called it bread. No kerosene, so Callie had gotten out the candle molds and beeswax. To sustain life, she picked wild greens, and dug sassafras roots for tea. She garnered everything edible in the woods. As soon as he was able, John fished, trapped, and shot squirrels and rabbits. Turtles. Frogs. Quail. They had not one penny of cash.

Each fall, after that first one, John had hoped to have enough left after re-seeding and living expenses to pay off the loan. But usually, he was forced to borrow more. He never seemed able to do more than take care of the interest.

This year, John knew, it would be different. This fall, John McKinnon would begin to bring down his debt, for the first time since walking home from Virginia.

Down at Johnson's Corners, wagons were lined up at the gin. The men were calling greetings to one another, ambling up and down the line of wagons, making small talk as they waited their turns.

"Hey! John! You ol' horse thief! What's this I hear about you?"

"Well, Haskell, I expect what you hear is true, if you're meaning the new baby," John beamed proudly.

"Well, I wouldn't have thought it of you, you sly ol' fox! Congratulations! Another girl, huh? How old are you, anyhow?" Haskell Tompkins, spat out a long squirt of tobacco juice.

"Another girl would be fine with me, Haskell. Got no complaint about any of my girls. And for your over-curious information, I suppose I'm about thirty-six."

"Well, we'll just have to go do us some celebratin', when we're finished here!"

The men continued to talk, until their turns came. John could scarcely wait for the tallying up to be done, to hold the money in the palm of his hand. He counted it several times. A hundred and fifty-three dollars. The most money John McKinnon had ever held in his hand at one time. He looked furtively around, tucked it safely into his back trouser pocket, and buttoned the flap.

Then John headed for Johnson's General Store and Mill, to pick up some needed supplies.

As John came out of the store, Haskell Thompkins insisted John join him in a bite of lunch from the brown paper bag he had brought. John declined, knowing Haskell probably brought only enough for himself. But John sat with him beneath the big oak tree.

The chicken and biscuit all consumed, Haskell produced a jug out from beneath the bench of his wagon, and offered John a swig …to celebrate the coming baby.

John knew immediately it was corn-squeezings, and shook his head, determined to refuse the drink—in a polite way. But he knew that in the mountains of North Georgia, just to be sociable, a man must take at least *one* sip.

The two men sat in the shade of the spreading water oak at the edge of the creek, behind Johnson's General Store and Mill, Haskell Tompkins talking and laughing, listening to the splashing of water spilling off the giant wheel that groaned and strained—and sipping from the corn-squeezings. Time slipped past; the sun grew warm.

It had been a while since breakfast, and the corn-squeezings did not set too well in John's stomach. Stumbling a bit, he arose after a while, and made his excuses. His head, when he attempted to stand, felt light and dizzy. He leaned against the huge tree trunk, to steady himself. He hadn't drunk that much. But John was unaccustomed to alcohol. He was not a drinking man. Maybe one sip of blackberry wine at Christmas time.

John staggered over and climbed groggily onto the seat of the borrowed wagon. He needed to get the wagon and horse back to their owner—

—Afterwards, he clearly recalled passing through Rhyersville, and turning the team toward home. But by then, his head had begun to ache abominably, his vision to blur, and his leg to ache. Then his stomach began to roil. Feeling worse and worse, John decided to pull off to the side, in the shade of a big tree, just for a few minutes.

John awoke retching and heaving all over himself, and all over the bed of the borrowed wagon. He had somehow been lying in the back of the wagon, on the sacks of cottonseed. John realized that his clothing was soaking wet.

I must have fallen asleep, John realized with a jolt. What time of day was it? He gazed towards the west. But …no …the sun was just coming up …in the *east—!*

—*He'd been here all night!*

He felt in his back trouser pocket, for his money.

It wasn't there!

Please, God, he prayed. What had he done with his money?

He had to find it!

John crawled down from the wagon, shivering and shaking from the chill in the fall air—and from the awful realization that he could *not* put his hands on all that money he had just gotten for the cotton crop!

NO! NO!

John got sicker. He began to panic, and to tremble in earnest.

How *could* he have been so stupid!

Why didn't he tell Haskell Tompkins to take his jug—

No. It wasn't Haskell's fault.

John was a grown man. He'd take full blame for his stupid mistake. He fought to clear the fog from his head, push down the panic. Try to recall the events of yesterday afternoon—

—He had to find that money!

Until the sun stood high overhead, John searched the wagon, the ground about the wagon, beneath the leaves.

Nothing.

By now, John was truly sick.

He had to get home. Get into some dry clothes. Surely, the money would turn up.

John started the team towards McKinnon Valley. At the creek ford, John got shakily down from the high wagon seat, and attempted to wash some of the vomit from his clothing. This only chilled him more, plunging him into violent spasms of shaking and trembling.

He remounted the seat, and somehow drove through the gap. The house was just ahead ...if he could just make it to the house ...

Maggie came flying out to meet him. A shawl about her shoulders, she had just stepped out to begin the long walk to Rhyersville, in search of him.

Maggie would never forget that day. Not as long as she lived. It came back to her over and over ...like a horrid, surreal nightmare.

Papa. Sitting on the wagon seat. Not looking at all like Papa. His bearded face was pale and slack. His eyes were sunken back into his head, and appeared sad, and haunted. His clothes were soaking wet, and stank of vomit.

Papa had been sick all over himself. And from the look of him, he had been out in the rain all night—and had fallen into the creek besides.

What Maggie would recall later, most of all, was the look in Papa's eyes. It was as if all the fight had gone out of him. Always he had been so strong, so positive that everything would be all right.

Now, he looked as if the world had just ended.

"Papa! What on earth happened to you?"

"Maggie!" John croaked, *"I can't find it! The money's gone!"*

Chapter 16

They had Papa in clean clothes, propped up in bed. Some black coffee with no cream. A few bites of steamed oatmeal. This was all he could tolerate.

Callie was pale as a ghost. She stood clutching her round middle, and staring at her husband, as he explained to them that he had somehow lost all the money for the precious cotton crop.

Then, she had turned and left the room—so none of them could see her cry.

Darkness was fast falling. The woodbin in the kitchen was empty. The water bucket on the washstand needed filling. The cow had to be milked.

Maggie had driven the borrowed wagon around to the back of the house, and scrubbed it of Papa's vomit, and let it dry in the sun.

Then she had driven it back to its owner, thanking him profusely for the loan of his fine rig and one of his horses for hauling all their cotton to the gin. She had unhitched Job from the twin harness, and walked him home. Job needed rubbing down, feeding.

The cow had to be milked. Supper put on the table. Barbara Jo had taken to her bed—with a bad headache.

"I can't believe that Papa *did that*!" she wailed into her pillow.

Now, it was full dark. Maggie sat alone at the kitchen table, a bowl of milk and bread before her. She was too tired to go fetch an onion or a late tomato from the garden. She stared at the bowl of bread and sweet milk—and thought of the sparrows. Slowly, Maggie began to eat.

Maggie banked the fire in the fireplace for the night. Took the kerosene lamp and went upstairs to check on her parents. They seemed to be resting.

Exhausted from her all-night vigil, the anxiety-ridden day, Maggie fell into bed.

Maggie awoke early. She was anxious to talk with Papa, as soon as he had regained some strength—and some of his senses. They had to find that money.

But John only looked at her, and smiled weakly, "I'm sorry, Maggie. You worked so hard."

"But, Papa! Can't you recall at all—what you did with the money for the cotton?"

"I've already told you, sugar," John heaved a great sigh. "I put it in my back trouser pocket. And buttoned the flap shut. But it's not there now."

"How could it *not* be there, Papa? I don't understand?"

"Neither do I, Maggie. I just know," John hesitated, looked as if he might burst into sobs, "that when I woke up ...the money wasn't there. I searched all about. In the wagon. Beneath the wagon. All in the leaves. For *hours*."

Maggie could see that John was getting agitated. He began to tremble. His face was flushed. He looked as if he had a high fever. Maggie walked over, took John's hand. It almost burned her palm.

"That's all right, Papa. I'll hitch up Job. Go back along the road. I'm sure the money's just laying there, somewhere. I'll find it. Then I'll bring back Dr. Ellis."

"No, Maggie. No doctor. We can't afford it," John's eyes brimmed with tears. He wagged his head. "No doctor!"

"I'll find the money, Papa. Then, we can afford it," Maggie leaned forward and gave John a peck on his burning forehead.

First Maggie rode into Rhyersville, and left a note for Dr. Ellis, that he was urgently needed at the McKinnon farm.

Then she rode slowly back toward home. Papa said he had the money when he left Rhyersville. She scanned both sides of the road. She climbed down from the wagon seat. Leading Job along at a slow walk, she searched the ground. *Nothing.*

She stopped beneath the tree where she could see the leaves all ruffled up. This was where Papa has spent the night. She moved every leaf—twice. No money.

After fruitless hours of searching, Maggie turned Job towards home.

It was almost dark that night before Dr. Ellis arrived. By then, Maggie was beside herself with worry, as were Callie and Barbara Jo.

Dr. Ellis prescribed quinine for the high fever, Laudanum to help John rest, and some sort of blue pill for the congestion. "I don't believe in bleeding and purging, anymore," Dr. Ellis remarked, wagging his head, gathering up his things. "Some still hold the notion that they release bad vapors, drive the phlegm humor from the body, and do a world of good. But, they never seemed to afford much relief to any of my patients. I gave both up, years ago."

As Dr. Ellis climbed into his rig, he told Maggie, "That's about all I can do, unfortunately. The rest is up to John. Make him stay in bed. And I mean *in bed*. Not up chopping wood, or pulling fodder. I know how John is. He thinks the world will suddenly stop turning, if he isn't out in the fields, or at the woodpile, or the barn. But I'm serious about this. Getting fatigued or overheated could put John six feet under. Keep plenty of fluid in him. See that he gets the medications. I'll be back tomorrow. Let me know, if you need me in the night."

Suddenly it dawned on Maggie—*Sunday* had passed. And she had not even realized it was the Lord's Day.

Papa coughed almost all night, every night. Then slowly, bit by bit, the awful coughing subsided. The Laudanum seemed to help him rest. And John seemed to be slowly improving.

But Maggie didn't like the look in Papa's eyes. The haunted look on his face.

She knew he was grieving himself to death—over the loss of the money.

"I don't know how a man of thirty-six could be so stupid," he said to her one day. "I never thought I would come to this."

"Papa! Stop fretting," Maggie chided him. "Everything will be all right. We'll be all right. Tomorrow's a new day. We'll grow an even *better* cotton crop next year. You just wait and see. We'll keep a journal. And decide which fields yield the most from what crops. Maybe we'll put in more Indian corn? What do you think of that, Papa?"

"I know what you're trying to do, sugar," John smiled at her weakly.

But John did not have the heart to tell her. There'd be no money—to even pay the interest on the loan. No money—to buy supplies for the entire year. No money—to put in next spring's crops. He'd be lucky—just to hang on to the farm.

Thomas Beyers still came each afternoon. Together Thomas and Maggie were slowly gathering a bit of the Indian corn, pulling some of the fodder, tying it into bundles, throwing it onto the farm sled, and storing it in the barn loft.

One afternoon, at almost dusk, Maggie and Thomas came driving the farm sled in from the field, laden with corn and fodder bundles. And there was Papa, out behind the barn, at the woodshed, swinging the heavy axe, splitting firewood.

"Papa!" Maggie shrieked at him, stunned at the look of John.

His face was pale as ashes. He was wringing wet with sweat. His eyes were glassy and fixed. When he saw Maggie and Thomas, he gasped, and collapsed in a limp heap.

"Help me, Thomas!" Maggie screamed, "Help me get Papa into the house!"

"Well, John," Dr. Ellis sighed, "you've really done it this time. You've got double pneumonia. Some more Laudanum might help dampen the cough. Some more quinine might help quiet the fever. And it might not. Pneumonia's something that's difficult to do much with, I'm afraid. You just try to take it easy. Rest. Eat and drink what you can. I'll ...see you in a few days."

But downstairs, with Callie, Maggie and Barbara Jo, all Dr. Ellis did was to wag his head.

"Just watch him. Give him the medications. And pray. We should know ...one way or the other ...in a few days. I'll try to drop back by ...tomorrow."

"Papa will be all right, won't he, Dr. Ellis?" Maggie insisted, walking the doctor all the way to his buggy.

"Maggie, I'm afraid that's between John and the Good Lord. Go on back in the house, Maggie. You don't want to catch a chill out here."

But John's condition did not improve. It steadily worsened. Dr. Ellis would visit each day, feel John's pulse, listen to his breathing, and give him more Laudanum and more quinine. More of the blue pills.

John's fever raged. He became delirious. Maggie and Callie took turns now, sitting with him through the night.

Work in the fields was suspended. Barbara Jo had taken to her bed entirely, complaining of terrible headaches.

Maggie did the morning milking, all the washing, cooking and cleaning. And Thomas Beyers came in the afternoons, to chop wood, do the milking. Help draw water for cool baths for John. Thomas also gathered several barrels of apples to store in the root cellar. And he planted some turnip seeds in the fall garden.

The remainder of the Indian corn stood rotting in the fields. None of the groundnuts had been pulled. Not one stalk of the syrup cane had been cut.

Maggie was almost past being able to think clearly.

All the long nights of sitting up with Papa, coupled with days filled with work and worry about Papa.

On a Saturday morning, she stormed into Barbara Jo's bedroom, carrying a straw broom in her hands.

Her face flushed with anger, with one hand she reached and flung the covers off Barbara Jo. With the other, she waved the broom threateningly.

Barbara Jo sat up with a jerk, and shrank towards the iron headboard, pulling her quilt up about her throat, as Maggie hissed at her:

"Thomas Beyers, who is *nothing* to this family in the way of blood relations, is working his fingers to the bone, while you take your ease. I want you *out* of that bed. Dressed and *ready for work*. In *five* minutes!" Maggie turned toward the door, then back to the foot of the bed. "You eat from the same table as the rest of us. And from now on, if you don't work—you don't eat!"

Maggie turned on her heel and stalked out, slamming the door with such a bang that the entire upper floor shook for several seconds. Barbara Jo's eyeballs fairly rattled from the vibrations.

"What was that?" John asked, staring at Callie with fevered, unseeing eyes.

"Nothing, darling," Callie soothed his brow with a cold cloth. "It's nothing for you to fret yourself about. There. There. Just ...lay ...back ..."

Callie had a general idea what was going on. And she was relieved to see that from that Saturday morning onward, Barbara Jo revived up from her bed of suffering, and took on her full share of chores.

Sunday morning, John was much worse. He sank in and out of consciousness. His fever was so high, he would burn Maggie with a touch. He was raving and incoherent. Wildly tossing about. They were hard put, both Maggie and Callie together, to keep him in bed and decently covered.

That evening, Dr. Ellis looked at his patient, then summoned Maggie out of the room. Descending the stairs, Maggie followed the doctor. Down to the front room. *Why didn't he speak!*

Reaching the first floor, Dr. Ellis turned. He ran a hand nervously through his thinning hair. Bearded face creased with sadness, he took Maggie's small, cold hand in his large warm one:

"Maggie. I hate to tell you this. I'd rather take a beating with a bullwhip, than to tell you this. But …I'm afraid your Papa won't make it through the night. I'm so sorry."

Maggie sank down on top of the huge brown leather trunk. She wanted to shriek. She wanted to rave. She wanted to weep and howl. But she felt totally unable to do any of these. She could only gasp for breath, like a person drowning. She wasn't even aware that Dr. Ellis had left.

Thomas Beyers knocked lightly on the front door. Like a wooden person, Maggie rose to let him in.

She fell into Thomas's arms and clung to him.

"Maggie! What's the matter?" Thomas muttered into her hair.

"It's Papa, Thomas! *Papa's dying!*"

Thomas stayed that night. He offered to take turns sitting with John.

Maggie sent Callie to bed. But Maggie refused to leave the room. Thomas forced her to sit down, and covered her with a quilt against the night chill. He kept a fire going in the downstairs fireplace, so the heat would rise to the second floor.

There seemed to be nothing in the room—except the labored breathing of the shrunken figure on the bed.

Maggie would rise, and stand by John's bed, holding his fevered hand in hers. Thomas would shoo her back to her chair.

Thomas heard the clock on the downstairs mantel strike three. He knew John McKinnon would not live to hear it strike four.

Maggie was dozing fitfully in the chair by the window.

John opened his eyes, and looked straight at Thomas. "They're calling me," he said in a calm, measured voice, "I have to go." He smiled.

Thomas Beyers went out to the barn, fetched the cooling board and placed it over the rails of the back porch. Then he brought Papa down from upstairs, and gently laid him on it. He sat there with Maggie, the remainder of the night.

When daylight came, and John had cooled, Callie washed him, rubbed him with camphorated oil, and dressed him in a new black worsted suit and a white shirt. She parted his hair in the middle, and water-combed it to each side. She carefully trimmed his beard and moustache. Maggie thought he looked particularly handsome. His face looked relaxed, and happy. Almost as if he would sit up, any minute now, and laugh with her, and talk with her, and sing with her ...and play the fiddle ...

Neighbors were coming by. Offering their condolences. Bringing platters of food.

Maggie welcomed them at the door. Thanked them for their prayers and kind thoughts. Took the food and put it in the kitchen.

She wasn't sure if Thomas Beyers even went home during this period of time. He seemed to be there, every time she looked up. Maggie wondered if Thomas was doing all this because he somehow felt guilty about taking Nellie Sue from them. Or was he just being nice? At any rate, Maggie thanked him, over and over, for his kind help.

Some of the neighbor men nailed together a fine pine box. Several of them grasped hold of it, and hefted it up the hill, to the little cemetery. The grave lay open, beneath the sweetgum grove.

The thin fall sun filtered through the trees. The sunlight did a strange little dance, atop the pine box. Maggie watched the sun dancing across the lid that hid Papa. Mama was crying softly. Thomas Beyers had his arm around her shoulders, trying to comfort her. Barbara Jo stood like the little wooden Indian Papa had once carved for Maggie. Unseeing. Unmoving. Maggie felt about the same.

She vaguely heard the reading of some verses of Scripture, from the Book of Job, she later recalled. *"If a man die, shall he live again—"*

The little congregation was singing a hymn. Then folks were drifting away.

The grave was being closed.

Thomas Beyers was ushering the three women back down the hill.

Thomas watched Maggie. He was worried about her. As far as he knew, she had not shed one tear since her father died. Though Thomas knew her heart was breaking.

She marched straight-backed, almost unseeing down the hill, back toward the house. Behind her, Maggie could hear the clods of dirt—hitting the top of the pine box.

"Maggie?" Thomas caught up to her, gazed at her questioningly, "Is there anything you would like to talk about? I can stay on, if you need me."

"No," Maggie replied tiredly. "You go on home, Thomas. You've done more than you should have, already. Your own place, your job must be suffering because of it. We'll …we'll be fine. I'm just going to go on in now …and see to Mama. Get her off her feet. See to the evening chores. Fix some supper. You just …go on home, Thomas."

"Can I at least see to the ordering of your Papa's headstone?"

"I wish I could answer 'yes,' Thomas, but …there's no money. Papa …misplaced …the cash he got for the cotton crop. I …haven't been able to find it, yet. I fear …I never will."

"Oh, Maggie! How incredibly awful, for you and your family! How …? Where …?"

"Somewhere between the cotton gin—and home. But I searched, several times—until I was blue in the face—and found nothing. I am much obliged, to you, Thomas," Maggie muttered, "More than you'll ever know. You go on home."

Everyone had gone. The house was empty. Barbara Jo was, for some reason, sitting out on the back doorstep. Maggie had put Callie to bed.

Maggie walked back up the hill, to stand beside the gravesite. On the way up, she gathered a handful of wildflowers, which she laid gently atop the fresh dirt. She looked down into the valley below. The house looked so welcoming, so peaceful. Out in the pasture, across the road, the cow had come up to the gate, wanting to be milked.

Maggie wondered what lay ahead. She shouldn't be thinking about things like that now, but she would *somehow* have to raise enough money to get them through the winter. She would *somehow* have to keep starvation from the door—from Mama, and Barbara Jo, and the baby—

The house had settled down for the night. Maggie went into her room, and slipped on her nightgown. Across the room, Barbara Jo snored softly.

Maggie climbed into bed. But she couldn't stay there.

She rose, walked to the window, and stood looking out. She could see everything clearly in the side yard and barnyard below. She knelt, pushed up the window, and gazed up. The stars hung stark and brilliantly vivid against the night sky. Papa had gone to Heaven, she had been told. And Maggie fervently believed that. But *where was* Heaven? Was it up there, beyond those stars? *How could Papa be dead?* She had never once in her life imagined Papa as being dead! He was so full of life! So full of love! How could all that be *gone*?

She thought then of the baby Mama carried. In all the horror and grief of Papa's sickness, Maggie had almost forgotten the baby.

Life goes on, Mama had said. It is passed from one generation to the next.

Maybe Papa's life would be passed to the baby Mama carried. Maybe it would be a boy, the way Maggie hoped.

They could name him John Thomas McKinnon, Jr. And he would laugh, like Papa, and love, like Papa. And John McKinnon would live on—

Chapter 17

Maggie sat at the kitchen table, with a lined tablet, and a stub of lead pencil. She was totaling up their assets, weighing them against their liabilities.

The assets column was pitifully short. The liabilities column, pitifully long.

They would need to pay Dr. Ellis. They all needed new shoes and coats for the winter, but Maggie failed to see how they could get them. There would be things needed for the baby soon to be born, but he would probably have to make do with what Mama could scrounge up. She needed to pay for the new suit and shirt for Papa's burial, and for the camphorated oil for Papa's final laying-out. The black stuff coffin lining she had bought on credit, also, at the Rhyersville Store—

And, of course, Papa must have a headstone.

They would need money for lamp oil, and matches. Coffee and tea—if they were to have any. Sugar.

Maggie had already decided to sell the pipe organ, to pay for Papa's headstone. She had prepared two notices, one to hang at the Rhyersville Post Office, the other down at Johnson's Corners, at the General Store. There was still corn waiting to be harvested in the field. And the syrup cane still stood, waving its full tassels at the sun. She wondered if she could sell those crops as they stood. But that might take several days. She needed money in hand—now. She certainly had no desire to run up debts she had no hopes of covering.

The bank had money ...lots of it, she knew. And she knew the bank manager, Mr. Franklin Purtle. She saw him every time she attended church. He had been a good friend of Papa's. Tomorrow, Maggie determined, she would go to the bank, and see about procuring a small loan …just to see them through the winter. And next spring, when the crops were put in, she would need proper seed. The growing plants would need fertilizer, and side-dressings, or the crops would not yield enough to be worth the bother.

She had never plowed! Could she put in next spring's crops, even if she had the seed, fertilizers and side-dressings? She had no idea she could rely on Barbara Jo for a great deal of assistance. Mama had plowed during the War—but she had known that Papa was coming back. Now, Papa would not be coming back. A chill crept up Maggie's spine. She wouldn't think about spring now. She'd just get them through the winter. Spring could take care of itself.

Maggie dressed very carefully. She must look as mature as possible. After all, she turned sixteen years old this past spring.

She rifled carefully through her dresses; there weren't that many of them hanging behind the curtain in the corner. She chose the darkest, most somber one she could find. The one she wore to Papa's funeral.

Gazing at herself in the mirror, she wondered whether she should perhaps put her hair up? Or pull it back. Usually only married ladies put their hair up. She left the back down, putting up only the top and front. This particular style, she felt, gave her a very mature appearance. But she was unaccustomed to this look, and thought it make her neck appear too long—and too white. But it would have to do.

Maggie had already hitched up Job, and he stood waiting patiently for her in the side yard. Heaving a worried sigh, she climbed onto the seat, drove out into the road, and through the gap. On the drive to Rhyersville, Maggie ran through her mind the amount she felt they must have, and what it should be stretched to cover.

Tying Job to the hitching post in front of the Post Office, she walked quickly inside, and asked permission to hang her advertisement about the pipe organ. Then she drove on to Johnson's Corners, to post the second one.

When Maggie arrived at the bank, she sat on the wagon seat for a moment, mustering the courage to go inside. The bank building loomed suddenly larger than Maggie had remembered. But she was here, and she must go inside.

Maggie entered, attempting to stretch herself as tall as possible. She approached a barred window, with a young man inside.

"I would like to see Mr. Franklin Purtle, about applying for a loan," Maggie said crisply, cleared her throat and waited.

The young man behind the bars stared at her. What a gorgeous young woman! Her dark hair lay piled atop her head in shining coils. A perfect face—and such perfection could not be marred by a small frown.

"Excuse me?" the young man stuttered.

"I would like ...to see ...Mr. Purtle ...about ...getting a loan," Maggie repeated coolly.

"Well ...yes ...Mrs.... Miss ...Mr. Purtle ...just a minute please."

The stammering young man disappeared, and reappeared a few moments later, tagging along behind an older gentleman whom Maggie had never seen before. He was quite heavily built, dressed in what Maggie knew was a very expensive vested wool suit, with an immaculate shirt and a dark tie.

"Good morning, Miss." The man stared at Maggie, a little frown knitting his thin brows together in a round face.

"I would like to see Mr. Franklin Purtle, about applying for a loan," Maggie repeated for the third time.

"I'm sorry, Miss, but I fear the good Mr. Franklin Purtle is no longer with the bank. He has moved to Tennessee, I believe, to establish a business of his own. Why don't we step into my private office, where we can discuss this more comfortably?"

Heaving his bulk gallantly aside, Mr. Phillips motioned Maggie towards a door at the back of the bank, marked in black letters *Private.*

It was a very nice office, Maggie thought, as she entered with a graceful swish of dark skirts. A richly furnished room, with a fine leather chair behind a huge mahogany desk. Files and bookcases lined the walls.

The heavy desk was stacked with papers.

Maggie was quite impressed.

"Won't you please have a seat?" he showed Maggie to a matching leather chair, across from the fine desk.

"Now, young lady," he smiled at her. "What, if I may ask, is your name?"

"Margaret Ann McKinnon," Maggie answered promptly, looking the man square in the eye.

"Well, I'm Theodore J. Phillips, manager of this fine establishment. I'm new to Rhyersville."

He beamed at her, his smile seeming to imply that with the propitious addition of himself to the town, the small community had raised a notch.

"How do you do, Mr. Phillips?" Maggie said solemnly.

"Fine," he smiled. "Now, Miss McKinnon, what may we do for you?" He leaned forward slightly, across the broad expanse of the desk. His eyes appeared kind, but small, in proportion to the face.

Feeling a bit uneasy, Maggie cleared her throat, "My Papa …just passed …and I …find that I need a small loan …until the family can get back on its feet."

"And *what* was your Papa's name, Miss McKinnon?"

"John …John Thomas McKinnon." Maggie heard her own voice saying the name, but it sounded strange in her ears. Papa should be in the wagon. Papa should be here, taking care of this business—

"What do you have in the form of collateral, to secure this loan for which you wish to apply?" Seeing the frown on Maggie's face, he asked, "What do you own?"

"We …have …a farm, a few miles east of town. A horse and cow—"

"Would you excuse me, for just one moment? I must check on something." With shallow, rapid breaths, the heavy-set, richly dressed man heaved himself up from his fine chair, and browsed with plump fingers among the files stored along the shelves behind him. Slowly, he withdrew a brown folder, retook his seat, and opened it. His voice became suddenly very low, very sad.

"I …thought I recalled the name. I see …from checking our records, Miss McKinnon, that there is already a loan outstanding …to a Mr. John Thomas McKinnon. A loan of rather long standing, I fear. Mr. McKinnon must have had a *very* good friend at the bank—as Mr. McKinnon has paid *none* of the principal, since the loan was initiated, on *February 2, 1866.* Yes, he must have had a *very* good friend. Not only is the principal outstanding, there has accrued interest for the past year—which has just come due. The interest, it seems, has usually been paid each fall. But …let …me …see …other small amounts were, through the years, added to the loan—and never repaid."

"Papa …owes the bank money?" Maggie could not believe her ears. "He has owed money …since he came back from the War?"

"You shouldn't find it that unusual, my dear. Many men returned from the War with *nothing.* These have been lean years. Since the War, the bottom has fallen out of the cotton market. Many farmers have found themselves swamped by debt. Many have lost their farms. Yes. I'm afraid that is the case. It appears that Mr. McKinnon put up his farm for collateral. And now that Mr. McKinnon is deceased, the entire amount will be due and payable immediately upon liquidation of his estate. Did Mr. McKinnon leave a Last

Will and Testament, as to his wishes for the dispensation of his worldly goods?"

"Liquidation? Will? No—"

"Yes, well, Miss McKinnon," Mr. Theodore J. Phillips pursed thick lips, wagged his head sorrowfully, "then, the rendering to his creditors of the amounts legally due them, must be accomplished, upon Mr. McKinnon's assets being—"

Maggie blurted out abruptly—

"How much does Papa owe?"

"Four hundred and fifty dollars, plus this year's interest—"

"*Four hundred and fifty dollars*?" Maggie felt her knees begin to tremble. It might as well have been a thousand.

Maggie stared at the heavy-set figure, the florid face. He kept moving his lips. She heard not a word. She knew she was about to be sick.

Maggie leapt up, and fled outside. She fairly leapt onto the wagon seat, and slapped Job's rump with an angry snap that sent him loping rapidly down the rutted dirt street.

Not only would there be no loan to get them through the winter—the land was mortgaged! *The farm was mortgaged!* And there was not a penny of money! Except for a few dollars and a bit of change Callie had found in John's trouser pockets. All these years, Papa had been in debt! And he had said nothing! No wonder poor Papa had been so dejected and upset—!

Reaching home, Maggie walked slowly up the stairs, into her room, changing into an old dress.

It would just be a matter of time, she knew, until the farm would be lost to them. With what was owed at the bank, plus a year's interest, they would be fortunate if the farm covered the debts.

Where would they go? What would they do?

She would have to find work. Where? There was no work in Rhyersville. There were only single family farms.

Nothing else. For miles around.

Maggie sank down to the edge of her bed. For just an instant, she thought of collapsing onto the bed, and pulling the quilts up over her head.

But, that she knew, would only add to their problems.

Mama and Barbara Jo would have to know about their situation.

Just then, Barbara Jo's voice came ringing up the stairs.

"Maggie? Thomas Beyers is here to see you!"

Thomas, Maggie thought. She reached up, removed the pins from her hair, let it fall over her face. She felt absolutely overwhelmed. Her heart might burst. She *couldn't* see anyone, not now. Later, when the horrible shock had passed, she could face Thomas—

—Thomas, with his handsome young face, his eyes so filled with …with what?

What was it Thomas felt? Pity? Sympathy? Just at this moment, Maggie didn't think she could face either. She loved Thomas Beyers like a brother. But she just couldn't see him. She couldn't see anyone—not just now.

She lifted her head, swept back her hair. Softly, she crept to her door, and eased it shut. Leaning against it, she closed her eyes. She heard Barbara Jo's voice. Heard the front door close.

Maggie wanted to rush down the stairs, out the front door. Let Thomas take her in his arms, and hold her tight, as he had done the night Papa died.

But, no, her problems were not Thomas' problems. She seriously doubted that Thomas Beyers' salary for an entire year would be equal to the debts they now owed.

This was something she would have to work out on her own.

Maggie lifted her chin, opened her door, and walked slowly down the stairs. If God cared for the sparrows, surely He would help Margaret Ann McKinnon carry the load that had been thrust upon her.

Mama was sitting in the front room, her head laid against the back of the rocker. The room felt cold. Maggie laid a fire, and set the kindling ablaze. Then she slowly turned toward her mother. *How could she tell her this?*

Callie sat, her eyes half closed, her hands in her lap holding a small garment she was knitting. A cap, Maggie could see. A small blue cap.

"Mama," Maggie said softly, approaching Callie's chair, taking one of her hands from the small cap. "I'm afraid I have …bad news."

"What is it, Maggie?" Callie asked calmly, as if asking what the hour of the day might be.

"Papa …Papa borrowed money on the land …after he returned from the War. It's never been repaid, Mama. And interest is due on the money."

Callie stared at her daughter, her blue-green eyes stunned, "What does this mean, Maggie?"

"It means, Mama, that we will lose the farm. I'll have to find work. We will have to move."

"*Move? Where?*" Callie asked, like a frightened child asking her parent.

"I don't know yet, Mama. But something will turn up. What is it you always say, Mama? We must pray …and have faith."

"Yes," Callie said softly, new thoughts circling in her head. "I'll write to my cousin, down in Cumming. See if she knows of anything."

"You have kin …in a place called Cumming? I never heard you speak of this cousin."

"We have, I'm afraid, lost touch over the years. She's a rather distant cousin at that. But we were close as children. Then Mildred's family moved away. And we wrote a few times, for a while. Other than Mildred, I haven't much family left."

Callie said this very matter-of-factly, hefting herself up from her chair. "I'll go now, and write to Mildred."

"You do that, Mama," Maggie smiled at her mother, wondering what could possibly come of contacting a distant cousin. Wondering if Mama really knew the import of what Maggie had just said.

Maggie then found Barbara Jo in the kitchen, looking over several small sacks, rowed up on the kitchen table.

"What's all this?" Maggie asked quickly.

"I don't know. Some things Thomas Beyers brought. When you didn't come down, he just left them on the front porch—without saying a word. He was very hurt. I could tell. I must say, Maggie, you were very rude to Thomas. After all he has done for us—"

"Barbara Jo," Maggie cut in angrily, "I think I have every right to be rude. I have just learned that this house we are standing in now—which has always been our home—will soon no longer belong to us. I think I have every right to be rude and upset!"

Barbara Jo stared at her sister, "What are you talking about, Maggie? Is this one of your tall tales, just to upset me? Well, I don't find it very funny."

"You will find it even less funny, Barbs, when we begin packing our things to move out of this place! To *who-knows-where!*" Maggie fairly screamed at her.

Maggie knew she was being unreasonable. It wasn't Barbara Jo's fault that Papa owed the money.

"You're serious …aren't you?" Barbara Jo had gone pale as ash. "How did Papa let this happen to us? Why did Papa let this happen to us? How could Papa be so careless?!"

"Blaming Papa isn't going to do any good, Barbara Jo! Papa is dead and buried up on the hill back of the house! Papa isn't going to get us out of this mess! The spilt milk cannot be put back into the jug!"

"You sound just like Mama! Well, you're *not* my Mama, and I won't take any of your lip! Don't you *dare* shout at me! I'm *tired* of your ordering me around! None of this is *my* fault!"

"Barbara Jo, you sound like a spoilt child Have you heard one word I just said? We are about to lose our home. *The roof over our heads!* We have to stick together. Not blame one another. Come up with some sort of sensible plan—"

"You expect me to come up with *some sort of sensible plan?*" Barbara Jo screeched.

"No," Maggie said, letting her voice sink to a normal level. "I expect you to help me look after Mama. And the baby, that will be arriving any day now. I expect you to keep a cool head about you. To help me with the work. To help me pack up, when it's time to move. Right this minute, I expect you to go draw up the milk from the well, then a cold bucket of fresh water. That's all I expect from you, Barbara Jo, is that asking too much? Oh," Maggie added as she glanced around the kitchen, "and maybe you could churn the milk, in the morning."

Barbara Jo wagged her head furiously. She looked as if she might burst into tears, or go hide beneath the bedcovers. Maggie was determined to deny her sister the privilege of doing either.

"Good," Maggie said in a stern voice, fixing her gaze firmly on Barbara Jo's pale blue eyes. "Now, let's just see what Mr. Thomas Beyers has brought us. Mark it down, on a piece of paper, each item and what it might cost, so that I can remember to repay him, the first chance I get. Then, go draw up the milk. And the water."

"Repay him with *what?*"

"Leave that to me, Barbara Jo. You just make the list."

Maggie checked around with some of the neighboring farmers. They would buy the crops still standing in the fields—the Indian corn, and the fine field of syrup cane stretching two acres along the river bottoms.

To feed his horse during the winter, Dr. Ellis would settle for ten bushels of Indian corn, and three dozen shocks of fodder already gathered by Maggie and Thomas.

That was fine with Maggie. *Where ever* they moved, she knew she could only take along foodstuffs. *When ever* she arrived *where ever* they were going, she would probably have to sell Job and the one-horse wagon. She could not envision herself ever farming again.

The Rhyresville Bank sent out the shy, stammering young man—to post the foreclosure sign in the front yard of the farm. And serve notice on the McKinnons—they had thirty days grace, before they had to vacate the farm. But the days passed, and no prospective buyers showed up. It was a fine farm that had fed and sheltered the McKinnons for four generations. But Maggie knew there would not be buyers knocking down the Bank's doors. The farm was too small, too isolated. It was out beyond the edge of nowhere.

Now, Maggie began to kick her plans into high gear. She thought of hanging a notice, "Employment Wanted" down at the Rhyersville Post Office and the General Store. Then she could imagine all their neighbors standing around them, rolling their eyes and clacking their tongues—at the state of abject poverty into which the poor McKinnon family had lately fallen.

She had witnessed just such abject pity, when she hung the two flyers for the sale of the pipe organ.

But the flyers were not up two days, until word came from the Rhyersville Post Office, that there was a buyer for the pipe organ. Maggie had immediately returned a note that the offer was accepted, and she was waiting for the new owner to pick up his instrument.

She was afraid she would not be so fortunate with an advertisement for employment. She knew she would have to look for something farther away. Where, she still had no idea. But Maggie clung persistently to her faith. Something would turn up.

It did, in the form of a reply from Callie's distant cousin, down south, in the small town of Cumming, down on the Chattahoochee River.

Cousin Mildred had written back a glowing report of the town:

Dearest Cousin Callie,

You will love it here, in Cumming. The town is laid out about a square. In the center of the square, sits the log courthouse. There are several licensed businesses in operation. A grog shop, which, of course, you and your dear family, Cousin Callie, would have no interest in, but I am only telling you this to give you an idea of the potential of the town. In addition, there is a tavern, unfortunately also selling spirituous liquors, and a hotel—which does not. A public stables, several tobacco manufacturers, a carriage dealer, two distilleries, and a wool carding establishment. We also boast a fine general mercantile.

In the nearby vicinity, there are two cotton gins, and two grist mills. And more than a dozen ferries transport wagons, surreys, buggies, horses and riders, back and forth across the Chattahoochee—such is the proliferation of roads.

Should it not work out for either of your young daughters to find employment at the address I shall supply you at the end of this letter, perhaps something might be found at one of these establishments—excluding consideration, of course, of those having to do with spirituous liquors.

I write you this letter, in point of fact, to inform you of an invalid lady of gentile family of some note and standing in the community. She is in search of a companion and serving lady, to see to her needs during the day, whilst her dear husband is away at his work. This employment could start immediately, and would pay quite well—ten dollars per month. But with no board or found. You would have to provide lodging for yourself and your daughters. But, if you have any interest, you may write to this lady, her name and address are shown below. I have already informed her that you are a dearly loved relative, and your family is of highest moral standing in your present community.

I remain, your loving cousin. Come to visit us soon.

"What do you think, Maggie?" Callie searched her youngest daughter's beautiful face. Maggie was sixteen. Maggie, the free spirit, taking work as a serving maid—!

"I'll write to her tonight, Mama. Give me the address," Maggie replied without a moment's hesitation. Reaching out one slender hand, she took the letter from her mother.

Maggie fervently prayed that a reply would be forthcoming, before their thirty days of grace had expired.

Maggie had received payment for the Indian corn and the syrup cane crops, and was on her way to town, to pay off their debts at the Rhyersville Store, and to repay Thomas Beyers for the sacks of coffee, sugar, and brown rice he had so generously left on their front doorsteps.

Maggie found Thomas at home. He answered the door in his shirtsleeves. Maggie refused his invitation to step inside, for a cup of coffee and a scone. Thomas was a single man. Maggie was a young, single girl. It simply would not do—even though he was a member of the family by marriage.

"I only came by, to pay you for the supplies you left, Thomas, and to tell you goodbye." Maggie said in as level a voice as she could manage.

This had been Nellie Sue's husband. This man was her last link with Nellie Sue. But, then, Maggie realized with a jolt, she was on the verge of breaking more than her ties with Thomas Beyers. She was on the cusp of breaking away from everything she had known and held dear her entire life.

"I ...heard ...about ...your ...about the bank."

"Yes. Well, that's all in the past now. Past and gone, as Mama would say. And tomorrow's a new day. We'll be moving to a new town. Starting a whole new life. I'm looking forward—"

"No, you're not, Maggie. This is Thomas," he said softly. "You don't have to lie to me. You can lie to yourself. Maybe even to your Mama. But you can't lie to me. I know you too well. I ..."

Thomas seemed on the verge of saying something else. Then he changed his mind, "I'll be so sorry to see you ...and your family leave. I ...love ...all of you."

"Yes, well, we all love you, too. And you're right, Thomas. I lied just now. But I hope the Good Lord will forgive me. I'm trying to put the best face I can on a very sorry situation. And, as Mama says, things will look brighter tomorrow. Anyhow, I want to pay you for the sugar and coffee and stuff you brought out—"

"Keep your money, Maggie. You might need it. And if you need me to help you with moving, if you need me at all, you know all you have to do is let me know."

"I'm—" Maggie's voice caught. She felt her lower lip begin to tremble. She glanced down, then brought her steady gaze back to Thomas's face. She hadn't dreamed it would be this hard—to say goodbye to Thomas Beyers, "I'm much obliged for all you've done for us. And I sure would appreciate some help with the move. Right now, I feel I can use all the help I can get."

Maggie went next to the Post Office, and mailed her letter to Mr. and Mrs. Earnest Phelps, Baldridge Ferry Road, Cumming, Georgia.

Callie had also written to Cousin Mildred, thanking her for her kind letter, her kind invitation, and sending her three dollars in cash money, to maybe find them a small house to let, in walking distance of where Maggie would be employed.

Cousin Mildred wrote immediately back. She had found a small four-room cottage, for two dollars per month, and was returning one dollar along with her letter. The address of the place she had rented was enclosed. It said simply:

> *Four-room plank cottage with small yard and front porch, small garden plot out back, at the corner of Davis Mill and East River Roads.*

A few days later, a reply came from Mr. Earnest Phelps.
If she could begin within a few days, Maggie had the job.

Chapter 18

Slowly, Maggie climbed the hill behind the house. Papa's headstone had arrived, for she had placed the order the day she learned the pipe organ was sold. She had to do this for Papa before she left. She knew how much it meant to him, the marking of a grave with a granite reminder that *this person resting here had lived.* She would never forget the day, two summers past, when they had finally hauled granite markers for Grandpa Thomas and Grandma Mary Margaret up the slope to the little graveyard. Papa had decided that even though Grandpa Thomas lay in a field or forest somewhere in Virginia, he deserved a memorial stone—placed beside that of his dear wife.

Maggie glanced down towards the house. Today, the new owner was to pick up the grand pipe organ. She recalled the day Papa had ripped into those logs like a man possessed. She could not bear to be there, in the house, when the pipe organ was hauled away.

She heard the unmistakable rattle of a wagon. Her heart sank. Then she recalled Papa's fine headstone. Her head held high, eyes dry, Maggie watched, as a fine black wagon that looked as if it had never traveled a dusty road, drawn by a pair of grand horses, came rolling through the gap.

Although she could see the approaching rig, from her high vantage point, she could not yet make out the people in it. Then she could just make out, as it rounded the bend in the road beyond the low rock wall she and Barbs and Nellie Sue had built to plant with flowers, she could just make out two men. The driver appeared to be a Negro man. An older Negro man, perhaps, from the way he sat the seat, the way in which his thin shoulders hunched forward, the way his hands held the reins.

Riding regally beside him, was a finely dressed man, perhaps a bit younger than the Negro, but not a young man. He had on a fine, wide-brimmed felt hat, which he kept lifting now and then, to draw a hand through his hair—white as snow in the autumn sunlight.

Callie met them at the door. They exchanged meaningless pleasantries. The organ was loaded into the fine wagon and lashed securely down. Callie bid them good day, and shut the door, dropping the latch with a little flourish. What a relief! She heaved a little sigh. At last! That huge, hulking thing was gone!

"Tie it good, Jacob," William Bartram Hurston had said to his colored helper. Then he'd lifted the brim of his wool felt hat, bowing politely to the pale, heavily pregnant middle-aged woman standing on the front steps of the farmhouse, her gray-streaked blond hair tightly braided, pulled back from thin temples and wound about her head. It made her appear far more stern and severe than William felt she actually was, because she had kind eyes ...sad ...tired ...but kind. Climbing stiffly back onto the wagon seat, he lifted his hand to the woman. Then, for some reason, his gaze swept up past her, past the steep, oak-shingled rooftop, up the mountain behind the house.

"Wonder who the young lady is, Jacob? Way up there on the hillside."

"I wouldn't be knowin', Massa William. A young lady of the house I 'spose."

"I wonder what on earth she's doing ...up there on the side of the mountain."

"I'm sure I wouldn't be knowin', Massa William."

"Anyhow, it has been a good day, hasn't it, Jacob? We got Eleanor's *pipe organ* back! Did you ever think you'd see the day that I'd actually bring that thing back to Cottonwood?" William Hurston slapped one knee with a gloved hand, laughed ruefully, as if he'd just made a huge joke.

"No, Massa William," Jacob smiled, "I sure didn't 'spect to live to see *this* day."

"Well," William Bartram Hurston removed his felt hat, took a clean handkerchief from the breast pocket of his rich wool jacket. "I couldn't bear the thought ...now that Eleanor's gone ...I didn't know where it might end up ...and I just thought ...the *boy* might want it, since it was his mother's. He won't be at that university forever, Jacob. He'll be coming home, one of these fine days."

"Yassa, Massa William, I's sure hope Massa Bart'll be comin' back home—some day."

William Bartram Hurston's brow drew into a slight frown, but he did not correct Jacob. Jacob could not seem to bring himself to address the male members of the Hurston family with anything other than 'Massa,' though he'd been a free man for nearly a score of years. William then forgot Jacob. He grew silent, his mind on the grand organ, then flowing back to the day— almost six years past—when the terrible news had come—

—Eleanor and Robert Logan had made plans for an extended trip to Europe. They had booked passage on one of the luxurious screw-propelled steamships that had begun making transatlantic crossings. But two weeks out of port, the ship had gone down in a violent storm. There were no survivors.

Immediately upon the loss of his parents, his patriarchal grandparents had sent young Bartram to a prestigious preparatory school. Following that, William Bartram Logan was enrolled at one of the nations earliest and most respected institutions of higher learning—the University of Pennsylvania.

His grandfather hoped, now that the boy had little family left, he might, perhaps, one day make Cottonwood his home.

––––––––––––––

Maggie knew little about birthing of babies, but she knew that her mother's steps were becoming slower. She knew the baby was dropping lower.

Maggie forbade Mama to come downstairs, but Callie was adamant, insisting: "I will *not* add to the burden of the house, by becoming an invalid before my time."

Maggie worried about the timing of the baby's arrival. And how it would fit into the forced move. They only had two weeks left.

Come on little one! Maggie wanted to call to him. Come on out and greet the world.

And as if he heard her, John Thomas McKinnon, Jr. complied.

He arrived that night, almost before Maggie could get her mother laid down in her own bed. Callie had just reached the upstairs landing, when the pains began.

"It's coming!" Callie gasped, and Maggie, at her side as she climbed the stairs, tried to guide her mother to her bed before the infant came popping out.

"Barbara Jo!" Maggie screamed to the top of her lungs, "Put the kettle on!" Maggie didn't know exactly why, but she knew hot water was needed. She was soon to find out.

The tiny boy emerged covered in bloody mucus, that Maggie had not had time to anticipate. Maggie snatched for an old sheet, but too late.

Little John Thomas McKinnon, Jr. popped out onto one of his Mama's best unbleached bed linens. But, he had a lusty, hearty cry, and all his fingers and toes, so none of them cared.

Barbara Jo appeared with a basin of hot water. Maggie sent her for the scissors.

Following her mother's instructions, Maggie cut the cord, placed the baby on a clean blanket, and carried the placenta and disposed of it.

Maggie gave little Johnny his first bath.

Exhausted, Callie lay back on her pillows, her eyes filled with tears. If only John was here! Callie gazed lovingly down at her newborn son. Joy should have filled her heart to overflowing, but, somehow, all she could feel was a deep, empty sadness.

John—!

—John would have been so proud.

But Maggie could not contain her joy. All the problems. All the sorrows seemed to simply melt away, in that one moment when new life came into the world, in the form of *John Thomas McKinnon, Jr.*

Chapter 19

Maggie tried to pack things as tightly as possible, onto the one-horse wagon. Thomas Beyers was handing things to her, as she attempted to place them to best advantage. Thomas had already heaved the iron cookstove into the front of the wagon box. Then he helped Maggie disassemble and load the three iron bed frames, that, when laid flat, did not take up too much space. The feather mattresses were piled on top, and weighted down with the kitchen table, turned upside down. The benches and chairs they lashed tightly between the table legs. The two front room rockers they tied to the side planks, beside the table and chairs. Two small washstands were tied to the table legs. The two dressers and the pie safe, Maggie had been forced to sell. They were the nicest, most ornate furnishings in the log house. But they weighed far too much, for Job to handle. The front porch rockers, Maggie and Thomas now decided, would also be left behind. Thomas Beyers moved the porch rockers inside, to protect them from the rain.

Thomas had kindly offered to drive his buggy, to provide smoother transport for Callie and John Thomas, Jr.—and to haul the huge brown leather trunk of Katherine Ann's. He had lashed it securely to the back of the buggy.

Bags of potatoes, yams, apples, corn meal, wheaten flour, and rolled oats were piled in amongst the scant furnishings, along with smaller sacks of salt, sugar, and coffee. Water buckets, washtubs, pans, kitchen utensils were piled here and there, amongst the other items. In the huge brown leather trunk, Maggie packed personal items, clothing, and bed linens and quilts. Also in the trunk lay Shawn's Bible, and Papa's fiddle.

"Well, I suppose that's about it," Maggie said tiredly.

Thomas Beyers walked around to the side of his buggy, and returned carrying a small package tied with a pink ribbon. A broad smile on his face, he handed it to Maggie.

"What's this?" Maggie asked.

"It's from me, Maggie. You can just call it a going-away present."

Slowly Maggie took the package, untied the ribbon and removed the brown-paper wrapping.

As she laid back the paper, she exclaimed, "Oh, my, Thomas! It's lovely! It's such a beautiful Bible! It must have cost a fortune! I can't accept this—"

"I *want* you to have it, Maggie. And …when you read it …think of me."

"Thomas, how sweet. But, really—this is too costly. It's bound in real leather!"

Opening the front cover, Maggie saw written on the fly inside, in a fine, neat hand—the inscription:

To Maggie—From Thomas

With tears in her eyes, Maggie, took a step towards Thomas, stood on tiptoe, pulled his head down, and gave him a quick kiss on the cheek.

It was a Saturday morning, when the little caravan pulled out of the yard of the log house, and rolled slowly through the gap. Maggie was determined not to look back. If she did, she knew, her heart would simply break. The farm lay behind them, deserted and empty. The cow, chickens and pigs had been sold off several days ago. Even the bee gums had brought in a few much-needed dollars—as well as the wood Papa had chopped.

The morning was fine. Only a few fluffy white clouds floated high up over the vast, rolling ridges of the mountains. The roadsides were strewn with colorful fall leaves. The nights, Maggie knew would be cold. But they all had their coats, such as they were. And they had Mama's quilts in the huge brown trunk. Come night, they would bed down beneath the wagon—and pray it didn't rain.

They drove into the small town of Cumming the following Monday afternoon. The town was much as Cousin Mildred had described it. The town square, with the fine log courthouse. Around the square, a clustering of one and two story buildings of log and plank construction. All unpainted. All with oak-shingled roofs. The streets running about the square were dry and dusty, deeply rutted red clay.

Thomas pulled his buggy to a halt before a store bearing the sign *Moss' General Mercantile*, on the north side of the square. He tied his horse to the worn hitching post out front, walked up the broad wooden steps, and disappeared inside. Maggie noticed that it appeared to be the largest retail establishment about the square. Next door stood a hotel, a narrow, two-story affair. And directly across the square, a huge barn-like structure bore in large black letters the sign—*Trimble Carriage Company*. A shiny new buggy and a brand new surrey could be seen through the broad front doors, swung wide. Next door to that there stood a wheelwright and stables. Two horses, tied out front, dozed in the sun.

Thomas soon reappeared. Close behind him was a thin, balding man in a white shirt and dark trousers. He stood on the porch and stared at them with open curiosity. This, Thomas told Maggie, was Mr. Fredrick J. Moss, proprietor of Moss' General Mercantile.

Maggie did not like Fred Moss, from the first moment she laid eyes on him.

Thomas said he had found the place, climbed back into his buggy, and led the way—east, out of town. Fred Moss stood on the porch of his store, and stared, until they drove out of sight.

Just a short drive from the store, and they drew up in front of a small, ugly, square house with nothing to recommend it to a human soul, that Maggie could see. The windows appeared dirty and the walls dull and dingy. The yard was a desert, barren of any sign of life, either weed or flower.

Maggie's heart sank. She thought of the welcoming warmth of the familiar log house, and felt the almost overwhelming urge to break down and sob.

This? This was to be their new home?

Instantly, her good sense prevailed, and reminded her that they were practically penniless—and fortunate to have any sort of roof over their heads at all.

"Okay!" Maggie called cheerily, bouncing down from the wagon, "Everybody out. I suppose this is it!"

By nightfall, Maggie and Thomas had everything unloaded, the beds assembled and the feather mattresses thrown on. Barbara Jo was ordered to make the beds.

The cookstove had been connected to the flue in the kitchen. With the scant bit of wood he found out back, Thomas laid a fire in the front room fireplace, a small thing of mud and river-rock. Then he and Maggie walked out into the back yard.

"Have to lay in a supply of wood, real soon, Maggie," Thomas warned, wiping his tired face with the back of one hand. "I ..."

He ducked his head, then met her gaze and asked, "Well, how do you like the place?"

"You don't *really* want to know, do you Thomas?" Maggie wagged her head and raised smooth brows as she looked up at him. Thomas' heart broke.

"No," Thomas sighed, but he couldn't restrain a wry smile, "not really. It's just that, I do so hate to leave you here. But ...I have to get back. I'll miss you. Are you going to be all right?"

"We'll be fine, Thomas. Can you at least stay the night? Sleep beneath a roof, such as it is?" Maggie returned Thomas' weak smile. "Your horse really needs to rest."

"I suppose you're right about the horse. But, first thing in the morning—"

When Maggie awakened Thomas Beyers was gone. And it was still dark.

Maggie fixed them all a bite of breakfast. Mama seemed too quiet, but otherwise she and Johnny seemed no worse for wear after the trip. The weather had been almost perfect. Not a drop of rain—an answer to Maggie's fervent prayers.

Before the sun was up, Maggie bathed and dressed for her walk to the house where she was to be employed.

But first, she went out back to feed and water Job, tied to a post of the back porch. Sadly she stroked him. She'd have to sell him, and soon. There was simply no place, no feed for him here.

Maggie went inside. Found a sheet of brown paper, and wrote in big, neat letters:

Horse & Wagon for Sale
Corner of Davis Mill & East River Streets
Any Good Offer Accepted

While Mama, Johnny and Barbara Jo were still asleep, Maggie picked up her shawl, her worn gloves, tied on her bonnet, and with her *For Sale* sign in her hand, walked out the door.

She'd swing by Moss' General Mercantile. Her notice would probably get more exposure there, she reasoned, than at the stables or the hotel. She *would not* enter either the tavern, or the grog shop.

She opened the front door of Moss' General Mercantile, and stepped inside. Immediately, Maggie was struck with the abundance and variety of merchandise along the shelves behind the counter. And all along the back of the store stood rows of churns and jugs and washbasins and pitchers of every color and hue. Yard goods covered a large table off to one side—lovely silks and cottons of every color and weave. Spools and hanks of thread were rowed on a shelf back of the yard-goods table. Some ready-to-wear garments hung neatly in one corner—dresses, shirts, and suits, trousers.

Men's, ladies' and children's rich leather shoes sat neatly paired on a shelf near the ready-to-wear corner. Lamps with brilliantly decorated globes, clocks, small and large, all wound, all exact to the minute, ticking and chiming away.

On the far side of the store stood a large supply of farm implements—plows, shovels, hoes, singletrees and horse harness—even an English style lady's side-saddle.

She had never seen a store with such a plethora of goods. *Fine* goods.

The moment Maggie stepped inside, Fred Moss was there to greet her.

"Settled in all right, have you?" he inquired, his dark brows shooting up towards his receding hairline.

"Yes, thank you, Mr. Moss, isn't it? Yes. I was just wondering if I could receive your kind permission to hang a handbill in your store? I have a horse and wagon for sale."

"I usually don't permit personal advertising," Fred Moss surmised, wrinkling his broad brow, pursing his thin lips importantly, "But …seeing that you're new in town …just this once, perhaps."

"Thank you *so* much for your kind generosity." Maggie made no effort to keep the sarcastic edge from her voice. "Perhaps I could offer you a small fee?"

"That *won't* be necessary, Miss McKinnon." Fred Moss' pale, pointed chin came up, as if he'd been highly insulted. I have all the money in the world, and I certainly don't need any pennies from *you*, his haughty eyes seemed to imply.

"Well, then, thank you again." And Maggie was gone, glad to be out in the fresh morning air.

As Maggie strode lithely down the steps of Moss' General Mercantile, and off down the rutted clay street, a tall, handsome young man came riding a beautiful golden palomino around the corner of the log courthouse.

Seeing the young beauty descending the steps, Len Evans pulled his mount up short—turned, and watched the girl until she was out of sight. Tying his horse to the hitching post in front of the adjacent hotel, he dismounted, and strolled over to Moss', his shiny black boots making small clicking sounds on the wooden steps and porch. The heavy oak door banged resoundingly behind him.

Inside the store, Len removed his wide-brimmed hat, ran a long-fingered hand through a mop of tightly-curled dark-brown hair. His clean-shaven face bore the faintest trace of a smile. For the first time in a long while, the smile even reached the dark eyes.

Holding the big felt hat before him, Len strolled over to the long counter. Fred Moss greeted him with a beaming smile.

"Well, Len!" Fred extended his right hand. He always figured it did no harm to stay on the good side of the county's leading family. "Good to have you back! It's been a while. How's your Pa?"

"Fred. Been a while, yes," Len said shortly. "And, thank you, Pa's fine. I was just wondering ...the young lady that just left the store? Who *is* she?"

"Oh, that's one of the *McKinnon* girls. Family just moved to town. I believe she's working for the Phelps over on—"

"Yes," Len interrupted curtly, "I know where that is. She just moved to town?" Len mused, leaning forward, his dark blue eyes boring into Fred Moss.

"Just yesterday, matter of fact. Didn't buy anything just now. Came in to hang that handbill over there. Got a horse and wagon for sale, she said. Quite a sight, isn't she?"

"I really didn't notice," Len Evans lied coolly.

He turned abruptly, and strode toward the sign.

"Don't think they're anything *you'd* be interested in, Len." Fred Moss gave a snorting laugh, hitched up his thin frame importantly. "Not given *your* taste for horseflesh."

"What d'you figure they're worth?" Len Evans turned to gaze at Fred quizzically.

"Not much, from the glance I had of the horse and rig when they stopped by here yesterday asking for directions. Won't get a lot for that outfit—maybe fifty dollars." Fred Moss gave another short, snorting laugh.

Len Evans took one long stride, reached up a tanned hand and ripped the handbill from its nail. Folding it carefully, he stuck it in his coat pocket.

"Thank you, Fred," Len smiled and walked out.

Chapter 20

The home of Mr. and Mrs. Earnest Phelps set a bit back from the street, with a low picket fence edging the narrow yard. A lightly graveled drive led from the dirt road into the side yard, and on into a neat carriage house.

The house was large, but not as large as Maggie had expected. Maggie didn't know exactly what she had expected.

Maggie walked up the graveled drive, to a small curved walk. Then up the steps onto a wide veranda that spanned the front of the two-story house. She took a deep breath, and reached for the ornate brass knocker.

"Who is it?" rang a sharp inquiry from inside.

"Mrs. Phelps? Mrs. Earnest Phelps? It's Margaret Ann McKinnon. I trust you received my letter?"

"Come on in, Miss McKinnon. The door is open."

Tentatively, Maggie turned the brass knob, and swung the oak door wide.

Her eyes were greeted with a fine entryway with highly polished, dark wood flooring. Just beyond, lay a parlor, where a low fire glowed in a huge fireplace that spanned half the wall. Overstuffed chairs and settees covered in rich, wine-colored horsehair damask were arranged about the room, and in front of the fireplace.

On one of these, reclined a slight figure, half covered with a light hand-woven afghan that hid the lower part of her body. Her legs rested on the settee in front of her.

"Well! Don't just stand there like a simpleton! Shut the door! And come on in! You're letting out all the heat!"

"Oh, yes, excuse me," Maggie muttered. Having no idea of what she should do next, or how she should proceed, Maggie gently closed the door.

"Well, don't just stand there. Come over here, where I can get a good look at you!"

Maggie stepped forward a few feet, and then paused uncertainly.

"Hmmmmph. Don't appear too strong to me. Why, you're no more than a child! You expect me to pay a full wage, for the services of a mere child?"

Suddenly Maggie got her bearings. She lifted her chin, and with quick, sure steps, strode up to Mrs. Phelps.

"Mrs. Phelps, I am *not* a child. I am as strong as any grown woman. I am sure you will find my services adequate, and *more* than adequate. Now, if you would allow me to put off my shawl and my bonnet, perhaps we can get down to the business of just exactly where all this strength of mine is to be applied."

"Well!" Mrs. Phelps remarked tartly, "I see that you have a mouth on you! Hang your things on the pegs, behind the front door. And then we can get better acquainted. Margaret, is it?"

"Yes, Ma'am," Maggie replied politely, as she hung up her shawl, tucked her gloves securely into her bonnet, and swung it over a peg.

She walked quickly over, stoked up the fire with a few deft motions, threw on an additional log, swept her gaze about the room and announced:

"Need to bring in some more wood. Have you had your bath, and your breakfast, Mrs. Phelps—?

"—No? Well, we'll soon see to that. Let's get these heavy curtains open, here. Let a little sunlight into the room. This rug could use a good sweeping, and I see that there are leaves drifted against the sides of the house. Dangerous. An open invitation to fire. I'll start a fire in the cookstove, fix you up some warm oats, with cream and lots of butter and sugar, and some hot coffee. As soon as you've eaten, I'll go out and draw up some water for your bath. Get your hair combed. Clean clothes. Perhaps some of those apples from the tree out back would be good …baked for your lunch. Or in a few tarts …I noticed a stand of fall turnips with good-looking greens out by the carriage house. Do you, perhaps, have some slices of ham, or a good ham bone? Or, we could fry up a chicken, make creamed gravy and biscuit. What time is Mr. Phelps in for supper? Or we could boil up a pot of dried beans, or peas, to go with a—"

Mrs. Earnest Phelps sat stunned and open-mouthed, as her new young employee rattled on, and on, and on.

Slowly, Len Evans rode the beautiful palomino back to the big farmhouse where he was reared. Riding into the yard, he sat staring at the house. It was a fine house, one of the finest in the county, with its looming two stories and the wide, well-shaded veranda stretching along the front. Its grandeur was enhanced by the lovely gardens his mother, Ida, had planted and faithfully tended.

Len's father, Big Carl Evans, was the richest man in Forsyth County. Even during the anarchy of the occupation of Georgia by Union troops those five years immediately following the War—when Big Carl had been tagged by some of his neighbors as a Republican and a scalawag—Big Carl somehow managed to maintain his holdings, and keep a finger in every economic and political pie. Big Carl Evans owned a good deal of the farmland in the county, as well as a cotton gin and a grist mill. And although he never officially was licensed for a banking operation or a loan company, Big Carl received hundreds of dollars each year in interest—on loans he made to struggling farmers. His hundreds of acres of farmland—now that slavery had ended— he let out to sharecroppers. This allowed Big Carl to take his ease. He felt he had earned it.

Despite the war, or perhaps partially because of it, Big Carl Evans was a very wealthy man. He had a shrewd eye for a deal. He never personally believed in banks, and kept his money, it was said, where he could keep an eye on it.

But Big Carl, if one met him on the street, would not appear to be a wealthy landowner. He was tall—six feet, three inches. His dark, curly hair had begun to gray at the temples. He wore the usual attire of Georgia farmers—heavy cotton trousers, a cotton work shirt, a straw hat, his big feet shod in rugged, high-topped leather work boots. He was never seen about town in a fine suit. It was not Big Carl's style. He smoked roll-your-own cigars filled with homegrown tobacco, and sometimes chewed on a wad. He was a tough, demanding man. Very few people came up to Big Carl's expectations, and those who didn't, Big Carl never failed to let them know about it.

The only luxuries Big Carl allowed himself:

A large, finely cut diamond set in gold, which he wore on his right hand.

A fine buggy, and a grand surrey—with equally fine horseflesh to pull them. He owned several saddle mounts that were the envy of his neighbors and acquaintances, as well.

Len Evans rode his horse into the barnyard, unsaddled him, rubbed him down, and led him out to pasture. Then he strode up to the house, and walked into the kitchen. He gave his mother, Ida, a little peck on the cheek, and a quick hug.

Ida came from a fine family. Her Pa, Zechariah Hawkins, one of the first settlers in Forsyth County, had been a gentleman farmer from Virginia. Zechariah, with two dozen slaves, had planted almost everything under the sun, to test the suitability of North Georgia soil and climate. Everything from grape vineyards to rice fields to flax. He even planted an extensive grove of mulberry trees, for the nurture of silk worms.

Tobacco and Indian corn were Zechariah's principal crops.

But the War Between the States had dealt a harsh blow to Zechariah Hawkins. It had broken him financially, and broken his spirit. Neither of Ida's parents lived to see the end of the conflict. Whatever assets remained to the Hawkins family fell to their only child, Ida. And disappeared into the holdings of Big Carl Evans—including this fine farmhouse. It was in fact, Zechariah Hawkins who gave Big Carl Evans his start in Forsyth County. He took Big Carl, a penniless orphan of eighteen, on as a hired hand.

From the day he began work on the Hawkins' Plantation, Big Carl set his eyes on Ida. And on Zechariah's holdings.

"Well, Son, how did you find things in town?"

Her son, Len, Ida knew, had changed. Since the day he ran Jenny and the child off, Len was a man of sad countenance, and of few words. *Nothing* seemed to bring him joy or pleasure.

"Changed. Grown. Quite a bit," Len replied tersely.

"Want a bite of lunch?" Ida pasted on a smile. She could recall better days. When she was a child. When the sun shone every day. And crops grew and rain fell. And her father, Zechariah sat on the front veranda, and doted on his only child.

Len walked over and washed his hands, leaned against the dry sink, studying his mother for a moment.

She was far too pale. Far too thin. She worked too hard. Her light-brown hair that had once gleamed in lovely coils atop her head was now worn in a tight, faded ball—on the back of her head. The faded cotton dress hung on her spare frame. He wondered absently why his father didn't buy her some decent clothes. Why his father didn't hire help.

But Len knew how Pa was. Pa lived mostly for *Pa*. If his own needs were met, he didn't give much thought to anyone else's. When it came to Ida, he expected perfection. Perfection in the way the house was tended, in the way his clothes were washed and ironed, in the way his meals were prepared. He allowed no excuses, put up with no slacking. And gave no quarter.

Ida had borne Big Carl seven children. And with the War—which Len could recall, being nine years old when the surrender finally came at Appomattox—Ma had lost her household help. And Big Carl, bitter and angry at *all* freed slaves, was bound and determined not to extend aid or succor to a single one of them.

What Negroes hadn't fled during the conflict and emancipation, Big Carl drove off the place with a loaded shotgun. He swore that none of those ingrates, those rebels and turncoats would ever receive one *crumb* of subsistence from *his* house. Not if they all starved. And Len wondered if any of them did. Most of the freed slaves, Len knew, stayed on familiar land, working as hired hands or sharecroppers.

A few were able, with the help of the Federals, to get their own places.

Len ate lunch, and then wandered about the house. He never saw any of his sisters or brothers. They had all left home as soon as they were old enough to make it on their own. Two of the boys, Len knew, were in Alabama, and a third one was in Mississippi. Len had visited them, on his recent travels.

The girls had all married young, to escape the house, and Len had no idea where any of them were.

Len often disagreed with his father, but never openly. His feelings for Big Carl were ambiguous, wavering between disdain and hatred, when Pa mistreated Ma. But Len never spoke out in his mother's defense. He dared not incur his father's wrath. On the other side of the coin, Len felt a deep respect for Big Carl. One had to admire a man who came into the county as an orphaned, penniless youth when the Indians were still here, and now owned a great deal of Forsyth County. Besides, Len was his youngest child, and Pa had always been good to Len.

The old house was empty. And Len felt that he rattled around it in, like a rock in an empty gourd.

The house—just like him—

—Dry—

—Empty—

—Bereft of life. Or joy. Or hope—

—Until he rode around the corner of the Cumming square, early this morning.

Len pulled the crude handbill from his coat pocket. He had gone immediately out to the place. A middle-aged lady had appeared at the door, an infant in her arms. A younger version of the lady appeared behind her, light brown hair, mildly pretty.

Her daughter, she told him, had the horse and wagon for sale. Her daughter was at work, and would not return, until late afternoon. Len knew *this* would be the girl he had seen leaving the store.

He planned to ride out there again, this afternoon.

After lunch, Len walked up the stairs to his old room. Five years, he thought, five years since he had climbed these familiar stairs—until last Friday. Maybe he'd just ride on out, now, see about the horse and wagon. No. It was still early. He'd stretch out on the bed. Have a nap.

Len stepped out into the back yard and drew up several buckets of fresh water. He would need a good bath, a shave, and shampoo, and a change into his best suit. Some toilet water from Moss' General Mercantile. He heated the water in the washpot, and put the tub on the latticed back porch, where the sun filtered through the slats.

Len Evans was definitely what most people would term 'handsome.' He had Ida's fine eyes and smooth complexion, her almost delicate features. He was an inch taller than his father, standing six feet, four inches. He had a quick smile, the few times he was in a particularly good mood. He was lithe and lean, moving with the strength and grace of a big cat, from years of hard work—

In his father's fields—

—Then on the road, picking up whatever odd job offered itself—from Georgia to Alabama to Mississippi, then to Texas. On the railroad—now creeping across the continent.

At age eighteen, Len married his high school sweetheart, Jenny Overby, a pretty blond girl. Len fell for Jenny the first day he saw her at school. They were both in their senior year. Jenny's family had just moved into Forsyth from the neighboring county of Gwinnett.

Len would never forget the first day Jenny attended school. All the boys were bug-eyed over the flirty, pretty little girl from Gwinnett. All the girls were green-eyed with envy. Jenny had a few things on them, as far as it went towards attracting the opposite sex. They were all nice girls, from strict Baptist families. They had all been taught that nice girls didn't throw themselves at boys. They did not bat their eyes and wiggle their bodies provocatively. They did not approach boys, and stand too close, and begin silly, witless conversations.

But none of these restrictions seemed to apply to Jenny. She openly flirted. She wore her skirts short enough to show some ankle. She wore her blouses low enough to show some young cleavage. She flitted from boy to boy, like a lovely butterfly swoops from flower to flower. A little kiss here, a little kiss there.

On the afternoons that he met Jenny in the woods out back of the schoolhouse, she swore undying love, and Len was in heaven.

But the very next day, she would come sauntering across the schoolyard on the arm of Ben Johnson or Todd Everly, or both.

By the end of the school year, Len Evans was half-crazed with jealousy.

And when the school year finally ended, Len, haggard and desperate, approached his father, and laid out his problem.

"Sure, Len, you want to get married, I'll set you up on one of my places. But, I've heard some bad tales on the Overby girl, Son. But you want her—go after her," was Big Carl's solution to the problem. "She don't buckle down to business, after the marriage ceremony, there's always ways of bringing a woman or a horse into line."

So Len married Jenny. But when Jenny continued to give him trouble, Len didn't hold with Pa's way of bringing women or horses into line.

Len was too much like his Ma, Big Carl warned him with a thunderous frown, so look out, because he was sure there was trouble to come.

Jenny became pregnant. Len didn't dare tell Pa—that he wasn't even sure it was his, lest Pa accuse him of being weak-kneed and bested by a spit of a woman. Besides, he'd never actually caught Jenny with another man. But the way the wind was blowing, who could tell what Jenny was up to during the day?

Big Carl had set Len up sharecropping on one of his farms, to provide a home and livelihood for his new young wife. But from the first day, Jenny was very unhappy.

She never did the wash. Never cleaned the house. Seldom cooked.

Jenny was sorely disappointed.

In Len—

—In the home and living he was offering her—

"—You want to know why I married you? 'Cause your Pa's as rich as Job after his restoration! So why do we have to live in this *dingy little shack*, out in the back of *nowhere*? Why can't we travel? Go somewhere? When can I get a decent dress? Or a decent carriage to drive! Or something decent to eat! I'm tired of salted side meat and boiled greens! Why don't you act like a *man*! Stand up to your Pa! Demand some of what is rightfully yours! Rightfully *ours!*"

To avoid Jenny's angry tirades, which grew more vicious and more strident the bigger with child Jenny got—and totally beyond Len's control— Len took to staying more and more over at Pa's, with the excuse that now that Pa was a bit older, he needed Len's help about the place. Chopping wood. Mending harness. Shoeing horses

Len spent longer hours in the fields. More time at the smithy shop he had set up out back of the small barn.

Anything, any place, to escape Jenny. But despite it all, though Len cursed himself for it, he still loved her.

He still wanted Jenny.

Then the baby came—a thin, pale, blue-skinned little thing. A tiny little girl, that didn't look quite real. Every time Len looked at the child, he wondered if she was his. He felt oddly repulsed by her, could never quite bring himself to touch her, to hold her, to feed her—despite the angry tongue-lashings of Jenny.

"You expect me to do *everything* for the child? She's yours, too, you know. *You* got me into this! I didn't bring her into this world all by myself! Now, act like a man. Assume some of your responsibilities!"

Now that the baby was here, Jenny always slept in each morning.

Len was up early, getting breakfast for them. He started a fire in the cookstove, washed his face and hands. He stirred up a hoecake, poured the batter into the skillet to fry, while he put on some coffee. The hoecake rose gently, filling the pan, filling the tiny kitchen with the smell of freshly baked bread. Len turned the hoecake out onto a plate, stirred some eggs into the skillet, and scrambled them up.

Len broke off a piece of the hoecake, slathered it with blackberry jam Ida had put up, ate his eggs, and drank his hot coffee. In his mind, he was planning the day's work. He knew it would be up to him to milk the cow he had bought to provide milk for them. He'd also have to feed the few chickens, and gather the eggs. Jenny most likely wouldn't be up until noon. He wondered if she ever took the trouble or effort to feed the child? He wouldn't even think about that.

He washed his plate and cup in the pan in the dry sink, and then walked into the tiny bedroom, to fetch his work gloves—and to check on Jenny. Holding the leather gloves, Len looked at his young wife, and wondered how anyone who looked so pretty could be so lazy, and so rotten inside. He reached out, let one of the soft blond curls twine about his finger, then slowly, softly, Len crept from the room, quietly closing the door.

When Len broke for lunch, he decided to walk over and eat with Ma. Ida heard the wagon drive up. She was half expecting him, and had food hot, on the back of the stove.

"Ma," Len entered through the back door. Ida walked to meet him, offered her cheek. Len gave her his usual cursory greeting, his usual peck on her thin cheek. Len often looked at Ma's face that had once been very pretty, and wondered—about the long scar—running from beneath her left eye ...to the tip of her chin. No one had ever mentioned how it got there. And Len had never dared ask. He thought about the heavy diamond his father wore on his right hand, and wondered ...if his father had anything to do ...with that scar. But Len pursued this unpleasant thought no further.

They ate their food, and then sat at the big table, sipping black coffee.

"How's Jenny?" Ma asked, out of kindness.

"About the same," Len replied, his heart twisting painfully in his chest. Don't get into that. He figured Ma had about all she could handle, without giving her grief over his sorry state of affairs.

"Tell Jenny to come over for a visit," Ida offered with a faint smile.

"Sure," Len replied curtly, tapping a fingernail absently against his coffee cup, "I'll tell her."

Ma was always inviting Jenny over. Jenny never came. What did the two of them have in common?

"Guess I'll be going. Want me to chop you up some wood, before I go?"

"Whatever you think, Son, will be fine with me. Len, is everything ...all right?"

"Sure, Ma," Len lied, pulling a stiff smile. "I'll go chop that wood."

"Thank you, Son." Ma accepted everything with gratitude. She asked nothing.

Back at the little sharecropper's house, Len found the child, Lisa, with a neighbor lady.

"Where's Jenny?" Len asked angrily, feeling his gut tighten.

"She didn't say. She went somewhere. She's been paying me real well, to sit with Lisa most afternoons. She's usually back before this time. I have things of my own to look after."

"You go on home," Len offered, without a word of thanks, or an offer of pay.

Len started a fire in the stove, and put on a pone of corn bread. He drew up the sweet milk from the well out back.

He fixed a bowl, and pushed it over to the child. She looked at Len with pale faded eyes. She began to cry. She looks like a little ghost, not a living child, Len thought dismally. How he wished she would cease that howling! But Len felt frozen inside, when he was near the child. So he made no effort to touch her, to comfort her. He just sat eating his corn pone and milk, the sorrowful wails swelling up inside his head. Just as darkness fell—

—Finally, in came Jenny. She became highly upset, raging at Len. How dared he question her about her whereabouts the past few afternoons! He didn't own her!

"You expect me to stay shut up in this dreary piece of a farmhouse, while the world passes me by? Not on your life, Buster!"

Len was tired. He had no wish to fight with Jenny. "I'm going on out to the barn," he said wearily. He had no idea what else to do.

"Well! Go on! And good riddance!" With a fierce scowl on her pretty face, Jenny slammed the door behind him.

Len redoubled his efforts to make his marriage work, to make the farmstead profitable. He felt he owed that to his Pa. The next afternoon, one of his plow lines broke, and Len brought the horse up to the small barn, to repair or replace the line. As he led the horse into the shadows of the barn, he heard loud laughter coming from the house.

A chill creeping up his back, his mouth set in a hard line, Len tied the horse, and walked slowly up to the house. The child was sitting alone on the front step. Len stepped quietly onto the low front porch, and eased open the door. He stood for a moment, letting his eyes become accustomed to the low light. Behind him, he could hear the child, beginning to cry softly.

There were sounds, coming from the tiny bedroom. Len crossed to the bedroom door, and flung it wide.

Jenny was on the bed. A man was desperately clawing his way out the window. He disappeared headfirst. Then there was a flash of naked feet, running down into the woods back of the barn.

Len couldn't trust himself to speak. He couldn't breathe. He could only stand in the door—and gape and stare. He dared not step forward. He was afraid, if he got close to her—afraid of what he might do.

"I want you dressed ..." he paused, sucked in a painful gasp, "and out of this house. Take whatever you want. And take the child with you. You have five minutes. *Then I'll be back.*"

Len came back. He took his clothes from the small farmhouse. He saddled up his horse. Then he rode over to Pa's—and said goodbye. Before it ever got dark, Len Evans had put some distance between himself and the town.

He was not to see his mother or father again, for five long years.

Five years Len spent drifting from town to town, from job to job, and from woman to woman. But no job, no town, no woman could hold Len Evans long. And Len drifted on. He would grow tired, and think of settling down, but nothing could hold Len.

The ghosts of Jenny and the child haunted him, wherever he went.

The child—*was she really his?* Had he ordered *his own child* out of her home—what would become of her?

Why hadn't he kept the child, and tried to see that she was raised properly? But ...what if she *wasn't* his? Only a fool would assume the responsibility of raising some other man's child!

He had stayed the longest stretch of time in Texas. He was wrangling cows on a big ranch out in the middle of nowhere. The Indians had all been cleared out, ranchers had moved in. There was nothing here—but the western cattle trail. Then there was talk among the ranchers, of a railroad coming through. In January, 1881, the *Texas and Pacific* arrived at a site they decided to name *Abilene*, after the cattle town in Kansas. And Len went to work for the railroad.

The work was hard. The pay was good. Abilene grew. Families moved in. Churches and businesses sprang up along the growing rail line that pushed steadily westward.

But one day Len looked about, over the raw, dry, dusty frontier town called Abilene—

—And he almost choked—

—On the desire to see home, and to feel the cool breezes off the old muddy Chattahoochee, where he had spent so many happy afternoons as a child, swimming and fishing. To see the rolling slopes of the foothills of the Blue Ridge Mountains, growing thick with tall trees. To sink his boots into the thick, rich dirt of a Georgia field.

So Len had packed up cowboy shirts and trousers, loaded his hand-tooled Texas saddle and his gorgeous palomino onto a freight car, and headed home.

Maggie couldn't wait for Mr. Phelps to come home. She had been on her feet all day. Mrs. Phelps, Maggie had quickly decided, was like a badly spoiled child. She desired constant attention. She not only desired it, she demanded it.

Maggie tried to be kind and patient, but by late afternoon, her patience was wearing thin. She had bitten her tongue, until she felt it might begin to bleed profusely. Mrs. Phelps reminded Maggie of an *old* Barbara Jo. If she didn't get out of this house—and soon—she would—

—Then Maggie heard a key in the front door.

Oh, yes! Mr. Phelps was home!

"Good afternoon to you, sir. Did you have a good day? Fine. See you at eight in the morning."

Maggie snatched her shawl, her gloves and bonnet, and was out the door.

Breathing clean, fresh air. Free!

She even enjoyed the walk back to the ugly little house. Maggie popped in the door, "Hello, Mama!" she chirped as cheerily as a bird. "Yes, the first day went fine. Mrs. Phelps is …a peach of a lady. Sweetest little thing you ever did see. A breeze to care for. But I would like a hot bath, and a—" Maggie hated dishonesty with a passion. But how could she tell Mama how she felt?

"Maggie?" Callie was staring at her youngest daughter. "Didn't you hear what I just said? A young man came by, earlier today, asking about the horse and wagon, said he would be back, tonight, when you'd returned from work."

"Oh, Mama," Maggie moaned, feeling the tiredness and frustration settling deep into every bone. "Not tonight!"

"But, Maggie," Callie gazed at her inquisitively, "I thought you just said …I could have told the young man to come back another day. If I had known—"

"It's okay, Mama. Don't fret yourself. How is Johnny?"

"If we were all doing as well as John Thomas McKinnon, Jr." Callie brightened, "we'd all be in fine fettle. He does nothing but sleep and eat. And in between, he's charming the birds out of the trees, with those blue-blue eyes of his and that sweet smile."

"Where is he? Can I hold him?"

"I just put him down, Maggie. Maybe you can after supper. Are you going to draw up water for your bath?"

"Where's Barbara Jo?" Maggie asked, "I thought I might bribe her—"

"She walked down to Moss' General Mercantile. Said she'd be back in a minute."

"What's she doing down there?"

"I don't know, Maggie. I think she just got bored, hanging about the house all day."

"*Bored?*" Maggie fought to hold her tongue, but she couldn't stop the angry thoughts whirling about in her brain. She *could* have busied herself washing the *pail full of dirty diapers* that accumulate every day, with a small infant. Or the clothes that have piled up since we left the farm. She could have planted the rose cuttings we brought from the mountains, Maggie fumed, her irritation mounting. But she didn't want to upset Mama; she'd had enough to deal with lately.

Maggie sighed wearily. She would have to speak to Barbara Jo. Mama had given birth not even three weeks past. Barbara Jo should be sharing some of the chores of looking after the baby. Barbs had no money. What on earth was she doing down at the *store*?

Mama was in the kitchen, trying to stir up the rest of the supper.

"Go sit down, Mama," Maggie ordered. "Let me do that."

"I know you're tired," Mama smiled at her. "But I must confess, a few minutes rest would do me a world of good. Johnny will be awake, again, wanting to nurse."

"Go sit down in the front room, Mama. Put your feet up, and close your eyes for a spell. I'll call you, when supper's ready."

Maggie hated the tiny, cramped kitchen. She hated the tiny, cramped house. She hated—everything. She was homesick—for the mountains, with the cool morning fog hanging in the valleys and over the creek and the river. She wanted to break down and cry. But Mama was sitting in the front room, exhausted from birthing a little boy. And the baby was asleep in the bedroom—

"Maggie? The young man's here again, about the horse," Callie called from the front door.

Maggie took a deep breath. She dried her hands on the apron tied about her slender waist, removed the apron, hung it on a nail on the wall, pushed the damp hair back from her forehead, and walked to the front door.

The young man stood staring at her. Not speaking a word. Just standing there. He took two steps backward.

Maggie followed, he moved backwards, down the front steps. Maggie stood on the low porch, her face even with his.

"Yes?" Maggie said.

He stepped back again. Maggie walked down the steps, and stood staring up at him. He sure was tall.

Still he didn't answer. Strange fellow, Maggie thought. The eyes were large, haunted. But the features were delicate, almost like the face of a little boy. She squinted up at him in the dimming light.

"You're interested in the horse and wagon?" Maggie asked. Still he made no reply. "Sir!" Maggie heard herself shouting at him, maybe he was hard of hearing, "You interested in the horse and wagon?"

"What?" he was stammering, "Yes …oh, yes …the horse, and the …wagon."

"How much you willing to pay?" Maggie inquired shrewdly.

Len Evans smiled, for the first time in a long while, showing a row of fine white teeth.

He has a beautiful smile, Maggie thought tiredly.

"What do you think they're worth?" he kept smiling at her.

Maggie, very quietly, "I doubt, sir, that all you *own* would be equal to what they're *worth*. But we must speak here in terms of what you are willing to pay. A fair market price."

The young man stared at her intently. He seemed rather set back on his heels. The smile faded. Perhaps he was not accustomed to young women who spoke their minds. That was neither here nor there. Maggie was responsible for the family. She wanted a fair price, and she intended to get it.

"I take it," Maggie heard him saying, "you are quite fond of the animal."

"*Fond* is not the word. Job is like a member of the family. Yes, you might say *quite* fond."

"But, you do want to sell him?"

"No, quite frankly, I *don't want* to sell him. But I *must* sell him." Then seeing the perplexed look on the young man's face, Maggie added quickly.

214

"I must sell Job, because, I simply cannot afford to feed him."

"Oh, I see. I'm sorry."

"And, as you can see," Maggie explained, "I have no place to keep a horse. So, how much you willin' to pay?"

The little smile played about the corners of his mouth. Then he said very softly, bending forward just a bit, "I think you said that before."

Maggie smiled, "So I did, sir, but the question still remains—how much?"

"Could I hitch him up? Drive him around a bit? I'd like to see how he handles himself."

"Well," Maggie said, on the verge of exasperation, "All right." She disappeared into the house, and returned with the lines and trappings.

Together, they hitched up Job.

The young man climbed onto the high seat, and extended a slender brown hand toward Maggie.

"Aren't you coming with me?"

"No. I don't think so," Maggie shook her head.

"Oh, come on. We'll just trot him around the block. Be back in a moment. Maybe you can give me some tips, on handling him."

"You're not familiar with horses?" Maggie frowned up at him.

"Well, not *too* much," he shook his head, as if he lacked any sort of experience with driving a rig.

Again, he extended his hand, which Maggie took—not daring to let Job out of her sight with some greenhorn that might drive him into the ground.

"Mama?" Maggie called.

Callie, who had been listening, poked her head out the door.

"Mr.?" Maggie looked over at the young man questioningly.

"Evans," the handsome young man smiled. "Len Evans, Miss McKinnon."

"Mr. Evans wants to try out Job. Be back in a minute."

Callie waved an acknowledgment and closed the door.

As soon as he picked up the reins, Maggie knew he had lied about knowing how to handle horses. But she was simply too tired to question why.

"He's a good strong horse," Maggie said, wanting to close the trade and let the young man be on his way. He said nothing, kept staring at Maggie.

"He's a real hard worker." Still he said nothing.

"Real steady—

"Mr. Evans? Are you listening?"

"Yes ...of course. He's a *real fine* horse. I'll take him. And the wagon."

"How much you willin' to pay?"

He laughed, spontaneously, uproariously. He laughed.

Then, seeing the look on Maggie's face, he hastened to say, "Oh, forgive me, Miss McKinnon, I'm so sorry. It's just that," he attempted to control his mirth, "I think you've said that about three times, now."

"So I have, Mr. Evans," Maggie said slowly, feeling anger seep into her voice, "And here goes *number four*! *How much?*"

"Seventy-five dollars."

Seventy-five dollars?

Maggie couldn't believe her ears! Maybe Job was a better horse than she gave him credit for. But Job was no two-year-old. And the wagon had some years on it. And it was a one-horse wagon.

"Seventy-five dollars?" Maggie inquired tentatively. She wanted to make certain there was no misunderstanding here.

He nodded.

"And you'll give him a good home?"

"I'll feed him almost every day. And I won't beat him over twice a week."

"You're right. I'm being silly. It's a deal."

"I don't have that much money with me, of course. I'll pay you a deposit, to seal the deal. Say fifty? Could I bring the rest of the money ...and pick him up ...on Saturday?"

"Saturday!" Maggie frowned. Saturday was her day off! She had planned to do the wash! And spend time with Johnny. Have a *good* talk with Barbara Jo. And maybe get some of her flower cuttings into the ground—!

"Saturday will be fine. Okay. All right. That's ...fine."

Len Evans reached into his coat pocket, and pulled out the fifty dollars he had intended to pay for the pair. "I'll be back Saturday," he smiled, "with the other twenty-five."

Finally, it was Saturday. Maggie awoke, stretched, turned over and pulled the covers over her head. The bed felt warm and inviting. It was Saturday, and she had the day off! Closing her eyes, she drifted off into a drowsy, dreamy sleep.

"Maggie! The young man's here again," she heard Mama calling.

"Oh, no!" Maggie muttered, her eyes only half open. Why did he have to come back today! But she needed the remainder of the money. She needed to get Job a good home, a barn and pasture.

Reluctantly Maggie swung her bare feet out from beneath the warm covers. Why did he come so *early*, she wondered. Slowly, she dressed, dragged herself into the kitchen, still asleep.

"He's in the back yard," Mama said.

Maggie moved slowly to the back door. He was standing on the porch, watching her through the partially open door. Maggie pushed the door open and stuck her head out.

The sleep was still in her eyes. She looked like a little kitten, Len Evans thought. She was stretching, yawning and rubbing her eyes.

Touch her, Len thought. *No! It's too soon!*

"Oh, hello," Maggie mumbled.

He just stood there, staring at her.

"Good morning. I mean, how are you, Mr. Evans?" *Good grief!* Why doesn't he just pay me and go away! I haven't had breakfast, or even washed my face!

"Lovely day, isn't it?" he was smiling.

"Yes," Maggie sighed, "Just lovely. I didn't expect you ...so early. I—"

"I thought we might drive around a bit more today. I'd like to see how the horse handles on the open road?"

"Open road?" Maggie asked. "I thought we already had a deal, Mr. Evans."

Maggie's voice had taken on an angry edge, and Len could see that she was more than a bit put out with him.

"Oh, we do," Len hastened to say, "It's ...uh ...just ...uh ...you being so familiar with the horse, and all ...maybe you could show me best ...how to handle him."

It's Saturday, Maggie thought. I wanted to help Mama in the house and spend some time with Johnny. And plant the flower seeds in the barren little yard. Make an excuse. Make any excuse.

"It's a bit early. And I had planned on doing some yard work."

"Please? We won't be gone long. I know what the horse means to you. And I think it would be best for him, if I knew a little bit more about the animal."

"I think not, Mr. Evans. I've not even had breakfast yet!"

"You go right ahead. And I'll wait for you. Take your time. All the time you need. I'm in no hurry ...got all day. I'll just wait ...out here on the porch." And so saying, he sat down on the back step.

Maggie heaved a loud, heavy sigh. Slammed the back door, and stomped inside.

"I can't *believe* that man!" she grumbled to Mama, who was just pouring coffee into Maggie's cup, and setting a bowl of steaming oats out for her daughter. "I simply can't believe him, Mama! He's just sitting out there whistling some senseless little tune, like he plans on spending the day!"

"You could have invited him in, Maggie," Callie chided in a hushed whisper, knowing the young man could probably hear every word her daughter was saying, "for a cup of hot coffee. That would have been the neighborly thing to do."

"He's *not* a neighbor, Mama! I attempted to conduct a simple business transaction with him, and now he …and I have so much to do today!"

"Try to be patient, Maggie," Callie said softly. "He can hear you. Go on and eat your breakfast. He'll soon be gone, and then you can get on with your day."

Maggie took her own sweet time. She brushed her teeth. Heated water and took a sponge bath. She combed her hair, and put on an old dress, for working out in the yard.

Finally, over an hour later, she came to the back door, and he was still there.

When she walked out onto the small back porch, he rose politely, and offered his hand. Job, Maggie noticed, stood hitched up and ready.

Suddenly, her hand was released, and in the same instant, she felt herself being lifted—and she was on the wagon seat.

He climbed up beside her, lifted the reins and with a practiced flick, sent Job into a gentle trot.

"I can *see* by the way you mount the wagon, the way you handle the reins, that you have *years* of experience with horses, Mr. Evans," Maggie said, a cool edge to her voice. She felt more than a little annoyed with him.

He offered no explanation for his obvious lies.

"So. *Now*, exactly what it is you wanted to know about Job?" He smiled at her annoyance, not speaking, and drove on. Maggie felt the blood rising hot into her cheeks. For some reason this man had deliberately lied to her. She was getting quite upset.

"Mr. Evans! Would you please be so kind as to afford me the courtesy of an answer?"

"All right, Miss McKinnon. So I lied to you, and I admit it. But I wanted to see you again. But I told you the truth about the money." He hurried on in an effort to somewhat redeem himself, "I really didn't have seventy-five dollars with me." He looked at her imploringly, like a little boy. Don't be mad he was saying, with his lovely, dark eyes.

Maggie did not reply. She was sixteen years old. What could she say to such a statement?

Scarcely without Maggie knowing it, they reached the river. She should have known, by its name, that the road by the house would lead to the river. But since the move, Maggie had found neither the time nor the energy to consider such things.

Maggie sat stiffly on the wagon seat. Ahead, she could see the river, flowing swift and clear beneath the trees along either bank. Directly ahead a long iron-girded plank bridge rose and spanned the stream. A feeling of unease stole over Maggie. She should not be here, like this, alone with this man. It was not proper. She knew *nothing* about him.

He had gotten down from the seat, walked around the wagon, and stood, offering his hand, to lift her down.

"I think we'd better be getting back," Maggie said with a cold little lift of her chin.

There was no one in sight, nothing but the sound of the rushing water, and the cool green of the trees, lush and towering, along the road and the banks of the river. And the young man, standing tall and tanned and handsome in the clear morning sunlight. His face, so clean and open and honest, and when he smiled at her—he reminded her suddenly of Papa. She put out her hand; he lifted her down. He was very strong.

He strolled out onto the oak-planked bridge. He stood, leaning against the iron railing, watching the waters flow beneath the bridge. Wordlessly, Maggie followed.

Flowing water had always fascinated Maggie. With tears in her eyes, she recalled the river that flowed through McKinnon Valley, how she and Papa had sat on the bank that day—

They stood side by side, on the bridge, for several minutes, watching the river. Maggie began to feel slightly dizzy, from the sight of the water rushing along beneath her feet. Len put out a hand to steady her. Abruptly, she drew away.

"I really think we should be going, Mr. Evans," Maggie said brusquely, "It's my day off. I have a lot of work to do."

"All right, Miss McKinnon," he gave her a warm smile, took her arm, and guided her across the bridge. Then he lifted her onto the seat.

Expertly, he turned Job, and they headed back. I wonder, Maggie thought, how old he is? He's not a boy. Not from his height, and the breadth of his shoulders. There are a few lines about the eyes. But he's certainly not old. He may be twenty-five or twenty-six? He's still a young man.

But that was neither here nor there. Get home. Get rid of him.

He turned Job into the small yard, then lifted Maggie down.

He began to remove his light jacket.

"Mr. Evans, are you going to pay me the other twenty-five dollars?"

"Oh, yes, of course. But first, I'm going to help you in the yard. Exactly, what is it, you want done?" He stood there—smiling at her.

Maggie was too astonished to speak. Not, would you *like* me to help you? Or even *may* I help you, but simply *I'm going to help you in the yard*!

She *cannot* get rid of him! "That really isn't necessary, Mr. Evans," Maggie said firmly, "If you will just *pay* me the other twenty-five dollars, we can consider our business *concluded*."

"Going to plant fall flowers?" He asked, his voice low and gentle, gazing at her solemnly, talking on, so easily, "My mother has lots of plants and all kinds of flowers. She'd probably be more than happy to give you some seeds and cuttings."

"That won't be necessary," Maggie said, considering her small hoard of wilted cuttings and dried seeds. Oh, for some real rose bushes, a hydrangea, and a gardenia, some jonquils and lilies—!

"—Your mother likes flowers?"

"She's got 'em all over the place!" he grinned, "You should see …say, now that's an idea. We could ride out there. And you can see them for yourself. Many are still in bloom."

"Oh! No! I couldn't do that!"

"Sure you could. Ma'd be so proud to see you. You'd love her. Ma would love you. If you're going to live here in town, wouldn't hurt to learn a few folk, now would it?"

"No. Really, I have too much to do. Perhaps …I might visit your mother, another day." Maggie made her excuses.

"How about tomorrow? Some time after church? You goin' to church?"

"I don't know. I'd love to, but …what with selling the horse …and it might be quite a ways to the nearest church. And after working all week, I don't think so."

"No problem!" he smiled, "I'll be by to pick you and your family up. Say about ten?"

"Really, Mr. Evans! I wasn't asking you to transport us to church!"

"I know you weren't asking, but I'm offering, Miss McKinnon. I'll be here at ten. Now, what's to be done in the yards?"

So Maggie fetched the only tool brought from the farm—a garden hoe. And Mr. Evans planted the black-eyed Susan seeds in two rows beneath the windows in front of the ugly square house. Then he put in the cuttings of climbing roses, to hopefully twine up the front porch posts.

The job completed, he carefully wiped his hands on his fine pants leg, paid Maggie the remaining twenty-five dollars, shook her hand very solemnly, and assured her he would see them in the morning for church. Then he drove Job out of the yard, and down the road towards town.

Sunday dawned clear and crisp. It was a lovely fall day. Maggie felt her blue dress with the white tatting trim was the only one she had left that was actually nice enough for church. She really must try to pick up some piece goods for Mama and Barbara Jo and ...she wondered if Mama was up to doing any sewing.

This morning Mama said she didn't believe it would be wise, to carry Johnny out. He had a slight cold. And Barbara Jo complained of one of her headaches.

Maggie was sure Barbara Jo wouldn't be walking down to Moss' General Mercantile, for it was Sunday, and she was sure the store would be closed. So, dragging her sister out of bed, Maggie forced her into her clothes. Maggie was not about to ride to church alone—with that man.

When Mr. Evans drove into the yard, promptly at ten o'clock, Maggie's mouth fell open.

He was not driving Job and the farm wagon he had just bought, but he wheeled a beautiful black surrey into the ugly little yard. The team pulling the surrey was as black and shiny as the surrey itself. It was a stunning sight.

Mr. Evans—Maggie couldn't recall his Christian name, though she was sure he had given it—but Mr. Evans looked very handsome. He had on a different suit. He must own half a dozen, Maggie thought sarcastically. It must be nice to be so rich.

He escorted the ladies to the surrey, helping Barbara Jo into the back, and then lifting Maggie onto the front seat covered with rich, soft black leather.

The surrey flew along behind the grand pair of blacks, as if it had wings.

Maggie thought how wonderful it was, to be dressed up in her best dress, and riding in a lovely black surrey, even if it was a one-time event. Just for today, she would enjoy herself. How long since she had actually enjoyed herself? She couldn't begin to recall. Today, she would forget all the heartache, all the grief, and just enjoy the sun, and the ride. And being in church.

It was a small, white wooden church, somewhat resembling Shiloh Baptist back in Rhyersville. The benches were about two-thirds filled, just about like back in Rhyersville.

They even sang the same hymns.

Maggie sat on the wooden bench, between the handsome young man in his fine suit, and Barbara Jo, whom Maggie elbowed twice in the side, in order to keep her sister awake.

All the people seemed inordinately interested in her, Maggie thought, after the service ended. Or did their interest lie in Mr. Evans? Evidently his family was of some standing in the community.

Finally everyone said their hellos and their good-byes, and they were in the surrey, and headed back to the ugly little house on East River Street.

Maggie felt strangely at peace, on the ride home. It had been good to be with people again. To sing and smile and shake hands. Even if she had not known a person there, she felt the familiar Christian kinship.

Len was pleased and happy on the ride back. Everyone had liked his girl. All the ladies, he could see, were envious of her looks. And all the men ...had envied Len. But they must all remember—*she was his girl.*

Len helped Barbara Jo down, then he turned and smiled charmingly at Maggie, "Ride on out to the place with me, Miss McKinnon, and have Sunday dinner. Ma's expecting you."

"What?" Maggie stared up at him, murmuring, "I ...couldn't possibly—"

About that time, Callie opened the front door and called:

"Maggie? Ask the young man in to Sunday dinner. I've fixed plenty!"

"Why, thank you kindly, Ma'am. I'd be happy to stay!"

Len Evans stepped lightly up on the front porch, and stood, huge hat in hand, holding open the door for Maggie and Barbara Jo. A strong hand on her arm, Maggie was steered firmly into the little house. He gave a nod to Callie, as he stepped inside, "I am much obliged to you, Ma'am, for your kind invitation."

Len Evans sat at the kitchen table, smiling at everyone in sight, and often laughing aloud. He could not have been more handsome, or more charming, engaging Mama and Barbara Jo in lively conversation—upon any and every subject that came to mind—

—While Maggie sat stiff and silent. There was a man at the table. Talking and laughing, with dark hair, and dark eyes—and with his heart in his eyes. Maggie felt as if she would choke. She had to have some air. Without a word of explanation, she pushed back her plate, rose and hurried outside.

She heard him walk up behind her. He stepped past her, and off the low porch. He stood facing her. His eyes—

"What's wrong, Maggie? May I call you Maggie? You don't like me?"

Tears flooded Maggie's eyes. Her emotions were in a jumble. She wanted to scream at him. *Yes I like you! I like you too much! And I don't want to like you! Please leave me alone! Please go home!*

But being the polite person she was, she said instead, "I'm sure you're a very nice young man, Mr. Evans, and I like you. It's just ...that ...never mind. It's not important."

"It *is* important. To *me*, it's *very* important. You're upset. Let's ride out and let you get a look at our place. You don't want to just sit around the house all afternoon. Get out into the country, get some fresh air."

So, he wasn't leaving. But it would be nice ...to see the countryside, smell a farm again—

"Only if Barbara Jo will ride along," Maggie insisted, cocking her head aside prettily.

"Your sister is more than welcome to come." He smiled. Maggie had never seen such a man.

Barbara Jo sat silently in the back of the surrey.

Fall leaves littered the road. But more than a few still clung stubbornly to the big oaks and hickories along the red banks and up the slopes of the rolling hillsides. There were no mountains visible here, but the countryside was lovely, Maggie thought. She wished Barbara Jo would *say* something.

"I hear you're from the mountains?" Mr. Evans said, as if reading Maggie's mind.

"What?" Maggie gave a slight start, "Oh, yes," and then came a long, heaving sigh, "Yesss."

Len glanced over at her. He saw her brush away a tear. She felt his gaze, and turned to give him a faint smile. She was so lovely Len's heart almost stopped beating. Her eyes were deeper than any well he had ever looked into. Her skin, her hair, she was a dream. But she was sad. *Please God!* Len began to pray for the first time in a long while. *Please, let her like me!*

Len wanted to comfort her, but how? Frantically, he searched his mind. He knew so little about her. He knew nothing about her family. She loved her baby brother. Mention him.

"You have a beautiful little brother," he remarked, in an effort to break the silence, lift the sadness he could feel in her.

"Oh, yes!" She smiled. "Isn't he adorable! So precious!"

"Oh, yes," Len agreed wholeheartedly, "Adorable. Beautiful. Very precious."

Maggie flashed him a beaming smile. Her eyes were alight with joy at the thought of little Johnny.

He *likes* babies, she thought to herself. He *is* a nice young man.

She's smiling at him. Len sits a bit taller. The horses' steps are a bit lighter. The sun's a bit brighter.

Maggie liked Ida Evans, the moment she laid eyes on her. She was a charming, gentile lady, with a soft, slow voice, and a gracious, hospitable manner. And she did indeed have a lovely yard, filled with all sorts of flowering plants, for every season of the year. Ida Evans' gardening kept her sane. She fairly glowed, and smiled unceasingly, as she gave Maggie a tour of her extensive gardens.

Len heaved a sigh of relief. He was glad Pa was not at home.

They sat on the wide veranda running the entire length of the big house, and talked a while. Ida rose at mid-afternoon and served them fresh China tea with lemon, and little frosted cakes. The cups and saucers were almost translucent, too delicate, too lovely, Maggie thought, to be real. She said as much to Ida Evans.

"They were my Mother's, brought over from England," Ida beamed. So nice, to have real company.

Duly impressed, Maggie gave a return smile, and offered to help her in the kitchen.

Bustling about in excitement as they washed the few dishes, Ida Evans offered Maggie a host of cuttings and seeds, and whatever else she desired from the gardens surrounding her home. "This being the Sabbath, though" she pulled a slight frown at the inconvenience, "I suppose we must wait. I'll send Len over with them," she smiled at Maggie.

Len, that's his Christian name, Maggie thought absently, as she hung the dishcloth on its peg.

The afternoon was winding down, and Maggie began to think about Mrs. Phelps …and tomorrow.

She tried to push these unwelcome thoughts aside, and concentrate on today. The sun, the gracious lady, the sweet China tea. An afternoon of leisure on a wide front porch—

—But the sun was lowering in the sky, casting shadows over the huge oaks and the giant magnolia trees in the front yard. Reluctantly, Maggie rose from her rocker, "We really must be getting back. Mama will begin to worry. Thank you so much, Mrs. Evans. It was a lovely afternoon. You must come to see us, sometime. Mama would love to have you. Thanks for the lovely tea and cakes. I don't know when I've ever tasted anything half so delicious." Impulsively, Maggie reached out and drew Ida Evans into a warm embrace.

Tears flooding the faded blue eyes, Ida's thin face stretched in a lovely smile.

Ma's almost pretty again, Len thought, as he gave his mother his usual peck on the cheek.

Ida waved briskly from the porch, as the lovely surrey drove down the graveled drive.

The drive back was quiet. Barbara Jo had acted like a sulky clod all afternoon. Maggie would have a talk with her.

Len helped Maggie down. She thanked him briefly, for a lovely day. He took her hand, and shook it solemnly. Then he was gone.

Maggie went into the house. She was tired. Her feet hurt. Tomorrow, there would be Mrs. Phelps. She was too tired to talk to Barbara Jo.

Maggie tried not to watch the fancy eight-day clock on the high mantel. But she felt her eyes straying more and more in that direction, as the afternoon progressed. Afternoons for Mrs. Phelps were always the worst.

Finally, she heard the key in the lock, just as the clock struck five.

Maggie snatched her shawl, bonnet and gloves, and was out the door. She dreaded even the short walk home.

Len waited in the wagon. He saw Phelps enter the house, and then Maggie was coming out the front door. She was tired. He hated it, that she was tired. He gave the reins the slightest touch, and Job moved up the street towards the Phelps' house. But he mustn't say anything, not yet. Give her time. She was young, skittish. He didn't want to lose her. He pulled Job to a halt, in the shade of a tree, just up the street.

"Maggie?"

Maggie thought she heard someone calling her name. But it couldn't be. Then, she saw Job! Standing under a huge oak, just up the street!

"Mr. Evans?" Maggie was stunned. "What are you *doing* here?"

He was not wearing a fine suit. Today he was wearing fine stuff trousers and a blue shirt, open at the neck. A light tan, wide brimmed felt hat, the crown deeply creased in the center.

"Care for a ride?" Without waiting for a reply, he was down, and lifting her onto the familiar seat.

It was good to see Job, and their old wagon—no, not *their* wagon. It was *Mr. Evans'* wagon …but *what was he doing here?*

Maggie's head was spinning. He was speaking, saying something about his mother wanting her to have the plants now. Fall, his mother insisted, was the time for getting plants into the ground, he was explaining. Get their roots well established during the winter, before the hot Georgia summer arrived.

Maggie glanced back at the wagon bed. It was literally *full* of plant materials.

Maggie looked over at Mr. Evans and frowned. "Straight home," she ordered.

He smiled.

Why today? She didn't feel like setting out and watering all those plants! There was a *week's* worth of work back there in that wagon bed! What was wrong with this man? You didn't transplant all that many plants—all at once!

Then Maggie sighed, determined she was too tired to bother with the plants this afternoon. If they died, they died.

"Just put them by the corner of the house," she directed Mr. Evans curtly, "and thank your mother for me."

Maggie marched inside, hung up her shawl and bonnet, gave Mama a kiss and picked up Johnny and showered him with hugs and kisses.

"I need a bath," Maggie said, putting the baby down, picking up the water bucket, opening the back door.

Mr. Evans was still here!

"Let me do that," he insisted, taking the bucket, drawing up the water, talking all the while, filling the bucket, and heading into the house. She followed him in. "Where do you want it?" he asked.

"In the back room," Maggie said tartly. "Just pour it into the tub. I plan on taking a bath."

"Oh," he smiled. "You'll need more. And some to heat on the stove," and with that, he went back to the well.

Maggie stood waiting. As soon as he entered the back door, she took the bucket of water from him, carried it into the backroom, and splashed it into the tub.

The next bucket, Maggie took from him, and stood holding it. He smiled and went back out. Maggie filled the kettle and set it on the cookstove. One more bucket, and with the hot water from the kettle, that should be plenty.

Maggie waited, listening for any sound from outside. She went out. He still hadn't finished unloading the wagon! He turned, smiling, and reaching for the bucket.

"You sure do use a lot of water."

"Yes, Mr. Evans," Maggie replied in a tired, angry huff, "*especially* when I take a bath!"

She stomped into the house.

"Yes," Len smiled at her show of anger. She sure was something!

He brought in the last bucket of water. Maggie snatched it from him, spilling some onto the kitchen floor, "*Goodbye*, Mr. Evans," she said very pointedly, walking over and opening the door.

Bowing slightly, Len said nothing. He smiled and walked out the door.

Maggie sat in the tub of warm water, soaking away the tiredness and frustration of the day. Mrs. Phelps had not felt well. Her legs had ached all day. She had been very testy, hard to deal with, demanding of Maggie at one point:

"Well, why don't you go ahead and ask me? Everyone else does! People are *so* rude! Why don't you just go ahead and ask?"

"Ask you what?" Maggie had inquired sweetly.

"How I became a cripple! *That's what!*"

"Mrs. Phelps, it's your life, and your legs. I figure if you want me to know what happened, you'll tell me."

"Well!" Mrs. Phelps replied tartly, "Some people couldn't care less!"

She appeared to be miffed with Maggie all afternoon.

Maggie lay back in the water, savoring the warmth. Thinking about *all those plants!*

She wouldn't think about them. She wouldn't think about them tonight. Mama must have supper about done.

Then she heard it. Soft whistling. From outside.

He was still here!

Maggie stepped out of the tub. Furiously she began to scrub herself dry. She heard Mama asking Mr. Evans to *supper*.

Maggie dressed, and stepped into the kitchen.

227

As she entered the room, Len Evans pushed back his chair, rose with a polite little flourish, saying, "Oh, Miss McKinnon, I thought we'd put the roses on the street side of the house, and then we'd set the lilies along the south side. I'm sorry …is that all right with you?" He smiled.

"That sounds fine, Mr. Evans," Maggie said resignedly taking the chair he held, "just fine." Her mother was passing Mr. Evans the mashed potatoes.

He labored strenuously, for hours. Half the plants were in, and well watered.

Maggie loved flowers. She really did appreciate Ida Evans' generosity in sending so many. She knew they would be gorgeous, come next spring.

"We can do the rest, tomorrow afternoon," Mr. Evans was saying, "right now, dark's coming on." At last, he rose from the table.

"We'll just leave them to soak their roots, in that tub. I put in a bit of water," Maggie heard him saying, as she stared at her half-finished plate.

She raised her eyes—and felt almost ashamed of her sulky behavior. His brow was covered with perspiration. His dark curly hair and fine shirt were wet. He really had worked so hard. She rose, and followed him out. Thank goodness! Finally, he was walking to the wagon.

Maggie searched for something gracious and appreciative to say. "Thank your mother for me, Mr. Evans. She really shouldn't have been so generous. And …I would like to thank you for …for all your work. It was …really …much more than I had expected."

"You're more than welcome," he replied, reaching up to the wagon, taking his broad brimmed hat from off the seat, "I'll tell Ma you sent your thanks. I'll be seeing you, tomorrow."

He took her hand. His hand felt warm, and strong. He shook her hand, very solemnly.

Mrs. Phelps' feathers were still in a considerable ruffle the following morning

Apparently, she wasn't telling the cause of her affliction—though she apparently wanted to tell—unless Maggie specifically asked. Which Maggie was determined she would not do.

And so, at this impasse, the two of them passed the day.

When the clock struck five, Job was back, beneath the shade tree at the end of the street. Almost gratefully, Maggie felt herself being lifted into the familiar wagon. Mr. Evans was smiling at her.

He put in the rest of the plants, and then watered them all thoroughly.
Maggie hardly spoke to him.

The following morning, Mrs. Phelps looked up as Maggie was doing her
hair, and said defiantly, "It was a riding accident. My husband shot the
horse."

"Was it the horse's fault?" Maggie asked quietly.

"What does *that* have to do with anything?"

"Well, it seems to me a bit heartless, to put down a poor animal for
something, if it wasn't his fault."

"You think it was *my* fault? You think *I'm* the one who should be
punished?"

And so the day had gone.

Every afternoon now, Job was waiting, beneath the big shade tree, though
the tree had by now lost most of its leaves. It was early November. Most of the
plants in the Phelps' yard had been frost killed, except for the few that were
evergreens, and one large pink-blooming camellia.

Maggie looked over at Mr. Evans. He was clean-shaven. He was in heavy,
black twilled cotton pants and a blue muslin shirt. He had a sort of colorful red
bandana about his neck. His black, broad brimmed felt hat cocked over one
eye. He didn't dress like any of the men Maggie knew. He seemed to have a
different hat for every day of the week. She wondered where he had acquired
this particular style of attire.

He looked over and smiled at her. She simply could not get rid of him!

This afternoon, his mother had sent over a chicken, already killed, gutted
and plucked and singed, and dressed for the pan.

The following day, there came a sack of yams. The next day, he brought
a mess of fresh turnips with tops and following that, a pie. There seemed to
be no end to Ida Evans' generosity—

—And when a man brought over such nice gifts, one could not in all
common decency, Callie insisted, fail to show Christian hospitality, by not
asking him to supper.

Sunday morning, they all went to church, in the shiny black surrey, pulled
by the high-stepping team of blacks.

Monday morning, Maggie went to the store for Mrs. Phelps, and caught a
glimpse of Mr. Evans, riding about the square on a beautifully prancing

golden horse with white mane and tail. Maggie had never seen such a horse, even on the Stillwell farm! Maggie ducked into the shadow of the hotel, and watched—the way Mr. Evans sat him, the way he handled him—as if horse and rider were one. Maggie had never seen a man ride like that.

This horse was evidently not a working horse. It was not a farm horse. Maggie had never known of such a luxury, not in Rhyersville, a horse that was kept for any other purpose—than to help earn a living for his owner.

Maggie became accustomed to Job's being in front of the Phelps' house, every afternoon. She became accustomed to being lifted into the wagon, and then the quiet ride home, to a man sitting down with them at the supper table—laughing, talking, so darkly handsome, so charming, holding the baby and nuzzling him close. It was almost as if—

But, *no*, this is *not* Papa! She knows next to *nothing* about this man. He never tells her *anything* about himself.

She must not allow this to go on, must not allow him to become too fond of her. She will have to tell him, and soon.

Sunday, he is there in the yard, with the lovely surrey.

But Mama says the day is cold, and she doesn't want to take Johnny out. Barbara Jo has one of her headaches. She absolutely refuses to get up, get dressed, and go to church.

Len Evans says good morning to Callie, then, "Ma has packed us a picnic lunch, if that's all right with you, Mrs. McKinnon? We might be a little late coming back from church. I'll take good care of her."

From the calm, accepting look on her mother's face, Maggie has the sudden, sinking feeling that this has all been arranged. They have all conspired against her, behind her back.

As soon as Maggie was seated in the surrey, she saw the huge basket, covered by a snow-white cloth, setting atop *two* colorful cushions.

Maggie heard not a word of the hymns, or the sermon. Her mind was too occupied with what she would say to Mr. Evans. She would have to do it today. It was clear now, that Mr. Evans felt he was more than a friend. It was clear that he wished to be more than a man bearing gifts from his mother.

Len watched Maggie, the way she took in the picnic basket, the two cushions. She didn't seem that pleased. She was frowning.

During the service, he sensed her unease. Like a trapped cat, she kept looking this way and that for a way of escape.

But she *had* to like him! He couldn't bear it if she didn't! But, she *did* like him! He could tell! What was the *matter* with her?

Len fervently wished that he had set aside some of the money he'd earned during his five-year stint on the road. But there had been the women, the gambling, the whisky, the fine clothes and horses. And there'd been no reason to save.

But all that was behind him. Anyhow, there'd be no problem …getting the money. There'd be no problem in setting up housekeeping …with Pa's help …on any of Pa's farms—

—Get a milk cow and some laying hens, some farm tools. I'll work my fingers to the bone. I'll do *anything*, to make her happy. I'll ask her today …at the picnic.

Thankfully the service was over. Maggie could not wait to escape the confines of the small church. The man sitting so close beside her, touching her hand, now and then, in such an intimate fashion, it unnerved Maggie. She felt frightened and confused.

Len was anxious for the service to end. He said quick good-byes to the people crowding around them. He was anxious to have Maggie alone. He had to talk to her. To discover what was bothering her.

She scooted as far from him as she possibly could, when he lifted her into the surrey. Len felt his heart dropping. He recalled vividly what he had said to his mother.

"Len," Ida had said to him, "She's a lovely girl. Charming. But, Son, she's so *young*. She's scarcely more than a child."

"I love Maggie, Ma. I can't imagine living the remainder of my life without her. If I don't have Maggie, I'll just *lay myself down and die*."

This dire prediction ringing in his mind, Len drove without speaking, pushing down the awful, empty feeling, planning what he would say to her, anything to allay her fears.

He drew the surrey to a halt, in a sunny spot. Maggie could hear water rushing over rocks. He lifted her down. Then he fetched the huge basket and the two cushions.

Maggie stalked about the creek bank, gazing into the frothing water, dashing over the smooth, stony slope of the shoals. Her head felt light. Maybe she was just hungry. Her palms felt sweaty. She kept wiping them nervously on the tail of her dress.

"Maggie?" she heard him calling her.

She turned. He had the tablecloth spread on the grassy bank. It was laden with fried chicken, potato salad, boiled vegetables, and apple pie.

Maggie felt as if she were about to be sick. How could she eat any of this?

"Come here, Maggie. Sit down," he was saying.

She walked toward him. He took her hand, seated her on the green cushion.

The tail of her blue dress spread demurely out to cover every inch of her ankles, Maggie looked at the spread of food. And suddenly, she was very hungry. She wouldn't worry about telling Mr. Evans she couldn't see him again. Not until after they had eaten. Maggie looked up, and smiled at him.

Len's heart did a flip-flop.

He gave a soft, pleased laugh. Then he began a low, meaningless conversation about the creek and its history. The Indians, it seemed, had once had a village on this very spot.

Maggie listened, recalling how she and Papa had sat on the riverbank that day. She nodded her head, and made short replies, in all the right places.

Then she realized what was happening. She was forgetting what she must do. She must tell him she could not see him any more. She did like him, but she could *not* see him. *Nothing* could ever come of this. She must tell him, before she liked him too much—

Suddenly Maggie stood up.

Slowly, Len rose. He did not like the look on her face.

"Mr. Evans, I ...need to tell you ..."

"Yes, Maggie?" Len's heart stopped beating.

"Oh, I'll tell you later." You're a sniveling *coward*, Margaret Ann McKinnon!

Maggie flounced away, to sit on the creek bank, staring into the water. *Why* must life be so complicated? This man, she knew, was becoming too attracted to her. He might even ask her to marry him. She liked him, but she was *not* ready for anything so permanent or so binding. There was Mama, and Johnny, and Barbara Jo. And she was only sixteen. She knew nothing about men. She had a lifetime ahead of her.

He came and sat down near her. He was picking up small stones, and skimming them across the water.

"Maggie? May I speak with you very frankly?"

"What? Oh, of course," Maggie replied absently.

"Maggie, I think you're aware that I love you. I want you to marry me."

Maggie leapt up. *"No!"* she cried. Her vision blurring, she dashed toward the surrey.

"Maggie!" He caught her, turning her to face him.

"Maggie, I know you haven't known me very long, but I *do* love you. You'll never know how much I love you! I care for you more than my own life! I'll be *good* to you. *Marry, me, Maggie!*" The handsome face was so earnest. The dark eyes filled with passionate pleading.

Maggie pulled away. She went to stand on the creek bank, watching the water, so fast, so free.

He came up behind her, "You do like me, don't you Maggie? I know you do. I can see it in your eyes." His voice was low, choked with emotion.

"No!" Maggie whirled about, screaming at him suddenly, "You don't know *anything* about me. You don't know *anything* about the way I feel! *I don't like you! I don't like you at all!!* Now please take me home!"

Angrily Len took her by the shoulders, forcing her to look at him.

"You're lying! And you know it!"

"Please, Mr. Evans, please just take me home," Maggie could feel the tears, hot, just behind her eyes, waiting to fall. But she determined not to cry, not here—not now.

"My name is not Mr. Evans. My name is Len. And no, I'm not taking you home. Not until you tell me the truth."

"What's the *matter* with you?" Maggie shouted up at him. "Can't you accept a simple reply? All right, I *do* like you!"

Len wanted to reach for her. He wanted to hold her, but—not yet.

"So, then, let's have the truth here. No more lies! No more maundering around!"

"I like you, Mr. Evans. But I have a Mama, a baby brother, and a sister! And they're *all* depending on me. On *me*, Mr. Evans, for clothes on their backs, food in their mouths, a roof over their heads! *I'm* the one who pays the rent and buys the necessities. Mama's got more than she can handle, with Johnny only a few weeks old. And Barbara Jo ...well, Barbara Jo is Barbara Jo."

"Do you like me enough to marry me, Maggie? I don't ask that you love me. Not the way I love you. But do you like me enough to marry me? I'll take care of you, *and* your family. I'll see to it that none of you ever wants for anything!"

"Mr. Evans! I couldn't expect you to do that—"

Len wanted to shake her. "Don't you understand, Maggie? I *love* you more than anything. I'd give my *life* for you! I'd do *anything* you want, just to make you happy!"

Then he was reaching for her, holding her close, "Maggie! I can't *live* without you! Say, *yes,* Maggie! Say, *yes!*"

"Yes," Maggie heard herself saying, scarcely more than a whisper.

Len picked her up and carried her to the wagon. She had said *yes!*

They started the drive back home. Maggie looked over at him. He looked so handsome, so at ease. "You're sure, Mr. Evans, Len ...about taking care of the family?"

Len could hear the doubt, very evident in her voice.

Len reached over and took her hand, squeezing it tightly, "Yes, I'm sure. I'm *very* sure, Maggie. I'll take good care of them." Right at that moment, Len would have promised her the sun and the stars, tied up in a neat little bundle, had she but asked.

Callie was overjoyed at the news. She knew how much Maggie had lost. How much they had all lost. And though Maggie never complained, Callie knew she hated working for the Phelps. Since losing her Papa, Maggie had been so unhappy, it broke Callie's heart.

Now, Maggie would have someone. And it was very evident, had been since that first day, that *this* was a man of considerable property. But more importantly, Len Evans was a church-going man of good family—a man who worshiped Margaret Ann McKinnon.

Maggie lay in bed that night, her mind in a whirl. She had begun the day, Sunday, determined to end their relationship. Now, she suddenly found herself *engaged*! *How had this happened?*

She had promised Papa, she had promised herself, that she would take care of the family. She mustn't let them down!

But she hated her job. She could not imagine growing old, arguing with Mrs. Phelps.

But, *marriage*! It had such a final ring to it. She was *sixteen*! What did she feel for Mr. Evans? Was it what they called *love*?

She was so relieved—that no date had been set for a wedding. She needed time to think.

What should she do? If she married Mr. Evans, she could escape the Phelps. But it would be *sinful*, to marry Mr. Evans, just to get out of doing a job she despised.

How did she *feel* about Mr. Evans?

She was right back where she had begun.

Maggie got up, pulled on her heavy shawl, and walked out onto the front porch. A full moon cast thin white light over the rutted dirt street out front. How she would *love* to leave this little house behind her! They could all be together, maybe in a big house, like Ida Evans had, shaded by giant trees. She could see Mama and Johnny, all day, every day. Be free, to help Mama with the baby, the housework and laundry. Mama looked so tired. But that was not reason enough to marry Mr. Evans. She couldn't marry him—she wouldn't marry him—even for her family.

What if he didn't like having the family in the house with them?

What if he grew tired of the burden of them? They weren't *his* family. He barely knew them.

The wagon was there, beneath the now bare tree, waiting for her.

He lifted her in. She was very quiet.

Maggie knew she must keep her wits about her. She must not let things get out of hand, the way they had on the creek bank.

She couldn't marry him—not now. Not any time soon.

Len spoke softly to her, "Maggie? Somethin' wrong?"

She didn't answer.

"Hard day?" She remained silent.

He turned Job into the little yard of the square, ugly house, lifted Maggie down. She was cold, unresponsive. She behaved as if he was a complete stranger.

They walked inside. Len Evans presented a fine ham. Callie accepted it graciously, "Tell your Ma we're much obliged for the ham, Len. Now if you two will go wash up—"

Len watched her carefully, all though supper. She was too quiet, avoiding his eyes, avoiding his touch when passing the food. Len felt anger, hot and suffocating, beginning to rise. He reminded himself what was at stake. Stay cool, try to find out what was bothering her. Maybe she had a hard day at work. She'd soon be done with that place, thank goodness. She'd soon be cooking for no one but *Len Evans*.

Len could scarcely wait for the table to be cleared. He took Maggie's arm, guided her firmly toward the front door, telling her mother, "We're going for a drive."

He drove toward the river. He lifted her down. They walked out onto the bridge. She said nothing, just stood at the iron railing, staring thoughtfully into the waters flowing far below.

"All right, Maggie, what is it?" The words came slow and measured. "What's wrong?" *If it's another man,* Len thought, anger choking him, *this time, he won't escape! I'll kill the fool*!

"I don't know," Maggie muttered, "I just don't know, Mr. Evans."

"Maggie, will you please stop calling me *Mr. Evans*!" Len insisted, attempting to keep the anger from his voice, "You're about to become *my wife*!"

"I ...don't ...think so, Mr. Evans," Maggie said, in a cold, deliberate voice—

"—I've been giving this some thought. And I just don't think marrying you, at this time, would be the right thing for me to do. I was wrong, to give you an answer so soon. I hardly know you. It would be a mistake—"

She broke off, stunned by the look on his face.

He was staring at her, his face set as stone. His eyes had narrowed to tiny slits. His nostrils flared.

When he spoke, the words were so low, so filled with rage, Maggie could not make out what he had just said.

"What?" she asked.

"You heard me!" he rasped, anger making his voice sound strange, as if it were coming from far away, from some other person, *"There's another man, isn't there? Who is he!?"*

"No! There's no one! It's just that—"

"Then why?" he hissed at her. *"Why?"*

His face dark with fury, suddenly he seized her by the arms, giving her a shake, accusing, *"You're lying to me again! Now who is he?"*

Who was this man? Always, he'd been so kind, so gentle. Now, his hands held her in a vice-like grip.

Maggie felt frightened.

"Let go of me!" she lashed out at him, angrily pulling away. "I'm *not* lying! How *dare* you accuse me for no reason? I'm not *married* to you, *yet*, Mr. Evans. *Nor* do I think I *wish* to be!"

Suddenly Len changed, became very contrite, pleading softly, "Maggie! Forgive me! It's just, that, I *love* you so much. I can't *bear* the thought of losing you. Of course, I understand. You just need more time—I'll make it up to you!"

Then he was drawing her close, and Maggie let him kiss her, for the first time. He was very tender, holding her face between his hands, gazing at her as if she was the answer to all his dreams.

And at that moment, standing on the iron-girded river bridge, the twilight deepening around them, Maggie was very happy—and very much in love with Len Evans.

Len drove her home. And for him, everything was settled. He should have expected this. She was young. She was very much a lady. She had no experience with men. Maybe he should have waited a bit longer, to ask her to marry him. But, no, he couldn't take that chance. She was too beautiful, too tempting to any man who rode into town. He couldn't wait. He couldn't take such a dangerous chance.

He would not lose her—to anyone—or anything. Not ever!

Maggie glanced over at that handsome face that appeared so calm and placid now. What *was* it she had seen, there, for just an instant, on the bridge? Or had she imagined it? Was there something in him, something dark and brooding? Just beneath the smooth surface of that handsome face ...

Maggie couldn't be sure, what she had seen—or whether she had seen anything at all. Perhaps she was being overly dramatic. She'd never been in love before—

In love! She was in love!

But, then, if there were ...problems ...

"Mr. Evans ...Len, may I ask you something?"

"Of course, what is it?"

"Promise you won't get mad with me?" *Why did she say that?*

"I could *never* be mad with you, Maggie," was the soft, reassuring reply.

"Then, let's not see each other, for a few days." Such a stunned looked crossed his face, that she hurried on, "Not for five days ...until Sunday. There are some things I need to do. I need some time."

Len felt as if she had hit him. Not see her *for five full days?* How could he? He had hoped they might be married Sunday. Everything was ready. The house, he had all the furnishings. All meant as a surprise for her. Now, here she sat beside him, saying she didn't want to see him—for five full days!

She was looking at him, waiting for an answer, expecting an answer. He must stay calm. Len waited for the crushing pain in his chest to subside. He drew in a deep breath.

"All right, Maggie," he looked at her, and lied, very convincingly, "if that's what you want. I'll see you then, Sunday, for church."

Back at the house, he lifted her down. He didn't trust himself to attempt to hold or kiss her, just a light peck on the forehead. Then he drove away.

The next afternoon, Maggie half expected Job to be there, beneath the bare branches of the big oak. But, no, he wasn't there. What was it she felt? Relief?

But, if she loved Len, shouldn't she *want* to see him?

She thought she heard something, turned, but there was no one there. Maggie hurried towards home. She needed to talk to Mama. She needed to speak with Barbara Jo. But first, she needed to stop by the store, to pick up a box of matches.

When Maggie entered Moss' General Mercantile, she couldn't have been more surprised. There was Barbara Jo! Perched on a stool, at the end of one of the long wooden counters, speaking animatedly with *Mr. Fredrick J. Moss*!

Barbara Jo was leaning over, almost in his face. Fred Moss was leaning forward, his eyes locked with hers. Their voices were low. Suddenly Fred Moss gave a soft, snorting laugh. He reached out—and touched Barbara Jo's hand.

Maggie felt blood rising hot in her cheeks. How dared he! How dared he touch her sister, in such an intimate fashion! He must be almost *twice* Barbara Jo's age!

Maggie felt a twinge of guilt. She was spying on them. She must make her presence known. Maggie cleared her throat loudly.

"Oh, good day, Miss McKinnon," Fred Moss straightened suddenly, took a step backward, color rising up his neck, past his expensive double-breasted vest, and tie, into his thinning hairline.

"Mr. Moss," Maggie replied, her voice cold with rage. Maggie could see that Barbara Jo had a piece of yard goods spread out from the bolt before her, a very expensive piece of yard goods. Nothing that she could afford, not now or in a million years—

—A piece of light green silk taffeta, lovely and shimmering. Even in the dim light of the store dancing across it, it was beautiful beyond belief. Barbara Jo gave the barest glance around at Maggie. Then she picked up the lovely piece of taffeta, raising it to her cheek.

Maggie thought, for the first time, that Barbara Jo looked very pretty; the taffeta flattered her light skin, gave her eyes a green tint. Her cheeks were flushed a rosy hue.

"Planning to make a purchase?" Maggie fought to suppress her anger, to keep her voice low, controlled.

"It doesn't hurt to look," Barbara Jo lifted her chin defiantly, her blue-green eyes challenging Maggie.

"No," Maggie replied shortly. "It doesn't hurt to look, just as long as you recall the nature and manner of your circumstances."

"What do you mean by that?" Barbara Jo demanded. She straightened, her color deepening. "You think *I* can never have *anything really nice, of my own*? You think that *I* can *never afford anything really nice of my own*?"

"I meant nothing of the sort, Barbara Jo," Maggie replied, "and you very well know it. I meant that now, at this moment, given our present situation, such a piece of rich yard goods seems sadly beyond our reach."

"Perhaps, Maggie," Barbara Jo gave a toss of her light brown hair, "it may be out of *your* reach, but mayhap, in the not-too-distant future, not that far out of *mine*."

"Excuse *us*!" Maggie grabbed Barbara Jo by the arm, and steered her firmly out of the store. At the door, she turned on Fred Moss, who stood staring after them, "We may or may not, be back to your fine establishment!" With that departing barb, Maggie dragged Barbara Jo down the front steps.

Once out of hearing, she turned on her sister, "And just, *what*, was that supposed to mean? Have you suddenly come into some *riches*, of which I am *totally unaware*? I hope you haven't run up a bill for goods—at this store!"

"Maggie! What's wrong with you? Where are your manners? You embarrassed me to death, just now! Back there!"

"You're embarrassed about what I said in front of *Fred Moss*? That we are not floating in money? What is he to you? He's old—"

"He is not—"

"He is not *what*, Barbara Jo?"

"He is not …old enough to be my father! Isn't that what you were going to say?" Tears filled Barbara Jo's light-blue eyes.

"No, it isn't. But, *you* said it, didn't you? Because *that's* what you were thinking. What *I* was about to say, is that he's old enough to have been married many years ago, and why isn't he? Why, now, would he suddenly be taking an interest in some young girl without a cent to her name, that has just shown up in his store?"

"Why *would* he, Maggie?" Barbara Jo demanded, her blue eyes narrowed, "Such a girl is *not very pretty*, is she? And she's *not* at all what would be called a *witty* person, is she? And *heads* don't turn, when she enters a store, or the church, or simply *walks down the street*. She's not very *good* at anything. In fact, she's *good at nothing*! Even her own Pa never cared a *rotten fig* for her! Never knew *she was alive*. He only had eyes for—"

"Don't you *dare* bring Papa into this, Barbara Jo. This has *nothing* to do with Papa! And *no one* ever thought those *horrid* things about you. How'd you ever *get* such nonsense into your head? You're quite …pretty. And good at …lots of things."

"Like what? Go on, tell me Maggie, what are all these *things* I'm so good at? How many times have you, or anyone else for that matter, told me how *very pretty* I am? Fred Moss *likes* me. He *looks* at me, and *he* thinks I'm *pretty!* He *likes* talking to me. I …I think he's going to ask me to marry him!"

"Oh, Barbs! Do you *love* that man?"

"No. But, I'm eighteen years old! How many men do you see, lining up to ask for my hand? He has a fine store. He has lots of money. He has handsome living quarters over the store."

"*Living quarters?* " Maggie squawked. "You've seen *his handsome living quarters?* "

"You have your man—"

"You didn't' answer me! And I do *not* have a man. I don't *know* whether or not I'll marry Mr. Evans."

"Oh, you'll marry him, all right." Barbara Jo eyed Maggie, while vigorously nodding her head up and down. "*He'll* see to that."

"Barbara Jo! What a thing to say! You think I have *no* decision in this?"

"You don't, Maggie. Mr. Len Evans has made up his mind—for both of you."

Maggie stood, speechless, hurt and stunned.

Barbara Jo flounced off down the street, well satisfied

For once in her life, she had gotten in the last word with Margaret Ann McKinnon.

No, she didn't love Fred Moss. So what? She wanted some life other than the one she had been leading for the past few months. She couldn't envision herself taking a job as a *serving maid*. Even less, could she envision herself living off Maggie's meager earnings for the remainder of her years.

So that left Mr. Frederick J. Moss. So he was a bit stingy. A big tightwad.

She had heard the whispers behind his back, how he scraped the manure from his store yard, and carried it each night to the garden back of his store. Maybe he just wanted his store yard to be clean! He had some annoying habits—that snorting, horse-like, laugh. And he was always running one hand through his thinning hair …not only drawing undue attention to his approaching baldness, but, no doubt, hastening the thinning, by his constant rubbing.

But he was a decent man, a deacon of the church. And he was comfortably well off. If she married Fred Moss, she'd never have to worry about work, or money, the remainder of her life.

Maggie strode along a few steps back, making no effort to catch and confront Barbara Jo. She couldn't *believe* her sister—openly flirting with that awful storekeeper! Maggie found him terribly unattractive, even repulsive, with his thin face and horse-like snort. She wondered how long this had been going on. She'd have to talk to Mama about it. They couldn't, they just *couldn't* let Barbara Jo marry some older man, just to get herself into a better situation.

Maggie's anger flared again. Why *hadn't* Fred Moss married all these years? He was *over thirty*, if he was a day. Surely Barbara Jo wasn't the only girl to notice that he was rich.

Mama had nothing to offer, when Maggie repeated the story about Barbara Jo, leaving out the part about the two being engaged in intimate conversation, their faces only inches apart. About Barbara Jo openly flirting with the man. More than hinting at receiving dress goods for which she could not possibly pay. Saying, *no, she did not love him!* Going on about *his handsome living quarters*!

Mama would be mortified!

"Maggie, I gave my blessing, when Mr. Evans asked for your hand in marriage. I want you to be happy. That's all I want for you. And I want the same for Barbara Jo. I won't always be with you. You'll both need someone …someone to cling to, when the nights are long and dark and cold. When life seems impossibly hard. When things don't go right. When—"

"Mama! Don't talk like that!" Maggie cut her mother short. "You're—"

"I'm not saying I'm likely to pass away tomorrow, Maggie. What I'm saying is that you girls are grown. And it's time you lived your own lives. What I had with your Papa—" Callie's voice broke, "I want that for you and Barbara Jo. Do you see what I'm getting at, Maggie?"

"Yes, Mama, but—"

"Barbara Jo will have to make up her own mind, about Mr. Moss. She could do a lot worse. He's neither a thief nor a drunkard—that I've heard. He has a good reputation in the community. Good upstanding member of the local church."

"Is that any reason to marry a man, Mama? Just because he's not a *thief* nor a *drunkard?* "

"Mr. Moss isn't perfect. None of us is perfect, Maggie. Your Pa and me, we had our differences. You know that. But we always worked them out, because we loved one another. It's love, Maggie, that you should seek. It's love that cushions us against all the cold, harsh realities of life. If you have someone *who really loves you*, together, you can overcome almost anything."

"What about Mr. Evans …and me, Mama? I don't think he's perfect. I don't know whether or not I should marry him. One moment, I think I should. The next moment—"

"I can't answer that for you, Maggie. No one can answer that. It's a decision you will have to make for yourself. Marriage is a *very serious* commitment. You're pledging everything, everything you are—to this *one* person—for the entire remainder of your life. The question is, do you love this man? Do you love Mr. Len Evans, Maggie?"

"I *think* I do, Mama. At least *part* of the time, I think I do."

"Maggie!" Callie couldn't restrain a surprised little laugh. Then she said in a serious tone. "I'd like to see you married, and settled, with a good strong husband that loves and can provide for you, a home of your own, and children. But, be very sure you know what *you* want, before you say *I do*. Don't marry to please *anyone*, but *yourself.* "

Children! Mama had said, *children!*

Maggie kissed her mother goodnight, and went to bed.

Len had followed her, as he did every day now, keeping well back, as she walked home from the Phelps' house. She stepped up onto the low porch, reached for the front door latch. A rich buggy came rolling down the street, and turned in at the little McKinnon house.

It was that storekeeper! *Fred Moss! What was he doing here*!

Maggie barely spoke to Fred Moss, but she did hold the door open. And she invited him in.

His rage mounting, Len waited, for several minutes, until he was on the verge of thundering over, bursting down the door, dragging Fred Moss out, and beating the living daylights out of him.

Then, the front door opened. Fred Moss stepped out, his fine hat in his hand. He put on his hat, reached towards the door. A slender white hand appeared, and behind it, Maggie's sister emerged. Barbara Jo, wasn't that her name?

Len heaved a sigh of relief. He felt the anger draining away. Still he felt frightened, and empty, almost sick from the old feelings that came crowding back at him.

Maggie snuggled down beneath the covers. She had helped Mama with the dishes, bathed Johnny, started a fire and boiled out his diapers in chips of homemade lye soap, in the black iron washpot, rinsed and hung them on the line. Mama had not regained her strength. It worried Maggie. It also worried her—how Barbara Jo had gone out riding with that storekeeper.

Finally, her lamp was put out. Len Evans stepped lightly into the Texas-style saddle, wheeled Golden Boy out from behind the house where he had been hiding. Feeling anxious, restless and unsettled, he decided to ride down the river road, get out into the open air. Yes, to cool his temper, he'd take the palomino for a good run in the country. Then he'd come back by Pa's—

—That would at least kill the remainder of the evening. Then he'd ride back to the house he was getting ready for his wife. And wait.

The day had suddenly turned cold and windy. Late in the afternoon, a slow rain began to fall, becoming heavier as the afternoon progressed. Maggie had not expected this. She had not brought a slicker, or even a heavy coat. The past few days, the weather had been warm for November.

She heard the key in the lock. Reaching for her shawl, bonnet and gloves, she spoke briefly to Mr. Phelps. He seemed to be a good man. He was as patient with his wife as if she was a baby. He paid Maggie regularly, with no questions asked. He seemed well pleased with her services.

He should be, Maggie thought wryly. She stood on the wide veranda, dismally looking out through the rain. She'd be soaked to the bone, by the time she got home! She might wait for a few moments, see if it slacked up. But, it could rain for hours. It was coming down in cold, drifting sheets.

Nothing for it, but to make her way home the best way she could. Tying her bonnet securely beneath her chin, clutching her shawl close about her shoulders, she stepped onto the graveled walk.

Before she reached the street, Maggie was soaked and shivering. If she didn't move faster, she'd be frozen stiff by the time she reached home. She felt frozen drops of sleet stinging her face.

At the corner, Maggie paused, looking this way and that, for any buggy or wagon traffic. Then she saw it—the fine buggy. It was parked at the end of the street. Then it was coming towards her, the black stallion in a high-stepping gallop.

The buggy drew near, and Maggie felt herself being lifted into the snug, dry warmth beneath its cover.

She was wet and shivering. He threw a heavy blanket about her, and drew her into his arms, holding her close. Suddenly, Maggie felt very safe. Very secure.

The wedding was the following Sunday. Maggie's extraordinary beauty was heightened by the gorgeous wedding dress Len had bought for her— white organza over silk.

Len Evans was completely bewitched. Like a man in a trance, he spoke his wedding vows with gentle sincerity, meaning every word, as he spoke them. It would be different, this time, Len was certain—

—Everything would be *very* different, this time.

Maggie had never been happier. He was handsome. He was strong. He loved her more than his own life, he kept assuring her. He would do *anything* to make her happy.

And Maggie believed every word.

Chapter 21

They left the little church, and Len drove toward town—then through town. Then he turned back east, and drove several more miles.

"Len," Maggie heard herself asking her new husband, "is it this far out? Our place?"

"It's not that far. Just seems like it. Be there in a minute."

Finally, they drove into the yard.

The house was tiny. Smaller even than the little ugly rented house on East River Street.

They couldn't all live here! Not in this tiny place! Whatever was Len thinking! Maggie looked at him, as he came around to lift her down from the buggy he had driven to their wedding. Len had made arrangements for Mama, Johnny, and Barbara Jo to be driven to the church by a neighbor.

Maggie thought that since it was their wedding day that was all well and good. But this house—

He carried her inside. Maggie's eyes adjusted to the dim light. There were few windows. It was a veritable shack. She could see cracks through the back door, where the sun was shining through.

Len put her down. Maggie stood there. Stunned. She felt out of place. Lost. She felt like bolting for the door.

But ...she was *married*. This was her *husband*, standing here beside her, waiting for her to say something. She took a few steps forward. She could see there were three rooms ...no, only two, really, as the third was not that large, and had evidently been hastily added on. It was more of a storeroom, she could see, peering in at a conglomeration of cardboard boxes and wrapping papers strewn about the floor.

"I'll clean that up, tomorrow," Maggie heard Len saying. He seemed ill at ease, embarrassed about the mess in the storeroom

Maggie looked about the front room. It would serve, she could see, as both kitchen and front room. She stepped into the part that would be the kitchen. It was a tiny space, with a small table, barely large enough to accommodate two people. She immediately understood that there would be no family dinners hosted here.

A full-sized iron cookstove. Brand new, from the look of it. No, he had built a few fires in it. A small iron skillet sat on one of the eyes. He had evidently fixed himself some breakfast. Then there was the bedroom, barely big enough to accommodate a full-sized bed.

Holding back the tears, Maggie turned to look at him, waiting for him to speak.

But he was watching her, she could tell, carefully gauging her reaction to his efforts.

Maggie flashed Len a brilliant smile. "Well," she put on a cheerful air, "this will do very …nicely, in fact. Some pretty curtains, perhaps, for the windows, and a warm cotton rug to go on the floor in front of the fireplace. A colorful tufted counterpane for the bed—"

"You don't like it," he said bluntly, his voice low, his eyes dark and accusing.

"No," Maggie hastened to say, "I mean, yes …it's fine …it's just …that …every woman wants to put her own touch onto her home …to feel …that …it's …really hers. And I was just wondering …if it's large enough for …all of us?"

"Maggie," Len gave her a puzzled frown, "there's only you and me."

"But—" Maggie began.

Then, it dawned on her.

Len didn't expect them all to live here. He was going to leave Mama and Barbara Jo and the baby, right where they were, eight or ten miles away, on the other side of the county, in that little ugly house on East River Street. It wasn't *even within walking distance.*

Maggie felt a chill creep up her spine.

Why? Why would Len choose a place like this? When did he buy this place? He must have been living, up until now, with his mother and father. Surely, he hadn't actually paid money for this place. Surely not, or he would have gotten something …larger …sturdier. She couldn't imagine what they were doing here. Surely price wasn't an issue; Len always had money.

Then Maggie had a troubling thought. But, did *Len* have money?

In a confused rush, all these thoughts tumbled into Maggie's mind. Why didn't she think to *check* out any of this, before she married him? She had assumed, by the way Len dressed, the fine suits …the carriages …the fine blacks that pulled them, the golden yellow horse and finely tooled leather saddle …the shiny black boots. Maggie walked to the back door.

There stood a barn, clapboard, weathered to a dull gray, so dilapidated it looked as if a stiff wind could topple it over. Not the sort of barn a man built to shelter a *rich black surrey*, a *fine buggy*, and a *grand team of black stallions*. Maybe the golden palomino would fit into one of the tiny, run-down stables—

"Well," she turned and smiled at him, her mind in a confused jumble, "I suppose I should change, and fix us some supper."

"I'll bring in your bags," Len said shortly. He turned, and walked out.

When the initial shock and disappointment had passed, Maggie was almost ashamed of herself. She had not married Len Evans in order to live in a big house, but she did expect one large enough to accommodate Len and herself, and her family. She did expect one where the wind wouldn't come whistling through cracks in the back door. No, this was not what she had imagined.

But even at the age of sixteen, Maggie had learned that life often handed you things you did *not* expect. And when it did, you took whatever came, and made the best of it that you possibly could.

Maggie felt sure they would work out better living arrangements—once she had a chance to really talk to Len.

Len was the perfect husband. He was gentle, kind, thoughtful, and considerate. He helped her fix their first supper. Then he helped her fix their breakfast the next morning. But sometimes, when he looked at her, it almost frightened Maggie, there was such intense emotion, such passion in his eyes—she felt as if she was spiraling down into a deep well—with no bottom.

But Maggie was back on a farm. *A farm!* There was a cow out in the little barnyard. There were chickens clucking about her feet, wanting to be fed. They were *her* cow, and *her* chickens. That should be worth something. She would speak to Len, later, about their housing arrangement, about getting something larger, so Mama and Johnny and Barbara Jo could live with them. Or at least mention moving close enough that Maggie could walk over and help Mama look after the baby. Honestly! You'd think Len Evans didn't have a brain in his head—sticking her way out at the end of nowhere like this.

Maggie wondered where the little rutted trail led to, that ran past the house. She asked Len about it that night, and he said, "Nowhere much. It dead-ends, down at the river. There's nothing at all down there. You don't want to go walking around here, Maggie. Exploring ...or anything. There have been panthers spotted on the riverbanks. Sometimes, black bears wander down from the mountains. It's not safe, for a woman alone to be walking the roads. And it's just not seemly."

"Seemly?" Maggie smiled at him, "Surely, you're jesting?"

"No," Len said, anger lacing his voice, "Maggie, I meant exactly what I said. I won't have you walking the roads."

Maggie had always felt free to go walking wherever she pleased. She had walked to school, all those years. She had walked to church. She had walked to the store, when the occasion called for it. All farm folk—all country folk—walked the roads, especially the women and the children. How else were they to get about, when the man of the house had the horse in the field plowing, or when the horse was tired out from the plowing, and needed to rest?

But—no, he was in no mood to jest, and from that dark look in his eyes, Len did not appreciate her questioning his choice of words.

Staring into his eyes, it became evident to Maggie—what Len was saying to her: I don't want *you* walking the roads.

This meant that Maggie would be virtually confined to the place, unless Len accompanied her.

She tried to push this thought away. She stayed busy. There were lots of things to do, even on such a small place.

But after the first week or so, almost every afternoon, Len would come in from the fields, saddle up the horse he called *Golden Boy*, and ride off—over to his Pa's, he said.

And he would leave Maggie behind. She had not even *seen* Ida Evans, since the wedding. She had not seen Mama, or Johnny. She had not heard a word from Barbara Jo.

She wondered just how far it was to the Evans' place? Why didn't Len ever invite her along? He was quick enough to take her before they married!

"How far is it, over to your Pa's place?" Maggie asked Len at supper that night.

"Why do you want to know?"

"Do you realize, Len, that I haven't been off this place, since the Sunday of the wedding?"

"This is a working farm, Maggie," he explained to her, as if speaking to a small child, "Pa expects this place to produce, just like any of his other tenant farms. I have to make this place pay, in order to provide us a living."

"So, this is …your *Pa's* place? Did you ever think of getting your own place?"

"Why on earth should I? Pa's got more farms and more land that I could ever hope to acquire. And I'm welcome to work his land as long as I want."

"I was reared on a working farm, Len," Maggie felt anger at his lack of concern for her feelings, "but we found time for other things. We found time to go to church, and to town. We don't even go to *church*, anymore. I'd enjoy walking over, and visiting a spell with your Ma. I could—"

"No! Don't you *ever* go over to Ma's by yourself, do you hear me? Don't you even *think* of doing that!"

"Why ever not?"

"Don't ask foolish questions, Maggie. You want to visit Ma, I'll take you over. Sometimes, you act just like a child! I'm your husband. You will do as I say! I've already warned you, it's not safe."

"Warned me?" Maggie heard her voice rising, "How many panther and bear attacks have there been lately?"

Len rose from the table, his face black as midnight. He towered over her, so close she could see the blood pulsing through his temples.

"Are you calling me a *liar*?" He knocked his chair against the table, strode out, slamming the plank door so hard the shingles on the roof rattled.

Maggie felt shaken to the core. She could hear him, out in the barn, flinging things against the walls. Then the golden palomino came thundering out the open barn door.

Maggie was fast asleep when he came in. Or so Len thought. He slipped into his side of the bed, careful not to wake her.

Maggie lay wide awake, her heart pounding so hard she was sure he could hear it. What had become of the man she *thought* she married? What had she gotten herself into?

The next morning, when she awoke, he was already gone. Maggie dragged herself out of bed. She walked over to the stove. The fire was still hot. Coffee, eggs and biscuit, all waited on the back of the stove.

Len had made breakfast for her!

Suddenly Maggie felt guilty, about—she didn't exactly know of what. But surely some of this must be her fault. There must be something she wasn't *doing*, to make this marriage work. If only she could talk to Mama—

She mustn't brood on that. She needed to get bathed, dressed, get out of the little house, and get to work. She milked the cow. Fed the chickens. Looked about for some seeds. She could plant a winter garden. Maybe after lunch, she'd kill and dress a frying chicken. Len, she knew, loved fried chicken, biscuit and gravy. Some fine mashed potatoes. Maybe she could scare up some apples and make a pie? Was there any sugar on the place? She needed to go to the store.

Len came in for a quick lunch. Maggie was smiling. She seemed happy, for the first time since he had brought her here. Len came up to her, took her in his arms. She laid her head on his shoulder, felt the strength of him, smelled the fresh earth on him, the good clean sweat. Just the way Papa had smelled when he came in from the fields. Len always looked nice, even when he came in from the fields. He was always dressed in his good shirts and fine twill trousers. Maggie clung to him. Len pulled her close, hoping this moment would never end.

The next morning, they had just finished breakfast. Len was reaching for his broad brimmed hat. Maggie came up behind him; put her arms around his waist.

"Len, I need some things from the store. I thought if I could get a cotton rug, maybe. Some curtains for the windows—"

He disengaged her arms. "I'll take you in. Soon as I have time," he said shortly, and walked out the door.

Len carried her in to town, on Saturday. He stood and watched as she picked out a few things. Maggie asked Fred Moss about Mama, Barbara Jo, and the baby.

"They're all fine, as far as I can see," Fred Moss looked at Maggie queerly. Why was she asking *him*, about her family?

Maggie could see that Len was angry, as soon as he lifted her into the wagon.

They had been so close, just last night. She had thought things were going to be better. But, whatever it was, it was *back*—the dark veil that so often dropped between them. She wanted to rip at it, and claw at it. She wanted to fight against it, but she didn't know how. She felt her heart sink. Maggie felt as if she was drowning. She had never known anyone like Len.

"Why were you asking *Fred Moss*, about your mother and your sister? I'm your husband, you want to know anything, you ask me," Len finally spoke, the anger all too evident in his voice.

"But, Len," she tried to reason with him. "If he's courting Barbara Jo—"

"He's not *courting* Barbara Jo. They got married. Last week."

"They—*what*? And no one told me? Barbara Jo got married, and *you* knew, and *you didn't tell me*?"

"Didn't seem to me you two were all that close." Len replied tersely.

"She's my sister!" Maggie heard herself shouting at him, *"She's my sister!"*

Nothing else was said on the ride back to the little sharecroppers' house. Maggie didn't wait for Len to help her down. She leapt off the high seat, hitting the ground with a thud. Right now, she didn't want Len Evans to touch her.

Maggie stalked into the house, leaving him to bring in the few things she had bought.

She was so angry. So hurt. So confused. Was she crazy? Or was Len?

Len came walking in, carrying her few purchases. Maggie turned her back on him.

She heard him slam the door on his way out. Then she heard the rolling of hooves, as Golden Boy came tearing out of the barn.

Oh, how I would *love* to shoot that grand mount, Maggie thought.

The following afternoon, Maggie walked to the front door, to get a breath of air. She couldn't believe her eyes. A woman was walking up from the road, walking straight for the little house.

She's coming *here*! I'm about to have *company*!

"Hello? Anyone home?"

"Oh, yes! Please, please, come in! I'm Maggie McKinnon ...I'm Maggie Evans."

"Sarah Greene," the woman extended one plump hand, her ruddy face breaking into an engaging smile. "Glad to meet you. Been meanin' to pop over. But been lot's to do. Meant to come over when you first moved in. We live 'bout a mile or so up the road, towards town. Not actually on the road, just down a little dirt trail off to the left. This place had been deserted for quite a while. You been knockin' down cobwebs, and drivin' out field mice?"

"Len must have done all that, before we moved in," Maggie smiled, attempting to make polite conversation. She didn't want Sarah Greene to know about her troubles with Len. She didn't want to think about that now. She had company! "Oh, please do come in, Mrs. Greene!"

Maggie was beside herself with joy. "Please take a seat. I'll heat up the coffee. There might be a—"

"Call me Sarah. Don't be going to no trouble on my account. Don't have that long to stay. Just wanted to drop by, leave you this pan of gingerbread, let you know we're in the neighborhood. Me and my husband Clem."

"Oh, please sit down, and stay for a while. I so seldom …that is …"

"Oh, all right. Guess Clem will figure out where I am. He was out back, piddlin' around with somethin', and I just sort of walked off. He won't have a heck of a notion where I disappeared to, should he miss me."

I just walked off, Maggie thought, what freedom. But she said, "Well, men get busy doing their thing …whatever it is men do out at the barn, or wherever, and time does get away."

"Not with Clem. Helpless sometimes as a newborn colt. Thinks he can't turn a hand, if I'm not there to hold the other one …and admire his handiwork."

"Have you been …married long?"

"Twelve years, come December. But we've only lived here two or three seasons."

"Twelve years, that's wonderful," Maggie heard herself saying. Twelve *years*, and Clem Greene couldn't be away from Sarah—

"You're new married, or so I heard?" Sarah smiled.

"Yes. Just, a few weeks, now."

"Well, I should be going," Sarah Greene rose, extending her work-roughened hand.

Maggie wanted to clasp her hand, not let go, beg her to stay.

But, she couldn't do that. So Maggie relinquished the warm hand, said, very politely, "It was so nice meeting you, and please do come again, when you can stay longer."

"You come on over to our place. Door's open. Any time."

"Yes, well …I might …just do that," Maggie smiled, walking her to the door, watching her disappear down the road.

Strange, Maggie thought, they had neighbors living only a mile down the road, and Len had never mentioned them.

Sunday came, and Maggie desperately wanted to get out of the house, go to church. She missed the Sunday gatherings, the quiet comfort of the worship, the friendly chats with other folk. She approached Len, soon after breakfast. He seemed in a good mood.

"Len, lovely *Sunday* morning, isn't it."

"Fair enough," Len replied, gazing at her with those dark, dark eyes. She could almost see her reflection in them, so intense were his emotions.

"Could we go to church, today? We haven't been, in quite a while."

"Horse's too tired. Been workin' all week. Cruel …to hitch him up on Sunday …such a long drive."

"What about the palomino?"

"What about Golden Boy?"

"Couldn't you hitch him up—"

"Don't talk so daft, Maggie. He's a saddle mount. He's not a draft horse."

It was a poor excuse. Maggie knew about horses.

"Len," Maggie walked up behind him, as he sat at the table, finishing his coffee. She laid her head on his shoulder, close to his ear, thinking she would charm him into going.

She tickled his ear with one fingertip. Immediately, Maggie felt him stiffen.

He was on his feet instantly, whirling about, his face contorted with rage. For an instant, Maggie thought he might strike her. He was hissing at her, "Don't you *ever do anything like that again*! You *hear* me! I won't have you acting like some *cheap little tramp*!"

Maggie felt all the blood drain from her face. No one had ever spoken to her like that. She felt faint.

Immediately Len was contrite, "Maggie! I'm sorry," pulling her into his arms, holding her close—

"Forgive me. You know I didn't mean that. It's just that—"

"It's just *what*, Len? *Tell me*!" Maggie pushed him away. She could hear the anger, trembling in her own voice.

Len gave her a peculiar stare, reached for his hat, and spent the rest of the day over at his Pa's.

The following day, Mama had a neighbor drive her out. Ecstatic with joy, Maggie flew to the door and flung it open, "Mama!"

Callie walked slowly in, a tight little smile on her face, Johnny clasped in her arms.

"Who's that with you, Mama? Tell her to come on in!" Maggie insisted with a smile.

"She'll just wait in the wagon, Maggie," Callie hesitated, "I wanted to talk with you alone."

"Oh, Mama! I'm so glad to see you!" Maggie clung to her mother, almost smothering little Johnny between them. He shot out fat little arms and let out an angry yelp. Maggie took him in her arms.

"Oh, look at you!" Maggie cooed, "Do I know you? I don't think so! I don't think I know this big boy! Oh, he's so beautiful, Mama. Please, sit down. Can I get you—"

"No, Maggie, I can only stay a minute. I had the neighbor drive me over. It's so far. It took half the morning to get here."

"I know it's a long way, Mama. I'm so sorry. I've been meaning to speak to Len about that, about moving us closer. Or moving you—"

"It's all right, Maggie," Callie gazed about the tiny house, heaved a sigh, "I …don't want to cause you any trouble. I just thought, well, the truth is, I learned something …that …I think you should know."

"What is it, Mama? Is something wrong? Is it about Barbara Jo? I didn't even *know* she was married!"

"I know, darling. It's not that. Nothing's …wrong. It's just that …Len's been married before, Maggie. There. Now. I've said it. There was a child."

"*What?* No, mama!" Maggie was wagging her head in disbelief, "No, that can't be true. You're wrong—"

"No, Maggie. I'm *not* wrong. Her name was Jenny Overby. And there *was* a child, a little girl—named Lisa."

"Where is she? What happened to her—and the child? Len has a little girl?" Maggie felt as if she was about to swoon.

"She and the child vanished. No one seems to know what became of either of them. Len's father arranged a quiet divorce. Len went off out west somewhere for a good long stretch. Some say he was at a place called Abilene, in Texas. Working on a ranch, or was it the railroad—"

Callie's face was thin and pinched; her hair lay in limp plaits atop her head. She looked as if she had aged twenty years, since Papa died. She looked as if her heart would break. "Darling!" she wagged her head, "I'm so sorry …to have to tell you this. But I thought that if you knew, it might help. Help you understand …Len."

"What happened?" Maggie asked, her voice quavering as this horrid news sank in, "What happened, between Len and his wife?"

"They said he found her with another man. Len was devastated."

"How on earth is this going to help me, Mama? Learning that the man you thought you married …is not that man at all? He's someone completely *different*! With a whole other life! He had a *wife! He has a child*! He's never *once mentioned these people!"*

"I don't know what to tell you, Maggie. But …sometimes people keep their deepest hurts inside, and it—"

"It what, Mama? It turns their hearts cold and pulls a dark curtain over their souls!" Immediately Maggie wished she hadn't said that. Not to Mama.

"Something like that, Maggie. I wish I could stay, and spend the afternoon, but I have to go. I can't keep Mrs. Justice waiting. She was kind enough to spend her day, driving me."

"Mama, there's so much I want to say to you. So much I need to know. How have you been? Is Len …do …you have everything you need?"

"I'm all right, Maggie. Len pays the rent, and he sends Fred Moss out with supplies. You just take care of yourself. And maybe you can come to see us soon. It's almost Christmas." Tears pooled in Callie's blue eyes. Maggie could see how hard this visit had been for her.

Maggie clung to her mother, dreading to see her walk out the door.

When Len came in, Maggie feigned a sick stomach, turning away from him. She felt as though she had been stabbed through the heart, multiple times. All through supper, she avoided his gaze—she avoided his hands. She couldn't bear the thought of his touching her. She couldn't bear the thought of his *not touching* her. Maggie went to bed early, telling Len she was still sick.

Len awoke several times in the night, calling her name softly, to make certain she was all right. She never answered. She seemed to be sleeping.

Dawn came at last. Len stared at her, making sure her color was normal. She looked all right. But something was wrong. Maggie wasn't herself. She was pale and withdrawn.

"You going to be all right today?" he asked, taking her hand, gently rubbing it between his own, his love so strong, so compelling, it almost frightened Maggie, "You want me to stay around the house today, to make sure you're going to be okay?"

"*No!*" Then, in a softer, less desperate voice, "No, you go on and do whatever you need to do." She wanted him *out* of the house. She wanted him to *leave*. She wanted to be alone. So she could think.

"Well …I want you to at least eat something. I'll take care of the milking before I go."

Maggie ate the food he offered her. It lay like stones in her stomach.

He kissed her tenderly, holding her close for a moment, "You know I love you, Maggie," he whispered into her hair. "No matter what happens, I want you always to remember that. I love you! You're all I ever want in this world!"

What about Jenny? Maggie wanted to ask. *Was she all you ever wanted?*

After what seemed an eternity, he released her, and was gone.

She had planned to put some plants in the yard, but now, her mind was not on plants. Her imagination was crowded with images of Len—Len with another woman. Len—fathering a child.

Where was Len's daughter? What age was she? *What had become of her?* Did he ever *see* her? Did he *love* her? She needed to *talk* with him about this.

But she was afraid. Afraid of what she might hear.

Maggie felt as if she was going to choke. She had to get outside. She wanted to feel the sun on her face.

She walked down to the little creek just back of the house. It wasn't a very large creek, but Maggie loved the sound of running water. A few clouds drifted by in the fall sky. She *had* to know! How could she live with Len, now, and not know?

She didn't know how long she had sat on the creek bank. She needed to get back to the house. Len would be coming in for supper. She walked along the creek bank, she was probably far past the barn now, she decided, and turned to walk out of the woods.

She came upon a tiny hut, set back in the edge of the trees. It was small. Only one room. Maggie lifted the latch and walked in. A little rock-and-mud fireplace. No glass windows, only two wooden shutters that could be opened to let in light and air. She thought it had probably been built as a temporary shelter, until the farmhouse could be constructed. She walked out, pulling the door closed behind her.

Len decided to knock off early, and go in and see about Maggie. It frightened him, to think of her being sick. Len knew that life was precarious.

The thought of her having some serious illness, something that might take her from him, sent chills through his very bones. He walked the horse to the barn, unhitched him and led him out to pasture. He went on up to the house. She wasn't there. Len's heart began to pound. He ran out the back door, shouting frantically:

"Maggie! Maggie!"

Then, there she was, coming across the pasture from the creek, her dark hair long, and flowing behind her.

Len ran to meet her. He folded her in his arms, whispering her name over and over, spinning her around, "Maggie! Oh, Maggie! Thank goodness! You're all right!"

Len was so worried about her; he couldn't take his eyes off her. He insisted on helping put supper on the table. Maggie hadn't seen him like this, since just after the wedding.

Her heart began to sing. He was like a different person. Everything was going to be all right! She had misjudged him. They laughed and talked over their food. Len poured them some hot coffee. Then he built a roaring fire in the fireplace, and pulled Maggie close beside him in the glowing warmth. Maggie shut her eyes, and almost, almost she could forget about …*Jenny* …

"Len," almost without realizing it, Maggie whispered softly, "tell me about Jenny …"

Instantly, Len was on his feet, towering over her.

His handsome face twisted with rage, he shouted, "Don't you *ever* mention that name in this house! *Do you understand?*"

Maggie shrank back, frightened. Then, despite her fear, she leapt up, and shouted back at him.

"Len! If you had another wife—*I have a right to know!*"

Len clinched his fists. For just an instant, Maggie thought for certain he was going to strike her. Then Len spun and slammed out of the house. She could hear the palomino's hooves, beating their way to the Evans' place.

Maggie lay in bed, crying softly. Finally, she heard him coming in. He lay stiffly beside her, his face to the wall. She could feel the tears, hot, scalding her cheeks, slipping silently down her face wetting the pillow.

Maggie never mentioned Jenny again.

The light had just begun to show in the eastern sky. Maggie lay quietly in bed, listening to the sounds of Len moving around in the kitchen. She heard the door of the cookstove clang shut, and knew he had built the fire in the stove so she could begin cooking breakfast. Then she heard him lift the latch to the outside door and go out, pulling the door shut behind him.

She threw back the covers and slowly sat up, swinging her feet to the floor. She felt her stomach rise up into her throat. She fought back the waves of nausea that threatened to engulf her, as they did most every morning now. She sat absolutely still for a moment, waiting for the sickness to subside, then got to her feet and dressed

Maggie was always up early, getting Len's breakfast so he could get an early start in the fields. He had finished the winter plowing, breaking the ground for early spring planting. Spring was just around the corner. Time now for planting the money crops—upland cotton and Indian corn, and maybe a few acres of tobacco.

She took the biscuits out of the oven, poured the steaming black coffee into the cups, and sat waiting for Len to come in from the barn. She waited with growing apprehension. She had meant to tell him earlier, but there never seemed a proper time. And she knew that any day now it would be all too apparent to him—as well as to everyone else. Maggie had known for several months that she was pregnant. She had to tell Len.

Len stepped up on the porch and knocked the dirt from the barnyard off his work boots. He opened the door and stepped in, going over to the washstand, splashing cold water over his face and hands. He dried on the towel hanging on a nail, crossed and sat down at the little table.

Maggie dipped the wooden spoon into the bowl, and placed the scrambled eggs onto Len's plate. She passed the hot biscuits, and he took two. Maggie sat in the chair opposite him. She didn't feel as if she could eat one bite. She cleared her throat.

"Len, I have something to tell you, and I don't quite know how."

"Oh?" Len gazed at her, his eyes dark, his face set. How well Maggie knew that look—as if he was expecting the worst.

"We're going to have a baby."

Len paused a moment, his eyes on her, his fork hovering in the air. Slowly he lowered the fork, put the bite of eggs into his mouth, and began silently to chew.

"Aren't you going to say anything?" Maggie asked.

Maggie wanted to shout at him, *Say something!*

Instead, she asked quietly, "Len, did you hear me?"

"I heard you," he said curtly, staring down at his plate.

Then, without another word, he laid down the fork, pushed back his half-finished plate, picked up his hat, and went out.

Chapter 22

Somehow Maggie made it through each morning. She fed and milked the cow, slopped the pigs, gathered the eggs, swept the floors—anything to keep busy. She didn't want to think. If only she could just switch her mind off, and avoid dealing with all these painful, heart-wrenching thoughts.

Finally, it was eleven o'clock. Maggie knew that Len would soon be in for lunch.

Maybe today, maybe today Len would mention the child.

Maggie had been taught that no matter what, life goes on. So she baked a pone of corn bread, and heated up the beans left from supper last night. And there was the cake she had baked yesterday.

The little clock on the mantel struck twelve, and still Len had not appeared. Maggie wiped her hands on her apron, stepped nervously to the washstand, and drank a dipper of water. Crossing to the window, she pulled back the curtain, looking out for some sign of her husband. He was nowhere in sight. She sat down at the table for a few minutes. Then she heard his step on the porch.

The door opened, and Len stepped inside. He hung his hat on the nail just inside the door. "Hot day," he said, crossed to the washstand, splashed water over his face and hands. He dried on the towel, came and sat down at the table.

Maggie sat there opposite him, slowly putting bites of food into her mouth, automatically chewing and swallowing. As if it knew there was a problem, the child inside her stirred. The food lay like heavy lumps in her stomach. She felt so empty, so alone, although her handsome, viral husband sat across the table from her.

Len finished his meal, rose from the chair, took his hat, said simply, "I'll be working in the north field this afternoon." He turned and walked out.

Maggie cleared away the lunch. Her eyes felt hot and dry. She felt jittery as a cat. She had to get out of the house.

She decided to tackle the weeds growing among the bean vines. She walked down to the barn, got a hoe and entered the vegetable garden.

The bean vines were up, sleek and green, heavy with blooms, just beginning to put on little pods. Grass and weeds dotted the middles of the rows.

Maggie worked steadily, vigorously attacking the weeds. Suddenly her throat caught. She came to a complete halt, the hoe poised in mid-air. All at once, she hated the garden. She hated this place. She hated the bean vines. Wildly she began swinging the hoe in high frantic arcs, viciously, furiously, flailing at the vines. Methodically, she made her way down each lush row.

She continued without letup, until the bean patch was completely leveled to the ground.

Then she slouched down in the midst of her crumpled bean vines, and began to weep, hugging herself, weeping and rocking back and forth, until she felt dry as a shuck. Then she picked herself up, knocked the dirt from her dress, walked down to the barn and put away her hoe. It must be four o'clock by now. Len would be coming in, and he would expect his supper.

Len never once mentioned the baby. Maggie's time drew nearer. She knew she would need some sort of little cradle, or bed.

The next time they were at the store, Maggie chose a little cradle, wordlessly brought it and set it on the counter. Len ignored it, as if it did not exist. He paid for their purchases, picked up everything but the little cradle, and walked out of the store.

Maggie was acutely aware of Fred Moss watching them, and how she despised him. His shrewd eyes seemed to be seeing, even relishing, all the terrible things that had gone wrong in her marriage. Fred Moss sidled from behind the counter, a knowing little smile on his face, as if he was going to be forced to carry the cradle out for her.

Maggie snatched up the cradle as best she could, carrying it in front of her awkwardly, out the door, and down the broad steps. To her great wonder, she made it down the steps, without tripping and breaking her neck. Safely on the ground, she lowered her burden to the dirt yard beside the wagon with a thump.

Len stood with his broad back to her, not even offering to lift the little cradle into the wagon. Fred Moss stood in the door of the store, leaning nonchalantly against the doorjamb, smirking. Maggie reached down, grabbed up the cradle. With an angry heave she hefted it over the side planks. It hit the wagon bed with a clatter. She hoped nothing was broken. She stalked to the far side of the wagon. Before Len could reach to help her, Maggie gathered up her skirts, and pulled her growing bulk onto the wagon seat.

Maggie brought out the box, where she had been hoarding small garments sewn in her spare time. A little quilt she had pieced and quilted by hand. Some cotton outing she had fashioned into little gowns, blankets and diapers. All these things, she squirreled away in the cradle, in the corner of the spare room. Then she pulled the door shut.

With great effort, Maggie got out of bed, walked to the cookstove, heated up the coffee Len had made earlier. She ate a cold biscuit with a big slab of sweet butter. She really wasn't hungry, but knew she should eat something.

She walked out into the morning sunlight, and noticed that leaves had drifted close against the side of the house. She walked slowly down to the barn, came back, carrying the rake.

With small, short motions, Maggie began to rake the leaves away from the house and into a pile. As she worked on, the pile mounted, until finally she decided she would have to somehow dispose of them, or the leaves would simply blow back against the gray clapboard house.

Maggie decided to burn the pile of leaves.

She walked into the house, returned carrying the kerosene can and a few matches. She sprinkled some kerosene onto the middle of the pile, and threw on a match. The fire caught, and shot quickly upwards. Maggie sat down on the back doorstep, to keep an eye on her fire.

Maggie has failed to notice the clouds gathering in the sky to the north. Within a few minutes, a slight breeze began to stir, lifting some of the burning leaves from the pile, and sending them skimming harmlessly away into the barren little yard.

As the burning leaves were snatched up by the breeze, and began to drift higher into the air, and farther from the fire, Maggie became a bit concerned. She took her rake and began pushing the leaves from the outer edges into the center of the pile, in an effort to contain the fire.

The breeze continued to freshen. Maggie heard a strange crackling sound from behind her. She whirled, to see that the oak shingles covering the little spare room were ablaze.

Maggie rushed inside, grabbed a blanket from the bed. She came out, clutching the blanket. She would need the ladder.

Dragging the ladder up from the barn, it was all Maggie could do to heft the heavy thing against the side of the house. She climbed up, and tried beating out the flames with the blanket. Seeing her efforts were futile, she wondered if she should get help. But it was too far to the Greene farm. And Len had gone into the woods to cut winter firewood. She had no idea where. He probably wouldn't be in until dark.

She ran to the well, and began frantically drawing up water, pouring it into a bucket, hefting it rung after rung, up the ladder, then dumping it onto the fire.

Maggie continued to fight the fire, drawing up bucket after bucket, until her arms and back ached. She was so tired she could scarcely stand. The clouds continued to gather. She was standing at the top of the ladder, just emptying her bucket, when the rain began.

It fell in sheets. Maggie climbed slowly down, pain now a continual thing. Like something alive, it was sitting astride her. She almost fell off the bottom rung, landing in the yard with a heavy thud.

Len saw the clouds, the rain moving in from the north. He decided to call it a day. He had almost a load of wood. He climbed up on the wagon seat, and drove along the worn field road.

Coming out of the trees, through the blowing sheets of rain, he thought he saw a figure, huddled in the yard.

Maggie!

Len thundered into the yard, flung down the reins, ran to pick her up. She was moaning, soaked to the skin. Her hair lay plastered to her head in soggy strands.

He got her inside, got the wet clothes off, drew a nightgown over her head, and covered her with warm quilts. All this time, she was moaning in pain.

The doctor! Maggie needed the doctor.

Frantically, Len grabbed his slicker, hurried Job to the barn, threw a halter on Golden Boy, and mounted him bareback. He came tearing out the barn door, leaving it open and banging in the rain, and went racing down the muddy road toward town.

Dr. Jeremiah Holt heard the furious pounding on his door, just as he was sitting down to supper.

"Oh, Len, something wrong?" he asked peeking out to see Len Evans dripping all over his porch.

"It's my wife! I think it's …the baby."

"Oh? I didn't know Mrs. Evans was expecting. She hasn't even been in to see me. I'll get my things. Maude, put my supper on the back of the stove …I'll be back …whenever."

Len thought the doctor would never get the rig hitched up, even with Len's help. Len's usually supple and capable hands—that had hitched up a rig hundreds of times—seemed numb and all thumbs. Len tied his mount to the back of the doctor's buggy, leapt onto the buggy seat, snatched up the reins, and sent the horse tearing out of the yard at break-neck speed.

Doctor Holt hung on for dear life, his heavily mustached face going pale as cotton, as they left the yard and swerved onto the road. Len Evens was driving like a lunatic. The light rig careened dangerously up on two wheels.

It rained so hard Len could scarcely see the road. He heard the doctor shouting at him, "Slow down! Len! Good grief, man! You're going to kill us, before we ever reach your place!"

Len pretended not to hear. He never allowed the horse to slacken its pace, until they turned into the yard.

Rain still coming down in torrents, Len drove the rig right up to the front steps, was down in a flash, and ushering the doctor inside. Len drove the buggy into the shelter of the little barn, and made a mad dash back to the house.

As soon as he entered the house, Len noticed water coming from beneath the door of the spare room. He opened the door and looked up—to see rain pouring through a gaping hole in the roof. Len muttered a string of soft curses.

"Len?" the doctor was calling, "Better put on a big kettle of water, and a big pot of coffee. Looks like this is going to be a long night."

Len stoked up the fire in the cookstove—again. Then he went to throw more logs in the little fireplace. He had heard no news from the tiny bedroom for hours. He could hear Doctor Holt speaking reassuringly to Maggie. But she never once made a reply, only the horrible moans.

Unable to bear the suspense a minute longer, he walked over and eased open the door. The doctor looked up and wagged his head sadly.

"Sorry, Len, but I couldn't save the child. And your wife's lost a lot of blood—but I think she'll be all right."

Ducking his dark head to hide the smile on his face, Len closed the door. He couldn't have had better news—

—Maggie was going to be all right.

Maggie was barely conscious, when they told her. She begged to see the baby. She begged to hold the baby. But Len said very adamantly, "No, you're too weak. It's better this way. The doctor took it away."

"*Took it away?*" Maggie recalled crying.

Maggie never knew what became of the child. *The doctor took it away!* What did that mean!

Where, or whether, they buried it, she never knew. Len refused to discuss it. She never even knew if it was a girl or a boy.

It was spring, of the year 1883, and Maggie was seventeen years old.

Chapter 23

To fill the emptiness, Maggie worked from daylight until dark. She worked side by side with Len in the fields. She kept the house spotlessly clean. Sweeping, scrubbing the bare pine floors until Len wondered she didn't wear out the planks.

Len carried her over to the Evans' place, for a visit.

They sat in the front parlor, on faded settees that had seen better days. Len and his father sat on one side of the cavernous fireplace, Maggie and Ida Evans, on the other.

Carl Evans kept eyeing Maggie with a veiled, measured gaze, as if she were a filly for sale. Ida Evans was quiet and withdrawn, quieter than any mouse, her eyes scarcely lifting from her hands, clasped nervously in the lap of her faded apron. She and Maggie exchanged not more than a few dozen impersonal, meaningless words in the hour or more they sat there.

Len kept watching Maggie from the other side of the fireplace, his face dark and unreadable. But whenever Big Carl spoke to him, Len's face broke into a smile, as if he were a child, Maggie thought angrily, waiting for some word of praise to drop from his father's venerable lips.

Maggie did not mention visiting the Evans' place again. But Ida Evans sent over some cuttings and some flower seeds. Maggie cultivated a little flower garden, along the front, and down the sides of the house.

Len worried that Maggie worked too hard. She was so thin. But she was even more beautiful, Len thought, than the day he first saw her. Len never tired of looking at her.

It had been almost a year since the death of her baby. Maggie tried not to constantly envision the child in her mind, but found this almost impossible. If only she knew, if it was a boy or girl. What had become of the little body? But Len adamantly refused to discuss it. It would do her no good, he said, to dwell on what was over and done.

It was Saturday, and Len said he was going to the store for supplies. Maggie wanted to come along. Len hesitated for a moment, then finally agreed.

On the drive to the store, Maggie brought up something she had been intending to mention.

"Len, several times now, I thought I saw smoke, rising from that tiny hut in the trees, out past the barn."

"Forget about it, Maggie, or you'll have us in a hornets' nest."

Some vagrant's living in the little cabin, Maggie thought, and Len doesn't want his Pa to find out. Maggie forgot about it.

Fred Moss greeted Maggie at the door, "Mornin', Maggie."

"Mr. Moss. I have a little list of things. It's just some sewing notions. Len's filling the kerosene can."

"All right, let's just see what we have here. Just got in a new shipment, thread and materials, from Atlanta."

"Is Barbara Jo around?" Maggie never saw her sister anymore.

"She rode out to visit with her Mama."

Maggie browsed around the store. A sign posted by the front door caught her eye. It read in fancy letters:

Farm for Sale
1 Mile North on Dawsonville Road
House and 40 Acres
See A. Denton
Attorney at Law

A farm for sale! Maggie reached up and took the little sign, folded it, and put in into her reticule.

"Maggie?" she heard Len speaking, at her elbow. Maggie gave a guilty start.

"What? Oh—"

"Got what you need?" Len asked.

"Mr. Moss is getting the things together."

"What do we owe you, Fred?" Len paid for the order, reached for Maggie's bundle, and walked her outside. When Len lifted Maggie into the wagon, she gave him such a dazzling smile, that Len couldn't help but smile back.

It always amazed Maggie. The way Len never asked the price of anything.

He never told her there was not enough money to get this or that item. The farm must be doing better than she had supposed. This fit right in with her plans.

This Saturday, Len had gone over to his Pa's to split wood. Maggie knew he would probably be gone the entire day. She packed a picnic lunch, walked down to the barn, and against Len's express orders, hitched up Job. As she drove out of the yard, she saw again that telltale drift of smoke, coming from the little one-roomed cabin. Maggie wondered absently who the vagrant was. What he looked like. Why she had seen Len sneaking armloads of firewood and supplies—on a regular basis—into the edge of the woods. Couldn't the poor vagrant do anything for himself!

But Maggie wouldn't think about that. She wouldn't think anything unpleasant today. It was a beautiful fall morning. Maggie had the *For Sale* notice from the store tucked beneath her skirt, on the wagon seat. The sky was a clear cerulean blue. The leaves danced on the trees along the side of the road. The grasses waved rich and thick. The world seemed perfect. Maggie was going to see a fine little farm that was for sale. They had a good harvest last fall, expected an even better one, this fall. Maggie knew they would have the money to buy a small place of their own. That was Maggie's dream, a place of their own, where Len wouldn't always be under his Pa's thumb. If she could get Len out from beneath his father's influence, if he wasn't always riding off, over to his Pa's, maybe then, she thought, things would be different.

There seemed to be a magic about the morning. Maggie passed a couple of farmhouses, cows grazing in pastures beside the road. She rode through beautiful, gently rolling countryside.

Finally she topped a slight rise. And there it was.

The house set far back from the road. It had been painted yellow, and looked to be in good repair. There was a big grove of hardwoods out front. Some of them Maggie knew, were nut-bearing trees.

Far back from the house sat a large barn with a cluster of several small outbuildings near it.

Maggie drove the wagon down the rutted drive beside the house. She climbed down and walked up to the front of the house. There was a large porch. The place showed no signs of life. The house, no doubt, had been empty for some time.

Finding the door unlocked, Maggie walked inside. It was not a large house, but much larger, much more sturdily built, than the little sharecropper shack. There were four good-sized rooms, a hall running down the middle, then a light, roomy kitchen that ran all along the back. Maggie loved it.

She walked out onto the back porch. A well curb with a wide shelter stood not far from the wide porch steps. Maggie walked out into the yard. A small orchard had dropped down fruits—two apple trees, two or three peach trees, and a pear tree.

Out at the barn, she peeked into the wide hall, running the entire length of the structure. Two stables on one side, a harness and tack room and a smithy on the other. She climbed the narrow ladder to the loft. A small stack of hay lay in one corner, as if ready to be thrown down to hungry livestock below.

Behind the barn, she discovered a creek, twelve or fifteen feet wide. Enough to water all the stock they would ever own. Clean and clear. Thick grass growing along the banks.

Maggie grew hungry, retrieved her lunch from the wagon, and sat down on the creek bank. She could see small children, wading in this creek. She could hear their voices, echoing along the hall of the sturdy yellow house. She could see them, running and playing in the grove of hardwoods shading the front yard.

The way Nellie Sue, and Barbara Jo, and Maggie had done, in McKinnon Valley.

Maggie had known for months that another child was on its way. She didn't want her next child to be born in Carl Evans' little sharecropper shack.

Maggie's head felt almost giddy from all the excitement. This would be just perfect, just what she and Len needed. And it was only a mile or so from Mama's.

Busy with all her plans, Maggie forgot the time. Suddenly she looked up, to see the sunlight slanting through bright red and orange leaves. She must get back! Before Len came home! Maggie leapt up, brushed herself off, and walked reluctantly to the wagon.

She fixed a wonderful supper. She wanted to get Len into a good mood, and then break the news of her wonderful farm to him.

They finished eating. Maggie cleared the table. Len had built a small fire in the fireplace, although the night was not really that cold. He sat before the fireplace, long legs stretched out before him, shiny black boots resting on the small stone hearth.

Maggie pulled a chair up close. She smiled over at Len.

"Len," she began softly, "I saw a sign, of a farm for sale, the other day, at Moss'. Wouldn't it be wonderful, if we could buy a fine little place of our own, where we could—"

"What, Maggie?" he looked over at her, his eyes dark and inscrutable. "What in the world are you babbling about? Why on earth would I want to buy a farm?"

"So we could make a life of our own, Len," Maggie replied, attempting to keep the anger, the disappointment from her voice. "We could—"

"We could go *broke*!" Len glared at her, wagged his head in frustration and mounting anger, "We could *starve* to death! We could *lose* the place for the *taxes*! I've seen too many good men do just that! Why on *earth* would you want to saddle me with that kind of burden? How do you think Pa got all his land? I'll tell you how, from *poor fools who bit off more than they could chew*—and lost their land for taxes and debts! Pa would *never* put us off this land, even if we never paid a *penny* in rent! Why would I want to give up such security? Besides, Pa would *never* forgive me, if I moved off and left him, after all he's done for me!"

"If you *left* him! Listen to yourself, Len! *Most* children leave their parents, soon or later!"

"Well, *I* won't be leaving!" As his rage mounted, anger darkened Len's eyes, deepened his voice. "And you can just get such fool notions right out of your head. Why can't you *ever* be *satisfied* with what you have? Can't you just *leave me alone*! *Stop hounding me*!"

Len stomped out of the house in a black rage. Maggie heard the barn door slam back against the wall. She heard the palomino come roaring out.

Angry and sick with disappointment, Maggie sat staring at nothing, and decided Len Evens would learn about this baby on his own. She wouldn't tell him *anything*.

Maggie sat there that evening, running over and over in her mind, exactly what Len had said.

Pa wouldn't put us off this place, not if we didn't pay a penny of rent. Why would I give up such security ...

Len didn't want the responsibility of a place of his own. Len was emotionally and financially dependent upon his father. Len would *never* get away from *Big Carl Evans*.

And why should he? Len could drive the rich surrey, or the fine buggy. They weren't his. But Len didn't seem to mind.

Len didn't mind living in this little shack. All he had to do was saddle up his fine horse, and ride *home*, to the security of the big house!

Maggie knew now, that Len could have chosen any house his father owned. But he had chosen *this place*. Because it was far out the river road. Isolated. Nothing within comfortable walking distance.

Maggie wondered why she had worked so hard. What had all her back-breaking labor accomplished! Why should she do *anything*!

Because she had been taught that every person swung his own weight— and did not become a burden to others. Because Maggie McKinnon did not want *one crumb* that fell from Big Carl Evans!

No, she would not mention the baby to Len. In a short while, he would become aware of it ...and she wondered ...just how Len would feel.

It rained for days. Finally, it had stopped. Maggie pushed the supper to the back of the stove. She took her milk pail, and walked down towards the barn. The cow, she saw, was not standing, as she usually did this time each day, with her head hanging over the fence. Ready to be fed and milked.

Oh, no! The stupid rogue cow was out again! Maggie would have to go and round her up.

Low clouds scudded across the sky, shutting out the sun. Maggie knew that in an hour or so, it would be dark. Perhaps she should wait for Len. But Len probably wouldn't be back until late.

Maggie took the battered feed bucket, dumped in two handfuls of sweet oats, and started off. She would walk along the fence, and see if there was a break, where the cow could have gotten out.

She moved through the tall grass, along the fence, then into the tree line, and on across the creek. Once across the creek, she found where a fence post had leaned far over. On the other side, she saw the cow's track in the soft mud.

With all the rain for the past few days, the ground was saturated. That's probably why the post had come loose. Maggie pressed on, following the tracks.

Ahead lay a large patch of granite outcroppings. And Maggie lost sight of the tracks. She skirted the granite slabs and boulders, and picked up the tracks, very clear, on the far side. She followed them, and knew that soon, she would be coming to the river.

Ahead lay a patch of thick cane, some of the stalks as thick as Maggie's wrist. But the tracks led straight into the canebrake. Maggie pressed on, using the feed bucket before her as a sort of battering ram to part a path through the dense growth.

By now, Maggie could hear the roar of the river. Usually the river ran by here with a mere whisper of sound. But not when there had been several days of steady rain up in the mountains, and all down the long Chattahoochee River basin.

Today, it was a roaring torrent, tearing at the banks.

The tracks led on, right to the river's edge. Then they turned and started up the bank, only inches from the foaming, frothing torrent. Maggie thought of turning back. But they needed the milk. They needed for the cow's sack to be emptied regularly, so that she would stay freshened.

Maggie turned, and stepped carefully along the muddy bank. Suddenly she felt her right foot slipping. The bank was giving away; then she was falling.

Frantically she clutched for something to break her fall. Her hand grabbed onto a small sapling, its roots barely maintaining their tenuous hold on the red clay bank.

Maggie hit the fast flowing water. It swirled and sucked at her, hungrily attempting to draw her down. She clung to the little sapling, wondering frenetically whether she could paddle her way back to the bank. Then maybe she could find something more secure to hold on to, and clamber out.

But Maggie found that her right arm refused to do her bidding. She had either broken it, or sprained it badly, when she fell. She clung to the slender little sapling—

Until the roots came loose—

Then Maggie was swept madly downstream.

Bobbing and tossing, she was flung like a rag doll against a tree limb jutting out over the river, almost in midstream. She thought about pulling herself, hand over hand, along the branch, to the bank. But found her arm would not cooperate. It was all she could do, just to hang on.

Surely, Len would come in, she thought, miss her, and come searching.

But Len would not be in until almost dark, and by then, Maggie doubted he could follow the cow's tracks, as she had done.

Maggie began to shiver—from the chill of the river, and from the frightening prospect of full darkness descending. Clinging to this precarious tree limb.

Len came to the house. He drove the wagon into the small barn, unhitched the horse, fed him and glanced up towards the house. Maggie wasn't in sight.

He noticed that the cow's trough was empty. The cow was nowhere in sight. Usually, this near dark, she hung close about the barn, wanting her sweet feed, ready to enter her stable for the night.

Len walked on up to the house. He found the supper, cooked, and growing cold on the back of the stove. He walked back to the barn. He found the empty milk pail, sitting near the trough.

The cow must be out again, and Maggie had gone in search of her.

And darkness was falling fast.

He should go for help. No, it would take too long. By the time he got back with help, it would be truly dark. And Maggie had probably been gone for a while. Something could have happened to her. Len's heart began a harsh, tumultuous pounding.

He took down the kerosene lantern from the barn wall. Lit it, and began to walk along the fence, looking for a break. But he noticed the clouds had drifted past overhead, and there was just a bit of light.

After half an hour of diligent searching, he finally came upon the downed fence post. He could see that the heavy rains had created a sort of gully, washing the dirt from about the post, and loosening it so that with the slightest push, it toppled over.

He stepped over the downed fence, and followed the tracks, as best he could in the gathering darkness.

He came to the granite outcroppings, lost the tracks, picked them up again.

Now, it was completely dark. Len crept along, almost on his hands and knees, trying to follow the fading trail. He came to the massive canebrake. He could hear the river. He knew it was nearing flood stage. It would be rising steadily, throughout the night, until all the rains from upstream had drained out of the river's basin.

He pushed his way though the cane, his heart hammering madly. *Please, God*, he prayed, *let Maggie be all right! Let me find her!*

Now he was creeping along the riverbank, following the barely discernible tracks. The river was rising, moment by moment. Soon, Len knew, it would crest, and overflow its banks.

He found a deep hole in the muddy bank, where it appeared someone had stepped too close to the edge—

"Maggie! Maggie! Answer me!"

Len heard nothing—nothing, but the tremendous roar of the water.

Maggie felt as if she was about to lose consciousness. It would be so easy, she thought, just to let go, and slip away with the river. The river seemed to be rising, the waters picking up momentum as they clawed and ate away at the banks. Then she felt a sharp kick from the baby. Maggie jerked instantly awake, fully aware. She mustn't let fatigue and the cold lull her into a stupor. She must hang on—for the baby's sake. She *had* to survive!

Overhead, she could see the clouds had drifted away. The stars were becoming visible, bright pinpoints of light against the deep blackness.

Not a sparrow...falls to the ground...

"Maggie! Maggie! Where are you?"

"Len! Len! I'm here!"

Len held the lantern as high as he could. Out in the middle of the river, she was clinging to a tree limb that hung over the water!

"Hang on! I'm going to get you out!" Len yelled over the roar.

He looked about, for anything he could extend to her, but he knew that was hopeless. She was ten or twelve feet from the bank.

He would have to make his way along the limb, and hope it would hold both his weight, and hers.

Len hung the lantern as high as he could on a tree limb, and stepped into the raging river.

Instantly, he felt the powerful pull of the river, tugging at his clothes. He inched his way along the limb, felt it sway, then become still. He waited for a moment, then inched forward, very slowly, trying not to make any sudden move that might snap the limb, and send it crashing down the river.

"Hold on, Maggie! I'm almost there! Are you all right?"

"Cold! Oh, I'm so cold! And my arm—"

"It's all right! You're going to be all right! I'm almost there! I've got you. Now, just hang on to me!"

"I don't know ...whether I can. My arm—"

"Here, hold with your other arm. I've got you. Here we go—"

273

Slowly, Maggie clinging about his neck with her good arm, Len made his way toward the riverbank. It seemed at least a mile away. Over the dark rush of the waters, he kept feeling for the limb. Every time it swayed, terror gripped him. He could see the dim light of the lantern, waiting on the safety of the bank.

"Almost there!" He kept talking to her. "We're almost there!"

Then Len was clambering out, pulling Maggie along behind him.

Once his feet were solidly planted on the bank, Len drew her to him. "Oh Maggie! Oh, Maggie! Thank you, dear God!"

Len took the lantern and set it on the ground. Maggie was trembling like a leaf, and Len knew she could never walk out of here. He lifted Maggie into his arms, then reached a finger down and hooked the wire handle of the lantern.

The kerosene lantern swinging precariously against his right thigh, Len made his way through the canebrake, around the granite outcroppings, along the fence. He felt he would never arrive at the barn.

Then at last they reached the house.

He sat Maggie on a chair, stoked up the fire in the cookstove and the fireplace. Stripped off the wet clothes, dried her vigorously, and wrapped her in a warm quilt.

"Drink this," he ordered, offering her a cup of hot liquid, half coffee, half milk.

Len put her to bed, and covered her, then he lay down beside her, and held her, never wanting to let her go.

"I couldn't live without you, Maggie!" he whispered into her hair. *"Don't ever, ever leave me!"*

Early in the morning, two days later, Fred Moss rode out to tell Maggie that her mother had died.

Len took Maggie to the ugly little house. It took over half the morning, to make the drive. Barbara Jo was there, waiting, in the little front room. Maggie was horrified, to find that Mama lay alone, cold and already stiff, still in her nightgown, still on her bed.

Maggie washed her, rubbed her with oil, dressed her in her Sunday best, while Barbara Jo sat in the other room. She could not, she told Maggie, abide the thought of touching the dead. Giving Barbara Jo a scathing stare, Maggie declared:

"That's not *the dead*, lying in there, Barbara Jo. That's *our Mama*."

They buried Mama behind the little white church where Maggie and Len had gone those few times. Maggie sat numbly during the funeral, scarcely hearing a word. *Mama was gone.* And Maggie had scarcely seen her since her wedding to Len—only when Mama made her one unpleasant visit, then once at Christmas and once at Easter.

Now, it was too late.

Johnny sat beside Maggie, crying softly.

Maggie felt the warmth of him, the life of him, and somehow, she endured the horror that was her Mama's funeral.

Back at the house, Barbara Jo told Maggie they would have to empty the place, make some sort of disposition of Mama's things. She also said she wanted none of them.

She didn't even want Johnny.

"That's all right," Maggie told her coldly. "I'll take Mama's things—and Johnny will have a home, as long as I do."

Maggie asked Len to load Mama's things onto the wagon. They hauled them back to the little sharecroppers' house, and stored part of them in the barn, and part in the little storeroom.

Chapter 24

Now that Johnny was in the house, Maggie felt renewed strength. And hope. He was so like Papa, so filled with open affection and energy.

She also felt a grave responsibility. Johnny had no playmates, no one to share the adventures and games that made childhood such an exciting and special time. She prayed that God would help her to keep the dark shadow of her marriage from falling across Johnny.

Maggie searched her mind, calling up all the games she and Barbara Jo and Nellie Sue had played, back in McKinnon Valley—

—Ring around th' roses, hopscotch, tag, jump-rope, marbles, dress-up— and each day, Maggie planned a bit of her time for Johnny.

She cut wild muscadine vines. They played jump-rope with them, Maggie jumping and skipping rope just as vigorously as Johnny.

She drew hopscotch patterns in the sands of the back yard. They leapt from block to block, valiantly attempting to put the correct feet into the correct blocks—snatching up their own stones, never missing a step—for fear of being counted out.

She and Johnny played tag amongst the few trees left standing in the back yard, and hide-and-go-seek wherever their spirits carried them.

Len watched all this gleeful activity with dark and glowering rage.

Since the boy had come, Maggie had no time for him.

Since the boy had come, Maggie tore about the place like a five-year-old, and not like a wife. Her face was often flushed, and her pulse racing—but not because of Len Evans. The boy consumed all her time and energy.

What *Len* wanted, and what *Len* needed—didn't seem to matter any more. Len felt frustrated, forsaken, left out, shoved aside—like some old cast off boot.

The two of them came walking out of the woods behind the house, their arms laden with little bundles of roots and plants and nuts.

"Just what do you intend to do with that mess?" Len demanded, leaning against a front porch post, a surly scowl on his face, as Maggie and Johnny came walking up towards the house.

"These are *medicinal* herbs, Len. We're going to make healing potions and teas."

"Who's sick?" Len snorted disdainfully.

"Well, no one that I know of." Maggie said quietly, her uneasiness growing. She didn't like the look in Len's eyes. Had he been drinking? No. Len never drank.

"You see, Len," Maggie went on, trying to defuse Len's rotten mood, "Johnny's planning on becoming a doctor—so that he can make lots of sick folks feel better. So, he's interested in—"

"Well, I don't want you bringing that mess in the house. Might be *poison*, for all I know."

"Why, Len! What a strange thing to say. Surely you know I have enough sense to tell the difference between a poisonous plant—"

"You heard what I said, Maggie." Len whirled and walked down to the barn.

"Is Uncle Len mad at us, Maggie?" Johnny asked, his little face anxious.

"No, Sweetie, it's nothing to do with you and me. It's just that …sometimes your Uncle Len …doesn't really mean a lot of the things he says. Well, never mind that now. Why don't we just tuck our things away, under your bed, in the corner of the spare room, and in that little box I gave you? And we'll just keep these treasures …*our* secret."

On Sunday mornings, Maggie brought out the lovely Bible that Thomas Beyers had given her, and she and Johnny had church.

"What are we going to play today?" Johnny asked, his little face very earnest as he gazed at Maggie across his bowl of warm oats and sweet milk. "Are we going to play church?"

"No, Sweetie, you don't *play* church—you *have* church, or you *attend* church. Church is very serious. It is not a game. The Bible teaches us who we are, and how to live in this world."

"That sounds very important," Johnny surmised softly.

"Yes, sweetie, it is, *very* important. Now, let me see …what did we study last week …and what should we read this week?"

"Maggie?" Johnny inquired, his blue eyes very wide. "Why don't Len and you and me do what you said?"

"What's that, Johnny?"

"Why don't we a—ten church? Like Mama and me?"

"Well, you see, Sugar, it's quite a long way from here. And the horse is tired—let's just go on with our reading, shall we? What would you like to hear today?"

"About the man with the name of a horse."

"A horse?"

"Uncle Len's horse."

"Golden Boy?"

"Not that one, the other one."

"Oh, you mean Job! The man who had such terrible problems?"

"Why do we have so many problems, Maggie? Why did Mama die?"

"Papa always said it made us stronger, honey. The harder we push back, against the bad things in life, the stronger we become, Johnny. It's like making your legs stronger, by running."

"Is that why we play jump-rope and—"

"Yes, sweetie. Exactly. Now, shall we read about Job?"

When Len came in, he noticed the Bible. Maggie had forgotten to put it back in the trunk. An expensive book he knew by the richness of the cover, the red velvet binding and ribbon—

Slowly, almost absently, Len reached out and picked up the book. With one brown fingertip, he flipped open the cover, revealing the inside flyleaf.

His handsome face in a deep scowl, Len called, "Maggie!"

Maggie turned from the cookstove, where she had a chicken in hot grease in the heavy iron skillet.

"What is it, Len? I'm sort of busy right here—"

"I think this is more important. Come here, Maggie."

"What on earth, Len," Maggie wiped her hands on her apron, and turned from the hot stove—to see Len Evans—holding her precious Bible—a black scowl on his face—she had forgotten to put it back in the trunk!

"I want you to tell me, Maggie, and I don't want any lies from you. *Who is Thomas?*"

"Why, Len," Maggie smiled sweetly, slowly wiping her hands on her apron, "Thomas Shawn McKinnon was my Grandpapa. He's gone to Glory, now."

Len stared at Maggie for what seemed to her an eternity. Her blue eyes locked with his. She kept her chin up and the innocent little smile on her face.

With an angry snap, Len slapped the Bible shut, and slowly placed it back on the table. He walked to the front door, and went out.

Maggie snatched her precious Book up into her arms. She closed her eyes, and leaned weakly against the little table. Waves of relief swept over her.

—When she had turned, and had seen Len holding the Book, a horrible vision had risen before her—of Len Evans walking over …jerking an eye off the cookstove …and shoving her precious Bible into the red-hot coals.

"*Thomas!*" Maggie whispered.

Maggie knew that sooner or later, the festering sore would come to a head.

She and Johnny were playing chase, and Len came in from the field early. She watched as he stalked past them, on into the house, to wash up. In a few minutes he was back out. He stood on the porch for several minutes. Then, slowly, deliberately, Len stepped off the porch—

—And came towards her. His face was dark as a thundercloud.

"I don't know who you think you are, Maggie. But I'm tired of watching you make a complete fool of yourself. I want you to know here and now—that I've had enough. *You are my wife!* And from now on, I would very much appreciate it if you would *act* like it. Now get your skirts down, and cover your ankles properly. Then get on in that house—and you stay there. I have a few words to say to Mister John Thomas McKinnon, Jr. here! He has to find himself another place to roost. And if he needs any help, I'm the man for the job."

With each sentence that came out of Len's mouth, Maggie's rage mounted.

Was Len *demented*? He ranted on—like a *crazy* man! There was no one in the yard, but Maggie and Johnny. No man to leer at an exposed ankle! And to say that Johnny had to *find himself another place to roost*! Johnny was two, going on three years old!

So filled with indignation she could scarcely see, Maggie's face felt cold, the blood all drained from it. She brushed down her skirt, and took a few steps towards this man she had married—

"My skirts are down, now, Len Evans! All the leering men lurking in the bushes can stop staring—and just go on home to their wives and mamas! I suppose I should also stop exposing myself so, by taking baths in the privacy of what I thought was my own home—!

"And as for my being your *wife*, much to my sorrow, sometimes I find that I have taken vows to a man who apparently has *no heart ...no soul ...*and not *one shred of sense—*

"*John Thomas McKinnon, Jr.—*is *my brother.* He is a two-and-a-half-year-old *orphan*—a baby! *With no one.* If he needs someone to find him a home, I think I know *just* the person! I'll take him *away* from this place! I'd rather scratch in the dirt with the *rats*, and live on rotten nuts and *weeds and acorns* in the forest—than to live with a man like *you!*"

As Maggie spoke, the dark, flushed face drained to a deathly pallor. Like a man awakening, Len moved toward her, his hands outstretched, as if in supplication.

"Maggie! I didn't mean ...you know I didn't mean to hurt you! It's just that ...the boy can *stay*! Maggie! I don't know why ...I said that! *I love you!*"

"You sure have a poor way of showing it! *Leave* me alone! *Get* out of my way!" Maggie shouted at him.

Maggie grabbed Johnny and fled past him, and in the door. She thought of dropping the heavy bar, but knew he would break it down. Frantically, she began flinging her things and Johnny's into the vastness of Katherine Ann's big brown leather trunk.

Len came in, moved toward her. Maggie backed away.

But his stride was longer. He was stronger. He had her in his arms, cradling her head against him, pleading and begging.

Maggie felt the strength of him. The warmth. The words filled with gentle, passionate love. Oh, how she had loved this man—! How she had given herself to him—

But these were the same words she had heard so many times before. Against her will, the familiar feelings stirred within her. She fought to push them down. It was no longer just *Maggie* that was involved here—

*There was Johnny—*Johnny, *with his whole life ahead of him—*

"Len!" Maggie finally managed to say, trying to get her head together, "Let me go! And just ...get away from me! I can't *live* like this. I won't have Johnny raised ...like this. I don't know what ...has happened in your life ...to make you ...but whatever it is, I can't let it ruin Johnny's life. *I just can't.* If it were just me, I might—"

Maggie broke off, trembling, uncertain what to say, or to do. She had broken away from him, and stood staring about the little house. She seemed at an impossible cross in the road. She would *not* have Johnny mistreated— not because of her mistake. *Not if it cost her life.* But if she truly *left* here, *where would she go*—?

—To Barbara Jo? And Fredrick J. Moss? With Johnny in tow?

"*Maggie!*" Len was pleading, "I'll make it up to you! This time, things will be different. Anything you want, Maggie! I'll do *anything*! Just don't leave me! *Don't leave me!* It's just that …you don't understand, Maggie! Without you, I'd have *no desire to live!*"

"No, Len, I don't understand," Maggie wagged her head sorrowfully. "And I don't know that I want to. All I know is that things *cannot* continue as they are. This is no longer just about you and me. Do you understand, Len, that *if I stay, Johnny stays*. I don't ask that you love him, but he is to be treated with decency—and respect. He is to be allowed to be what he *is*—a sweet little boy. Full of energy and in need of great care and love—which I intend to see that he gets. If *any* of this is going to pose some kind of *problem* for you—Len Evans, I will take him and walk out that door—and you'll never see either of us—ever again.

"You have my solemn promise on that. And Len," Maggie locked her gaze with his, as if seeing him for the first time. "While we're on the subject, what about the child *we're* soon going to have? What about *your* child? Will it be welcome—in its father's house?"

"Maggie, you didn't tell me …I didn't know …but I won't lie to you, Maggie," Len's face still pale, the passion had died in his eyes, his face was set and cold—

"—You should know me by now. You should know I never wanted a child."

"No, Len, I don't think I *do* know you. And no, I didn't tell you—because I didn't think you'd care to know. But, if you're not blind, I'm sure by now *you do know*! And whether you *like* it or not, this child *is* going to be born."

With a warm hug and a kiss, silently Maggie put Johnny to bed. She wasn't sure how much of what had just been said Johnny understood. But she noticed that for once in his life, Johnny was silent and subdued. In a low voice, Johnny repeated his prayers, and then he gave Maggie a long, tight hug, and snuggled silently into bed.

Leaving their things still in the big brown trunk, Maggie went to bed, and lay there weeping silent tears, until her pillow was soaked. What was *wrong* with Len Evans—that he had such a supposedly all-consuming love for her— but had *no feeling* at all for a sweet little boy like Johnny—and a cold, denying repugnance for his *own child*?

Maybe she should *leave Len Evans*. But she seriously doubted he would let her go. What was that he had said, about *not wanting to live*? Maggie shivered.

But if things got worse, and she *did* leave—Maggie was back to the same question—*where would she go?* With one child in hand—and another only weeks away? If she opened that door, *who knew where it might lead?*

On a fine spring day, in the year 1884, the spring Maggie turned eighteen, Katherine Ann was born—perfect, rosy-cheeked, with wide blue eyes. She was everything that Maggie could have dreamed.

When she was three months old, she would look at Johnny—pulling funny faces at her—wave her little arms and legs, and squeal and laugh out loud.

When she was five months old, she could already sit up unsupported, in the little tub Maggie had brought for her baths. She splashed and gurgled and cooed, swelling Maggie's heart with pure adoration.

When she was ten months old, like a perfect, miniature doll, Katie Ann was walking across the floor of the little sharecroppers' house, all by herself.

Maggie's days were full; her heart was content. She was happier than she had been, since marrying Len Evans.

Len fed them, and kept wood for the fires, and a roof, such as it was, over their heads—and Maggie stayed with Len.

Len stayed mostly out at the barn—or over at the big house.

Another spring awoke. The trees budded, the perennials came up that Maggie had planted in the yard, and bloomed in lovely rainbows of color. The rose bushes put on plump, colorful buds that had begun to open with the warming days.

Maggie put in her spring garden. She had fresh leaf lettuce, and radishes pushing their red heads through the soil, and scallions with a sweet odor and tangy taste. Her tomato plants were setting blooms—and this year, she did not chop down all the bean vines.

It was wash day. The children were playing chase around the trees in the back yard, their happy squeals rippling on the clean spring air, while Maggie was hanging out the week's wash. She glanced at them now and then, to make sure they stayed within the confines of the back yard. Johnny, his dark hair, the boyish face flushed with the excitement of the chase. Katie Ann, blond curls bobbing, as she tottered gleefully around, darting from behind this tree, then that.

Maggie heard the rolling thunder of the palomino's hooves. *Too close!* She heard Katie's scream—

Katie! NO! *Not Katie!*

Len leapt off the golden horse—

—He reached for the child—

"Don't *touch* her!" Maggie flew at him, screaming:

"Don't you *dare* touch her! You *never* wanted her!—

"—*But did you have to kill her?!*"

"Maggie! Surely, you don't believe I saw the child? I didn't see the child—!"

Ignoring him, Maggie picked up her baby, holding the little body close. But before she ever picked her up, she knew. She knew ...that Katie Ann was dead. Her back was broken.

"Maggie—!" Len pleaded, "Maggie, please! You've got to listen to me—!

"—*Listen to me—!*"

"Get *away* from me! Don't you *dare* touch me—!

"Don't you ever touch me again!"

Chapter 25

In an icy, petrified rage, Maggie strode past Len. She couldn't look at him. She couldn't speak to him. What was there left to say to this man?

Her heart racing, her eyes so filled with tears she could scarcely see, Maggie hugged the little body close, as she carried her inside, and laid Katie on the kitchen table. It would have to serve as her cooling board.

Very carefully, Maggie straightened the perfect little arms, the tiny little legs, still warm. Then she picked her up, hugged her close, and laid her back down. Blood had seeped through her little dress, forming a puddle on the tabletop. Maggie wanted to keen and wail. But felt if she once began, she might never be able to cease. She would simply shatter into a million unrecognizable pieces—

Remembering Johnny, Maggie walked back outside, got Johnny by the hand and led him into the house.

She had no idea where Len had gone. She reached and took her shawl down from a hook by the front door. As a sort of afterthought, she walked over to the table, and stood gazing at the exquisite little form,

Johnny sat in a chair in front of the fireplace, weeping softly. Wordlessly, Maggie walked over, took his hand, pulled him along, walked to the door and reached for the latch.

The door seemed to open of its own accord. A thin Negro woman stood framed in the waning afternoon light.

This, Maggie knew instantly, was the *vagrant* that had been living in the tiny one-room cabin tucked into the woods down past the barn.

"I's heerd the rackets. I's cum' to see, could I's be of any help."

"What's your name?"

"Liza, Missus."

"Liza, stay with my child, until I get back."

Maggie walked to the barn, hitched up the wagon, and lifted Johnny in.

"Maggie? What on earth are you doing here? Are you alone? Where's Len? You afoot? You walked all the way? No, I see you have the wagon out front."

Barbara kept staring at her younger sister.

"Maggie! For heaven's sakes, what's happened?"

"My baby. Katie Ann's dead. I want to borrow a wagon and team. I'm going to take her home."

"*Home?*" Barbara Jo asked.

"Yes," Maggie replied.

"To *Rhyersville*? Maggie! You can't be serious! You mean to *Rhyersville*? How did this ...what happened?"

"Len rode over Katie Ann, with his fine palomino."

"Oh ...Maggie! Oh ...no! Come ...sit ...down ..."

"No. I've got to go. She's there ...in the house ...all by herself ...except for the colored woman ...it's coming on dark. She hates the dark—"

"Maggie! *Colored woman?* Where on earth is Len?"

"I ...don't know. Over at his Pa's, I suppose. Maggie!"

"Whenever anything doesn't go to suit Len, he runs home to his Pa."

"*Home?*"

"I'll need a bottle of Calvert's Rubbing Oil, and some camphor balls. And a little pink silk dress and bonnet. I want the little box lined—no black—with the same pink—"

"Don't think about all that now. Of course, you can have whatever you need. Here. Here's the oil. And ...oh, dear God! I can't believe this. You plan to take her to *Rhyersville*? That will take at least three days ...two and a half ...if the weather's perfect."

"I'm taking her home. I *won't* have her put in *Carl Evans'* grave plot. *I won't!*"

"All right, Maggie. You can have the team, and the heavy wagon Fred uses to make deliveries ...the one that has a cover on it ...in case there should be rain. And I'll go with you."

"I want to send a message, by telegraph wire—I heard that you can do that now—to Thomas Beyers. So he can make arrangements. Maybe he'll ...help me put her near Nellie Sue."

"I'll do that, right now. Then I'll get the camphor balls. And I'll drive home with you."

Before leaving the store, Maggie took the bottle of Calvert's Rubbing Oil, uncorked the top, and dropped in several of the camphor balls, to let them melt. As she drove the wagon back to the little sharecroppers' house, she clutched the paper parcel tightly between her knees. She felt as if she might burst from the grief swelling up inside her, an all-consuming pain. But she couldn't. She had to keep her wits about her. She had to take the camphor home, and take care of Katie Ann—

As soon as they drove into the dooryard of the tiny sharecroppers' house, Maggie recognized the bulky form of Clement Greene, sitting on the front step.

He hurried forward to take Johnny, help Maggie step down from the wagon.

"Maggie, Len came over and told us. We're so, so sorry about this. Len is, too."

"Oh? Where is he?" Maggie asked coldly.

"I think …he said something about …going over …to tell his folks."

"She's been dead for two hours. It takes him two hours to go half a mile, and tell his folks?"

Clem Greene turned his eyes away. He couldn't bear to see it—all that pain in Maggie's eyes.

Maggie turned and walked into the little house. Sarah sat in a chair by the tiny kitchen table, staring at Katie. She rose, and clasped Maggie in her arms.

"Oh, Maggie! Oh, sugar! I'm so sorry!"

Maggie clung to her for several moments. Then she pulled away, took her shawl, and hung it back behind the front door.

She walked to the table, carefully put down her little paper parcel.

Barbara Jo came in the front door. "Sarah," she nodded, then, "Maggie, it's getting dark, since Sarah's here with you, I'm going to be going on. I'll pick you up at first light."

"Thank you, Barbara Jo. I'll pay you—"

"Hush, Maggie. I'll see you tomorrow."

Maggie heard the door close behind her sister. She undid the bottle of oil and the camphor balls, walked to the cookstove, kindled a fire, and put on a kettle of water. Then she began to undress the body.

Sarah and Clem stayed with her, throughout the nightmare that was the night of Katie's lying-in. Len did not show up, until the following morning, when Barbara Jo had arrived with the small coffin, which she had lined with pink silk, as Maggie had requested. He didn't come toward the house, but Maggie had seen the grand black horse, prancing into the barn. She immediately recognized it as belonging to Big Carl Evans.

Sarah lifted the lid of the little pine coffin. Maggie laid Katie Ann, dressed in pink silk, inside. Then she carefully placed the remainder of the camphor balls nestled about amongst the folds of the lovely pink silk that adorned the tiny body.

"She's so beautiful, in that pink silk dress and bonnet—just like an angel," Sarah whispered.

Maggie didn't say anything. She didn't dare. Afraid, if she opened her mouth, of what horrible sounds might come out. Unearthly wails of pain. Maggie bent her head, and gave her baby a final kiss.

Clement took his hammer, a few nails, nailed the lid securely shut.

Sarah fixed them a bite of breakfast, hot coffee.

Clement carried the little casket out to the covered wagon. Clem and Sarah climbed onto the seat. Johnny, dressed in his best little suit, sat between them. Maggie and Barbara Jo sat on empty kegs in the back, with Katie Ann.

As the covered wagon pulled out of the yard, a rider came out of the woods behind the little barn.

He was dressed in a fine black suit. He wore a fine black hat. He rode a gorgeous black stallion, the one Maggie had seen go into the little barn, the one that Maggie recognized as belonging to his father, Carl Evans.

But the rider dressed all in rich black, riding the beautiful black horse, stayed well back, most of the morning. Toward noon, like some stranger, he approached the wagon. He drew his beautiful black abreast of the driver's seat of the covered wagon, and spoke briefly to Clem Greene.

Maggie ignored him.

Barbara Jo had thought of everything. She had packed food and water for the journey. Warm blankets in case the nights were cold.

They ate when it was time. They stopped the wagon only when the darkness made it impossible to proceed. And the horses, Clem said, had to rest.

They camped by a little stream, so they could wash up a bit, and have fresh water for coffee.

As Clem saw to the horses, Barbara Jo, Maggie, and Johnny trooped down to the little creek, carrying a washpan, soap and towels.

Clem led the horses to water. The horses grazed beside the road. Then Clem tied on the feed bags of oats Barbara Jo had brought.

Len hung about the fringe of their little camp. So lean and handsome, in his new black suit. Just like that first day, Maggie thought, the first time she ever laid eyes on Len Evans—when he came to bargain with her, about the horse and wagon.

But he didn't come near her. He didn't attempt to speak to her.

Mid-afternoon, on Saturday, Clem pulled the team bearing its precious cargo up to the hitching post out front of the Shiloh Baptist Church, in Ryersville.

Thomas Beyers came out of the church, and down the steps. He reached up for Maggie, and bodily lifted her down from the high wagon. Then he folded her in his arms, one hand holding her head into his chest.

"Oh, Maggie! Oh, darling!"

Len sat in the shadows, on the black horse, watching.

Clem took his shovel out of the back of the covered wagon.

Thomas Beyers lifted out the little pine casket that smelled so loudly of camphor it almost took his breath away.

He hefted it easily onto one shoulder, and carried it up the gentle slope.

Dressed in a new black dress from Barbara Jo's store, with a bonnet and veil to match, Maggie walked next. Barbara Jo walked beside her, holding tightly to one hand; little Johnny clutched the other.

Clem and Sarah walked behind them.

Several steps back, hanging in the shadows of the trees, finally leaning against a large oak twenty feet back, there came Len Evans.

Maggie could not recall for the life of her ...what happened after that. She recalled being seated in a small restaurant, some time later that day, turning a hot mug of coffee in her hands. Barbara Jo, Clem and Sarah, Johnny, all seated with her.

And there was Thomas Beyers. Blessed, sweet, Thomas—

"Won't you have a bite to eat, Maggie? Maybe some—"

"Thank you, no, Thomas. I'm much obliged for ...everything you've done." Maggie said. "The coffee is fine."

She couldn't help but glance around for Len. He wasn't there.

"I can't believe how this place has changed," Barbara Jo was rattling on, "I can't believe how it has *grown*! As we were driving in, I saw a *half dozen* new businesses. Looked like a cotton gin, and a mill of some sort. I guess Rhyersville has outgrown Johnson's Corners, and stolen all their business away—!

"And this restaurant! Did you ever think, Maggie, we'd live to see the day there would be a *restaurant*—in *Rhyersville?*"

"No, I didn't think." Maggie muttered numbly.

"Looks like there's a storm brewin' over th' mountains," the little restaurant's proprietor said, making friendly conversation. "You folks new in town?"

"Just here," Clem smiled thinly at the man, "for the afternoon."

"Well, you'd better be finding yourself somewhere in town to lodge. Some place that's good and dry. Looks like she's goin' to be a humdinger."

"Why don't you folks spend the night at my place?" Thomas Beyers offered.

"We couldn't possibly," Maggie said. "I've got to get back."

"Back to *what*, Maggie?" Barbara Jo asked shortly. "I say we accept Thomas' kind offer of hospitality. Some of us may have to make pallets on the floor; but if a storm's brewing, it'll sure beat overnighting in the wagon, even with its canvas top."

"Then it's settled. And we'll get a good hot supper, and then some breakfast into all of you ...and you can ...be on your way. Maggie?"

"Oh, yes ...that's fine. Whatever you want to do."

Thomas Beyers' house was small, but comfortable. Maggie knew it well. It was the house where Nellie Sue had died.

Sarah and Barbara Jo helped Thomas Beyers in the kitchen, while Clem sat at the table and tried to make small talk.

They sat down to a meal of fried steak and potatoes, and early vegetables from Thomas Beyers' garden, with more hot coffee, and some apples for desert.

Maggie fiddled with her food, forced down some of the hot coffee, as she gazed about the little kitchen where she had sat and talked with Nellie Sue—

Suddenly she felt she had to get outside, get a breath of fresh air.

"Will you excuse me?" Maggie rose and stepped through the front door, out into the small fenced yard with its ivy and lovely rose trellis heavy with blooms.

Immediately, Thomas Beyers followed.

"Maggie," he said, walking along beside her, their elbows almost touching, "you don't know how good it is to see you ...I'm sorry ...that's probably not the right thing to say. It's just that ...I've missed you ...all of you, so much."

Maggie almost smiled, in spite of herself. Thomas Beyers was as handsome, and as painfully shy, as that first night, when he approached Nellie Sue at the Bidwell's corn husking. He was such a nice man. How he had loved Nellie Sue! *Really* loved her. And Nellie had loved Thomas. Maggie wondered why Thomas hadn't married again. Fortunate would be the woman, to find a man ...a man like Thomas Beyers.

"It's all right, Thomas. I know what you mean. And you'll never know ...how I've missed this place ...the church, those mountains over there, this little dirt street, the store. The post office. And just down that street, the school ..."

"Why don't you come home, Maggie? This is where you belong. You don't ...that is to say ...have you ...been happy, Maggie?"

Of course, he had seen Len, the way Len slunk about in the shadows—the way Len was not with her. Maggie was certain Clem had told him exactly who that rakishly handsome, rather odd fellow was.

"I wish I could. Oh," Maggie whispered, "I wish I could."

"I wish I could. But I can't," Maggie told Thomas, again, the next morning, as she gave him a brief peck on the cheek, and he gave her a small hug.

"You know," Barbara Jo said, gazing about her as the big covered wagon rolled slowly down Rhyersville's Main Street, "This place has *real* potential."

"You folks leavin' out, are you?" It was Ransom Jones, standing in the door of his Rhyersville Restaurant, "If you'd hang around, I'd give one of you a job!"

Clem drew the team to a halt, "Well, I suppose we best be movin' on."

"You folks ought to stick around, help us solve the mystery."

"What mystery would that be?" Clem asked with a friendly little smile.

"Oddest thing. They found a *corpse*, fully clothed, over in the graveyard, back of the Shiloh Baptist Church. Fellow dressed to kill. And all laid out, hands folded on his chest and everythin'. Just layin' on top th' ground, by a fresh grave."

"Oh! Maggie!" Barbara Jo's face went ashen.

Maggie felt icy waves of shock—rocking her—

"—*Len?*"

"Where is he?" Maggie heard Barbara Jo ask the restaurant owner. "Got the corpse over at Dr. Ellis' office. But there was nothing could be done for him. You know how it stormed last night. But the Doc said he didn't think it was th' rain. He couldn't find any *real* cause of death. It was like the fella' decided it was time to go, so he went to the graveyard, laid himself down, and went."

Dr. Ellis had taken off the wet clothes, and hung them up to dry. Maggie recognized them instantly.

The corpse was wrapped in a clean white sheet. Dr. Ellis lifted the corner of the sheet, for Maggie to view him.

Maggie's hand flew to her mouth; she stood gazing in stunned disbelief.

Len Evans, cold, stiff, the handsome, familiar face, as if it was carved of ice.

"Maggie?" Dr. Ellis asked quietly, "You know this man?"

"He is ...he *was* ...my husband."

Thomas Beyers drew Clem aside. They huddled together for a few minutes.

"If you will see to his laying out, Doctor Ellis, until Maggie can make arrangements, I know she would appreciate it." Thomas Beyers spoke softly.

Then the four of them hustled Maggie out of the doctor's office, and down to the restaurant, for more black coffee, and hopefully a bite of lunch.

Len Evans was not buried where he had stretched himself out, not buried beside Katie Ann and Nellie Sue. Thomas Beyers was reserving that space for himself.

But he was buried in the little graveyard back of the Shiloh Baptist Church, at the edge of a pine grove some twenty feet away. The only plot, Thomas told them, that was available for immediate sale.

Maggie couldn't have told a soul what sort of funeral it was, or if there was indeed a funeral.

She just knew that she walked again, up that gentle slope behind the church, and saw another open grave, which was soon closed.

"I'll have to get some headstones," Maggie said, as if now that was the most important thing in her life.

Chapter 26

The little sharecroppers' house stood quiet and empty, as Maggie drove into the barren yard upon her return from Rhyersville ...and the funerals. She lifted Johnny down, and carried him inside. He was exhausted, and half asleep. She held him close, and felt the warmth of him. The enormity of being a young widow, left with this small boy to provide for, had not yet become a reality to Maggie. She had lost her child, and her husband. She was numb—from the traumatic events of the past week.

She started a fire in the cookstove, stirred up some eggs with scraps of cheese from the cupboard, and made a small hoecake. She drew up the milk from the well. It was fresh. Maggie quickly realized that Liza had been sneaking over, milking the cow, and feeding the chickens and the pigs. She had completely forgotten about the thin, emaciated Negro woman.

Darkness fell. Johnny was fed. Like all small boys, he had a ravenous appetite, wolfing his food down, and grinning up at Maggie between bites. Soon he was tucked into bed. Maggie sat alone, at the little table. The image of Len intruded itself into her mind, but she quickly pushed it aside.

Who was Len Evans?

She had married him, but she had never really known Len Evans. Who would ever have *dreamed* he would have done such a thing?

But Maggie felt no guilt, none at all, for his death. Len Evans had lived, and Len Evans had died—on his own terms.

Feeling confined and overwhelmed, the walls closing in on her, Maggie took her shawl, and walked outside. Overhead, the moon and the stars hung like bright coals from a winter fire, filling the night sky with soft light.

How lovely! And somewhere, up there, lived a God who, Maggie knew, had created all this. And breathed life into it, and declared that it was *good*—

And this same God, Maggie firmly believed, loved and oversaw His grand creation. Even to the smallest creature:

Not a sparrow...falls...

Maggie took a hard look at the little sharecropper cabin.

She knew she couldn't possibly stay here. She couldn't live in this place.

But the rent was paid through the fall harvest. She wondered if she could keep the upland cotton rows, the ribbon-like Indian corn rows, free enough of grass and weeds, to bring in a decent crop this fall—

And could she possibly *harvest* the crops—all alone. But—she would have to try; she needed money.

And she had nowhere to go. But after the harvest, she would have to come up with something.

The following morning, Maggie saw the thinnest curl of smoke rising out of the woods. She took Johnny's hand; they walked over to the little one-room cabin, where the bone-thin Negress, Liza, had been hiding out for the past year or so.

Maggie rapped softly on the door.

Liza opened it. She ushered Maggie and Johnny into the tiny room.

Gazing at Liza, Maggie was again struck with the vision of bones almost protruding through the paper-thin, dark skin.

"I came over to tell, you ..." Maggie paused, clearing her throat, "that Mr. Evans ...he won't be coming back ...Mr. Evans has ...passed away."

The thin Negress did not ask what had happened to Len, how he had died. She simply said, "I's suckled Massa Len, when he was furst born," tears spilling from the dark, sunken eyes, coursing down the withered cheeks, "I's eleven or twelve. I's had lost my furst baby."

"*Eleven or twelve?*" Maggie was horrified. So *this* was how Len knew Liza. She had been a *slave* ...at the Evans' place! She had a child ...at age eleven or twelve! Liza must still be in her early forties! With her protruding bones, and her thin, wizened skin, she looked to be ninety years old!

Maggie was afraid to ask—how many babies Liza had lost.

"Then, when Mr. Len were just a little thing," Liza was saying, "come the War, and then the War were over—his Pap, Massa Carl, says we has to move on. I didn't see Massa Len again, until I heard he had come home, and had got this place, and got married again."

"You knew Len's first wife?"

"Yes'm," Liza muttered, her eyes large, her lips pulled thin.

Well, Maggie thought, whatever lay there, just let it go. Len is dead. Maggie gave her a weak smile.

"Well, Liza. As soon as I milk, I'll bring you a fresh pitcher."

The cow had to be milked. She had to check on Job. She needed to bring in some water. And throw some Indian corn to the chickens. There might be eggs to gather.

And Johnny would need his lunch.

And there was Big Carl Evans's fine black stallion.

She'd almost forgotten about the stallion. The beautiful black was found, tied to the hitching post, in front of the Shiloh Baptist Church.

Clem had hitched him to the rear of the covered wagon, and he had followed them home—his head high, his powerful muscles rippling, in a perfect prance.

Maggie checked on the horse. She tossed him some hay, led him to the watering trough. He probably needed grooming. But he wasn't Maggie's animal. He belonged to Big Carl Evans. And Maggie intended to see that his property was returned to him at the earliest convenience. She wondered what had become of the golden palomino.

But the next morning, no more had Maggie started a fire in the cookstove and put her dough-tray on the kitchen table, ready to prepare breakfast, than there was a frenetic banging on the front door.

Barely dressed, her hair in disarray about her shoulders, Maggie called: "Who is it?"

"Who do you think it is? Carl Evans!"

"Mr. Evans," Maggie lifted the latch, and swung the plank door wide.

"You got my horse?" His face was flushed, his voice harsh and rasping.

"He's out in the barn."

"You'd better have brought him back in fine shape."

"If you will recall, Mr. Evans, I'm *not* the one who took him."

"Another thing, Miss High-and-Mighty," Big Carl lifted a meaty finger and wagged it in Maggie's face, "now that my boy's gone, I want you *off* my place. By the end of the month. Never did take to *your kind* of woman— woman who wants to meddle in men's affairs."

Maggie let that comment pass, but as to the other, "The end of the month!?" Maggie shouted at him. "You know good and well the rent's been paid on this place until *the harvest* is in!"

"Yeah, I know." Big Carl gave an angry jerk of his head. "But it was rented to *my son*! It wasn't *ever* rented to you." He turned and stomped off the shallow little porch. Suddenly he swung back, his fleshy face contorted with rage, his dark eyes hot with tears:

"Why didn't you bring my boy back? To be buried with his own kin!"

"It was Len who climbed the slope behind the Shiloh Baptist Church, Mr. Evans, laid down by his daughter's grave, put his hat over his face, folded his hands on his chest, and died. I think Len finally made his *own* decision."

With that, Maggie slammed the door shut.

She had until the end of the month!

Maggie cooked up some biscuits and ham. Spread butter on two biscuits to be kept warm for Johnny, when he got up. Set aside a slice of ham for him. He could have some fresh berries, and a cup of warm milk with his ham and biscuit.

She returned from the barn, strained up the milk, leaving a cup for Johnny, a little pitcher for Liza, lowered the rest into the well in the usual pitcher.

Johnny was up, rubbing the sleep from his eyes, with his chin propped on the table, grinning at her.

Maggie smiled, in spite of herself. She whispered a fervent prayer: *God, have mercy on us both!*

After she had choked down a bite of food and had a hot cup of coffee with fresh, sweet cream, Maggie sat down at the little table with a sheet of brown paper and a stub of a pencil. Her face was still unwashed, her hair swung dark and loose around her shoulders. It was May, of the year 1885. Maggie was nineteen. She felt as if she had lived a hundred years.

She needed to total up her assets.

Assets?

And her liabilities. *Liabilities!*

She owed Barbara Jo for the little casket, the pink silk dress, bonnet and casket lining.

She owed Barbara Jo for rent on the covered wagon …for a week.

She owed Barbara Jo for whatever she had spent on Maggie's food—especially at the Rhyersville Restaurant.

Then, there was the large bottle of *Calverts Rubbing Oil*—and the bag of camphor balls.

She had no idea about Len's funeral expenses. All that day had been an unbelievable nightmare, a horrid surreal vision of what *hell* must be like.

She probably owned someone quite a lot—for that.

She had one iron bedstead, one table, two chairs, one iron cookstove—that she intended to sell, even if Len Evans had paid for them. She thought that she had earned at least that much.

She had Katherine Ann's trunk, with her worn wool blankets still inside, her iron Dutch oven, and Shawn's and Papa's fiddle and Shawn's and Mama's Bible.

These things were surely *hers* by every right.

She had one horse—that had given faithful service—and a one-horse wagon, in which to haul *whatever* she took with her—to *wherever* she went. The beautiful palomino, she supposed, had disappeared into Carl Evans's big barn. That was just as well, for Maggie never wished to lay eyes on that animal again, even though the horse was not at fault for her child's death—but the rider.

She could take the iron bedsteads, the iron cookstove, the large table and benches the front-room rockers and washstands that they had brought down from McKinnon Valley. Packed the same way she had brought them down.

That left the trunk.

If she sold one of the mattresses and beds—

No, she might need the beds. She had plans.

She would definitely need the table, washstands, chairs, and benches. Wherever they went, she thought tiredly, they would still have to eat, and wash.

She would *definitely* not leave the trunk.

She would pack what few clothes and bed linens they possessed in Katherine Ann's trunk, and it still contained most of Mama's things.

Maggie stood and stretched her back, and paced the tiny room. She had to be gone—*by the end of the month.*

She was back to where she had begun. She couldn't possibly take everything.

And this, Maggie thought, is *the fifteenth.* She tried to think of anything else of value she might have.

The cow, the chickens, and the two pigs, she could sell.

What would they bring—the cow and the chickens and the pigs?

She'd ride into town, and ask Barbara Jo if they would be enough to cover a great part of her debt.

When she left here, and went …wherever …she would need some *cash money* …to put a roof over their heads, and to keep starvation at bay, until she found work.

She wondered about the money Len had gotten for the last crop. Several hundred dollars! What had Len *done* with it? He never discussed money, or crop prices or receipts with her. She had no idea what he could have done with the money. There was nothing of value on him, Dr. Ellis said, when he was found. Just a few loose coins in one of his trouser pockets. And a pocket watch.

Maggie had a good idea where the money had gone—to Carl Evans.

Did she have the watch? Did Dr. Ellis give her the watch?

She ran to look in her small reticule. She had the watch!

Maggie laid the watch on the little table. She turned and began to survey the house. She walked from room to room. She wondered if there was any money hidden in the house.

There was simply no place to hide anything—not in this house. It was too small, too sparsely furnished.

Where did Len spend most of his time?

The barn.

Maggie searched the barn thoroughly.

Nothing. But a pack of letters—hidden beneath the hay in one corner.

Letters …with *Mama's* handwriting on the envelopes!

Mama had written her letters—at least a dozen. Len had picked them up—

Maggie clasped them to her, tears flooding her eyes. What had Mama said to her, in these unread letters? Mama had never mentioned them to Maggie. Perhaps she was waiting, for Maggie to mention them, to answer them—which, of course, Maggie never did. So Mama had stopped writing.

Maggie determined to deal with the letters at some later time.

What about the tools—axes, plows, lines, the bellows and forge?

She knew the tools most likely belonged to Carl Evans—just the same as the house and land. Len had probably owned nothing—except his fine clothes, his horse and saddle. She didn't want *anything* that belonged to Carl Evans! They had brought down very few tools, from Rhyersville. Maggie would take only what she felt belonged to her.

Back in the house, Maggie looked down at her left hand.

Len had given her a small gold wedding band.

She took it off, and dropped it with a cold little flourish, into her reticule, with the pocket watch.

"The cow, pigs and the chickens will be enough, Maggie, more than enough," Barbara Jo assured her. Then Barbara Jo went into a deep study, pursing her lips, "In fact, let me see, you may have some money coming back to you. A good milk cow is a very valuable animal. She gives steady, does she?"

"Almost two gallons—both morning and night milkings. If she's well fed and tended."

"Let's see? How about ...I would say that you have at least ...five dollars coming to you. After we subtract the cow, the pigs and the chickens, you still have the iron bedstead, cookstove, small table, and two chairs. Maybe twenty-five dollars for those. Plus five, makes thirty dollars."

Thirty dollars was not much, but probably more than she was actually due, so Maggie smiled at Barbara Jo, and said, "Thanks, Barbs. For everything."

"Oh," Barbara Jo gave an embarrassed little toss of her head, "it was nothing. I might need your help sometime."

"Just let me know," Maggie smiled at Barbara Jo—standing behind the counter of one of the most prosperous businesses for miles around.

"Maggie," Barbara Jo said worriedly, "*where* on earth do you plan on going?"

"I thought I'd just ...go back home."

"Home? You mean ...*Rhyersville?*"

"Yes, Barbs ...Rhyersville."

"What will you *do* there?"

"Maybe Reliance Ransom Jones will give me a job in his restaurant. Who knows, I may end up owning that fine establishment some day." Maggie gave a dry little laugh, "I can't stay here. I have to start somewhere."

"You know, Maggs, I've been telling Fred ...about Rhyersville ...about the big gin and the mill, and all the other new enterprises there. We may just ride up that way, and let him have a look at the place. He says he's thinking of relocating."

"Are you serious? Are you *serious!*"

"Let me get back with you in, say ...a week or so. You might drive your wagon along with ours."

"Barbara Jo, are you sure about this? I've never heard a word out of you—about Fred wanting to *relocate*. That's so ...astonishing!"

"Well, to tell you the truth, Maggs, it's me. I *never* have liked it down here. I get so homesick sometimes I just cry my eyes out. It get's on Fred's nerves."

"You don't wail and moan, do you?"

"What? Oh, no Maggs, I'm not a child. I just miss the way the mist hangs over the mountains. And the way it's not really *that* hot—even on the hottest days of summer."

"I have to leave by the end of the month," Maggie said wearily.

"I'll let you know something, by tomorrow week."

"Would Fred *do* that for you, Barbs? Would Fred relocate his business, just for you?"

"Fred's a good man, Maggie. He's not perfect. But he's a good man. I'll let you know something, tomorrow week."

It had been ten days, since Katie's funeral. Ten days.

Maggie needed to get her mind together. To decide what foodstuffs she could possibly take along with her. The sweet potato vines were lush and green, but Maggie knew the tubers beneath the ground were still only roots, not real sweet potatoes. That would take all summer.

Maybe there were still a few yams left in the potato hill, from last fall's crop, and a few Irish potatoes.

She'd check on the potatoes, today. There might be some dried peas, a few dried apples. She still had some ground oats, a bit of flour, some Indian corn meal. That was about the extent of it.

Maggie found a few sweet potatoes, a few Irish potatoes still in the hill. She dug them up, and spread them out on the kitchen floor to dry. She dragged out a small sack of dried peas. She went to the meal chest, bagged up the last of the flour, the oats, and the Indian corn meal. She set them on the top of the cold cookstove, where any mice couldn't get to them.

Before Maggie knew it, the day was over, and darkness was again descending. She fed Johnny and put him to bed.

She was clearing away the dishes, when she heard a wagon drive up out front. Who on earth could that be, she wondered, at this hour?

Maggie drew back the thin cotton curtain. She couldn't believe her eyes. It was *Fred Moss*! And he was fetching a box out of the back of his wagon.

Maggie lifted the latch, and swung open the plank door.

"Fred? You alone? Where's Barbara Jo?"

"Evenin', Maggie. Barbara had a meeting, or something, at the church. I was out this way, thought I'd just drop you off a few things you might be needin'."

Fred carried the box over and set it down on the little table. Then he took off his hat, and stood nervously twisting it in thin, pale hands.

How strange, Maggie thought, watching him carefully. Fred was known all over the county as about the stingiest man that ever lived—except perhaps, for Big Carl Evans.

Maggie stared at Fred Moss' shiny face, the hairline receding by the day, until now he was almost bald on top. She was unsure of what she should say.

"I didn't expect this, Fred. I'm very much obliged. How much do I owe you?"

"You don't owe me anything, Maggie," Fred was smiling at her, a crooked, stupid grin that stretched his mouth in an unnatural smirk. His eyes looked peculiar, Maggie thought, as if he were seeing her for the first time. Tiny beads of sweat popped out on his forehead. His thin face was flushed red as a beet.

"You all right, Fred?" Maggie asked, "You're not comin' down with something?"

He stood staring at her, twisting at his collar, then licking his lips.

Maggie had never seen Fred like this.

Suddenly he reached out, and grabbed her hand. "I just wanted you to know, Maggie, how I *personally feel* …about you …since that first day …when you walked into my store!"

Maggie quickly snatched her hand from his, wiping it on her skirt. She took a step backward. Oh, no! Not Fred!

Fred? Fred Moss?

Maggie took another step backward.

Fred Moss followed.

Maggie backed completely around the little table.

Fred was carefully stalking her; he reached for her.

The first sense of shock passed, as Maggie backed around the table. Now all she felt was anger—hot and sick rising in her throat. How dare he—! This was *her brother-in-law! Barbara Jo's husband!* He knew she had just buried her *child*! Her *husband*—!

That's why Fred Moss was here!

Maggie glanced about, for anything she could fling at him.

Her eyes fell on the box of supplies Fred had so generously brought her. She snatched up the small bag of flour, and swung it with all her might—

The bag burst on impact.

Flour went flying all over the kitchen, but mostly down Fred Moss' face, into his eyes and nose. Down his fine vest and jacket and shirt and trousers—down to the tips of his black shiny shoes.

He stood sputtering and gasping. He looked for all the world like a white ghost!

Suddenly, Maggie burst out laughing.

Fred Moss drew his thin frame up, muttered a few words Maggie did not catch, reached for his hat, flung the front door open, and vanished in a cloud of white.

The door slammed shut behind him, and Maggie collapsed into a straight-backed chair. She laid her head forward onto the little table. She was uncertain as to whether she should laugh? Or cry. What could possibly happen next, she wondered?

What next?

Following Fred Moss' unwelcome visit, Maggie kept the rifle loaded, and near at hand.

She kept it propped by the front door, when she was inside. She kept it propped by the feed trough, when she did the milking. She kept it propped against the well curb, when she went for water.

This was where the rifle was—

—When the stranger came walking down the rutted dirt road.

"Evenin,' Ma'am. Could I trouble you for a drink of that cold water?"

Maggie's initial impulse was to refuse. But could she in all good Christian conscience deny a drink of water to a thirsty soul? Reluctantly, she reached for the tin dipper that always hung on the rusty nail beneath the low well shelter.

Maggie dipped the bowl of the dipper into the bucket, handed the dipper to the man, and wiped her hand on her apron tail.

He raised the dipper to his lips, his narrowed eyes swiveling over Maggie, then over the quiet little house behind her—over the loaded rifle, propped against the well curb.

Maggie, meanwhile, kept one eye on the stranger, while replacing the well lid, and emptying the freshly drawn water into her bucket.

She needed to get back inside. She fervently wished he would hand her the dipper, and be on his way, back up the road down which he had just walked.

Why, she wondered, had he walked down *this* road? There was nothing down here. It dead-ended at the river.

Slowly, his eyes on her face, he handed her the dipper. His hands, Maggie could not help but notice, were none too clean. Nor was his face. He needed a good bath, a shave. He could do with a hair trim. His hat and his clothes could have well done with a good scrubbing in lye soap.

I'll scald the dipper, Maggie noted to herself, in a kettle of hot water, as soon as he leaves.

He made no move to leave.

Act naturally. Don't let him see he's making you nervous. Don't let him know how frightened you feel.

"If you will excuse me, sir," Maggie said in what she hoped was a firm voice of dismissal, "I have work to do."

"I was wondering, Ma'am, if your husband might be about?"

"Not at the moment," Maggie said quickly. Then immediately she lied, "But I expect him—any minute now. He'll be coming in from the field—any minute now."

He gave her a wicked little grin, said slowly:

"Well, I'd sure like to wait around, for a minute. See if he'd mind, if I slept in your barn tonight."

"My *husband*," Maggie said very sternly, "*does not* cotton to strangers. I can give you your answer now, mister. There'll be no sleeping in *this* barn. Tonight, or any *other* night."

He glanced around the well curb. Maggie saw his narrowed gaze resting on the loaded rifle.

He knew she was alone. Any woman whose husband is momentarily expected in from the field, does not go for a bucket of water with a loaded rifle.

Maggie had propped the gun close. She could probably reach for it, aim it, and get off a shot—

But could she actually *shoot a man*?

Her eyes on the stranger, Maggie took a step closer to the loaded rifle.

Yes. She decided. Yes. She could.

He saw the determination in her eyes, and gave a little nod. As if to acknowledge that she had won this round. But who would win the next?

"Well, Ma'am,' seins' how the land lays, I s'pose, then, I'll just be moseying off."

With one final glance at the rifle, he turned and swung away, walking off—down the road towards the river.

Weak with relief, Maggie snatched up the bucket of water in one hand, the loaded rifle in the other, and with the bucket banging against her leg—spilling water all down her dress tail, wetting her stockings and shoes—she hurried into the little house. Once inside, Maggie dropped the latch, leaned against the door a moment for support. Then she dragged the kitchen table against the door.

She glanced around. He had walked down towards the river. There was *nothing* down there.

He would be back.

Maggie began to wonder frantically, if there was anything else outside she needed to look after tonight? The milking was done, the pigs fed, Job was in his stall for the night. She had water—but she would need more wood.

Maggie eased the front door open. No one was in sight. Fear, cold and clammy, made her feel faint, almost nauseous. But she would need the wood. The nights sometimes were cold, and there must be fuel for the cookstove, for supper and breakfast—for Johnny.

She could hear Johnny, now, playing in the spare room. Leaving the door slightly ajar, Maggie slipped out to the woodpile, then back in, her arms laden. She made four or five trips.

One more armful, and she slammed the door shut, bolting it tightly. She should have enough for the entire night, if need be.

Maggie set about cooking the evening meal. Fear clung to her like a wet garment; it seemed to rob her of all her body-warmth. They ate in silence, Johnny sat across from her, making little boy sounds between bites, humming and muttering. Johnny never managed to stay completely quiet. Above Johnny's murmuring, Maggie, all the while, strained every fiber in her being, attempting to pick up any slightest noise from outside.

Automatically, she did what had to be done. She cleared the table, washed the supper things, drew the curtains, and lit the lamp, turning the wick as low as possible. She built a fire in the fireplace. Then she put Johnny to bed, having him repeat his prayers as usual. She didn't want him to suspect anything was wrong. She didn't want him to be afraid.

Then Maggie went to sit in a chair before the fireplace. Despite the small fire, the warm glow of the lamp, Maggie felt cold. She rose from her chair and checked the rifle for the third or fourth time. She threw another log onto the small fire.

Still, she felt a deepening chill, and wrapped her shawl tightly about her shoulders. The little clock on the mantel struck nine o'clock.

Suddenly, with no warning, there came a loud rapping on the door. Maggie gave a start. She had not even *heard a footstep*! Wily as a fox, he had waited, and then he had stepped across the porch, while the clock was striking the hour.

Reaching for the rifle, she raised it, and stood facing the front door. Would he go away? Or would he break down the flimsy door? Or would he try the even flimsier back door?

"Ma'am? You can't fool me. I know you're in there—" The voice was sly, suggestive of bad things to come.

The moments dragged past. Maggie stood petrified, afraid to move, or breathe.

"Ma'am?" the voice came again, more insistent, "I could use a crust of bread. You wouldn't deny a bit of bread, to a starvin' man!"

Maggie had made up her mind—if the door moved the first iota, she would fire—directly for his heart. Just one shot, she thought, just like shooting a wild turkey, up on the mountains back of the log house.

Finally, she heard light footfalls. He was walking off the front porch.

Maggie shifted her position, so that she could cover both the front and back doors.

She stood, her hands clenching the loaded rifle, for what seemed an eternity.

Out in the barn, she heard Job's frightened whinny.

He has gone to the barn!

What would he do, in the barn? Lie down, and fall asleep?

Or would he grow hungry—and be back, back at one of the doors—

Maggie waited. The minutes inched past. Maggie dragged a chair quietly over, so that she could sit, and cover both doors. She threw another log onto the fire. It was now well past midnight.

The clock struck three. Nothing, there was no noise from the direction of the barn. Apparently, the man had gone to sleep in the hay. Come the dawn, hopefully, he would move on.

But what if he didn't? But he *must*! She had to see to the stock!

Not daring to let her guard down for an instant, Maggie waited.

Finally, dawn broke in the east. She heard a loud commotion.

Out in the barn, Job was stamping and whinnying, raising a fuss.

He was stealing Job! He couldn't! She had to have that horse!

Maggie rushed to the front door. With one desperate motion, she shoved aside the table, flung up the heavy latch.

The rifle grasped firmly in her hands, in a flash, Maggie was across the front porch, down the steps, and hurrying toward the barn. The barn door was shut. Good. He was still inside, probably hitching up Job. And there was only one door. She waited—for what seemed to Maggie to be several minutes.

The door swung open. He was attempting to lead Job out. But, Job, his ears laid back, reared up, wild-eyed and quivering, jerking the wagon behind him noisily from side to side.

The paralyzing fear of the long night forgotten, Maggie's voice came clear and strong, full of conviction:

"Step away from that horse and rig, Mister! And do it *now*—or you're a *dead man!*"

His back to her, he said, "You couldn't shoot a man in the back, little lady."

"I could shoot a *thieving rat*, without batting an eye. Now, you just do like I said. Step on out of there, real slow. And set your feet to walking back down that road, the way you came. Should I ever catch the sorry sight of you out this way again, there'll be no warning—before the shootin' starts."

Wordlessly, he dropped the lines, stuck his hands high in the air, backed out of the barn, and headed down the road, towards Cumming.

Maggie watched him long out of sight. Then she put the loaded rifle down beside the wagon, unhitched Job, and led him out into the pasture.

There was no milk this morning. Barbara Jo had come out yesterday, and picked up the chickens and the cow. Clem and Maggie had the wagon almost loaded—Mama's iron bedsteads, feather mattresses, benches, table and chairs, cookstove. And Katherine Ann's trunk.

Sarah hugged her friend. Then she helped with the light loading, while not crying into her apron tail.

Maggie had scoured the barn and the house for any edibles she could safely take along. She had rounded up two sacks of dried Indian corn, half a sack of dried beans, a small bag of dried peas, some ground Indian corn meal, a big bag of oats, along with a few armfuls of hay. She would also take the last of her eggs—which she would have to use up the first day or so.

"Johnny? Just about ready?"

"I'm ready!" Johnny announced, his little face beaming.

I can't *wait* to be shed of this place, Maggie thought.

And she wondered suddenly, what has it been like for Johnny, here, in all the tension and sorrow and silence? He stood grinning at her, showing a fine row of white teeth in an apple-cheeked face.

Quite obviously, Johnny had not suffered the least bit of harm.

"Okay, Mr. John Thomas McKinnon, Jr.! Here we go! We're going *home!*"

Out the door, Johnny bounded, his cap falling off as he ran.

At the door, her small reticule in one hand, a pair of worn gloves clutched in the other, Maggie paused and took one final look about the little sharecroppers' cabin.

Then, quietly, she closed the door.

When she turned, she saw a thin, dark-skinned, dark-haired, painfully bony figure, stepping out of the woods from the direction of the little one-room cabin. A grungy, half-filled tow sack swung on her back.

She had forgotten about Liza.

"Mornin,' Liza."

"I's all packed, Missus. Where's you wish I's to sit, Missus Evans? In the back, on the hay?"

Maggie stared at her. How could she *possibly* take on the responsibility for this former slave of Carl Evans?

But, what would become of her …if Maggie rode off and left her standing here in this yard …barefooted …in a dress so worn and thin you could see the darkness of her skin through it, and carrying her pitiful bundle—

What would happen to her …when Big Carl Evans came riding over to inspect his property, after Maggie had gone …

"In the back will be fine, Liza." Maggie forced a smile, attempting to keep the worry and frustration from her voice. "Then if Johnny gets sleepy, you two can swap places." *Oh, Lord!*

Liza tossed in her bundle, and clambered into the wagon bed, sitting awkwardly, her bony body sprawled amongst the grain sacks and furnishings.

Maggie drove slowly out of the yard, letting Job set his own pace.

Lord, she prayed, as she lifted the reins and let them fall with a light flick across Job's rump, *I don't ask much of you—*

> *Just let Job handle this load I've put on him.*
> *Let the old wagon not cast any spokes.*
> *Let me be able to take care of this sweet child—*
> *And this homeless old woman.*
> *Lord, they're worth more than many,*
> *many sparrows. Amen*

They met Barbara Jo and Fred Moss at Moss' General Mercantile. Maggie could not actually believe the two of them were going to drive up and look over the business prospects in Rhyersville.

As soon as Maggie drove into the store yard, Barbara Jo came out the wide front door, and down the steps. She looked regal, in a royal blue traveling dress with a stylish bonnet to match, its ribbons tied neatly beneath her chin.

In her worn black dress that was faded to a charcoal gray from countless washing in home-made lye soap, Maggie felt dull and drab. And her bonnet— it was one she had made from a scrap of a black dress that had seen its better days, the hem tattered and frayed, the bodice giving away at the seams. Maggie couldn't actually recall when she had bought a new dress. Not since the one Len bought her, for their wedding. After she had married Len, somehow, things like *clothes* didn't seem to matter. Since she was seldom allowed to leave the house, what need had she of new dresses and bonnets?

Barbara approached the loaded one-horse wagon; she ran a critical eye over its jumble of contents. Of course, her sharp gaze couldn't miss Liza, perched in the center of the wagon bed between the table and the chairs.

Drawing Maggie aside, Barbara Jo gasped:

"*What* in heaven's name are you *doing*, carting along that old colored woman?"

"She has *no* one, Barbs. She has not a soul in the world. She's been squatting out at that place, in a little cabin hidden in the woods, for about a year now. I shudder to think what would happen, should *Big Carl Evans* find her there! Besides, I can't leave her to starve or freeze to death. With Len gone, who's going to bring her a sack of Indian corn meal, or chop her a pile of wood? Look at her! She's thin as a scarecrow. She won't eat much. But she does need a pair of shoes. You wouldn't happen to have any that would fit her, would you, real cheap?"

"Maggie! You do beat all! As if you didn't have enough on your shoulders!'

"It'll be all right, Barbs. The Lord will look after us."

"Well," Barbara Jo wagged her head in wonderment at Maggie's lack of judgment, "I sure do hope so. For it seems you don't have sense enough to look after yourself. As if the horse didn't have a big enough load to pull. And it's not as if you're going just around the bend."

"Liza doesn't weigh much, Barbs. She's nothing but hair and a few bones. Not more than eighty or ninety pounds soaking wet. But I would like to get her a decent pair of shoes."

"All right. Bring her inside. Let me see what we can do. I do declare—!"
Barbara Jo reluctantly disappeared into the storeroom, and reappeared,
carrying several boxes.

"Liza, sit here," she instructed the bony Negress.

Liza stood gazing at Maggie. Her dark eyes wide with anxiety and
disbelief, slowly she wagged her head at Maggie.

"No'm, I's cin't let you do this. I's never had on no shoes, not on these two
feets. And—"

"Liza!" Maggie ordered sternly, "Sit!" Pointing to the chair Barbara Jo
had set out, she issued her ultimatum:

"If you intend to ride with *me* in *my* wagon, you will do so with a proper
pair of footwear. I will *not* have you getting sick on me. Sit down, and try on
these shoes. Or you can just walk, barefoot, back to that little shack! Now!
Which will it be?"

Wordlessly, Liza sat.

"What do you think?" Barbara Jo gazed at the long, bony feet stuck in the
brown leather lady's lace-ups.

"Walk around a bit, Liza," Maggie ordered. "See if they pinch your toes."

"No'm!" Liza Mae beamed like a small child at Christmas, "They's jus'
fine! They's jus' *so fine!*"

"How much?" Maggie asked her sister.

"One dollar, and that's with a family discount."

"I have these, Barbs." Maggie pulled out her gold wedding band and Len's
pocket watch. "What can I get for them?"

"You're bartering off your wedding band, Maggie?" Barbara Jo stared at
Maggie. "Are you sure you want to do this? And Len's—"

"I'm sure, Barbs. How much?"

"Six dollars, for them both?"

"Take out for the shoes. And two pairs of cotton stockings to go with them.
And a bottle of turpentine. And a box of sulfur powders."

"What on earth are they for? Turpentine? And sulfur powders?"

"First chance I get," Maggie replied brusquely, "I'm giving Liza's head a
good scrubbing."

"Oh …" Barbara Jo nodded her head, "You think she might harbor—but
I never heard of that remedy."

"Neither have I." Maggie smiled thinly. "But it sure can't hurt to try. And
a bar of sweet smelling soap, to kill the smell. Afterwards."

Maggie dropped the money remaining after her purchases into her little reticule.

"Well, if we're through here, let me see if Fred will take off that heavy trunk. We can lash it onto the back of the buggy."

Barbara Jo couldn't immediately locate her husband, "He's probably out back, in the storeroom. I'll go and fetch him."

"Thanks, Barbs." Maggie walked outside to wait, Liza fairly skipping along behind her, in her new footwear.

Fred Moss stepped out the door of his establishment, wearing an expensive vested wool suit and white shirt, his half-bald head gleaming in the rising sun—until he slammed his hat onto his head when he saw Maggie staring at him.

A frown on his pale face, he kept his eyes lowered. He absolutely refused to meet Maggie's gaze, as he begrudgingly hefted the heavy trunk onto the rear of the buggy. Maggie noticed with delight that Fred was developing a hefty midriff.

"God bless you, Barbara Jo," Maggie gave her sister a quick hug, thinking, *perhaps I don't* really *know* Barbara Jo.

But I sure do know Fred Moss!

"I guess we're about all ready," Barbara Jo surmised. Fred climbed into his buggy and led out. He had left a trusted friend in charge of the Mercantile.

Job stepped smartly along, now that he was rid of the extra burden of the brown leather trunk.

They rumbled along the main street of town, around the log courthouse, which Maggie had heard there was talk of replacing, and then out onto the open road. Maggie's mind was flying. The watch and ring were the last items she had to turn into cash.

She might take some of Mama's dresses out of the trunk, and see if they would fit Liza, before her dress fell to shreds off her skinny frame. Maggie had not had the heart to wear them herself. Anyhow, Mama's dresses would have been too short for her. Maggie was two inches taller than Callie had been. And as for Liza's footwear, it had been well worth the one dollar and fifty cents, to see Liza stepping along in her new leather shoes and cotton stockings.

As the wagon rattled northward, Johnny fell asleep on the wagon seat, and his dark head bounced against Maggie's side. While in the back of the wagon, Liza hummed a lively Negro spiritual.

"Liza? Is that the only name you have?" Above the rattle of the wagon, Maggie made an effort at conversation to pass the time.

"Only's one I ever done had, Missus."

"I don't understand," Maggie frowned slightly, "You've been free for years now. Why haven't you taken a full Christian name?"

Confused, Liza could only mumble, "Missus?"

"Wouldn't you *like* to have a middle and last names? Like other folk have?"

"*Yesss,* Missus, but …wouldn't that be …too …?"

"No," Maggie replied shortly. "It's only fitting and proper. You should give it some thought. What other names you'd like."

"My son, he's called hisself 'Moon,' 'cause he likes th' light of it."

"Liza *Moon*! That sounds perfect. How about a middle name?"

"Like whut, Missus?"

"Well, what month is it?"

"I don' kno', Missus."

"It's May, Liza. How about …Liza Mae Moon?"

"Oh! My! Whut a grand soundin' name, Missus! I's gonna' be Liza Mae Moon?"

They had left Cumming on Monday morning. On Wednesday, the little caravan pulled onto the main street of Rhyersville. Just about in time for lunch.

"You think Thomas Beyers will put us up for a few nights?" Barbara Jo called to Maggie as they stopped before the Rhyersville Store and tied up their horses.

"I'm sure he'd be more than happy to," Maggie smiled. "Oh, me, Barbs, it's good to be home! Remember the day Papa bought us all two sticks of candy each? And we thought we were queens!"

"Yes," Barbara Jo laughed. "But as I recall, *you* got two sticks, and Nellie Sue and I got *one* each. And I recall another time, when *neither* of us got any."

"Oh? I don't recall that."

"No." Barbara Jo sighed. "I'm sure there's quite a bit Papa did that you don't recall."

"What?" Maggie asked. She thought she caught a note of—she couldn't decide what—in Barbara Jo's voice. Not *jealousy*? That had been such a long time ago. They had all lost so much. Papa. Mama. McKinnon Valley …

Then Barbara Jo was smiling at her, "Forget it, Maggs. Sometimes I'm still somewhat of a brat."

Fred Moss was up the next day, and out assessing the town's business opportunities.

Maggie was up and out, going to Reliance Ransom's Restaurant.

"Mr. Ransom?" Her heart banging against the wall of her chest like a sledge hammer, Maggie smiled as cheerfully as she could manage, as she entered the front door of the restaurant. "Do you remember me?"

"Oh, my, yes, pretty lady! A man doesn't soon forget such a face. Not so soon."

"Well. Thank you," Maggie smiled prettily. She *needed* this job. She certainly didn't wish to appear forward. But neither did she wish to appear shy and stand-offish.

"When last I was in here, you mentioned the possibility of employment?"

"You mean a job? Yes, Ma'am. The offer still holds. Pretty lady like you, you'd be more than good for business."

Maggie stared at him for a moment, quite taken aback. Then she noticed that his swarthy, bearded face was open, honest, and innocent. He had meant it as a compliment.

"What would the job entail? And what remuneration would I be able to expect?"

"'Cuse me, Ma'am?"

"What would I have to do? And how much would I be paid for the work?"

"Oh, helpin' to cook. Servin', cleanin' up—that sort of stuff. I could probably go high as five dollars a week. And you would get your meals. But I can't offer you lodging. Not a pretty lady such as yourself. There would be talk."

"I understand," Maggie smiled at him fleetingly. "I'll take it. When should I start?"

"There's an apron hanging on a hook just inside the kitchen door," Ransom pointed and grinned at her.

"There is one ...other thing," Maggie said slowly, her eyes on Ransom's ruddy face, to gauge his reaction.

"I thought this was too good to be true." He wagged his head.

"No. It's nothing like that. It's just that ...I have a little boy ..."

"He a good kid?" Ransom asked, as if envisioning broken pitchers, spilled cups of coffee, and cats let loose in the kitchen.

"One of the best," Maggie smiled.

"Bring th' kid along."

Her employment secured, Maggie strode about town later that afternoon. She had to find a place to live—for Johnny, Liza, and herself. She would not outstay her welcome with Thomas Beyers.

She met Dr. Ellis, in front of the Rhyersville Store.

"Am I seeing things, or is that really you, Maggie?"

"Your eyes do not deceive you, Dr. Ellis. I've come back home. I hope to stay. If I can find a reasonably-priced shelter for our heads."

"What sort of place, Maggie, would you be wanting?"

"Something dry, and cheap," Maggie gave a wry laugh.

"How big?"

"Big enough for three people to get inside it. As you can see, Dr. Ellis, at this point, I'm not very particular. I just need some shelter, until I can perhaps do better."

"I have a small one-room cabin, down at the end of the street. Stayed there temporarily, when I was attempting to get my practice off the ground. I did say *small,* didn't I? That *is* the operative word here. I have my doubts that it would comfortably accommodate three persons."

"Besides myself, one is a skinny colored woman, not much wider than a broom straw; the other is a child, Dr. Ellis, a very small child."

"Oh? I wasn't aware," Dr Ellis frowned slightly, "that you had another child."

Maggie was not sure why, but she made no attempt to correct Dr. Ellis' misconception, that Johnny was *hers.*

"Yes," she smiled. "I have Johnny."

"You want to walk on down and take a look at the place, Maggie? Won't charge you a cent, just to look? And not much more, if you decide to actually *live* in the place. Hasn't been used since I moved out. Gone to the rats and bats, you might say."

It was, as Dr. Ellis had warned Maggie, small. But it appeared to be sturdy enough. It was half-filled with junk. In one corner, there was a small iron stove that Maggie could see would have to serve for both heating and cooking. There would be no oven. Maggie could see no evidence of water having coming through the oak-shingled roof. There were, of course, no glass windows, only two or three wooden shutters that would have to be opened to let in light and air. But, then, they wouldn't actually be here that much. She'd be at work all day—and she hadn't yet decided what to do about Liza Mae Moon.

"If you want it, Maggie, I'll move out all this trash."

They settled on a rent of fifty cents a month. It was Dr. Ellis' way of allowing Maggie to retain some of her dignity, by actually paying a rent.

Already, standing in the door of the tiny cabin that afternoon, Maggie could see the placement of an iron bedstead, the big brown trunk, a washstand. Maybe two small chairs. That would be about it.

Barbara Jo walked over to the restaurant a few days after they arrived in Rhyersville, and announced proudly to Maggie that Fred had bought the Rhyersville Store.

"From henceforth, to be called: *Moss' General Mercantile!*" Barbara Jo announced proudly. "Fred's having the new sign painted this very afternoon. And besides that, Fred's donating a belfry to the little church. He's already ordered the bell, and as soon as lumber can be hauled in, they'll begin construction on the bell tower, and a little steeple. I think we're going to build a new house, back of the store."

"Just like that?" Maggie asked incredulously. "I'm …speechless!"

"Well!" Barbara Jo remarked with a grin, "Now, there's a first!"

Maggie could see that Frederick J. Moss had apparently lost no time installing himself as the leading citizen of Rhyersville! And probably, soon he'd be elected Chairman of the Deacon Board of the Shiloh Baptist Church—into the bargain!

Chapter 27

A slight mist hung over the mountains behind the little white church. The tall man climbed the slope behind the clapboard structure, its low, oak-shingled roof bathed by the sun just rising over the blue, rippling ridges of the eastern mountains. He had noticed a pile of timbers being unloaded out front, and wondered the reason for the materials. Then his eye picked up a large crate, and inside it, a huge iron bell.

He paused beneath a stand of giant oak trees bordering the narrow path, removed a watch from the inside pocket of his coat, and glanced at its face. Yes, he still had plenty of time. He was to meet his foreman at exactly noon. He raised his left hand, drew a snow-white handkerchief from the inside breast pocket of his finely tailored suit. He held it for the briefest period of time, against his right eye, then the left. This was *so* hard! Why did he *put himself* through this? It never failed to upset and depress him. Well, he muttered beneath his breath, I don't come that often. But the times I do come, this is about all I can stand.

He knew this little graveyard so well, he told himself. How many years had it been now? Four? It seemed like an absolute eternity—an eternity since she had sickened; and then she was gone. In a matter of days, the child followed her. He felt his chest constrict. His lips began to tremble, and moisture filled his eyes until he could scarcely make out the little graveled path. His breath caught on the giant lump stuck in his throat. He clutched the small bunch of wild violets he had gathered to put on their graves. One bunch, that was all it took. The woman had been so young, so fragile, with her long blond hair and fair skin, and the boy, his only child, just a few months old, never took his first step …

Stop it! Bart Logan warned himself, stop it! What's the use in torturing yourself over your loss? Just look about you, see all these graves?

He had absolutely no idea *who* lay buried in any of them. He didn't know the small town that well. When Sue Ann came down with the fever, they had been here on a visit with his grandfather. Then suddenly she was delirious, too ill to travel. Then the child was stricken. The quinine, the Laudanum, the poultices, the camphor rubs prescribed by the local physician—nothing helped. The weather worsened, and there was no hope of carrying her and the child home—home to Philadelphia, for burial.

He blinked his eyes, tried to clear his throat. The great lump would not move. Not for several days, now, he knew from past experience. Sometimes it came upon him, even in the night when he hadn't actually thought of his wife and son, or at least he didn't think he had. But they were always there, like two beautiful ghosts. After the loss of his father and mother, when that transatlantic steamship sank in that terrible storm, Bart didn't think he could ever live through such pain again. But he had lived.

Bart's ears caught a slight rustle in the leaves still left from winter. Was there someone else up here, in this remote little graveyard? He gazed around. He caught the slightest glimpse of a woman and a child. A young woman from the look of her, draped in a heavy shawl, an enormous black bonnet enveloping her head, completely obscuring her face. She was bent over a grave. She stroked the grassy soil with one slender hand, then spoke to the child, so softly Bart could not hear, then she turned, took the child by the hand. It was a boy, dark hair neatly trimmed, three or four years old, as far as Bart could see. About the age Joshua would have been—

He turned from staring at the two. Suddenly he felt like an intruder. She had come here to grieve over a loved one, not to be gazed at by a stranger. The woman and the boy were making their way slowly down the path towards him. She with her head lowered, the boy gazing solemnly up at the woman, then down at the ground. She passed within a few feet of him, but he did not look at her; he didn't acknowledge her presence. Nor she his. Then they were gone, down the path beneath the shading oaks, out the gate in the little fence ...

Maggie had seen the man coming up the path. Saw him pause as if to collect himself. She saw him take out his handkerchief, touch his eyes once or twice. She tried not to look. She had no wish to intrude upon his sorrow. She didn't know him. He must be a stranger in town. So few strangers came through here. So few climbed the hill to the little cemetery. She forced her mind away. It was none of her business. She knelt, ran her hand through the low grass growing over the grave, laid her bunch of wild roses atop the baby's tiny grave. Oh, God! Was she going to *die* of this grief! Wouldn't the pain ever *lessen*? She didn't even glance toward Len's final resting place.

She took Johnny's small hand in hers, clutching it so hard he gave her a startled look. She loosened her grip, tried to smile at him reassuringly.

They made their way down the path. She avoided glancing toward the man. She didn't want to witness his grief, not anyone else's grief. She had enough of her own. His face was entirely in the shadow of his hat brim, but Maggie could see that it was a fine hat. He was a rich man, by the style and cut of his clothes. No one in Rhyersville wore a suit like that.

She made her way on down to the tiny town, up the main street, towards the restaurant. Once inside, she removed her bonnet and shawl and hung them on a peg in the kitchen. The sun was up, over the misty mountain ridges. The air was warming. And the huge black iron cookstove in the kitchen out back soon had Maggie longing for the sweet morning coolness of the mountainside. But she shrugged off the discomfort. She had a paying job. She had work to do.

The dining room of the restaurant was crowded. She had never seen this many folk out this early in the day. They were mostly men. And most of them were strangers.

"Reliance?" she asked, as soon as she had an opportunity, "What on earth's going on?"

"Haven't you heard, Maggie? Thought I told you yesterday. There's to be a new business established a few miles up Eagle Mountain. A man named Logan is bringing in a lumber mill."

"That's why all these men are here, to find work at this lumber mill?"

"I expect so. Not much else to do hereabouts, unless a man's got land for farmin'."

"You, mean, Reliance, that this *Mr. Logan*—is going to *cut down the trees?*"

"How, else, Maggie, is the man to get lumber off the mountain?"

"But, Reliance, that's awful! To strip the mountain of trees!"

"You're not th' only one, Maggie, that'll hate to see th' old-growth timber cut. Them trees's been standing there since before th' Injuns walked these mountains. Seems a shame now, to go and cut 'em down. But, things're changin', Maggie. And, I suppose it'll be good for th' town. Bring in jobs, and th' trees'll grow back. We need jobs hereabout. Not much rain to speak of this summer, and some folks' crops are mighty poorly, from what I've been hearin', even in th' bottom lands."

Maggie had ceased listening. Some *timber man* was coming to Rhyersville! He was going to cut the giant pines, oaks, and hickory trees that had shrouded the mountains for hundreds of years. Trees that had been growing before Shawn McKinnon had ever set foot in this country. How sad! How frightening! Everything was changing.

"No time to think of that now, Maggie," Reliance was remarking pointedly, "There's biscuits to be baked, the ham and sausage to be fried, the hominy grits ..."

The morning passed slowly. The heat built in the valley. Almost noon, and more men pouring into town.

As the old clock on the kitchen shelf struck twelve, a tall, well-dressed man with a fine wool felt hat entered the small restaurant.

He took a seat at a table near the window. He sat gazing out at the traffic in the one street. The only traffic was a few wagons, a few men on horseback. The street was dry and dusty. No good rain for weeks now, but for a few precious sprinkles. Not their usual weather for this time of year, he had heard. A dry spring. Usually thunderclouds built up in the afternoon heat, boiling over the mountains, dropping precious rain on the crops in fields and gardens. But this year had been different. But Bart Logan didn't really know that. He hadn't been around Rhyersville that much. He kept watching the door, with growing impatience.

When the tall man had entered the restaurant, the men already seated at the few crowded tables began to mutter and nod.

"People sure are excited, about the timber man comin' to town," Reliance drawled.

"How *can* they be?" Maggie snapped angrily. "What will the mountains look like—stripped of trees?"

Maggie, of course, recognized the tall man instantly. It was the stranger from the graveyard. But they were so busy, she soon forgot him.

Finally, Bart saw the man he had been waiting for—Stephen Giles, the foreman of the Logan Lumber Company. He was late, at least ten minutes.

"Sorry," Stephen Giles apologized briefly as he removed his hat, extended his hand.

"Tardiness is not something I approve of, Mr. Giles." Bart smiled briefly. "But I'm sure, since you have worked with me for several years now, you're well aware of my feelings on that subject. And knowing you, I'm sure you have a very good reason for being late. So shall we dispense with the small talk, and let's get down to it, shall we? I have here a general layout of the camp—"

Stephen Giles bent his blond head over the diagram Bart Logan laid before him.

"This," Bart was saying, "is the cookshack. Mostly completed. Just here, about twenty yards away, will be the main bunkhouse—currently under construction. Should be ready by this weekend. Hold up to two dozen men. Here, a pine log corral is being put in, for the draft horses. There's a good, deep spring, just back of the cookshack, plenty of fresh water for drinking, washing up, and whatever. I'll have a little cabin, for myself, just here, out from the bunkhouse. And we can build you a little place to yourself, or you can bunk in with the men. The sawmill will be here, in this large clearing, far enough away from where the men will be living and eating. Close enough to the logging road we've cleared, and to the river—where I hope we can float some of the logs down from the highest peaks. We'll need to build sluiceways, with gates. You're familiar with that?"

"Yes, sir. And as to living quarters, I'd just as soon bunk in with the men as not, Mr. Logan," Stephen Giles surmised. "Then I can keep a keen eye on them. It can get pretty rough, sometimes, at a logging camp."

"Yes," Bart replied, a small frown kitting his brow. "But, as you well know, I'll abide no heavy drinking, no fighting, and *no women* will be allowed in the camp. These have always been my strict rules, everywhere I've placed an operation, and they seem to work very well. You think this, then, is a good, workable plan?"

"Looks good to me, Mr. Logan. When would you like me to report?"

"I've got to sign on a crew. I'm going to set up a hiring hall, or line, somewhere here in town. You might want to join me, to look over our prospects. But, first, have you had lunch?"

"No, sir, I might take time, just time for a bite, maybe. I just need to see to my horse." Stephen Giles disappeared outside, then returned. The two men had a quick meal.

"I have a couple of things to attend to. Then I'll meet you—?" Stephen Giles stared at his boss quizzically.

"Somewhere along Main Street probably. Small as this place is," Bart remarked dryly, "I don't think you could miss us, even if you tried."

Maggie noticed briefly that the man she now knew was *Mr. Bartram Logan* had been joined at his table by a tall, muscular man who appeared to be about thirty years of age. Dressed, not in fine clothes, but finer than most worn on the streets of Rhyersville. The man now known to Maggie as Mr. Logan, rose as the other man entered, extended a hand, and they shook.

Then he drew out of his pocket a paper, which he spread on the table between them.

Now both men had ordered and been served. The other man had disappeared back into the dusty street. But Mr. Logan lingered.

And lingered.

Until he was the sole remaining customer in the dining room.

Maggie wished he would *leave*, so she could clean up the little room and prepare it for the supper crowd. He seemed to be lingering inordinately long over his cup of coffee that *had* to be stone cold and bitter as gall by now. Still he lingered, studying the paper still spread before him.

Maggie watched him, waiting, ready to grab the broom and get to work on the biscuit crumbs adorning the floor. Would he never leave? Then Reliance left his station by the cigar box, where he placed the breakfast receipts. He sauntered over, wiping his ham-like hands on his apron. "Nuther cup of coffee, Mr. Logan? That'n must be gittin' mighty cold by now."

"No, thank you. But, may I trouble you for a moment of your time, Mr.—?"

"Jones. Reliance Ransom Jones. No trouble. No trouble a'tall. What kin I do fer ya?"

"Mr. Jones, as you're probably aware," the man began, slowly turning the cold cup of coffee in his hands, his steady gaze on Reliance's sweaty face with the chin covered in dark beard, "we're going to be setting up our logging operation on the mountain ridges north of here, just a few miles off, actually. And I'll be hiring a mess cook. Some good, sober reliable man, who can manage the job of cooking and putting up with the grumbles and complaints of at least a couple of dozen men. Would you know of anyone who might be interested in such a position?"

"No, sir. No, sir, I surely would not. I'll be closing this place myself, come the end of the week. Going back home to Kaintuck. Got my aged Mama up there, not doin' that well. I don't know of a soul that would put up with a logging crew for long. Not many men *I* know care to cook a'tall."

Bart heard Reliance Jones rambling on. Then his eye caught the shadow of a slight form. A woman, lurking in the shadow of the kitchen door, peeking out now and then, watching him. What the—

"If I hear of anybody, I'll sure let you know. When will you be hiring, should I hear of anybody looking for such a job? Is the pay good?"

"I'll be setting up a hiring line here in town, this afternoon. I need a man on the job come Monday morning. It would be good, in fact, if he could go on up to the site, say, Sunday afternoon, to get things ready for Monday's morning meal. The pay will be fair, and with meals and a cot thrown in."

"Mighty short notice, Sunday afternoon. And this is Tuesday. Good luck to you, now. Sure you won't have anuther cup o' coffee?"

Bart noticed Reliance Jones nodding at the young woman lurking in the shadow of the kitchen door, and got the distinct feeling they both wished he would leave. He saw the small shadow of a child dart past the open door. The woman shooed the child back. He glanced around. He was the sole diner still remaining, and they probably needed to clean up the place.

"Thank you so much," Bart said, quickly unfolding his lank frame from the straight-backed oak chair. He straightened his coat and tie, a bit much in the growing afternoon heat. He was in a small town. Why stand on ceremony? He removed the gray wool suit jacket, draped it over one arm, and with a deft flick of his hand slid the chair beneath the square oak table strewn with bits of ham and biscuit. Yes, indeed, they needed to clean up the place.

With a polite nod to the proprietor, Bart doffed his light gray hat and strode out into the sunlight.

He needed to see about setting up a table of his own. Some convenient spot where the men could get in line out of the hot sun …maybe there …

He walked slowly toward the end of Main Street. *Jonas Trap*, the faded sign read over the big double doors, *Wheelwright.*

Maggie watched the man go. Her heart thumped. He was looking to *hire* …he had said …to hire a good, reliable *cook! Of course*, he wanted a *man*. But what did most men know about cooking? *A job!* It would be a real job— with meals and a place to live thrown in for good measure!

Maggie flew about the tiny dining room, making quick work of the crumbs on the floor and the tables. She rearranged the chairs. Then she flung off her apron, donned her shawl …but it was so hot …still she wanted to look like a decent, well-covered woman for this very special job interview. She surely wouldn't want the man to think she was some wanton woman, openly displaying herself. No, it would definitely be the shawl, and her bonnet, the good one hanging in the kitchen, with the ruching about the face. What was she thinking? This man wasn't interested in ruch trimmed bonnets! He needed a good cook!

And she was certainly *that;* she was a *good* cook!

"Mr. Reliance Ransom Jones!" Maggie smiled at Reliance, and said teasingly, "Once you're gone from this town, you needn't fret yourself about Margaret Ann McKinnon Evans. She'll be cooking up at the new lumber camp!"

Reliance Jones, stood, his big mouth agape, his astonished eyes following Maggie's slender form, as she strode across the dining room, and then out the front door. Reliance still watched, as the slender young woman walked up the dirt street, her little leather boots sending up fluffy puffs of dust.

"He said a *man*, Maggie! He said a *man*!" Reliance ran to the door and yelled after her. She paid him no mind, just kept on walking.

"That fool woman *has lost her mind*!" Ransom muttered to himself, as he wagged his head in wonder, turned and went back inside.

Bart Logan—sitting bent over his hiring sheet at the hastily placed table under the big oak in front of Jonas Traps'—noticed that a sudden lull had fallen over the noisy line of men gathered before him and stretching far on down the red dirt street.

Bart glanced up. The line of men had turned to stare at a young woman, striding purposefully up the dusty street, in the direction of the hiring table. She was swaddled in a huge black shawl, and a huge black sunbonnet completely concealed her face.

As she came on, Bart watched in amazement, as the line of men melted back, giving way for the young woman. The way clear, she strode immediately to the front—straight for his table. She lifted her chin, and smiled, charmingly, at the stunned line of men, acknowledging their courtesy with a nod.

"Can I help you, Miss—?" Bart asked, cocking his head to one side, his dark brows lifting quizzically.

Despite the swaddle of clothing, he could tell she was slightly built. Where had he seen her before? Had he seen her before ...?

"I'm Mrs. Margaret Ann Evans," she was saying, her chin up, her voice low, well modulated, and sweet, barely audible. The way a *lady's* voice should be.

Bart was shocked at the change that had come over the line of men that had only moments before—their faces hard, their eyes determined—been catcalling and jarring and jostling for a place in line. Young men, full of themselves, full of loud talk and boasting brags—

Now that same line of men seemed to have totally forgotten why they were even here ...every man jack of them had given way to this one young lady.

And it was obvious to Bart that they considered her a *lady*—with her big black bonnet, her long black dress high up to her neck, down to her wrists, and her pale face, with her head held high.

A few of them mumbled curiously to one another. Bart could not hear, but could readily imagine. *Who is she!? What on earth is this woman doing here!?*

"Mrs. Evans ...did you say?" Bart muttered, "I don't believe I've had the ...pleasure ...of meeting you. What can I do for you?"

"I'm looking for a *job*, Mr. Logan." Her voice was firm, no wavering, no nonsense, no shilly-shallying about, just a straight shot from the shoulder.

"A ...*job*, Mrs. Evans?" Bart asked, his dark brows shooting up. He fought to suppress the smile playing about his lips. "I'm ...afraid you've been misinformed ...you're under some ...misapprehension ...you see ...these ...men ...these ...men ...are ...these men are—"

Why did he keep repeating himself? Did he think she was deaf? An idiot! A complete fool! She knew exactly why these men were here. For the same reason she herself was here!

"These men," Bart glanced over at his foreman. Giles had his head tucked down, in an attempt to hide the broad grin on his face. No help there. He heard himself clearing his throat, continuing to stumble along. "These men are hiring on for *logging* work, *sawmill* work ...you see, to *fell* logs, and *roll* them down to the river." Bart stared at her, and wondered incredulously what on earth was wrong with him. He sounded like a bumbling schoolboy, attempting to explain something to a child! "Hardly a job, I would think, a lady would be interested in," he finished, he trusted, with more than a note of finality in his voice.

"You need a *cook*," the young woman announced with a firm lift of her chin. "If you *expect* these *men* to *work*, they surely must *eat*. *That's* the job I'm interested in, Mr. Logan, if you please."

On the last words, she gave her chin another stubborn little lift. Her face, which had been shadowed by her bonnet, was now fully lit by the golden afternoon sun. And it was a shock to Bart.

She *was* young, not exactly the sort he had envisioned for a *mess cook* for a crew of rough and ready loggers!

"I'm sorry, Mrs. Evans," Bart wagged his head, heard his voice as if from a distance, "but we already—"

"I beg to *differ* with you," Maggie interrupted, anger making her voice tremble, her lips to draw into a thin line. How dared this man lie to her! She bent towards him, so her every word would be clear to this grown man who evidently had a problem with speaking. "I *heard* you, Mr. Logan, not more than twenty minutes ago, in Reliance Ransom Jones' restaurant. *Have* you hired someone?"

"Oh, I see." Bart replied cryptically, his voice filled with chagrin. He felt as if his usually quick mind was suddenly operating at a snail's pace. "That's where I saw you, in the restaurant." He didn't fancy being caught in an outright lie. It wasn't his style. But what did she expect? She was putting him on the spot. And he was attempting to be a gentleman, but she had not budged from the line. Nor, from the look on her face, did she intend to! The sun was hot, and the men were getting restless, despite the presence of the lady.

"Mrs. Evans, wasn't it—?"

"Yes," Maggie said, her blue eyes implying, 'Do you find that a difficult name?'

"Perhaps, Mrs. Evans," Bart raised a hand and loosened the black string tie that seemed to be strangling him. How did he tactfully get rid of her? He waved a hand strangely in an offhand manner of dismissal. His white shirt, which he had donned fresh only a few hours ago, now clung to him like a limp dishrag.

"Perhaps we could discuss this …your possible employment at some more convenient …time. Now if you would—"

"*When*, Mr. Logan, *exactly*?" Maggie demanded, in a voice that brought complete silence about her. She leaned forward again, the sun falling full on her face.

"Well …uh," Bart stammered. He'd never seen a woman put herself forward so. "How about …uh," he gestured helplessly again, with one hand.

The men were all staring at him. He glanced over at Giles. Giles had covered him mouth with his hand.

"I'll speak with you, as soon as I finish here."

"I'll *wait* for you," she announced. "*On* the bench. *At* the storefront."

Giving a polite nod first to Bart, then to the astonished line of waiting men, she turned and marched off.

More than a bit shaken, Bart watched her go. She was slender. She was scarcely more than a girl. *She wanted to work in* a *logging camp*? He hoped she hadn't somehow gotten the wrong impression—

"*Sir? Mister Logan, sir?*"

"Yes, yes, you look like a fine strong fellow. Had any logging experience?"

Bart turned and frowned at his foreman, said in a low aside, "What do you think about this man, Giles? You didn't provide much assistance, with the *female* applicant."

Stephen Giles wagged his head in disbelief.

Then he grinned and muttered to Bart, "Personally, I would have hired the *lady,* Boss, but I guess this man will have to do."

Bart frowned at Giles in exasperation, turned and said to the man standing before him, "Can you start the first of the week? Forty dollars a month, and found. You can stow your things up at the camp, as early as Sunday evening."

Forty dollars a month! It was a princely sum! Maggie sat on the hard bench at the storefront not far down the street, and listened.

Sitting alone on the bench, watching the line of men, she felt the fear, the anger, the utter *helplessness* of being a woman alone engulfing her. A cold, hard lump rose in her throat. An icy wave of sheer panic swept over her. Frenetically her mind darted about. What sort of impression had she made? Had she made *any* impression at all …on this man who could give her a *job?* The restaurant would be *closing* the end of the week. She was *desperate* for a job. Any job. *This job. She could do this.* She could cook for the logging camp. It was about her last hope. She *had* to have this job.

But Maggie knew that the mere fact that she was a woman was a gigantic detriment. It just wasn't fair—!

"Mrs.—"

He was standing over her, creating a shadow that fell across her and up the rough oak planks of the storefront behind her. How long had she been waiting? Had she fallen asleep! *Oh, no!* He mustn't think her some sort of slug-about, napping at storefronts in the middle of the afternoon—!

Maggie leapt to her feet, so quickly that the man was startled and stepped back, almost losing his balance. She was so near, almost in his face.

She actually bumped into him in her haste to rise. He regained his balance, caught her by the arm, righted her, and then moved back from her a few steps. What should she *say* to him? What *could* she say to him?

"Mrs. Margaret Ann Evans," Maggie finally blurted out, her voice sounding high, unnatural, strained.

The man was literally towering over her. How tall was he? What did that matter! Here he stood ...her *only* chance to find employment! What could she say to him?

"Mister Logan, I realize that you don't know me." She heard herself babbling in a desperate rush, *"But I can cook. I'm a good cook.* And I'm strong, and I can do the cleanup. Ask anyone who frequents the restaurant. I'm sure I'm more than qualified—"

"Mrs. Evans," he was shaking his head, "Certainly, it's not your qualifications that are being called into question here."

He paused uneasily. That wasn't the thing to say. What was the thing to say? Maggie's heart sank. He was going to say no, because *you're a woman*—

"Then, what *is* it, Mister Logan, exactly what *is* it that's being called into question here?"

Maggie was so angry she could scarcely see his face. She was angry with him. She was angry with herself. She was angry with Papa for dying. She was angry with Len ...

She was angry, Bart could see. More than angry, she was frightened. Did she actually need work so badly, as to put herself into a *logging camp* with a couple dozen mostly unwashed, unshaven young men?

"I was thinking more of your ...safety." Bart finally managed to say, rather lamely he thought.

"My *safety*, Mr. Logan?" Maggie asked in a too sweet, too cool voice. "But, of course," she attempted to recall what was at stake here, "I would stay well away from where the trees were being felled. I do have the sense of an *addled* goose!"

"Well, yes, Mrs. Evans, I'm sure you have, a good deal, no, that is to say ...a *great deal* ...of sense, but ...that's not the sort of ..." He hesitated, raising one hand helplessly, continuing slowly, "Not at all the sort of danger that comes to my mind."

"Exactly what sort of '*danger*' does come to your mind, Mister Logan?" Maggie! What are you *doing*! *Watch your temper*!

She certainly didn't shrink from speaking her mind. If there was a woman who could manage herself at a logging camp, it just might be this one! But— what did she expect from him! He couldn't *possibly* take her up to that logging camp ...isolated in the mountains ...the men—

—Bart lifted one hand, blurted out in growing frustration, "A young woman—like you—why would you *want* to put yourself into such a *position*? I could not *possibly* take responsibility for—for—"

"*Mister* Logan," Maggie cut in, her voice angry, barely audible. Bart did, in fact, find himself forced to lean down a bit to catch the words that came from her mouth, in something like a soft hiss. "I have taken responsibly for myself—for quite some time now, and I can assure you I fully intend to continue to do so in the future."

"What about your husband?" Bart heard himself asking. "And there was a child with you at the restaurant—?" Why was he asking these questions? What had gotten into him? He couldn't possibly allow this woman on the mountain, with or without a child or a husband.

"He ...he's ...away."

"He? Your husband? Away?" Bart leaned forward slightly, staring at her. Her face had suddenly gone pale. "Away," Bart repeated. "Where? For how long? What would he say—?"

He continued to talk, but the words went completely over Maggie's head. She was deliberately *lying* to this man! *Where had that lie come from?* Why had she lied? What did she say now? One lie always called for *another*—to cover it up, Mama always said—

"—He's at the gold fields," she blurted out without thinking.

"The *gold* fields?"

"Yes," she said defiantly. Better to let Mr. Logan—and the loggers—believe that she had a living husband. Yes, better for them all.

"I have no idea," Maggie kept lying, "when he'll be back. Not until he's ...struck gold, perhaps."

"I ...see," Bart said slowly. He didn't see at all. None of this made any sense. A man didn't leave a woman like this, and strike off for ...wherever ...not if he had any sense.

Bart heard himself saying, "Well, regardless of your ...family situation ...we couldn't have *a woman* up at the logging camp. The cook will have to *live* there, you see. There's a cookshack, with a small room at the back, with just a bunk and a table—"

"It sounds perfect!" Maggie gave a little lilting laugh, relief sweeping over her. "A cabin! A cabin! Johnny will love that!"

"Johnny? Then, you *do* have a child?"

"Yes, Mr. Logan. But, I'm sure that won't present a problem."

"The little boy I saw ..."

"Yes," Maggie heard herself saying sweetly, "Johnny is ...an absolute dream of a child. He has never given a problem a day in his life. And I heard you tell the others to report this Sunday evening! So! That's just fine, then. And I intend doing the same. Now, good day to you, Mr. Logan."

Bart found himself standing alone on the narrow wooden porch of Moss' General Mercantile. His mouth half open.

Did he miss something? What just happened here?

Bart shook his head, reached up and removed his hat, as if it was suddenly a heavy burden atop his mop of dark hair. Did that woman actually think he had just *hired* her?

Well ...after she'd had a few days to think it over ...he was sure she'd forget the whole ridiculous idea. But ...she sure could wind a person's senses up in little knots.

A man would be *wise* to avoid women of her ilk! Frankly, he hoped he'd seen the last of Mrs. Margaret Ann Evans.

Chapter 28

Maggie gazed about the tiny cabin Johnny, Liza Mae Moon and she had called home for the last two months. Yes, there was Liza Mae. Eating a regular and sufficient diet, Liza Mae had filled out, and with her dark hair washed and combed, and clothed in some of Mama's dresses, Liza Mae no longer appeared emaciated to the point of death. Thomas Beyers had agreed to take her in, just until Maggie returned from the logging camp. In return, Liza would do a bit of cooking and cleaning for Thomas.

What would Maggie take with them up to the logging camp? Most of her things she would be forced to leave with Barbara Jo.

Not the trunk. She couldn't *imagine* not seeing Katherine Ann's big brown leather trunk every day. It would be just what she needed, she told herself. She could pack in it most of their belongings. Their clothes. Katherine Ann's Dutch oven? Maybe, she'd leave that with Barbara Jo. But Great-grandpa Shawn's fiddle and Bible—would ride safe inside the trunk. *Medical Methods for the Treatment of Burns, Scrapes, Cuts and Bruises,* the huge medical volume Dr. Ellis had given Johnny, would also be tucked into it.

And she would take her accounting book along.

Mama's best dishes and jars and jugs were already stored safely away with Barbara Jo.

And the oaken bucket brought from the farm—the one she, and Nellie Sue and Barbara Jo had despised drawing up out of the depths of the well—she'd decide about that later.

She took the bucket, now, in one hand, clasped Johnny by the other, and walked to the town well.

She washed and dried all their clothes and their bedding, then packed what Johnny and she would need, into Katherine Ann's trunk. She placed the fiddle on top. With the clothes—and two of Mama's hand-stitched quilts—the trunk was practically full.

Maggie closed it with a firm thump.

She would walk down to speak with Thomas Beyers, and see if he would agree to drive Johnny and her up to the logging camp.

She did not find him at home. She became frantic. Doctor Ellis? He was not in Rhyresville this week. He had mentioned going down to Gainesville, to pick up some medications.

It was Sunday night before she found Thomas Beyers at home.

"I would be more than happy," he smiled at her, "to escort m'lady and her knight, up to the logging camp. But, Maggie," Thomas shook his head and gazed at her with dark, solemn gray eyes. "Are you dead certain …that this is something you want to *do*? *A logging camp*? That's *no* place for a lady."

"Now, don't you start with me, Thomas Beyers." Maggie wagged a finger in his face,

"This is *exactly* what I want to do. Tell me of *one* place in Rhyersville— or anywhere nearby for that matter—where a *woman* can get any job at all, much less one that pays so well, and with meals and lodging thrown in? I'm far too proud to beg—or live on handouts. I plan to save all my earnings. This job is only temporary. I know that when the bigger trees are cut, Mr. Bartram Logan will pick up his sawmill, pack up his bags, and move to another mountain. But, by that time, I intend to have put aside enough money to put down rent, hire a helper, and stock the restaurant with fine food. Margaret's Meals—or whatever I name it—will not deal just in fried ham and grits and biscuits and gravy. There'll be roasts and beefsteaks, buttered potatoes, fresh greens, fruit pies, puddings, onions and whatever vegetables are fresh in season. Even roast duck, now and again."

"It sounds to me, Maggie, as if you have this …all figured out. But, if things don't go well …up there …"

"Things will go well, Thomas. Things *have* to go *very* well—for *I* intend to see that they do. There is one other thing I wanted to mention to you. It's about Liza Mae Moon. I hope she won't be too much of a burden. I did so hate to mention her to you, but—"

"Forget it, Maggie." Thomas raised a hand in dismissal, gave Maggie his usual sweet smile. "Liza Mae Moon and I will make it just fine. I won't let her starve to death. And maybe she'll keep all my dirty shirts picked up off the floor."

"Thomas! God bless you!" Maggie gave him a quick hug. "I don't know what we'd do without you. Now, what time shall I expect you in the morning?"

She would be *a day late*, Maggie realized, stewing about it fitfully as she lay on the feather mattress attempting to get some sleep, Liza snoring softly beside her. And Johnny's soft breathing could be heard from the thick mat of quilts and blankets, atop the big brown leather trunk. What tomorrow would bring, Maggie had no earthly idea. Mr. Bartram Logan might just meet her at the door to his cook's shack, an ugly scowl on his face—and send her and Johnny and their big brown leather trunk packing—back down the mountain.

Maggie arose early, despite having slept very little. This was the day—the day that would determine, to a large extent, *the remainder of her life*. The trunk sat by the door, where she had dragged it before finishing her packing.

She washed Johnny's small face, giving him several teasing kisses into the bargain. He wiggled and twisted, wanting to play.

Liza sat watching them, her dark eyes filled with terror, at the thought of Maggie leaving her.

"Do stand still, sugar, and let me finish the job. We want you spick and span and all dressed and shining when Thomas gets here." With one fingertip, Maggie gave him a playful poke in the stomach.

Johnny giggled and poked her back. She poked him again. Then, "That's *all* the playing for now, young sir. Jump into your clothes. Jump! Jump!"

Maggie dressed herself very carefully. She tried piling her hair atop her head, as was usual with a married woman, going out into the public.

Her thick hair in heavy coils atop her head, she gazed into the only mirror she had. She didn't at all like the effect. She looked too much like she was headed for church, she thought.

"Why're you frowning, Maggie?" Johnny asked, his little face tilted to one side. "You don't like the way you look?"

"It's not what *I* like that matters much today, sugar. It's what *Mr. Bartram Logan* might like—or more likely—*not* like."

"You don't think the loggers will like the way you look? I think you look pretty," Johnny said very solemnly.

"Well, sugar. That may just be the problem. Today, I'd rather not look pretty."

"I don't understand."

"Today, sweetie, I'd like to look like a cook for a logging camp."

"How would that look?"

"Like a two hundred pound man—with a wrinkled face, an unkempt beard, and long, shaggy hair."

Solemnly Johnny stared at Maggie and wagged his head. "I don't think you're going to look like that ...no matter how many times you comb your hair."

Now, Maggie wound her hair in tight plaits, the way Mama always wore hers. But Maggie's hair was thicker and darker than Mama's, and her face was young, and smooth, with fair skin. Critically, she studied her image.

"I'm afraid you're right," Maggie sighed. Giving herself a final glance in the mirror, she turned to finish her packing.

On top of everything else in the big brown leather trunk, Maggie laid in her mirror, her comb and brush, a few black-tipped hairpins, some plain wire ones, and a half bar of soap. At the last minute, she shoved in the battered tin washbasin, along with an earthen pitcher of her mother's. Surely Mister Bartram Logan had some place in mind from which his employees could fetch clean water.

"Well, Johnny, I think our ride is here. And, Johnny—" Maggie hesitated just inside the door of the tiny cabin, "I want you to play a little game with me, sugar."

"What kind of game?" Johnny looked up at Maggie. She had mentioned a game—now she really had his attention.

"It's about you ...calling me *Maggie*. Let's pretend, just for a while—just while we're up at the logging camp—let's pretend I'm your *Mama*, and you're my little boy. You think you could call me *Mama*, for just a while? For just pretend?"

Johnny gazed at her very seriously; then he shook his head, 'no.'

"Okay. Well, that's okay," Maggie smiled at him. "How about, if you just don't *tell* anyone up at the logging camp that you're my little brother? It's ...just for a while ...just a game ...between you and me? You don't tell them a lie. You just don't tell them *anything*."

"Can I still call you *Maggie*?"

"Yes, sweetie. I know you wonder why, but I thought it might be nice to fool the men at the logging camp. Men don't take too kindly to women who have little boys at their skirt tails."

"You don't want the men at the logging camp to like you?"

"Not too much. Just a little—just enough to say good mornin' and good evenin'—you understand? And nothing more."

"You want them to think I'm your little boy, so they won't want to kiss you, or walk with you, or anything."

"You are so smart!" Maggie smiled. "It just a game, just for the logging camp, okay?"

"Okay!" Johnny smiled, hoping he could remember.

"Good! Now, we'll just see what kind of job the two of us can make of cooking for a wild bunch of woolly-bearded loggers!"

Johnny lagged back, "You seem worried. Are we goin' to be all right, Maggie, up at the logging camp? I'm scared. I don't know anybody. What if Mr. Logan and his loggers don't like me?"

Maggie bent and planted a wet kiss on Johnny's forehead, "Everything will be just fine. We'll *make* it fine, sugar. How could anyone in his right mind not like you, John Thomas McKinnon, Jr.! And don't you *ever* be afraid! Fear makes you not think straight—and you have to think straight, in this old world. Just you always remember: *Are not two sparrows sold for a farthing? And not one of them falls to the ground without your Father!"*

"Liza," Maggie took Liza Mae Moon's dark hand between her own, and gave it a warm squeeze. "Thomas Beyers is your friend. You remember that. He's a good man. You can rely on him. You need anything, you tell Thomas. Okay?"

"Does you hav' ta' go, Miss Maggie? I's don' know—" Liza's dark eyes swam with tears.

"You just tell Thomas, if you need anything," Maggie insisted, giving the thin dark hand a final reassuring squeeze before releasing it. "And I'll see you, from time to time, when I can. When I get to town."

Outside, Thomas was valiantly attempting, single-handedly, to push the leather trunk onto the back of the buggy. Maggie put both her hands to the end of the trunk, and together they gave it a mighty shove.

"What on earth—? What on earth do you *have* in this thing, Maggie?" Thomas removed his hat and wiped his brow with a clean handkerchief.

"Everything in the world you can image, and then some," Maggie laughed.

She was in a fine mood. She had definitely determined, as soon as her feet hit that bare floor this morning:

She was going to make this work! And nothing was going to stop her!

332

A sweet breeze was moving down from the mountains, carrying the scents of wild sweet shrub and plum and honeysuckle, caressing her cheeks, swaying the full skirt of her black dress, the best black dress she had, and her best black bonnet. She wore her best black shawl, the fringed one, about her shoulders. She was headed up the mountain. She was headed for a new job, with fine benefits.

Suddenly, Maggie was filled with hope. Suddenly, the world looked bright again.

After they left the county-maintained road, the freshly-cut road up the ridges to the logging camp was a trial to the horse and buggy. Stumps. Roots. Limbs.

Finally, Thomas called the horse to a halt, glanced up the steep incline dotted with stumps, turned to Maggie and shook his head.

"I think this is about as far as this rig can make it. Afraid we'll have to conclude our journey on foot."

Thomas noticed that the farther they drove up the narrow logging road, the more quiet and subdued Maggie had become. She had begun the trip in such high hopes. Now, it seemed they couldn't even reach the camp.

"I'm sorry, Thomas. I had no idea—" It was one of those rare occasions in her life, when Maggie McKinnon was at a total loss for words.

"Well," Thomas glanced at the sun. "It's not yet noon. But the day is really warming up. We've come this far. It can't be that much farther. I'm game— if you and Johnny are?"

Already, before the words were out of his mouth, Maggie had hopped down from the buggy, and stood staring up the impossibly steep incline.

"That trunk of yours is big, but maybe I can—"

"It has handles on either side, Thomas." Maggie pointed to the big brown bulk. "Together we will carry it, or drag it the remainder of the way. Johnny, why are you taking your medical book out of the trunk?"

"I might need to have it handy, in case I get a patient—as soon as I get there. If there's lots of men up there, it may be that one of them is sick. And it'll make the trunk lighter."

"Well, that thing looks about as big as you are, young man. But, if you plan on being a physician, I suppose you'd better learn to handle your end of the load!"

"Right!" Johnny stuck out his chest. He had already taken off his cap, and had it tucked in a breeches pocket. His hair—so like Papa's—

"Maggie? You sure you're up to this? Ready?" Thomas gazed anxiously at her.

"Yes," Maggie asserted defiantly. Reaching down, she grasped the right handle of the heavy trunk, "Let's go!"

Half an hour later, the three of them staggered and stumbled into the edge of the logging camp clearing.

Maggie had thrown back her bonnet, and let it hang down her back by its straps. Her face was wet with perspiration, and tiny tendrils of dark hair were plastered to her forehead and hung limply about her ears.

"Well, Johnny," Maggie announced wryly, taking a deep breath, and sinking down on the top of the big trunk, "if it was my intention to reach the logging camp looking my worst, at least in that, I think I have succeeded."

"How do I look?" Johnny asked so innocently that Maggie wanted to cry.

"You look like the handsomest physician in the whole country. And just look, Doctor Johnny, you brought that heavy book—all the way up the mountain."

"I wonder what's going on? What's all that ruckus?" Thomas was mopping his face and drying his hair with what was left of his once-clean handkerchief.

"You think it's a fight?" Johnny piped up hopefully.

"Of course, not." Maggie didn't sound too convinced of her own words. "These are *grown men*, working up here, sugar."

"You are of the mistaken opinion that grown men don't fight?" Thomas smiled at her.

"Well," Maggie hedged, "maybe from time to time. Over really important issues, but what could be upsetting them so?"

"Just taking a quick guess," Thomas surmised slowly, "from the direction of the noise, I'd say it's the *cooking*."

As the three of them drew on into the clearing, they could hear a cacophony of sounds emanating from the pine-plank cookshack. A few men came spilling out, wagging their heads angrily. Some of them strode down the steps, and stood spitting into the leaves and pine straw littering the ground on either side of the pine plank steps that oozed fresh resin.

"*Worst* lot of food *I've* tasted in a while," one tall, thin logger concluded, wiping his mouth as if to rid himself of the horrid taste.

"I thought my wife was a poor sort of a cook, but what Alice turns out would put Tad Horton's' grub to shame," the man at his elbow wagged his head sorrowfully.

"I don't think I can work, not eatin' like this," another logger grumbled. "I thought Mr. Logan said *three square meals* a day. If that's what he calls a square meal, he must'a been lappin' up slop with th' hogs!"

Suddenly the door burst open to the small cabin sitting just to the left of the cookshack.

Bartram Logan came strolling out, slamming his hat onto his neatly trimmed hair as he came, his dark eyes flashing, "What's all the noise? What's going on here? Where's Giles?"

"Didn't you ask him, sir, to go on up—"

By the time he had uttered those three questions, Bart was past the man who made a reply. His long, angry strides had carried him to just outside the cookshack door.

"What's wrong with you men? You already eaten your noon meal? Ready to get back to work? We're already running *two hours* behind schedule!"

As Bart Logan strode toward the cookshack, Maggie stepped out of the trees, and followed him, a few feet back, almost in his shadow.

"No, sir. Begging your pardon, Mister Logan—" the man nearest Bart began, looking not at Bart, but down at the tips of his new logging boots.

"If you have something to say to me, Roberts ...isn't it?"

"Yes, sir."

"If you have anything to say to me, Mister Roberts, I would appreciate it if you would just *look me straight in the eye*, and say your piece. If a man doesn't believe in what he's about to say—enough to meet my gaze—then he needs to just go on back in and eat his meal—and keep his mouth shut. And then get back to work."

"But, Mr. Logan ..."

"Yes, that's better. Now what seems to be the problem in the cookshack, Mister Roberts?"

"Not ...you understand, Mr. Logan ...that any of the men blames you personally ...but, well ...the thing ...is ..."

"I'm growing a beard, here, Mister Roberts."

"We just can't work a day's hard labor—on the swill that's being ladled into our plates! Ask any of the men!"

"I thank you, Mr. Roberts, for that assessment of the food …situation. And as you will *all* remember, you *yourselves* voted for Mr. Tad Horton to be your temporary mess cook. Right? Until we can acquire a *real* cook?"

"Well, yes, sir, we did, but—"

"Then, what seems to be the complaint here? I told you when you voted for Mr. Horton, that his attendance at the job would be only temporary …until we can come up with …what's going on in there?"

Maggie fairly popped into the cookshack. One quick glance around, and she immediately assessed the situation. She had swung past Bartam Logan, as he stood attempting to reason with men who had no taste, right now, for reasoning, and more taste for a decent plate of food.

Her eyes adjusting to the lessening light, she saw a newly constructed pine slab interior. Turned bark-side out.

A huge black iron cookstove took up one entire corner. Two long rows of tables almost completely hid the puncheon floor. Long puncheon benches flanked both sides of each table. Plates of uneaten food littered the tables, cold lumpy piles on each and every plate.

As she swept inside, Maggie put out a hand in either direction, picking up as she moved, never missing a step, a plate of the goop in each hand. Reaching the corner cookstove, she unceremoniously dumped the cold mess back into what was evidently the original cooking pot. There were blobs of it drying along the bottoms and sides.

"Stoke up this fire!" she ordered the first man immediately to her right. He was staring at her—wide-eyed, bearded mouth agape.

"Yes, Miss!" John Perkins flew to do her bidding.

"Where's the salt and the sugar? Any butter on the place? Go and fetch it! And get the milk and cream while you're at it! You men—

"Gather the remainder of those plates! Bring them here.

"Tell the men outside to wipe their boots and get themselves in here! Quietly, and in order! That is, if they intend to feed their faces at *my* table! Is this all of you? Take off your hats! Get them off my tables! See the racks by the door?

"Now! Which of you would like to say *Grace*?"

Bartram Logan caught the last few sentences, as he stood in the door of the cookshack—which had, not five minutes before, been a place rocked by stomping boots, banging eating utensils, and loud complaints that could be heard at least half way up the mountain.

Like some mighty hand had swept through the place, quiet rows of men sat—hatless, elbows off the table, heads bent, a fork in one hand, a waiting cup in the other, as if nothing at all untoward had transpired.

To his even greater astonishment, *there by the huge black iron stove, stood the young woman—whom he had assured at least twice the Tuesday afternoon just past, that there was absolutely no way she would be allowed in his logging camp.*

Completely oblivious to him, she hefted the heavy coffeepot, and tipped it just perfectly, into each eagerly waiting cup. Placing the pot back on the stove, carefully she dumped in a new measure of coffee, added the perfect amount of fresh water. Then she was vigorously dumping this and that from bags and pitchers, into the big iron pot on the stove—that had just begun to bubble and hiss, sending forth a mouth-watering aroma.

Bart walked slowly up behind her. She must have known he was there, but she deliberately chose to ignore him.

"Mrs.... Evans, isn't it? If you will recall, this Tuesday afternoon past, when we spoke in Ryersville—"

Bart suddenly realized that the room had grown deathly quiet. He glanced around.

Every eye in the room was fastened on him.

"Mrs. Evans, if you will just kindly step outside, I think we need to have a little ...discussion. Evidently, I didn't make myself clear, this Tuesday past."

"Oh?" Maggie turned to face Bartram Logan—as if startled that he should be there. She hesitated, very prettily, for just the slightest moment, moistening her lips. Her smooth brows rose questioningly. A sweet smile played about her mouth, her head tilted, just so. Her blue eyes were so wide, so innocent.

"I'm *so* sorry this happened, Mr. Logan. *So* sorry I got you into this mess. It really wasn't anyone's fault—that I ran late and you had to draft a temporary cook! But not to worry!" she gave a quick little wag of her head. "All is well."

Bart could find absolutely nothing to say to that.

"But," she continued, blue eyes bright, still smiling, "you see, Mr. Logan, try as I might—and I did try—I couldn't get a ride up, until this morning. I called on my friend, and he was unfortunately—away."

She paused, as if this should explain her unexpected appearance out of nowhere, and set him clear in his thinking.

"Would you care to take a seat, Mr. Logan, and taste some of these delicious hot oats? With cinnamon and sugar? Or cream? Black walnuts? White sugar? A little milk and honey?"

Bart thought he could have heard a pine needle hit the puncheon floor, had one been dropped.

The men sat still, like wooden statues, their spoons and forks halted in mid-air. He knew that if he was not *very* careful, he'd end up with a full-scaled rebellion on his hands.

"I'll ...speak with *you* later, Mrs. Evans."

He stalked outside; his brain in a whirl. Devious! Conniving ...female!

She had sneaked in, behind his back, when he was otherwise occupied, wormed her way into his cookshack—now his entire crew was waiting with bated breath—to see just how he would handle this. He deliberately paused just outside the door, listening every moment for an eruption of the ribald quips and off-color humor that ran pandemic at every logging camp he'd ever known.

All that came out of the cookshack was the quiet scraping of utensils, the gentlemanly slurping of hot cups of steaming coffee. An occasional quiet clearing of a throat, followed by a polite-as-you-please, "*Yes, more, Ma'am. Thank you, Ma'am.*"

You'd think they were attending a ladies' social!

Bart swung his lank frame down the steps, and walked back to his cabin. All right. Let them have one good meal. Then he'd set them all straight.

Bart sat on the steps of his cabin. He waited. He lit and finished his pipe. His own stomach had begun to rumble. He could do with at least a decent cup of hot coffee! They must be eating everything in sight! And then licking the pots!

He strode down to look at what progress had been made on readying the sawmill site. It appeared they were getting the log deck constructed. He wanted everything ready here, when the first logs came twisting and bobbing and splashing down the sluiceways—which still needed constructing. So much work yet to be done. But, there was no hurry. Although the cross-cut saws had arrived, the steam engine, boiler, belts and pulleys, and the main five-foot circular saw wouldn't be arriving until the end of the week. The edger saw was expected the week following.

After what seemed an eternity, men began to filter out of the cookshack. Wiping their mouths, and brushing down their beards, they donned their hats from the rack just inside the cookshack door, and politely wagged their heads, "Mrs. Evans. *Thank you, Ma'am!*"

Just then, Bart saw his foreman, Stephen Giles, walking slowly down the cleared logging trace that ran on up the ridge.

"You had your breakfast?" Bart asked testily.

"No. Couldn't quite bring myself to—"

"Well, if you hurry, you might just get yourself a fit plate of oats with all the trimmings—and a hot cup of fine coffee."

"Have I just died? And gone to heaven?"

"As near about as you're likely to get, Giles, unless one of our *under cutters* or *fellers* makes a serious blunder—and a big tree lands on your lean carcass."

"Whose doin' this heavenly cookin'? What did you do with Tad Horton? Drown him in the river?"

"No, but I felt like drowning the whole lot of them. Traitors. You should have seen the ruckus they raised when breakfast was served. Then—since nobody ate *anything* at breakfast, and they were all starving—I let them break for an early lunch—! You'd have thought you'd never seen a man offered a pan of oats with absolutely no seasoning of any type, and a weak, cold, bitter cup of coffee—twice in the same day."

"What brought about all this peace and quiet?"

"Remember the little lady, by the name of Mrs. Evans? You recall her …big joke, huh? Well, she *just showed* up here, out of the blue. Utter pandemonium was breaking loose. She marched into the cookshack—with neither a *gun* nor a *knife*—and is still holding sway in there."

"You don't say!"

"I'm afraid I do say. And just what I'm going to do with her—you know my rules—how I'm going to *rid* this camp of her …the men are all looking at me like …*You dare send this little lady packing and you haven't seen anything yet!*"

"Sounds like you've got yourself a mighty knotty problem."

"If I'd hired her on—instead of you—as head foreman on this job—we'd have that boiler puffing, that engine steaming, and that five-foot blade whining like a freight train coming up the slope. You should have heard her in there barking orders. And all the men were dancing to her tune, like some jamboree!"

"Sounds like quite a lady."

"You're head foreman around here. Why don't you march on in there, and—"

"Not me, Boss! You're the one let the filly past the corral gate!"

"Don't remind me—"

"—Well, some of the men seem, at last, to have their fill of sweetened oats and *gourmet* coffee. Why don't you get yourself something to eat and a hot cup of coffee—if there's by some miracle any left—then get the buckers started to clearing off limbs on the logs already cut, up on the upper trace? We'll have to wait for the mill and the saws to cut some timber to build the sluiceways."

Grinning from ear to ear, Giles walked toward the cookshack.

Bart looked up, and there stood his *problem*, in the door of the cookshack. For some odd reason, she still had that huge black bonnet securely tied about her throat. The thing was so big that all you could see of her face was the chin, unless she chose to look up at you. Dressed all in black, she appeared to be in mourning. And that sweeping black dress, with the long shawl wrapped about her shoulders—as if it were the dead of winter, and about to spout a blizzard. If she got too near the stove with those voluminous garments—

—Bart wondered if Mrs. Evans was a member of some particular religious sect.

Slowly he rose, and approached her. She was standing in the doorway; he was standing on the lower step. Their eyes were about even. Then he heard her saying in a sweet voice, "I saved you a plate of sweet oats, and a cup or two of hot coffee. Why don't you come on in, Mr. Logan. And we can talk."

Well! Thank you, Mrs. Evans, for that kind invitation into my own facility! Bart thought, but was too much a gentleman to say. He wanted to end this confrontation with as little spit and spectacle as possible.

Bart sat down at the end of the table nearest the big iron stove. He noticed that the ash hopper beside the stove was filled with ashes still alive with hot coals. Behind the stove itself, freshly chopped stove wood stood stacked so high it was in mighty danger of crashing down on some poor unsuspecting soul.

The dishes had all miraculously disappeared into and out of the vast dishpans, and the pans hung on iron nails high up on the wall behind the second table.

Someone had *sure* been busy! And he didn't think all of this industriousness could be attributed to Mrs. Evans alone.

Slowly, gazing about him from time to time, as if this was the first time he'd seen the cookshack, Bart began to shovel the oats into his mouth.

No wonder the men looked daggers at him! He'd eaten oatmeal since he was a toddler, but never any that tasted quite as good as this.

But the problem still remains. She's a *woman*, albeit a very young and very pretty woman, and one obviously gifted in the arts of fine cuisine—and in winding men around her little finger. But *she would have to go*. He had his rules. A logging camp was a wild and dangerous world, to be inhabited solely by men. A *woman* could create all sorts of ...problems.

He couldn't possibly allow her to stay.

Suddenly Bart heard voices. They seemed to be coming from the small lean-to on the back wall, that held a cot for the cook.

Picking up his hot cup of coffee, Bart rose, crossed to the door leading into the tiny add-on.

Old Jacob lay abed. A small boy sat beside him. The child appeared to be rubbing some sort of concoction into Jacob's bony black chest. And Jacob seemed to be enjoying it immensely.

The little boy turned to look up at Bart. Bart's heart almost stood still. He was immediately struck by the shock of dark, unruly hair that he knew instinctively no comb or brush could tame, and a little face, fair-complected, beautiful and solemn, with startlingly blue eyes.

"You my next patient, Mister?" the child asked solemnly.

"No," Bart answered, just as solemnly, his heart beating again, "I hope not."

"Then please close the door. All patient doctor work is ...strictly ..."

"Confidential!" Mrs. Evans prompted cheerily.

Quietly, Bart closed the door. "Your son's a bit young, isn't he, for medical practice?"

"We all have to start somewhere, don't we? Now, Mr. Logan, what I wanted to speak with you about—"

Bart's dark brows shot up in surprise, "Yes? Mrs. Evans?"

"The larder seems rather sparsely furnished—with so many mouths to feed. And I haven't had a chance to check the spring house, for milk and butter—"

"There *is* no spring house, Mrs. Evans. Where is all this leading?"

"Well, it appears the evening meal must consist of dried peas or beans, and corn pone! And water!" She wagged her head vigorously, as if this was altogether unthinkable. "There's not even a yam, or an onion—both of which can be kept for *weeks* very well. And then there are dried fruits, for pies and fritters. Canning has lately been very successfully done—with new, self-sealing lids. And—"

"Mrs. Evans, this is not a grand hotel we're operating here. It's a *logging camp*. Men in camps such as this are not accustomed to such fancy fare."

"And why on earth not? It's just as simple to cook a good meal—as a poor one. And a body has so much more health and vigor. It's good for the constitution. There's less illness—fevers and agues and chilblains. And with just a bit of planning, these men can dine well at every meal. With a minimum outlay of funds."

"And just who, Mrs. Evans, do you expect is to put forth this 'outlay of funds.' And who is to do the searching out of all these fine victuals, purchasing them, and hauling them to the camp?"

"Well, Mr. Logan, it was my understanding—Didn't I hear you promise the men *meals*, as well as a fair wage …in return for the labor rendered you …to operate your business …so as to earn yourself a *profit*?"

"Mrs. Evans, the purpose of any business enterprise—not just mine alone—is to earn a profit. Now as to—"

"I have prepared these posters. We can put one down at the Johnson's General Store and Mill, and another at Moss' Mercantile in Rhyersville. Perhaps, one even at the Post Office, though traffic there is not as good as at the stores—"

"*Mrs. Evans!* How did we get into all this? I thought I made myself plain, the other day, on the porch of the Rhyersville store that you seem to be speaking about—"

"Yes!" Mrs. Evans nodded her pretty head at him, as if suddenly she was in a deep, deep study. "I think you're right, Mr. Logan. We *should* start with the Rhyersville Store, first. Then the word will, naturally, just drift out from there. What man can you spare? He could make it there by dark, and back in the morning. Just to put our posters up in some conspicuous location. Spread the word to all the farmsteads hereabouts—that the Logan Lumber Company is in the market for their freshest produce, their best cuts of beef, their fattest geese, fresh eggs—he could bring back, whatever is available on such short notice, from both stores—"

"Mrs. Evans! How—?"

"How, what, Mr. Logan? You could just set up a special fund. I'd be more than happy to act as your purchasing agent. I'm extremely trustworthy. I'm very good at selecting good birds, and fine fruits and vegetables. Some onions, definitely. Bushels of yams and Irish potatoes. We can make a hill back of the—"

"Mrs. Evans—!"

"We could build a wire coop, for poultry, and how about a *bee gum*? The men seemed to *love* the honey I brought up—with their oats, this morning. And honey is good to sweeten gingerbread and puddings, and—you can trust me, Mr. Logan, as God is my witness!"

"I'm sure, Mrs. Evans, that God is your witness. From where else would you be getting these out-of-this-world ideas! Next, you'll be asking the men to go berry picking, so you can bake them all cobblers!"

"Mr. Logan! That's an *excellent* idea! If you can't spare any of the men, then perhaps, with your permission, Johnny and I could go. We might even make it back in time to fix a cobbler for supper, and have some left for strawberry syrup for the men to spread on their buttered johnny-cakes, in the morning!"

"Mrs. Evans. Now …let me get this straight. You want …to go …*berry picking* …to cook the men some pies …for the evening meal."

"The way you put it, Mr. Logan, it sounds even better than when I said it. Johnny," she was summoning the child. He popped immediately out. "We're going berry picking, sweetie. Grab your cap. And get the big empty bucket setting there beside the stove. I think I saw some wild strawberries down by the path, as we were coming up."

Bart had risen, and was standing numb-faced staring at her. She turned to him and smiled. "You won't have to pay me now, for picking the berries, it can wait …until whenever you pay the rest of my wages. You have something you want to say, Mr. Logan?"

"You expect me …to pay …you …for picking …berries! What's the going rate, by the way, for berry picking? So I can enter it into my ledgers!"

"Oh, I don't know. How about ten cents for me, for whatever I'm able to pick this afternoon, and a penny for Johnny."

"I'm to pay *Johnny*, too? For picking berries?"

"You know, Mr. Logan, what the Good Book says about the workman."

"No, Mrs. Evans, but I'm afraid you're about to tell me."

"The workman, Mr. Evans—be he large or small—*is* worthy of his hire—

"—And, Mr. Logan—"

"Yes, Mrs. Evans?"

"You won't forget—to send a man with the posters. Probably since he's going, he could hit both stores the same day. So you won't have to send him back again—except to haul up the comestibles. From what I can see, you have a fine crew of men here. They'll most likely work their hearts out for you …if you do right by them …with their meals."

"Ah, yes. The …posters …" Bart sighed.

Bart stood for a moment, heaved another great sigh. She was gone! He opened the door to peer in at Jacob.

"How are you feeling, Jacob …now that you've been attended by the country's youngest physician?"

"Ain't that chil' *somethin,*' Massa Bart? The face of an angel. The face of an angel. I could feel it clean down in my soul, Massa Bart. That chil'—he's so ser'ous. So set on healin' all th' sick! Savin' all th' poor!"

"Saving all the poor? Since when do physicians do that?"

"Massa Johnny …now …he's no going to charge his patients one penny. Jest do his doctorin' out of th' love of his heart. And couldn't you jest feel it, Massa Bart, the very Love of God, comin' like a fountain, out o' that chil'?"

"You must have a fever, Jacob." Bart lifted a dark brow, "Your fine physician may practice his healing arts out of the goodness of his heart, but when it comes to his berry picking, the good doctor expects to be paid."

The evening meal consisted of black-eyed peas cooked tender with chunks of streak-o-lean, hot buttered corn pone, freshly dug sassafras tea sweetened with honey, and two of the biggest fresh strawberry pies most of the loggers had ever laid eyes on—dripping with butter and sprinkled with sugar and browned to a tasty crisp.

Bart ate wordlessly. He didn't look at the men. He didn't dare look at Mrs. Evans. He made sure he didn't get anywhere in her immediate vicinity …afraid she might set upon him …and want him to pay her for going frog-gigging, or coon hunting.

And then, she might ask him about those stupid flyers. Or posters. Or whatever she called them.

He had already planned—had already fully intended—to send a rider to post some letters, down in Rhyersville. And it really *wasn't* that far fetched, he supposed, to get a *few* fresh vegetables. A *bit* of fruit. A *roasting or frying chicken* or two. He even liked yams and Irish potatoes and onions. And did they really seal food up in jars, and keep it *all winter*?

Bart couldn't' help but notice that Mrs. Evans set aside an extra plate. He wondered what on earth she intended doing with it. Was it for the 'friend' who had belatedly driven her up to the logging camp? Who was this *friend*?

He appeared to be a bit older than Mrs. Evans. But he seemed to be on *quite* friendly terms with the boy. Almost as if he was family. Bart noticed that he had hung about, outside, obviously to see how Mrs. Evans had fared her first morning. Then he had unobtrusively walked inside. But the look in his eyes, when he gave that quick peck on the cheek to Mrs. Evans as he took his leave—not the look of a man who was family—

"Johnny? You finished your supper already? Then go on in, Doctor, and feed your patient. I'll bet he's just waiting for your sweet, sunny little face to brighten up that sick room! And you see to it, that Jacob eats every bite."

These were the orders issued by Mrs. Evans, to her small son.

Now, Mrs. Evans seemed to have taken it into her mind that she was somehow going to cure a dying old man.

Bart had watched Jacob's frail health decline, ever since his master, William Bartram Hurston, was laid to rest out at Cottonwood.

The old Negro had about grieved himself to death, since William Hurston passed, and left old Jacob in Bart's care. Bart was too busy to really notice the old man. Pour soul, Bart sighed, not that I'm that hard hearted, but what does he have left, now that his last friend on earth is gone? Friend? But, they *were* friends, those last few years. What a strange world it was.

It became clear to Bart, soon after his grandfather passed away, that Jacob had no desire to live—and every desire to follow his master. And he was sorely afraid this was one battle Mrs. Margaret Ann Evans would not win.

The next few days passed rather uneventfully. More uneventfully, in fact, than any of the days since Mrs. Evans had entered the camp.

Jacob seemed to be making amazing leaps in the improvement of his health. Now and again, Bart would find him out behind the mess hut, seated upon an upturned barrel—upon which someone had thoughtfully placed a thick blanket for padding—quietly enjoying the morning breezes, and peeling potatoes, or stringing beans!

"Well, Jacob!" Bart would stop and pass a few minutes of his valuable time with the old man. Poor Jacob …he had no one now.

Then on this particular morning, as Bart made his customary visit and his customary morning greeting, out the door of the cookshack bounded the boy.

He saw Bart, and immediately the smile faded from his beautifully childish face. His blue eyes got very wide.

"Won't you say good morning to Mr. Logan, Johnny?" Mrs. Evans called to the child from the door. In the shadows of the door, Bart could barely make out the bulk of the huge black shawl, the voluminous black skirts, the eternal sunbonnet.

"Mornin,' Mister Logan," the boy said in a muffled, subdued voice, as he sidled up beside Jacob.

"Look what I found for you," Bart heard Jacob saying to the boy. Jacob produced from somewhere in the folds of his clothes a tiny bird, which appeared to be crippled in some way. "You can take him, and doctor him back to health."

"Jacob! Why would you tell the boy such a thing?" Bart asked, his practical mind asserting itself. He detested anything that smacked of dishonesty. "You and I both know that bird's not got one chance in—"

The boy was staring at him with such concern, it caught Bart mid-sentence.

"Then, again …who am I to say. It …could be that the creature …might even …survive …given …eh …proper …treatment."

Feeling he had somewhat redeemed himself with that lie, Bart turned and quietly walked away. Why hadn't he kept his unwanted advice to himself? What did *he* know about children?

Three days later, when he stopped by to check on Jacob, there sat the boy, leaning sorrowfully against Jacob's slight frame, the cold, stiff bird laying in one little hand.

Neither of them was speaking, so Bart offered, "Well, good morning to you, both, gentlemen. Ah? And what do we have here?"

"He died!" The boy gazed up at him, his eyes filled with accusations, as if to say, 'It's your fault! You put a curse on him!'

"We thought, Mister Bart," (not *Massa* Bart?) "that we's would giv' th' poor thin' a funeral."

"Well!" Bart's eyebrows shot up, "That's …very commendable …a …matter entirely …I suppose …at your discretion. Since you seem to be the …only …next of kin."

"Are you making a joke at us, Mister Bart?" the boy asked, his little face in as much of a scowl as he seemed able to muster

"Well—" Bart began, staring at the child in amazement—amazed that the child had such a level of discernment. "And …why would I do that?"

"Because you don't *like* me! You don't *like* little children. And a person that doesn't like little children—"

"Whatever gave you such a fool idea?" Bart heard his voice rising against his will. "Or should I say, *whoever* gave you such a fool idea?"

The child only stared at him, his blue eyes brimming with unshed tears, his little mouth clamped tightly shut. Whoever it was, the boy wasn't about to divulge that little secret.

"Well!" Bart rose slowly to his feet from his perch on the empty fruit barrel, "I suppose I'll just leave you two, then, to your morning's work."

Neither of them spoke, the boy still fixing those blue orbs on Bart.

"Jacob," Bart said rather pointedly, "I will see you, after the ...funeral."

"Mr. Johnny, why don't you axk him? Now's the time fer ye to axk."

"Ask what?" Bart was suddenly very intrigued.

"Mr. Johnny would like a small box built, out of some scrap, big enough to bury his patient, here."

"Maggie always put her little rabbits in tiny boxes, before burying them! She told me that!" The boy announced soberly.

"Mrs. Evans? Buried ...little rabbits ...in tiny boxes?"

"I take, it, Mister Bart," Jacob added quietly, "this was some time ago. And these tiny critters ...wuz in the nature of pets."

"Oh! Of course! I see. Well, Johnny, isn't it? Well, Johnny, you just come with me, and we'll see if we can't rig up some ...sort ...of ...casket ...for your friend ...there."

"His name is Ruffles!"

"Yes, well, Ruffles shall have a very fine casket. Which we shall line with the softest of mosses ...just like his Mama made for him ...when he was first born! Then he can go to his final rest, cushioned in his—"

Their words faded as they rounded the corner of the cookshack, and Maggie could not tell exactly to what realm of the Eternal Mr. Bartram Logan was consigning poor Ruffles. But she couldn't help but give a tiny smile. *So.* It appeared that the cold, callous lumberman, with business for blood, Mr. Bartram Logan, possessed—somewhere in that finely-clad, entirely closed, chest of his—some sort of vestige of a human heart!

The 'casket' finished and properly lined, Bart intended to send the two mourners off to conduct their ceremony. He didn't feel that he could attend that—and keep a straight face.

Besides, he had dawdled away enough of his precious time this morning, seeing to the construction of the casket.

All the crew had watched, totally amazed, that Mr. Logan spent his morning in such a non-productive manner. But the boy seemed to be pleased with the box Bart himself had tacked together, and had watched as Bart tucked in the straw and moss. Then Bart had knelt, and handed it to the boy. His throat had caught, as he placed the crude treasure in the boy's tiny, upturned hands. This could be *his* son, *Joshua*, here before him. This could be *Joshua's* tiny hands—outstretched towards him. His vision blurring, Bart had leapt up, made some excuse. He couldn't hurry off fast enough.

Bartram Logan dreamed that night—of Joshua. Wreathed in drifting fog, Joshua came towards him, reaching out his little hands …reaching for him …
Bart awoke with a start, and sat up. His shirt was wringing wet. His face felt numb. His arms were cold and clammy with moisture.
He rose, crossed to the plank door, lifted the latch, and let in a rush of cool mountain air. Stepping outside, he slumped to the solitary step, and let his head sink into his hands.
"Oh! God!" he gasped out a halting prayer—
"—Oh! God—!"
He didn't think he actually wept. But his throat kept opening and closing, his shoulders heaving. It was some minutes before, exhausted and drained, he regained control of himself.
He walked back inside, closed the door, went over and lay back down on his cot. In the dream, the face was shrouded in fog. He saw …just a small form …and the hands. What, he wondered, would Josh *look like*, if he had lived? He would, of course, probably have dark hair, like Bart's, and a fair, child's face, since he would be only four. He would, probably, look like the boy—Johnny—
—Bart did not sleep the remainder of the night.
And the day following, and every day after that, he avoided the boy.

Maggie had watched with anxious eyes, as Mr. Bartram Logan made it a point, now, not to be anywhere near Johnny. She had such high hopes, that Johnny could soften the mercenary heart of Mr. Logan. But apparently, that had not happened. Nor was it about to happen. Mr. Logan's face appeared closed. Distant. Even his dark eyes had taken on a sad, harsh glint.
Maggie began to make it a point to place a plate for Mr. Logan, somewhere near where Johnny sat.
And Bartram Logan made it a point to snatch up that plate, and move as far as he could, away from the boy, preferably to the far end of the other table.

Bart ceased his morning checks on Jacob. And Jacob missed this few minutes with the man that in his heart he still considered to be his master—even if Miss Maggie insisted he stop using that offensive title.

"Now you listen to me, Jacob," she had chided him very sternly one day. "You have been a free man for many years, now. I've been meaning to speak with you about this. Though, you understand it's really *none* of my business. But, when I see one person subjugating himself to another, outside the proper and approved relations that are so clearly set forth in the Holy Scriptures, well, Jacob, how can I, in all good Christian conscience, not speak up?"

"It says that, in th' Holy Book?"

"Oh yes! And very clearly, at that!"

Then, very solemnly, Mrs. Evans explained the passage to him, how it forbade calling any man on earth your master.

"So, you see, Jacob. There you have it. We are permitted to call no man on this earth master. There is only one Master, and that is God Almighty, Himself!"

"He tried to tell me that, but I couldn't believe it—not after so many years—"

"Who, Jacob?"

"It was a long …long …time …ago …before the War wuz ev'r over."

"Well, at any rate, there's another thing I've been meaning to discuss with you, Jacob. It's the matter of a surname. Do you have a surname for yourself? A last name?"

"I's all'us had only one name. Only Jacob."

"But, you see, Jacob, the thing is, on your legal papers, if you ever owned property, you would need a full name. Or even on your headstone, when—in distant years to come, of course—you pass, you want a full name: Jacob *so-and-so*, and the date of your birth and passing, you understand, to carve into your headstone."

"I don't knows when I's born. Just that it were a long, long time ago."

"Then, Mr. Logan …no Mr. Logan wouldn't be that old. Mr. Logan's father might know?"

"Mr. Robert and Mizzzz Eleanor, God rest their souls, done sunk in the Great Ocean Sea, far out, more than a few years past. When Mr. Bart were but a boy."

"Oh!" Maggie gasped.

"Then, Mr. Bart's grandfather?"

"Himself is passed, too, and buried on his own plantation."

"Then, we can just guess at the age. But as to a surname, you will just have to choose one. What do you think?"

"I think," Jacob replied sorrowfully, "I wouldn't has any …monies to pay fer a headstone …when I pass."

"But, all these years, since the War, neither Mr. Logan nor his grandfather *paid* you?"

"No'umm. I"s mostly been sick and not workin,' since Himself passed."

"I see. But still, you should choose yourself a name. And I'm sure that Mr. Logan will be happy to see to it that …then, again …I don't know, whether he would or not. At any rate …just to have the dignity of being equal to other men, you should choose a name. So, what would you like to choose?" Maggie prompted, bending toward Jacob to look deep into his rheumy eyes.

"I don't know, Mizzz Maggie. Lot of th' other colored folk done took the name of they Massas."

"Then you shall be called *Jacob Logan*.

"What would you like as a second name …a so-called …middle name?"

"You don' think *two* names for old Jacob be plenty enough?"

"Why stop at two, when most men have three?" Maggie smiled sweetly. "How …about …" Maggie contemplated deeply, "choosing something from the Bible. What about the name of some great prophet of old? Then there are the disciples, and New Testament authors: There was Matthew, Mark, Luke, and John. Peter. Paul. Barnabas—"

"I's like *that* one!"

"Barnabas? Then …*Barnabas* it shall be!" Maggie got up and dashed to the door.

"Come here a minute, Johnny!"

Johnny came running in. Johnny, as Bart himself had always noticed, never walked.

"Johnny, com'on in, sugar! Isn't it exciting! We're about to have a little ceremony, to give Jacob his new name."

"Do I get a new name, too, Maggie? I don't *want* a new name! Is this like the game we're playing, about you not being—"

"No, Johnny, sweetie, this has nothing to do with you or me. This is all about Jacob. Jacob," Maggie announced, a huge smile wreathing her face, "has chosen himself a new name. Jacob, rise to your feet!"

Jacob raised himself slowly off the puncheon bench and stood away from the corner of the table. He stood straighter than old Jacob had been able to pull his frail frame upward for many a year now. His chin was high, and his eyes fixed on something far away, far distant from this little pine-slab mess shack.

"The man you now see standing before you," Maggie announced in a clear, calm voice, "shall from this day forth be known by the full and final name:

"Jacob Barnabas Logan!"

Jacob Barnabas Logan found it extremely difficult to hold back the sobs. At last!—

—After all those long, difficult, lonely years—

—The burden was lifted.

—At last—!

—He could lift up his chin.

—He could walk tall, and proud.

—He was a whole man!

—He was free!

Chapter 29

"Well, am I to understand, then, Mrs. Evans, that you have succeeded in delivering the message which our esteemed President, Mister Abraham Lincoln, was unable to deliver—with his grand Emancipation Proclamation—nor that the score or more of years of freedom following has conveyed?"

"And what would that be, Mr. Logan?"

"Why, you have single-handedly, and apparently quite effectively, set old Jacob free of his lifetime of slavery!"

"No document written on paper, Mr. Logan, no proclamation ever issued or set pen to by man, can set another man free. A man is only free, when he believes in his *own soul*, that such is the fact."

Feeling duly chastened, Bart took his plate, and seated himself at the far end of the table. He wagged his head slightly, and wondered why he *ever* made the slightest attempt to carry on any type of conversion with Margaret Ann Evans!

But, as Bart watched her sailing effortlessly about the cookshack—dishing out rice pudding with raisins and cinnamon and butter sauce, and refilling cup after cup of hot coffee, and sometimes now, China tea—he wondered to himself that she had still not, as yet, set herself ablaze—with that abundance of trailing and frothing garments flaring about her.

The long, swaying tips of the black-fringed shawl dangled more than a few times dangerously close to the red-glowing lids of the big black iron cookstove. And when she lifted one of the eyes, to shove in a short length of stove wood to keep the coffee or tea pots steaming hot, Bart often held his breath, ready to leap up and fly over and put out the flames, or fling her to the floor and roll her about like a sack of cotton—that swaying fringe—an inch or so above the leaping flames. Maybe he would dash water on her—or snatch off the flaming shawl, and plunge the offensive garment into the nearest water barrel—

This was ridiculous. He was the owner here! He was the employer! It was his responsibility—the proper running of the camp to keep everyone safe! He should establish the rules!

Bart drained his coffee cup, and determined in his mind he would speak with her, dreading the encounter, knowing Mrs. Evans' conversational style now, so well, having not the slightest notion as to where in the world she would run to—with his suggestion. No, not suggestion. *Demand.*

Bart set the coffee cup carefully, softly, down on the puncheon table, covered now with some sort of table linen—for which he had foolishly agreed to pay. His thinking was that the argument *against* paying for the table linens would cost him more in time lost from productive work, than the price for their actual purchase.

Bart waited until the crude building had completely emptied of men, then made his way slowly towards the black iron cookstove, his eyes on the puncheon floor, scrubbed clean every day, swept free of mud and dirt and crumbs.

He was almost to the cookstove, now. He slowed his advance, his mind wrapping itself around exactly the words he would use.

"Mrs. Evans," Bart tried to smile at her, most agreeably. He could see only the tip of her chin, from beneath the great brim of her black bonnet. How did she *bear* that thing in this oppressive heat? But the bonnet, as uncomfortable, as odd as it appeared—indoors, in the shade—was not the issue here. At least the big bonnet did not pose the threat of setting the entire camp ablaze.

"Yes, Mr. Logan?" she asked, meekly, as if willing, even eager to hear every word he had to utter. Red flags immediately popped up.

"I couldn't help but notice …every day …since you've been here, Mrs. Evans …that you are always and eternally swathed in that …I mean …to say …you always don your beautiful black shawl."

"You don't like my shawl, Mr. Logan?"

"Well, it's not that I don't *like* your shawl. I mean, it's a perfectly fine looking shawl. And in some settings—and on some occasions—I think it would be a perfectly acceptable piece of apparel—"

"But not here?" Maggie raised her face, and the blue eyes locked with the brown. "And why not, Mr. Logan?"

"Well, it gets so *deucedly hot* in here—"

He must watch his language ...she'd be after him—with her Scripture book he had seen laying around.

"You are, then, Mr. Logan, concerned about my bodily comfort?"

What does a gentleman say to that—?

"That is not what I meant to imply. Not in the least way am I at all ...concerned about your body!"

"What, then, Mr. Logan, seems to be your main concern?"

"I am concerned that *the camp will catch ablaze*! Every time you move about the stove, the thing dangles *dangerously* close! Like an unlit match! Just waiting to ignite into leaping flames! When you open the eyes of the stove, I *cringe* inside, waiting for the entire cookshack to explode in devouring flames! I live in constant fear ...of ..."

"Well?" Mrs. Evans cocked her head aside, waiting, peering up at Mr. Logan from beneath the big brim of her bonnet. She noticed how that, all the time Mr. Logan was scolding her about the big black shawl, his dark eyes were glued to the brim of her bonnet. She had the odd feeling that he might actually knock the thing clean off her head.

"Well ..." Bart hesitated. Mrs. Evans continued to peer up at him. He could almost feel the thoughts flying about inside that pretty head. He knew he should have kept his fool mouth shut. All his instincts warned him, but did he listen?!

"It seems, that what I'm gathering from what you just said, Mr. Logan, is that your *own* bodily comfort may be more in the forefront of your mind here ...than mine."

"What exactly does that mean?"

"Well, you yourself just said, that *you* feel thus and thus discomforts when I moved about the kitchen, in my shawl and bonnet. I said nothing, about any discomfort I felt, as I can recall."

"Mrs. Evans. Permit me just to speak plainly here. I *am* the *owner* of this operation. I am *responsible* for the welfare and personal safety of all the crew—which, it seems, by some odd quirk of fate, has come to include *you.*

"And I am putting you on notice—here and now—either you take off that huge blanket or shawl or whatever the thing is—and hang it somewhere *safely* away, or—" Unable to think of some viable threat, Bart continued, "But if you want to swaddle yourself in it like some Egyptian mummy when you're away from the cooking area, then well and good. But take that thing off—and hang it somewhere—before you succeed in burning the entire camp to the ground!"

Wordlessly, Maggie lifted the black fringed shawl from her slender shoulders. Wordlessly, she turned, walked over to the wall, reached up, and flung it securely onto a peg.

Very slowly, she smoothed down her skirts, and turned to face Mr. Bartram Logan.

Bartram Logan stood staring at her. *Why* had he ever mentioned the stupid shawl?

More than twenty young, stout, healthy men, with fine eyes in their heads, would all be watching Mrs. Margaret Ann Evans as she moved about the puncheon tables ...every day ...without the cloaking protection of her big shawl—

But he would *not* retract a word of what he had just said.

She stood looking at him, so calmly, so—

"What about my bonnet? Mr. Logan?" she cocked her pretty head aside and asked sweetly, "Does it also alarm you with discomfort?"

Maggie slowly undid the ties beneath her chin, and drew it off. Bart was stunned.

Without the shawl and bonnet, she appeared to be *an entirely different person.* Now Bart had a glimmer of an idea as to why she had shrouded herself in those uncomfortable things.

Why, he didn't know, but, still, Bart felt a compelling urge to have the last word in this matter. Slowly, he walked towards her. He stopped, not two feet away.

"You can take your bonnet, Mrs. Evans, and stuff it into the fire, for all I care. I am interested only in keeping this camp safe."

"And, now, Mr. Logan, that I have shed my shawl and bonnet, you think your camp will be safer?"

Well ...so much for the last word! And before he got himself in any deeper, Bart thought the smart thing to do was to simply bow, and back away.

Which is exactly what he did.

Her hair, without the constriction of the big bonnet, would now sometimes work loose, without Mrs. Evans even being aware of it. And it would swing down her back in dark, loose coils, ending just above her small waist.

Without the bonnet and shawl, she was a vision to behold. Though her dresses came up to her neck and their hems swept the floor, grace and beauty were undisguised. Always, now, Bart watched the men at the mess tables with wary eyes.

But the men seemed as subdued in Mrs. Evans' presence as ever. It was clear to Bart that they had such deep respect for this lady, they held her in such elevated esteem, that she hovered high above their heads, right up there in the clouds, along with the angels. And Bart assured himself that he personally regarded her only as a nuisance and a problem. And yet—

—Often he would return to his cabin for the night, feeling anxious and uneasy, as if a lit powder keg glowed in the camp—

—How he longed for the return of the days of the heavy black shawl—and the big black bonnet!

Maybe he should suggest to her—

Not if it rained *FIRE AND BRIMSTONE*!

Why didn't he just fire her!?

And lose every single worker in the camp? And probably even old Jacob along with the rest. Or should he say *Jacob Barnabas Logan*!

Upon laying aside the stifling bonnet and shawl, Maggie felt somehow liberated. Unfettered by the heavy, bulky clothing, she seemed to glide over the rough puncheon flooring, in a little dancing step, she felt that light.

And without the weight and bother of the heavy bonnet that had often obstructed her vision, she felt she was seeing the world anew.

The next time she was down at Rhyersville, she would speak to Barbara Jo, and ask if she had any brighter pieces of apparel Maggie could buy— *really cheaply*. How long since she'd had a new dress—?

As Mrs. Evans began to make some sort of metamorphosis before his very eyes, from a black clad caterpillar—to a brightly colored, prettily flitting butterfly, Bart slowly came to the painful realization that when she was enshrouded in the dark shell of her shawl and bonnet, Mrs. Evans had felt responsible for her own safety. Now that Bart had ordered her to lay these worrisome garments aside, he had unwittingly shifted that burden off her— and onto himself.

Stephen Giles stared at Bart, "Excuse me, Boss? You think we're just about ready to turn the water into the sluiceways? Everything seems to be about—"

"What's that? What did you say, Giles?"

"Is something bothering you, Boss? You seem sort of preoccupied of late."

"No, it's nothing. Just the usual problem I've been encountering every single day—since Mrs. Margaret Ann Evans set foot on this mountain!"

"What has she done now?"

"That's the problem, Giles, this time it's not so much what *she's* done, but what *I've* done that bothers me."

"Oh? You have feelings for Mrs. Evans?"

"Feelings? Oh, the *feelings* I have for Mrs. Evans would fill a book! An entire huge volume. But they're certainly not the sort of feelings to which you seem to be referring. She's about as attractive to me as a bad case of the plague. A nest of coiled vipers! A bunch of wild bees disturbed in their secretive hole. She's ...and she's—"

"She's very pretty, isn't she Mr. Logan? And such a lady. Not at all the type you would expect to find working in a mountain logging camp."

"There, Giles, you have put your finger squarely on the problem. You see, Mrs. Evans, is ...she ...did ...she ...said ..."

"Why don't you just fire her?"

"Oh! You think it's that simple, huh? I could not count on *all* my fingers and all my toes, the number of times I have actually 'fired' Mrs. Evans. She's like a child's rubber ball—"

"She is?"

"The more *pressure* I put on her to leave, the farther she bounces, and in all directions!"

"I see."

"Yes! Now you see my problem. The only way I'm going to get her out of this camp, and off this mountain—is if I *hog* tie her, throw her over the front of my saddle, and then try to heft the little boy up, while attempting to hold on to his mother. And all the while, the child is pummeling me viciously about the head and shoulders ...and she's fighting and screaming ...full of righteous indignation up to High Heaven—

"—And," Bart continued, "To say nothing of the reception I'd get from the men when and if I got back from such a trip. They'd probably burn me in effigy, and quit in flocks ...since their *nurse and cook* was gone and they'd get no more pampering and puddings and pies."

"I can see you've given this …a lot of thought. You could get one of the men, to take her down."

"Yes. Fine idea. And, let me see, Giles. Didn't I hire you on as head foreman? Didn't I already attempt to assign *you* the job—of getting Mrs. Evans and her son off this mountain? You seem to think it such a small thing to accomplish."

"Nooooo, thanks, Mr. Logan. You give me *that* particular chore, I think I'd just be forced to tender my resignation."

"Yes. Well," Bart said very thoughtfully with a slight wag of his handsome head, smoothing down his hair, reaching for his gray felt hat, "sometimes, Mr. Giles, I wish I could tender mine. Now, let's go see if those sluiceways will perform the way I designed them."

The sawmill itself had been delivered, hauled up the mountain on sleds, behind two giant logging horses, that had just arrived, amidst a crescendo of shouting, yelling and cursing that Maggie could hear clear from the beginning of the steep incline, until they drew into the camp yard.

The mill was set up, and soon the massive stallions were dragging logs into the camp clearing, to be fed to the giant saw. Maggie and Johnny stood watching, their eyes wide, the day the giant draft horses were first led into the campsite. They were both stunned at the sight of them. Now, every day when the giant horses were led out of their corral for exercise or feeding and watering, or hitched up to logs, Johnny made it a point to be standing in the cookshack door.

They were so huge! Both snow-white! Their hooves, Maggie told Johnny in a whisper, might not fit into the biggest of her dish pans. She wondered if the pine pole corral would hold them.

But they seemed docile enough. The loggers walking along beside them— tall men, but they appeared almost to be young boys, the stallions towered so far above them. Maggie calculated that they must stand nineteen or twenty hands high!

"Can I go out there to the coral, Maggie? And see them up close?"

"No, Johnny! Mr. Bartram Logan would have both our hides! You stay safely away from those giants! One could inadvertently step on you, and smash you like a tiny ant!"

"Can I stand here, then, and watch them roll the first log off the deck, and onto the saw carriage?"

"Where did you learn that, Johnny, about the saw and the carriage and such?"

"I heard Mr. Logan talking to the men."

"You haven't been spying on Mr. Logan! Tell me that you haven't been spying on Mr. Logan!"

"No, Maggie. I just wanted to learn how the steam engine works. How it drives the steam into the big chamber, after the fire is built up. And how the steam creates all this pressure, and drives the pistons forward, which moves the belt along the carriage and carries the log into the teeth of the big round saw!"

"Why! Johnny! I don't know quite what to say!"

Well, there's a first! Bart Logan thought, listening to this conversation as he leaned his tall frame into the shade of the cookshack for a minute. Good boy, Johnny! I can see you're growing up to be *just like* your mother.

Unseen to Maggie or Johnny, a pleased grin on his face, Bart made his way surreptitiously back to work, taking the round-about route, creeping in a circle behind his own cabin. And all that afternoon, those few words flew sweetly about in his brain. *Mrs. Margaret Ann Evans ...didn't know quite what to say!*

Bart sensed a different feeling towards the boy, now, a sort of warming, as if they were fellow conspirators—in the battle against the wit and words of Mrs. Margaret Ann Evans! And, the boy had somehow scored a victory. So the boy must be worthy of a small word of encouragement, now and again.

"How are you today, Johnny?" Bartram Logan actually smiled at Johnny, and laid a tanned hand, ever so slightly, ever so lightly, on Johnny's small shoulder. He even seemed to make a point of sitting beside Johnny at the breakfast meal.

Johnny peered up at the tall man beside him, very cautiously. Oh! How many cautions there were ...issued by Maggie ...about this man ...the owner of the mill ...the man who paid Maggie money to work ...the man who—

"And, how are all your patients, Doctor Evans? No more deaths of record, I take it?"

"Are you making fun of me, Mr. Logan?" The boy frowned at Bart.

"No! Indeed not! Why, Johnny, I would never do such a dastardly thing!"

"What's 'das ...ter ...ly' mean?"

"Well, bad. Rude. Out of order. That sort of thing."

"Then …you're my friend? And you're Jacob Barnabas' friend?"

"Why, certainly! Whatever would make you think otherwise?"

"Because of the way you treat me. And Jacob Barnabas."

"Treat you? I was not aware that I treated either of you in any unseemly fashion. But, I have?"

"You won't speak to Jacob any more. And you never look at me. Or speak to me. Since we buried Ruffles. I thought you didn't like us anymore."

"But, Johnny," Bart searched for words. How could he explain to this child, this beautiful, precious little child, that sometimes, the merest sight of his face, the hair flopping over his eyes, caused Bart immeasurable pain.

"That was nothing, *nothing* whatever to do with you, Johnny …or with Jacob. It's just that, sometimes …in …life …a man …has …there are …these feelings …but they have nothing to do with you."

"You don't have any feelings for me? You don't *like* me, do you?"

"That's not what I said …not at all …what I meant to say. I have an idea. Why don't we just forget the past, and start clean from here. You put out your right hand, and I will take it in mine. You see, then we will shake like this and I will look you straight in the eye, and I will say, 'I like you Johnny Evans.' And you will say to me, 'I like you, Bartram Logan.' And we will have declared between us—Johnny Evans and Bartram Logan—a pact of friendship."

The boy jerked his hand away, "That won't do," he frowned and wagged his head so hard his hair shook.

"Why ever not? You don't like me? Not at all?"

"I could like you fine, if you'd let me. I got to go, Mr. Logan. Maggie's calling me."

Bart got up from the table, slammed his plate down, rammed his right hand into his pocket as if it has just been burned, and stalked out of the cookshack. He could never recall in his entire life, having his offer of friendship so resoundingly, so clearly rejected. By a four-year-old!

Bart didn't make any further attempts to make amends, or to make friends, with Johnny Evans. He was beginning to wonder about his lack of expertise in the realm of human relationships. All those years, first his grandfather, and then he, after his grandfather's death, had attempted to instill in Jacob's scrawny black breast the fact that the Hurston family, then the Logan family, relinquished all title and claims ever held against his person.

But it took a conversation with one small woman—who was smart as a whip, well read, and could beat the devil in a debate, but most certainly without benefit of higher education—to convince Jacob—now Jacob Barnabas Logan—that he was indeed a free man.

Why couldn't Bart, with all his eloquent vocabulary, all those studies in philosophy, in probing deep within the human mind and psyche, why couldn't Bart Logan accomplish so small a task, with so fine a subject as Jacob?

With Jacob still on his mind, Bart looked up from his ledger books to find Mrs. Evans standing quietly in his office door.

"Am I disturbing you, Mr. Logan?"

"Why, no, Mrs. Evans. Won't you step in, and take that chair?"

"No, thank you, Mr. Logan." Her face looked set, her voice sounded cold as January rainwater. She appeared to be on the verge of tears.

"Is something wrong, Mrs. Evans? Has something happened, of which I'm apparently unaware?"

"I don't know…exactly how to put this, Mr. Logan. But if you wish it, Johnny and I will pack up, and walk down the mountain—tomorrow. I can send for our trunk—later."

Bart could instantly recognize from her voice, from the look on her face, that this offer of resignation—for which he had longed for so long and so often—had just cost Mrs. Evans dearly.

"What has happened?" Bart asked quietly.

"Johnny…" Mrs. Evan paused to collect herself, tears brimming in her eyes. Angrily, she swiped them away with the back of one hand. "Johnny tells me that you do not like him. That you no longer want him at the camp."

"*What?* Why, Mrs. Evans! *Why* would your boy say a thing like that?"

"You tell *me*, Mr. Logan, why *would* Johnny say a thing like *that?* If you want to yell at me, Mr. Logan…" Again the hand, brushing away the tears, the eyes bright, "If you want to make jests about me, Mr. Logan…if you want to make false proffers of supposed friendship—"

At that, Bart leapt up from behind the desk, knocking several objects off into the floor as he rose.

He exclaimed:

"*If I what!?*"

"Johnny told me…about your little conversation this morning. About even extending your hand—to supposedly seal the pact of a friendship that was not to be with him at all—but to some person of whom he never heard."

"*What?* In good faith and conscience, I *swear before The Eternal*, I offered *your* boy *my* friendship, sealed with a handshake. And he *spurned me.* He threw it back in my face. I was *roundly rejected*, Mrs. Evans, by a *four year old boy!*"

He watched her face closely, as she took in and digested his every word.

"What, exactly…did you say, to Johnny?"

"Well, I don't…know…something like…'Well, Johnny Evans, you give me your hand, and I'll give you mine…and we'll shake on it—and be friends!' Nothing more. He replied to me, 'No sir. That won't do!' and off he went! My hand still stuck up in the air like a fool!"

"Ooohhhh," her mouth made a little gasping sound. He could almost see the anger, the hurt, draining out of her. As some sort of *light* seemed to dawn in her brain.

"Oh, well, Mr. Logan, if *that* was *all* there was *to* it." And just like that, she turned to leave.

"*Mrs. Evans!*" Bart's voice reached out like a giant fist and drew her back.

She turned to face him. No tears. No hurt. Just that wary, defiant—*and now what*, Mr. Logan.

"Don't you feel, Mrs. Evans, that there is something more that needs to be said here! I would be much obliged to receive from you, just once, some sort of logical—"

"Oh, yes, Mr. Logan. There is a matter that we need to discuss. It's been on my mind lately, and I didn't know quite how to approach you on such a sensitive subject. So very close to your heart."

"I know…this may sound *foolish* of me, Mrs. Evans, but…exactly, what *is* this subject, that is, as you choose to put it, so close to my heart?"

"It's a matter of…money, Mr. Logan. Money. Pure and simple. Have you *never*, never after he was freed, paid Jacob Barnabas a *wage*? Not even a few pennies, to call his own, to buy him a piece of candy? I know it may be none of my affair, Mr. Logan, but it seems to me a matter of greatest import, that any man should receive a simple sum for his work…just for the sake of his human dignity…a workman is—"

Bart stood gazing at her in complete amazement, as she talked on. *How had they gotten onto this subject?! Money?* She was worried about old Jacob and *money?* Jacob had never held a red cent in his hands, and if he had he wouldn't have had *the slightest* notion what to do with the thing! Didn't she *realize* that everything had been *bought* for him, everything *furnished* to him, and *then some*, that he could ever use in this world?

"—And Jacob absolutely refuses to stand up for himself, and speak to you."

"So, you, Mrs. Evans, have decided to play *advocate* for poor Jacob? Excuse me—for *Jacob Barnabas*. Now that you have given him a full Christian name, you feel compelled to stand at the Bar of Justice of the *Unjust Judge*, being *ME*, and speak up for *poor* Jacob Barnabas. And just what is this *unjustly withheld salary* to be spent for? Do you receive just compensation, say, for your acting as Advocate to the *victim*?"

"No, Mr. Logan. If Jacob should offer money to me, I would, in *every* instance, refuse. I have no *desire* for, or *need* for, *any money* that I have *not rightfully earned*. If you must know, Jacob wishes to have a headstone erected, to give all passersby notice—of his *final resting place*."

Bart stared at her. Not really seeing her. "Jacob wants a headstone!" he muttered.

"Good night, Mr. Logan."

Bart had gleaned absolutely no information about the rebuff of his aborted offer of friendship to young Johnny. He ran the conversations with the boy's mother over and over in his mind. He could glean absolutely no clue as to what changed the tearful protector of the innocent into—

—Into the advocate of poor old Jacob. Jacob wanted a carved granite headstone, with his new name on it!

A few weeks later, what should appear to Jacob, when he made his morning trip out back of the cookshack, than a big object, standing beneath a huge pine that shaded the building. It was covered with some sort of gray cotton shroud.

Curiosity overcame Jacob. He took the corner of the rough cotton canvas, and lifted it ever so slightly, and gave a peek. As he lifted it, he began to keen and cry.

Maggie, hearing him out back, came flying to see what disaster had befallen Jacob Barnabas Logan.

She found Jacob, all hunched over, rocking and crying like a baby.

"Ohoooo, tell me, Mizzzz Maggie! Ohoooo, tell ol' Jacob Barnabas, what it don' says on this smooth shiny piece of stone!"

"Why, Jacob! It appears to have your name written on it. Well...! Just...look...at...that! It says:

Date of Birth:
When God in His good Mercies
Decided to bless us all
With
Jacob Barnabas Logan"

"Oh, Mizzzz Maggie! Ol' Jacob never dreamt of havin' hisself any headstone half so fine as this!"

Maggie gave Jacob a quick hug, and then flew inside, so nobody would see her. She pushed the door firmly shut, and let the tears flow.

Bart had heard the cookshack door slam shut behind her. Then, he thought he must be mistaken, but were those...*sobs*?

"Mrs. Evans? Is everything...all right?" He stood in his office door, staring at her.

She turned to face him. Her eyes were bright with tears. Her face was wet with a few that still dribbled slowly down her cheeks.

She flashed him the brightest smile he'd ever witnessed, her eyes fairly gleaming:

"Everything is *fine*, Mr. Logan. Everything is *just perfect*!"

Well, well! *And let us all pray*, Bart muttered to himself, *they stay that way!*

Chapter 30

Bart entered the office at the front of the mess hut, removed his hat and placed it carefully on a chair. His hair was soaked with perspiration; his face was dripping. It was hot today. Even in the deepest of the thick woods, not a breath of air stirred.

He stretched his back, flexing shoulder muscles and arms. He was tired. He reached out his right hand to grasp the handle of the porcelain water pitcher. A slight smile played about his lips. The pitcher and wash bowl—even on a private washstand in his office—were incongruously out of place, in this logging-camp shack thrown together from scrap lumber. But he liked to have them near. His parents had the set imported, from England, so the pitcher and bowl were particular treasures to him. Right hand firmly clasping the pitcher, he raised it, while lowering his head toward the beautiful porcelain bowl.

He heard, more than saw, the flying missile that struck the beautiful pitcher. The pitcher exploded into a thousand pieces, and went flying about the shack. Several shards smashed into the bowl, and broke it into half a dozen pieces.

Stunned, Bart stood holding the handle of the pitcher. What little remained of it, gleamed in his hand.

Bart straightened with a jerk, his gaze sweeping the room.

The boy…the small boy of Mrs. Evans, stood peeking in at the doorway, looking guilty—and more than a little frightened.

"Did you—?" Bart fought to control his anger, keep his voice low, "Did you just *throw* something at me? See this pitcher, what little is left of it?" He felt the anger, creeping up his neck, growing in his voice. It was one thing, to refuse his friendship—it was quite another to fling missiles at him!

"No! No, sir! No, sir! Not at you. Not at all!"

"But you *did* throw something?"

Reluctantly, the boy produced something from behind his back. It appeared to be a crude slingshot.

"It's all right, Johnny. I'll handle this," Mrs. Evans immediately intervened.

She pushed the boy behind her, as if to shield his small frame from imminent, brutal attack.

"Why must, *you*, Mrs. Evans, handle this?" Bart exclaimed angrily, "Why must *you* handle *everything*! Why don't you permit your *son* to grow up! Allow him to take some *responsibility* for his actions!"

"It's all right, Johnny, go on out and play." Mrs. Evans ignored every word he had just said. Would he really have expected anything different?

Bart, beside himself with anger, watched. Still ignoring Bart, ignoring the devastation the boy had wreaked, she bent towards him. Cupping his face in one hand, she smiled and bestowed a kiss—swift and light as a butterfly—on the boy's small forehead.

"It's *not* all right," Bart spat, stung by the dismissal in her voice. She let the boy get away with far too much. She was spoiling him rotten. Bart was also stung by the open show of affection. It struck a raw chord in him. Some feeling long dormant tried to push and struggle its way out of the dark sea of long suppressed emotion. How long since he'd received such a gesture—of pure, unadulterated adoration? Was he *jealous* of the *boy*?

"Whatever the pitcher...and the bowl cost," Mrs. Evans was saying, her voice cold, no hint of affection, not a shred of warmth or caring there, "you can take it out of my pay."

"Your *pay*?" Bart gazed at her and asked incredulously, "My dear Mrs. Evans, *your pay*, as you call it, for the *entire summer and autumn*, would not cover the bowl alone, much less the pitcher. Do you realize these were *finest English porcelain,* imported items? Do you realize...what we're talking about here—?"

Maggie felt the blood drain from her face. *All* the money she had earned thus far this man was saying—and more—to pay for this man's precious pitcher—?!

"What are such items, such expensive, precious possessions, doing in a logging camp, *Mister* Logan? Don't they belong in the fine parlor of your great house? Then a small boy, innocently at play, would not inadvertently smash them to bits!"

"Mrs. Evans," Bart began, but he had watched the feelings play across her face. Those she couldn't easily hide from him. At the mention of docking all her wages for the stupid pitcher and bowl, all the blood seemed to drain from her head and face. He feared for a moment that she might sink in a dead swoon.

Still pale, but apparently over the first shock of having just been stripped of all her pay, she made a valiant effort to recover. Now, there was only a sort of empty, devastated shock. As if someone—no something—had just died.

Bart felt his anger subsiding. She looked so bereft, so vulnerable, so completely at the mercy of a harsh cruel reality—with which she had just lost the battle.

Tendrils of damp hair clung to her forehead. Tears threatened behind the blue-blue eyes. She chewed her lower lip.

Then she lifted her chin, drew herself up, and stubbornly crossed her arms—as if daring the enemy to advance one step toward her line of defense.

"Don't you know *anything* about children, Mr. Logan? Do you not have any children of your *own*?" Maggie thrust out an angry jab.

Instantly, she realized her mistake.

Bart drew in a quick breath, as if he had been struck in the midriff.

Maggie knew this time she had crossed some line. Something swept over him. She had no idea what. Whatever it was, it was too much. She had really done it now.

His handsome face blanched. He drew in several more deep breaths, fighting for control. His well-tanned hand closed like a vice over the remnant of the pitcher handle. She wondered for an instant, if he would fling it.

But instead, he gazed at it for a moment, and then tucked it into his trouser pocket. Very carefully he gathered up the largest shards of the beautiful porcelain bowl. Holding them in his hand, he looked at her. He opened his mouth, as if about to speak. Then he picked up his hat, crossed to the door, pushed brusquely past her, and on out the front door.

Bart felt as if he had just been struck with a giant fist. He wondered if his legs would bear his weight. Since the deaths of his parents, and then later, of

367

Sue Ann and Joshua, he had been alone. To maintain his sanity, he had plunged into his schooling, and then his work. To maintain his sanity, he had kept his emotions safely locked away. What was she doing to him—*this woman?* She seemed to know *exactly* which chords to strike—

—Never in his life had he encountered such a creature. One instant, she was all sweetness, submission and grace. And then the next instant, she would reach into your chest, and carve out your heart.

Chapter 31

It was Sunday morning. Bart always gave the crew Sundays off. He didn't actually know why. Maybe it was a carryover from his childhood, when he had attended church regularly with his family, in an era when no one—no one—worked on the Sabbath, as Sunday was called.

Yes, he did know why, because the logging horses needed rest. The men needed a break. He needed a break. It had, Bart assured himself, absolutely completely been a *disastrous* week. He felt drained and empty. And Mrs. Evans was moving about the cookshack as if she was but a husk of her former self. No light banter with the men. No cheerful humming of some little ditties as she went about her work. No setting Bart Logan straight—upon all and every subject beneath the sun.

Now, there was only a sad, empty silence.

Now, he had to somehow make amends for his senseless threat—to dock all Mrs. Evans' wages. That cruel threat had devastated her. Didn't the woman know him well enough by now—?

"No," he murmured softly to himself, "she doesn't know me at all. She thinks I'm some sort of *hard-hearted, child-hating, money-grubbing tyrant!*"

Why was it that every time he attempted to speak to her—or to the boy for that matter—everything got all at sixes and sevens?

He'd have to fabricate some sort of tasks for her—so as not to rob her of her customary salary—to pay for that hateful bowl and pitcher.

"Mrs. Evans," he entered the cookshack, hanging his hat on a hook.

"Mr. Logan?"

How cold can it get!

"I have been thinking…the past few days. About the matter of the broken bowl and pitcher—"

"Yes, Mr. Logan? I have already assured you that—"

"I have looked at some past invoices. And I find to my utter amazement, that I vastly over calculated the value of the pair."

"Oh?"

"Well…yes…they were somewhat old…older…and worn…maybe even a crack or two…here…and there…you understand?"

"I thought they were some of your most priceless possessions? Brought over at huge expense, all the way from England?"

"Well…I have so many others…" *Why* in the world did he *say that?*! Now he sounded like a patronizing dolt!

"I'm sure you do, Mr. Logan. A man of your wealth and standing in the world, must own *quite a few* priceless works of art, along with rich carpets, and sculptured pieces by the great masters. To say nothing of—"

"*EXCUSE ME*, Mrs. Evans, can't you see what I'm trying to do here?"

"What, exactly, are you trying to do, Mr. Logan? Extend some sort of charity—to a poor widow—?"

"*Widow?*"

"Of course, not, Mr. Logan," Maggie instantly realized her slip-of-the-tongue. "Merely a figure of speech. You know, the poor—the widows and orphans—"

"*Orphans?*" Bart gasped, completely lost.

"You know what I mean."

"No, Mrs. Evans. I'm afraid you completely lost me, dunce that I am, somewhere back there…now…what was…it…about…*a widow?*"

Maggie raised her chin.

"If you can come up with some sort of extra *suitable work* that I can perform for you, Mr. Logan, then we will consider the matter of the pitcher and bowl closed."

"What sort…of…form do you…feel…this suitable work…might take, Mrs. Evans?"

"Well, you're always bent forward over that desk in there, far too long, for a man with so many and varied responsibilities. I scarcely know when you have time to sleep."

"You're concerned about my lack of sleep?"

"Of course, not. It's just that…I could…possibly handle the payroll…make entries into the journals. That sort of thing."

"You know what a *debit* is, Mrs. Evans?"

"Naturally. It's an amount owed. Or taken, and removed from one person's fund or account to that of another. I owe you. You, or the bank as your representative, debit my account for the funds you are due, by way of bank draft."

"How about…a credit?"

"I purchase something from you, for which I have no funds to pay. You extend to me…credit. I dissolve the debt, by paying you in full. You respond by giving me credit…to my account."

"Have you ever written a bank draft?"

"I did the payroll, what there was of it, at Reliance Jones' restaurant, did the purchasing, and made regular deposits to his account. Reliance was a good cook—but he never learned to read or to even so much as write his name."

"Mrs. Evans, would you step into my office."

Mr. Logan had lit a large, swinging kerosene lamp. Maggie, her heart flying, sat down across from him at the big desk.

She couldn't believe this sudden turn of fortune. He was willing to forgive the debt! He showed her all the records—the blank bank drafts, the ledgers, where he had extended credit to the loggers—until receipt of their next pay—and invoices for tools, machinery, repairs and supplies, to keep the lumber mill operating. There were numerous receipts for sales of different lengths and widths of milled lumber, hauled by wagon to the railroad depot for shipment.

Maggie didn't roll into her cot until late in the night. She had just been promoted! She was head bookkeeper for the Logan Lumber Company. The only thing—there was to be no pay—for how long, she wasn't sure. She'd have to straighten that out with Mr. Logan. She'd have to pinpoint the exact moment the bowl-and-pitcher debt had been paid in full—and her pay for bookkeeping was to begin.

Each night, Bart kept an eye cocked, for the lamp to be put out, in the company office. A week later, he felt he could bear it no longer. She was working much too late, and there were meals to cook and cleaning the next day—

Carefully, he lifted the latch and slid the cookshack door open. He certainly didn't want to startle her. The door to the office was open, so he stepped to one side, and knocked softly on the doorjamb.

Then he stepped inside.

"Oh. Mr. Logan. You're still up."

"I couldn't sleep. The night is much too beautiful to spend it sleeping. You're still at it, I see."

He slowly lowered himself to his usual chair, the one facing the door. For some unexplainable reason, she always sat in the one directly opposite. It was scarcely more than a backless stool, while his was an actual *chair*. Maybe he should offer her the comfortable chair—no, no! Who knew where that might lead?

"So, where have you gotten to? How much left to do?" Bart asked softly. She was bent over the ledgers, her hair loosened for the night.

Receiving no response, he tried again, "I thought that since I couldn't sleep anyhow, maybe I'd just lend you a hand. Just for tonight."

Dark hair falling loose about her shoulders, slowly she raised her head. She eyed him suspiciously.

"I thought the ledgers were my job now?"

"I just said, Mrs. Evans—*just* for tonight. Here, I'll take this stack, and you take that."

Wordlessly she moved her hand, and Bart retrieved a stack of invoices.

The tiniest bit of a frown wrinkling her brow, she worked in absolute silence, never glancing up for the slightest instant.

Bart watched her for a moment, and then bent to the work. Then he noticed the slender hand lying on the table. The left hand, the ring finger—

"You aren't wearing a wedding band, Mrs. Evans."

She looked up at him. "No, Mr. Logan. I…never had a ring," Maggie lied.

"Hard times," Bart murmured. "Country just getting over the war and all. I suppose most people couldn't afford jewelry."

"You mean, Mr. Logan, *most southerners?* It *wasn't* that my husband…*couldn't afford* to give me a ring, he just chose not to."

"Oh? He has the money for a ring? But he thinks it would be best spent in other quarters?" What sort of fool was this man? A man with money, and sense, bought a wedding ring for a woman like this. And he took care of her.

"Yes," she said sleepily, her anger dying, "I suppose that's what he…could…have thought."

"He *could have thought*? You speak of your husband as if he was…"

"What?" she raised her eyes and looked at him. Her eyes were tired, unguarded. Why, he wanted to ask her, do you speak of your husband, as if he is deceased?

Bart bent back to the work. He saw Stephen Giles entering the cookshack, moving towards the office door. Then Giles saw Maggie, bent over the desk. He stopped short. Bart gave him a look that said: *This is strictly business.*

Giles stuck his head in the door. "Couple of questions, Boss, about tomorrow's schedule. The *fellers* are set for the south ridge, and *buckers* are set for—"

Maggie scarcely listened. The logging talk meant less than nothing to her. She just wanted to get the ledgers completed, and get to bed. As Mr. Logan resumed his seat opposite her, she stifled a yawn,

"You look tired," he said. "Why don't you go on to bed? I'll finish up here. I won't even dock your pay."

He had meant it a joke, but instantly, her head jerked up. Fire flamed in the blue eyes. "I am more than capable, Mr. Logan—"

"Peace?" Bart raised a hand, "Could we just finish this then—so we can both go to bed?"

After a few minutes, Bart felt he had to stretch his legs. He got up, walked out of the office opened the front door and stood gazing up into the night sky for several minutes. Then he stretched his back and shoulders, walked inside, and moved back into the office. On his way back to his chair, he stopped beside Mrs. Evans' stool, peeking over her shoulder, to see how much she might lack in finishing her work. For some reason totally unknown to him, he reached out, and laid a hand, very lightly on her shoulder.

Immediately, he felt her shrink from his touch.

"Oh, I'm so sorry, Mrs. Evans. How thoughtless of me…it's just that…it's late…and I'm tired—"

"No need to apologize, Mr. Logan," she snapped crisply. "I'm not some giddy schoolgirl, who's going to fall in a dead faint."

"Well," Bart stammered, his tongue clinging to the roof of his mouth. He wasn't sure if he should just exit the office, or make some farther attempt at an apology. "Yes." he said, retaking his seat in the big office chair. "Well, I just want to say, Mrs. Evans. I never…what I mean to say is…you can rest assured, it won't happen again."

"I know it won't," Mrs. Evans replied as icily as if she were a stick of wood—

—And he, William Bartram Logan—who had once been the toast of the ladies from Boston to New York—was about as poor a threat of manhood as a pan of stale dishwater.

Stephen Giles, who knew the two of them mixed about as well as oil and water, was like as not to find both Margaret Ann Evans, and Bartram Logan, their dark heads bent over the company books, many a night, as the lamp burned lower and lower between them.

One day when Bart entered the cookshack, as he strode in, he couldn't help but notice that, as the boy exited their room, he left the door ajar. To preserve the privacy of the two, Bart felt it would be kindly of him to go over and gently close the door. As he reached for the door latch, his eye caught a glimpse of the interior of the tiny room that was so familiar to him. Since they had moved old Jacob out of here and into his own quarters, now some sort of colorful rug adorned the floor. Bright patchwork quilts in lovely patterns were draped carefully over the two bunks. Over the huge brown trunk he recalled from the day the pair of them arrived, to Bart's complete amazement, hung a beautiful violin, and below it, a finely strung bow. He was too far away to make out the name of the violin's maker.

"Can I help you, Mr. Logan?" Mrs. Evans appeared quietly at his elbow.

"Johnny left the door open. I was just closing it for you."

"Thank you, Mr. Logan."

"Mrs. Evans, I couldn't help but catch a glimpse of that fine musical instrument, hanging over the large brown trunk. Do you, perchance, play the violin?"

She shook her head.

"The boy, then?"

"Johnny?" she gave a soft little laugh, her head tilted wistfully to one side, "No, Mr. Logan, though he would dearly love to, Johnny can't get a decent sound out of it."

"Perhaps, then, his father—"

"Oh, yes!" her smile brightened, and became a thing of absolute beauty. Then the smile faded, and she shook her head, rather sadly, "Oh, no."

Regarding him inquisitively, she asked, "You show such an interest in the instrument, do you play, Mr. Logan?"

"Not since...no. Not for a long time now. Not any more."

Bart went to bed that night, with the lovely violin on his mind. The wood appeared dark, rich, and a bit dusty, but with a bit of polishing, it could be a thing of real beauty. It probably needed tuning. Did his father play? *Oh, yes!* Then, *Ohhhh, noooo!*

But the boy, Johnny, he wanted to play. And Bart would have bet half his fortune that the boy's father *did* play, and *very* well—from the way her face lit up at the merest mention of that grand music.

Bart always knew exactly where to find Jacob Barnabas Logan any fine morning.

"Jacob Barnabas! Good morning to you!"

"And to you, Mister Bart. How's you been doin'? Ol' Jacob has been missing our little mornin' chats. But, I knows you is a busy, busy man."

"Not that busy, Jacob Barnabas. And I'm totally ashamed of myself, that I don't talk with you more often. I just happened to notice in passing that Mrs. Evans and her son are the owners of a very fine musical instrument. Isn't that amazing?"

"How so, Mr. Bart? Peoples o' t' south are the world's best fiddle players."

"Neither of them happened to mention to you…who it was exactly…who played that fine fiddle?"

"Well, now that you axk, Mr. Bart, I do believe that little Johnny put out the brag that his Papa was the best fiddler in four counties."

"Thank you, Jacob Barnabas. You don't happen to play, do you?"

"Me? Noooo, sir, Mister Bart. I never had no chance to hold no fine fiddle in these ol' blac' hands."

"If you had wanted to hold one, Jacob Barnabas, you know, don't you, that all you had to do was ask? And you still can."

"I don't has no moosical abilities, Mister Bart. Can't sing a lick, either—not even my favorite hymn. But wouldn't it be so fine—if *I had a friend* who could learn to play it—and play it for my home goin' service!"

"And what hymn would that be?"

"Why, Mister Bart, it be the one Mizzzz Margaret Ann sings so sweet for me—ever' Sunday mornin'."

"Why would she do that, Jacob Barnabas?"

"Because I's always requests it. Mizzzz Maggie, she always stan's up, holding onto her Scripture Book, and axks:

'Now, what hymn would any of you care to sing today?' and I's always answers, 'Is there any other hymn in this world wo'th singing—?

"And then, Mizzzz Maggie being the sweet, kind Christian lady that she is, she starts to singin' it in her clear, sweet voice that must make the very angels of heaven sick wif' jealroursy."

"That sounds…almost like…a…*church* service."

"Why! That's right, Mr. Bart, that's exactly whut it is."

"And she always sings the same song?'

"Among others. Yes sir:
Amazin' grace, how sweet th' sound,
That saved a wretch like me!
I once wus lost—but now I's foun',
Wuz blind but now I's see—!"

She was in *his* logging camp—!
And—she was holding a church service!

Bart Logan sat down on the edge of the riverbank. Removing first one boot, then the other, he wiggled his toes inside the rich woolen socks. It had been a steep climb up the mountain, to check on the sluiceway and the gates, to see how they were holding up. There'd been a lot of rain the past week. He wanted to make sure that the flow of the river, diverted into the sluiceway, hadn't overstrained the system.

They had all looked good this morning. The men had done a good job. He glanced abstractedly about. What beautiful country this was! Sometimes, he almost hated the thought of felling trees that had stood for centuries, sheltered so many animals, and the Indians.

But, he tried to console himself, in just a few years, with the older trees removed, and the sun hitting the forest floors—which had seen no sun for a very long time—young seedlings would sprout and cover the mountainsides with fresh timber.

The country needed the timber. Needed lumber for building. The country was growing, pushing westward. Even here, along the eastern seaboard, buildings were sprouting up like mushrooms.

Bart listened for a moment, to the deep quietness of the forest around him, disturbed only by the slight rumbling of the falls high above, and the murmur of the river flowing past his feet.

What was that sound, high in the treetops, almost like singing, sweet, lilting notes of music, drifting in and out of the massive branches, and on down the river.

He felt almost as if he was in church.

Church! It was Sunday. *She was having church.*

Nobody invited *him*. Did *all* the men know? Were they *all* there? Why had he never noticed this before? Of course, they were probably all there, except for the ones who had family close enough to visit, with only one day off.

Bart made his way back down the hill. The forest lay silent about him. When he reached the camp clearing, he saw the men come filing solemnly out of the cookshack door—their heads down, their hats and caps in their hands.

He wasn't running a lumber camp! He was running a camp meeting! Not only had he *not* been invited, he hadn't even been *informed*—or asked for his permission.

In passing, the following day, Bart mentioned the 'church' to Mrs. Evans.

"Well, Mr. Logan," Mrs. Evans came right to the point, "you did say *Sundays* the men were not expected to do their usual work, but were free to follow whatever pursuits their hearts fancied. And, I suppose, *some* men's hearts fancy worshiping Their Maker—on a glorious Sunday morning."

"Well, I am so sorry I missed the service, Mrs. Evans. Perhaps, though, some day you might sing for me?"

"I…beg your pardon?"

"Jacob tells me you have a lovely voice. And he *particularly* admires your rendition of his favorite hymn."

"Oh, *Amazing Grace*."

"Yes, exactly. And since Jacob Barnabas is getting on up in years, and he mentioned to me, quite in passing one morning, that it would pleasure him greatly to know that one of his friends would play that hymn…at his final *home goin'*…I just thought—"

"I don't believe I get your meaning, Mr. Logan. I sing, a bit, but I don't play the fiddle, and as I believe I've already told you, Johnny could only put the birds all over this entire chain of mountains to frenzied flight."

"I play, Mrs. Evans."

"But you said you hadn't played for such a long time. I thought by that you meant you had no desire to play anymore."

"This wouldn't be for me, Mrs. Evans, or you, or the men who might attend Jacob Barnabas Logan's final home goin'. This would be for Jacob."

"Feel free, Mr. Logan, to avail yourself of our fiddle, whenever you feel the need of it for practice. And I will make myself available, whenever you have the time, to teach you the tune, to *Amazing Grace*. Did you then, Mr. Logan, never attend church?"

"Not for…quite some while, now, Mrs. Evans, and it was an Episcopal Church, in Philadelphia. And, as I've already said, I was a child, and not that interested in church. If they sang that particular hymn, I don't recall it."

"Your parents didn't take you to church, except when you were a small child?"

"No, Mrs. Evans. I'm afraid they couldn't." Bart had never discussed the death of his parents with a living soul. Now, for some odd reason, he felt compelled to.

"They were drowned at sea, when the liner they were sailing on sank in a storm, far out in the Atlantic. I was thirteen or fourteen, at the time."

"I'm...sorry," Maggie said, feeling very foolish, as she suddenly recalled that Jacob had told her—Mr. Logan's parents perished at sea.

"And you, yourself, Mr. Logan, I detect from your voice, sound like a man adrift—with no life jacket, and no certain port in mind."

Her remark, so blunt and personal, did not anger Bart, rather, it saddened him, he replied, "Yes, Mrs. Evans, I fear that's, oftentimes, exactly how I feel."

Then she asked softly, as if feeling a great sadness for him, "Are you, perhaps, the owner of a Bible?"

"Well, yes, Mrs. Evans, as a matter of fact, I am. I am the proud possessor of the Sacred Volume that belonged to my Mother."

"Then, perhaps, Mr. Logan, you should take it out now and again, and search its pages diligently—to be *certain* of that shore, and that lighthouse, that beckons to us through the storm."

"I...just...might do that, Mrs. Evans. Good night to you, now."

That night, Maggie couldn't sleep. She lifted the fiddle down off its pegs, and dusted it tenderly. She ran a fingertip along its length, and felt the tautness of the strings. They seemed to quiver and sigh, in response to her touch, as if Papa, Thomas, and Shawn McKinnon were all speaking to her. She wouldn't dare let a soul touch this precious instrument—except that it was for Jacob Barnabas Logan. With a sigh, Maggie replaced the beloved fiddle

Within a few days, Mr. Logan advised her that, due to the clouds and rain moving over the mountains, he had given the crew the afternoon off. Would she please lend him the violin? And would she consent to teach him the desired tune?

Maggie handed him the precious fiddle, pushing down her reluctance, pushing aside the memories it invoked—

Bart took it, gently rubbing one finger along the bowl of the fine wood. He'd never in his life seen a finer instrument, and just as he had supposed, it was crafted by one of the most eminent makers—*Antonio Stradivari.* He rested the instrument lightly—his chin just touching the chinrest. Then he ran his fingers over the fingerboard, the pegbox, and on down the neck to the bridge.

He ran the fingering for the chords quickly through his mind.

Then he lifted the bow and laid it against the strings.

Never in her life had Maggie heard anything so beautiful. She felt tears stinging her eyes. Papa played so well. Papa played so fine. But Papa's music stirred the hands and the feet and the blood—

Bartram Logan's playing stirred the soul.

When the music ended, Maggie said softly:

"That was *lovely*. What was that?"

"Something from Bach, I believe. It's been a really, long, long time—"

"Well, apparently you haven't lost your touch."

"You really liked it?"

"Liked it! It was wonderful! It was…very nice…yes, it was…very nice."

She would have *loved* to hear him play again, but felt it would be inappropriate, maybe even a bit forward of her, to ask such a thing. After all, he was her employer.

"Well," he was saying, "now, I suppose it's time to get down to the business of Jacob Barnabas' final home goin.'"

He gazed at Mrs. Evans expectantly.

"Oh, yes, of course. You want to hear the tune…to…*Amazing Grace*."

Maggie closed her eyes, parted her lips, and began to sing.

And the hair began to rise on Bart's neck.

He felt chills creeping up his spine, and little bumps forming on his arms.

When the singing stopped, Bart said nothing. He didn't quite trust himself to speak. Her singing seemed to come from some *other* world. And reach into this one. To tug at the heart, and then lift it—

Bart lifted the violin, placing it beneath his chin. He lifted the bow. The first few notes were so far off, it made him cringe. He shut his eyes, and said:

"That was…terrible! Could you…just hum…softly…the tune…Mrs. Evans, until it sticks in my brain."

Softly, Maggie began to hum.

Bart lifted the bow, and attempted to find the key, to match the notes coming out of her throat.

A few tries, and the rhythm of the bow, and the rhythm of the voice became one, the bow moving, the voice rising, falling. And the voice and the music, pulsing in a lovely cadence, like duel heartbeats, twining around, twisting and mixing and dancing and spinning in a marvelous harmony, a living, breathing thing, spiraling up.

"Well," with a semblance of a smile, Bart lowered the violin with an apologetic wag of his head, "I suppose that wasn't too bad, for a first practice."

"Why, Mr. Logan, you belittle your considerable talent. I found it...remarkably lovely."

Johnny, almost completely forgotten by the two musicians, slouched lower on the bench, finally laying his head down on his arms on the rough tabletop.

"You tired, sweetie? You sleepy?" Maggie asked softly.

"Nah."

"Then, what's wrong?"

"It won't ever happen for me. I'll never be able to play like that. And Papa would have been so proud."

"Your Papa *is* proud of you, John Thomas McKinnon, and don't you for one minute ever doubt it."

Suddenly Maggie realized who else was in the room. All these weeks, she had cautioned Johnny. Now, in one unguarded moment, her lie was laid bare.

She raised her head, to look at Bartram Logan. He was watching her very carefully, his face closed.

"Good night, Mrs. Evans," he said, "I'll let you know, when we can get a few moments, to practice."

The door closed behind him, and Maggie sank down at the table. Tiredness, frustration, a mixture of emotions overwhelmed her.

The way he had looked at her! All this time, she had been *lying* to him. And she with her *Holy Scriptures* and her fine singing of *Amazing Grace*!

She was a black lying sinner! *Why* had she done it? *Why* had she piled lie upon lie? Looking back now, over the past month and a half, it seemed so *unnecessary*. None of the men had ever shown the slightest bit of disrespect for her. Mr. Logan himself had always behaved in an utterly gentlemanly fashion, often going to extremes to let her know he had absolutely no interest in her.

All those lies! And for what! For *nothing!*

"We just told Mr. Logan, didn't we, Maggie? Wasn't that what we just did? Now, I don't have to pretend anymore—that I'm somebody else?"

"No, sweetie, you don't have to pretend. Not any more."

Maggie lay in bed, her head in a whirl. Maybe there hadn't been too much damage done. Mr. Logan, after all, had not been *personally* affected by all her lies. She hadn't actually *hurt* anyone. They were very *innocent* lies. And carried hardly any importance, if you really thought about them—

Who cared, whether she was a woman who had been deserted by an uncaring husband, or whether she was a widow? Who cared, if Johnny was her child, or if her child lay in a cold grave, pelted by leaves and rain and snow?

Those lies, she thought at the time she began telling them, were for the good of Johnny, and her, and the entire camp. They had somehow made her feel—safe.

Now, she could see that she was only deceiving herself. She had been frightened out of her wits. Scared to death to come up that mountain, and sleep in a flimsy log shack with only a latch on the door that a two-year-old could open if he could reach it. But far more than that, she was frightened that Mr. Bartram Logan would send her packing, back to a town that held *nothing* for her, had he known she was an *unattached female*! She had desperately needed a job. She had desperately needed a wall—to protect her. A wall behind which she could crawl—and hide in the darkness.

And like a frightened child, she had *lied* and *lied* and *lied! Until it became so easy!*

But all the excuses in the world didn't change one fact:

A lie was a lie. And a person who was a habitual liar in one thing, Maggie well knew, cast a long shadow of doubt—that he could be trusted in *anything*.

Chapter 32

The skies had cleared, no clouds hanging over the mountains. Early in the day, Maggie had left the logging camp for Rhyersville, with Tad Horton leading the three pack mules, to carry back their purchases of the day.

Waiting for the remainder of the produce to be brought into town, walking down the narrow street, so familiar, so replete with memories, she decided to push away the past.

Today, she would live for the present. What tomorrow would bring, she had not the faintest idea. Mr. Logan had yet to confront her about her flagrant misrepresentations of the truth.

But today, just today, she would do something that she really enjoyed. Down at the end of the street, she spied the livery stable. The huge oaken double doors stood open. A rig stood just outside, the horse tied to the oak hitching post.

Why not go for a ride in the country? But, if she did, she would be forced to rent a rig. She had lent Job and the wagon to Barbara Jo and Fred. Job was to work for them, to earn his keep, until Maggie returned and had need of him and the wagon.

A few minutes later, Maggie was headed out of town, down the rutted road she had ridden over so often with Papa—and Mama. Out through the countryside. Then she found herself taking the left fork in the road.

The miles fell away so quickly. The little mountain gap came into view.

What was she doing here! *But she was here*. No need to flee now. She saw that the *For Sale* sign had rotted and fallen apart in the front yard. She drove the rig into the shade of the grove back of the house. She climbed down, and stood gazing up the hill towards the little graveyard. Then she turned, and walked up on the back porch. Her eyes filled with tears, as memories came flooding back. Papa coming in from the field, washing up at the back porch wash shelf. Mama, coming out the back door, the milk pail in her hand. Nellie Sue, standing at the well curb, drawing up a bucket of fresh water—

—Almost, Maggie could hear their voices, their soft, lilting laughter.

She walked into the familiar kitchen. Cobwebs hung everywhere. She moved on into the front room. The porch rockers still sat before the fireplace, where Thomas Beyers had placed them the day they left the farm.

Overcome with emotion, Maggie turned and hurried back through the house, and out the back door.

Almost against her will, she found herself making the climb—into the cooling shade of the stand of sweetgums.

There were leaves scattered over the graves. A catch in her throat, Maggie bent over Papa's grave, and began to sweep them away with her fingertips.

John Thomas McKinnon
Born 1845
Passed to Glory 1882

Maggie felt the tears, wet and hot, coursing silently down her cheeks. But as quickly as they had started, the tears ceased. What was the need of weeping? Papa and Mama were both gone to rest. But Mama was not here—beside Papa.

The sound of rustling in the dry leaves on the mountainside above the grove brought Maggie's head up with a jerk.

"Is someone there?" she called.

A man stepped out of the trees—

What was he doing here!

Looking down the mountain, Bart saw her. Kneeling at the graveside. A woman he could tell. A heavy, dark sunbonnet.

Where had he seen *that* before? But it couldn't be...*it couldn't be!*

But it was—

"Mrs. Evans—?"

"Mr. Logan," Maggie replied. She made as if to rise, thinking surely her legs would fail her.

What are you doing here? The question flew through Maggie's mind—

He held out a hand to her, as if he thought she might topple backward, which Bart reasoned might be a real possibility. She had blanched absolutely white, at the sight of him.

"I might ask you the same question," Maggie heard him saying, and realized she had actually spoken.

"Are...you...related to these people?" He motioned towards the headstones. "Is Johnny related to these people?"

"These people?" Maggie muttered softly.

"The McKinnons. That used to own this farm."

"Oh?" Maggie muttered, as if totally caught by surprise. But—no. No more lies.

"For years, so I was told, it was in their family. But it's been deserted for some time, now. No market for it," she heard him going on. "The story goes, a McKinnon cut the logs for the first part of the house, with his own hands. He came from Scotland. If I'm not mistaken."

"No, Mr. Logan," Maggie said quietly, at last finding her voice. "You are not mistaken."

Maggie searched for words. But no more lies. She was determined not to lie. But she was also determined not to divulge her inmost secrets, her inmost pain—

Not to this man. Not to any man. Not ever, ever again—!

"Then you are related to them?" Bart Logan was asking.

"Umm," Maggie muttered. "You might say that."

"I did, in fact, just say that, Mrs. Evans. Would you mind telling me just *how* you are related to these McKinnons?"

"It's a long story, Mr. Logan. And I have a rented rig down there behind the house," Maggie hedged. "I really must be going. I only rented it for the day."

"Of course," Bart took a step backward, as if not to hinder her. "I can understand that." As usual, she wasn't going to tell him a thing.

She clasped her two hands tightly together, as if shutting out the world.

"And you, Mr. Logan, just *why* are *you* here?"

Maggie felt as if she had somehow been *violated.*

"Just looking the place over," he mused, studying her face closely.

She was suddenly angry with him. The cheeks flushed deep rose. The blue-blue eyes, sapphire, as if she was seeing him for the first time—and taking his full measure. She didn't appear to like what she saw.

"Looking the place over?" She lifted her chin with an angry jerk. "Whatever for?"

"I'm thinking of buying it. Well, maybe not actually *buying* it. Maybe, at first, just leasing the timber rights. But there's something about the place—I find it absolutely—"

"The *timber* rights!?" Maggie leapt backward, almost tripping over her own feet, in her haste to retreat from this man. This spoiler of forests! This—

"Well...yes...is there something wrong?"

Maggie stared at him. She felt the tears then, hot, flooding her eyes, coursing down her cheeks, until they almost scalded her face. She felt her lips trembling. She tried to clamp her lips tightly shut, to keep them still.

She found to her horror, she had no control—she could not prevent them. She threw a hand across her mouth, to hide the awful tremors. All her life, she had scarcely known what it was to weep. Now, she felt great wracking sobs escaping her throat, welling up from somewhere deep inside her being—great, ugly, heart-wrenching sobs that made her feel like some sort of blathering fool.

What was the matter with her? Her heart broke, but she had scarcely shed a tear, when Papa died. When Mama passed, there were no tears to cry. She was too empty, in too much pain. They were a human luxury she simply couldn't afford. When she lost the man she *thought* was Len Evans, and found herself married to a complete stranger, she had wept. But not like this—even when she lost Katie Ann—!

What was wrong with her! What foul fountain of sorrow had this man unleashed?

Staring at him through tear-filled eyes, shaking her head, still holding her mouth, Maggie backed slowly away. Then with her free hand, she gathered up her skirt and fled down the slope.

Bart was left standing on the hill, gazing first down at the graves at his feet—then his eyes following the puffs of dust flying up from beneath the steel rims of the speeding rig. The name she had called the boy, was exactly the same as the younger man, on the headstone. *This* John Thomas McKinnon had been born in '45. Johnny was about four. This man would have been thirty-five or thirty-six, when the child was conceived. This was probably Johnny's father.

The more Bart learned, the less he knew.

She was there, when time for the morning meal came. Pale, subdued. *She's sick!* This was Bart's first thought. He tried to watch her closely, but without being too obvious. What on earth—! What had he *said*? He'd asked her about any possible relation to the McKinnons. Then he'd said something about buying the place, or more probably leasing the timber rights. What about either of those statements had sent the woman into great wracking sobs?

"Mrs. Evans."

"Mr. Logan," the blue eyes downcast, as if she had absolutely no desire to look at him. What had he done to deserve this treatment? No, Bart told himself. Maybe it wasn't him, or anything he said. Something, perhaps, to do with the McKinnon place. *But what?*

"Grits with your eggs, Mr. Logan?"

"Yes, thank you very much, Mrs. Evans. And how do you—how do you feel today? Do you find yourself in good health?"

"As well as might be expected, Mr. Logan, given the circumstances."

What on earth did that mean! What circumstances? Afraid to ask, Bart passed on down the line. Finished his food and rose to pour a second cup of coffee.

"The coffee, Mrs. Evans," he bragged, perhaps that was not wise? "The very best you have ever made!"

"So glad it pleases your palate." *Pleases his palate!?* "Mr. Logan."

"Yes," Bart mumbled, feeling like a fool, "I do find the coffee very—pleasing."

He hung close about the cookshack most of the day, neglecting his other duties.

Despite all his resolve to steer clear of Mrs. Evans, he was really worried about her! Was she coming unhinged?

No. Those blue eyes when they finally met his gaze, ever so briefly, were filled with the quick intelligence, the same fire, but the fire was smoldering now.

It was *he*, who should be angry. All those *lies* she had told him. He had not yet confronted her about that. But it was certainly his intention to do so. When the time and the mood were right. Not that it mattered personally to *him*—one way or another—it had no effect on *his* life, whether she had no husband—or ten. No children—or half a dozen, or whether they were in fact, living or dead.

Unsure of exactly what to do about the ludicrous situation—had he somehow created a *situation*? Bart felt useless and adrift the entire remainder of the day.

She appeared in the door of the cookshack, dashed out the dishwater. She shook out the broom, and carried in fresh water. So busy, as if the world would come to a crashing halt, should she cease laboring.

The sun traveled on around the heavens.

"Five o' the clock, Mrs. Evans, time to knock off," Bart declared, entering the mess hut to find her down on her hands and knees, vigorously giving the puncheon floor the scrub of its life. "Mrs. Evans! There's no need for you to do that! Some of the men—"

With one slender hand, she pushed the damp hair off her forehead. She was gazing up at him—her eyes—completely unreadable.

"I am perfectly capable, Mr. Logan, of handling my work *by myself.* That is, after all, what you pay me for. And I know you are a man who wants *every single penny* to count. You are, after all, in business to make a *profit.*"

"Well!" Bart said, "As you wish! Good day to you then, Mrs. Evans."

Bart made as if to leave, and then turned about, facing her again, "Have I done something? Anything? Have I somehow—inadvertently offended you?"

"Not yet, Mr. Logan."

What did *that* mean?

Feeling more than a bit depressed—and thoroughly confused—Bart left the logging camp. He guided his horse down the steep slope of the mountain. On either side of the grade, the young saplings had already begun to rear their heads. Good, Bart smiled to himself. The mountain will recover quickly. This summer had seen adequate rainfall. Fine virgin soil, deep in leaf-loam. He had begun to like this part of the country—immensely.

At last reaching the town, he tied his mount to the little hitching post behind the white church. He noticed that the belfry for the church had been completed, the bell hung, and the entire church sported a new coat of brilliant white paint.

Bart walked past the church, and up the hill, for his monthly visit to the grave sites.

It couldn't be! *It just couldn't be!*

But it *was*!

It was *Mrs. Evans!* And the boy that he now knew was *John Thomas McKinnon, Jr.* Everywhere he looked! She was there!

Bart dodged behind a tall tombstone, waiting for her to leave. She mustn't see him here! He didn't think he could endure another of those episodes—the great wracking sobs—

Good...she was rising now...taking the boy by the hand...coming this way...move around to the other side...wait until she's gone...until she's out of sight. She was visiting that group of graves...over there...

As soon as Maggie disappeared from sight, Bart practically lunged forward, his boots making odd little muffled sounds in the soft grass. Let's see...there...no a bit farther...ah...there...

A small grave. Tiny in fact. Unmistakably a child. A small spray of fresh wildflowers.

Katherine Ann Evans
Beloved daughter
Born May 5, 1884
Died May 1, 1885

Did not live to see its first birthday. Bart removed his hat, ran a hand through his hair, strode around a bit more. Out in the outer edge of the graveyard, all by itself, he discovered a small block of granite, scarcely more than a foot square, lying flat on the earth, with the small, cryptic engraving:

Len Evans
1857–1885

It was evidently meant to be a grave marker. But Bart had never seen such a small, thin, insignificant stone to mark a man's passing.

Could this possibly be the illusive Evans, who was supposedly away at the gold fields?

Some instinct told Bart—*this* was the missing husband.

Not only was Johnny *not* her child, but there was a distinct possibility Mrs. Margaret Ann Evans had no living husband.

Bart felt as if he needed to sit down. He felt as if some giant fist had just struck him in his middle. Driving all the breath from his chest.

Had she lied about the husband? If so, why had she lied? What else had she lied about? Or did she tell him in so many words that Johnny was her son?

Well, she certainly knew that was what he believed, and she did nothing to dispel the misconception—and everything to encourage it.

He didn't go to the other side of the graveyard, where lay his own wife and child. He didn't feel at the moment that he could handle any more. The very thought that Mrs. Evans might be—

He needed to escape.

Bart mounted his horse, and rode slowly out of town.

The boy was running madly about the cookshack. As always, when Bart entered, he came up short, and disappeared.

Bart entered his office. He sat down in the familiar chair, picked up a pen and drummed it absently against the rough work surface of what surpassed for a desk. He heard her come into the main area of the building. Heard the rattle of the iron stove. She sent the boy out for fresh kindling. She was building up the fire. He would go out and speak to her. What would he say? Good morning, Mrs. Evans, and by the way, I just found out yesterday, my dear young lady, that you have possibly been lying through your teeth! You *have* no husband! Your loving Len is lying in the graveyard—that is he, isn't it? And his granite headstone is a poor, miniscule thing more suited for a pet turtle than a beloved husband! But, was he a beloved—*anything*? *Was* that her husband in the graveyard?

Bart shifted his weight around in the chair. He could just make out her form, out of the corner of his eye.

She was a cool one, that! Why had she lied? Did she have some sort of fantastic idea he might become interested in her?

If she had ever thought of him in that way, he mused, she had certainly hidden it well. She showed about as much interest in him as she did in the iron cookstove—

"Mrs. Evans! Good morning."

"Hello."

He received not even so much as the courtesy of mentioning his name, this morning.

"I was wondering, if you had heard from your husband—lately?"

"My husband?"

"Yes, Mrs. Evans. Have you heard from…Len?"

"Len—?" She blanched pale as a ghost, as she repeated the name, a mere whisper.

"Yes, Mrs. Evans, I was speaking of Len, your husband. I suppose he's not having much success then, is he?"

She looked pale as death. "Why don't you just come out and say it, Mr. Logan. So you've been to the graveyard. You've seen Len's grave. Were you following me?"

"Why on earth would I follow you? I've been to the graveyard...because I have a *wife and infant son* buried there."

"I didn't know. I'm sorry. What was his name? How old was he?"

"Joshua Bartram Logan. He would have been four this fall. I still miss him, and his mother, Sue Ann. They were both stricken with fever. They were both very...dear to me. I don't think the pain will ever subside."

"No," she said quietly.

"You lied to me. That *is* your husband, in the graveyard."

"I...didn't, exactly, *lie* to you."

"I don't know what else you could call it, but let's just say, then, you failed to tell me the truth, when you applied for this job."

"You want me to leave?"

"No! I didn't say I wanted you to leave!"

"Then what are you saying, Mr. Logan?"

"I'm saying that I don't appreciate being lied to. And in the future, please be truthful in all your dealings with me. Then...we'll get along fine."

"Fine," Maggie replied. Turning her back on him, she began to build a fire in the black iron cookstove. "Joshua would be about Johnny's age," she said.

"Yes."

Her back to him, she seemed to forget that he was in the room.

He hadn't said *anything* he had intended to say. He had learned *nothing* at all, about how she felt. He had lost a son. He *told* her he had lost a son. He told her his son's name. He had shared his pain. She had lost a husband—and possibly a daughter. She said not one word about either of them. He had lost a beloved wife. She had lost—? What *had* she lost? Who was this *Len Evans*, who deserved *a headstone the size of a shoe-box lid?*

Then it dawned on Bart—he was getting *far* too emotionally involved in something that was entirely none of his business. And he needed to put a stop to it—*right now!* He needed to clear his head. He needed to go on out to the mill site. Check on the drying stacks, and see how many board feet were ready for shipment. See that the sluice gates were opening and closing properly, up on the mountain. Do anything—but get entangled in the problems and lies of *Mrs. Margaret Ann Evans.*

Johnny saw the big draft horse coming down the slope, the giant oak log skidding along behind his magnificent hooves. He sneaked out the door, down the steps, and scooted across the open yard, into the edge of the few trees that remained standing east of the sawmill site.

Bart came out of his cabin. Saw the white stallion, and walked a few feet forward, being sure to leave the giant draft horse clear room for passage with his load.

Then just as the huge white came prancing along, lifting his hooves high in a perfect rhythm, his great head lifting and dropping in time with his hooves:

Something came darting out from behind the big pine across the clearing. The boy! It was Johnny! Headed straight into the path of those giant hooves!

Bart opened his mouth to shout. But he knew it was too late.

Bart hurled himself forward, into the path of the oncoming stallion, in a running, flying leap, snatched the boy to him, in a flash, saw the approaching hooves, that magnificent head. *God!* He prayed, as he hit the ground in a diving roll that barely carried him beyond the reach of those hooves. As he dived, he crushed the boy to his chest, one hand on the little head tucked beneath his chin. He glanced over, to see the granite-like hooves, pounding the earth in great loud Clumppph! Clumppphhh! Clumphhhhh! Just inches from his face.

The stallion, then the log passed. Bart staggered to his feet. The boy was safe. He hugged the child tightly to him, one hand pressing the child's face into his neck. He could feel the slight weight of the child, the rhythm of his heart, the warmth of his breath against Bart's neck.

Bart squeezed him even tighter. And the boy clung to him for what must have been only a few seconds—but to Bart seemed an eternity he wished would not end.

Maggie heard the shouting, ran to the cookshack door, just in time to see Bart grabbing Johnny up, protecting him against his chest as he made that plunging dive away from those deadly hooves.

Then they were clear, and Bart was on his feet, still holding Johnny.

The crew watched in fascination. Never had they seen Mr. Logan move so fast. Forming himself and the boy, in an instant, into a spinning ball of bone and flesh—that by inches and seconds had just escaped certain death.

Maggie ran to them, her face ashen. Bart instinctively reached out an arm, and she walked into it. He hugged both of them to him, a hand on Maggie's head as she bent into his shoulder near Johnny. He wasn't sure how long they stood like that, the three of them.

Then he released Maggie, gave her a smile of reassurance, and handed her the boy.

Not one word was ever said about that day. None of them mentioned how close death had come to the lumber camp. Johnny had not been scolded, not one word. They were so relieved he was alive. Bart tried to recall only one thing about that day: the feel of the boy, warm against him, his breath on his neck.

Maggie thanked God Johnny was still alive. He was all she had.

A few days later, Maggie pulled on her dress with the least awkward skirt for riding. Today was Saturday, the day for her usual buying trip into Ryersville and Johnson's Corners. She opened the door and peered out. Where was Tad Horton? He was always so punctual. Wasn't it time he was showing up, with her mount, and the pack mules?

She stepped back inside, giving Johnny his final instructions for the day.

"You are not, under any circumstances, to play in the front clearing, or to walk near the front clearing—where the great sawmill and the horses are. You are not—"

"He'll be fine, Mizzzz Maggie," Jacob grinned at her. "I'sll keep young Mr. Johnny outta mischief. Maybe he can practice on he's fiddle."

"Well, great! If you can bear the noise."

"Oh, No'nnnmmm. not noise. Not now. Not since he done been taking he's lessons, from Mr. Bart."

"Lessons? I haven't heard anything about any lessons!"

"Mr. Bart, he done bought some paper, with music on it. That he can read. Just like readin' a book. And he bin showin' Mr. Johnny how to read that paper, too!"

"Well!" said Maggie. Then she walked to the door, pulled it open—and: "Oh! No!"

"What's wrong, Mizzzz Maggie?"

"Why, it's Mr. Logan. I do believe he intends to accompany me into Ryersville."

"Weilll, whut's wrong wi' that? Mister Bart, he's bin a fine horseman?"

"Yes. Well. I suppose I'll have to go. We're almost out of at least a half dozen things. Johnny, you behave, now, you hear me!" This as Maggie exited the door, drew on her blue sunbonnet to shade her face, and stepped down to meet Mr. Bartram Logan.

"Horton's sick," he frowned at her and said cryptically, "Won't be able to make it today. I have to go into town anyway, get some drag lines mended, or replaced. You ready to go?"

"Yes."

Maggie strode forward. He made no effort to get off his horse and help her mount. Fine, she didn't need his help. He held the horse's reins until she was seated and had arranged her full skirts. Then he handed her the reins. And he rode off.

They made a quiet trip of it, down the perilous incline—he never speaking, never looking back at her—she not needing him to. Secure in her saddle, Maggie trailed along behind the pack mules.

Reaching the main street, they jogged slowly into Rhyersville. Bart rode on until he neared the building with the faded sign over the door:

Jonas Trap—Wheelwright.

Bart dismounted, led his horse over and tied him to the hitching post.

Maggie dismounted, brushed down her skirt, straightened her bonnet and followed Bart into the hall of the wheelwright's enormous barn. Several carriages waited in different stalls. There were two or three buggies, a beautiful surrey. Even a coach had been brought in for repair. Jonas Trap also boarded horses, and owned a few fairly decent ones that he offered to rent at reasonable rates.

"I'll just leave the horse here," Maggie said to Bart's back. "And go on over to the store, and see what's been brought in for the camp. Later, after that, I'll ride on down to Johnson's Corners. Should I go ahead and take a couple of the pack mules with me, down to the Corners?"

Over his shoulder, never turning to look at her, "I'll ride down there with you. Just let me know, when you're ready to go."

"You'll be—?"

"I'll be around."

"Yes. Well, I suppose I'll meet you later, then."

Bart gave the briefest jerk of his head. He knew he was acting like a cad, but he had decided it would be best for everyone concerned, if he kept his distance from Mrs. Evans. This was apparently what she wanted.

"Maggie! How good to see you! How's everything going on that fine job of yours?"

"Great! Just great, Barbs! And you? How are you…and Fred…doing?"

"Well, you know Fred. Always pretending to have a cold, or something. Me, personally, I just think he wants attention. He's spoiled as a child."

Then Barbara Jo smiled brightly at Maggie, "Listen to me! Listen to who's talking about being spoiled! Mama couldn't do enough for me! Let me get away with all sorts of mischief. And you! And your Papa!"

Impulsively Maggie reached out and gave Barbara Jo a quick hug. "I have missed you so!"

"You ought to come around more often."

"I really don't have the time. My travels and my job—"

"Still traveling a lot on your new job? Exactly what is it, Maggie, that you do on these trips?"

"I do—purchasing. Like the things I buy here, for the camp. And lately, I've been helping out a lot in the front office."

"Oh, it sounds grand! I'm so proud of you."

"Yes," suddenly Maggie wanted to change the subject. Why was she attempting to impress Barbara Jo about her work? Was she ashamed of being a cook at a logging camp? No, she wasn't actually lying. She just wasn't telling Barbs everything. And that was all right.

No. Not really.

But Barbara Jo had a big new house—on the new street back of the store. Fred had just bought her a new team, and a new carriage. She wore beautiful dresses. Her hats were the envy of all the ladies of the Shiloh Baptist Church—!

With a keen stab of guilt, Maggie realized that she was jealous of her sister.

Bart took care of his business at Jonas Trap's. Trap felt certain he could mend the lines and rigging as good as new.

Bart checked his pocket watch. Almost lunchtime. He took out the pack he had stashed in his saddlebag. One of Mrs. Evans' biscuits with a piece of country ham. She had insisted he also bring an apple. He had a canteen of water.

Maggie lunched with Barbara Jo—in her new house. The dining room overlooked a lovely garden—

Maggie tried to be glad for Barbs, and she was. Then she recalled how she and Johnny and Liza had lived in Dr. Ellis' little dirt-floored, one-room cabin.

Fred came in, and gave Maggie a curt nod. He had somehow absented himself from lunch. He's scared to *death* of me, Maggie smiled to herself, well pleased. He's scared I'll talk—about his generous gift of supplies brought to the little sharecroppers' house. Or scared he's going to end up with me and Johnny on his hands—the impoverished female relative, unable to support herself, cast upon some well-off but unwilling family member that only takes her in to save face with the community—

"—How are you, Fred?" Maggie smiled at him sweetly.

"Maggie," Fred nodded again.

"Do sit down, dear," Barbara Jo chided her husband. "And at least have a cup of tea with us. Maggie gets to visit so seldom. Sit here," Barbara Jo patted a polished mahogany chair bottom lightly, just her fingertips. "Surely you want to hear all about Maggie's job. She's buyer, for some big company."

"Got to get back over to the storeroom," Fred mumbled, his bald head lowered.

"Men!" As Fred walked out, Barbara Jo tried valiantly to cover for her husband's blatant rudeness. "He's—"

"It's okay," Maggie smiled at her sister. "We can just have girl talk. But I suppose that will have to wait. I need to get on, to the next buying assignment."

"All right, Maggs."

Maggie still hated it, when Barbara Jo called her that.

Maggie gave her older sister a peck on the cheek.

"Have you seen Thomas Beyers, this trip?"

"No. I never see Thomas anymore. How is he? How is Liza Mae?"

"Liza Mae's fine. Thomas, on the other hand, is lonely. I think he fancies you, Maggie. Ever since Nellie Sue passed, I think our dear brother-in-law has had his eye on you! Thomas Beyers would marry you in a heartbeat, if you'd just give him the slightest bit of hope. Why don't you—"

"Don't be silly, Barbara Jo," Maggie snapped, taking her shawl with a jerk from Barbara Jo.

"A man with an *eye* for me is the *last* thing in this world I need! Not even sweet, sweet Thomas Beyers!"

Bartram Logan was waiting for her, on the bench outside Moss' Mercantile. Maggie saw Fred, peering curiously out the big store window.

Maggie waved to him, as she walked off with the tall, extremely wealthy, strikingly handsome Bartram Logan. Let him look! Maybe he was jealous! She would never in her whole life forget the night he came to her little house down on the river, and left doused head to foot in fine white flour! Maggie put a hand over her mouth, to muffle a little giggle.

"Is something funny?" Bart asked in a surly voice.

"Yes!" Maggie laughed outright.

Bart wasn't about to ask.

All the way back from Johnson's Corners, the two of them had watched the sky, northward. Clouds were gathering over the mountains. It was mid-afternoon. If they left now, they could easily make the logging camp before dark. But they both knew that a storm was brewing.

"I don't think it would be wise, to ride off with the sky looking like this. Rain's coming, any minute now. Guess we'll just have to bunk in somewhere for the night. No rooms to let, that I know of, in this town. Place is growing. You'd think someone would build a small inn or hotel. I suppose Trap, here, would let us borrow a haystack or two for the night. You could take one side of the place, and I could take the other. I can assure you, Mrs. Evans, you will be perfectly safe."

"I don't doubt it for one moment, Mr. Logan." Maggie wagged her head in agreement, as if he posed no danger to any female on the planet, "But I don't exactly fancy a night with the rats and the mice and the fleas. If we're going to be stuck in town for the night, Mr. Logan, I plan to make my own sleeping arrangements."

"And what arrangements would those be, Mrs. Evans?"

"I have a…friend…I can stay with."

"Does your friend have a name?"

"No one who would interest you. I'll just go on, then, before the rain gets here. And I suppose I'll see you here, in the morning."

He gave her a curt nod. Then he felt forced to offer, "If you should need me during the night…if your *friend*…"

"Why on earth should I need you during the night, Mr. Logan? If my friend what?"

"Nothing, Mrs. Evans. Have a good night."

"I intend to."

"Yes, I bet you do."

Maggie gave him a curious stare. Wondering why he was being so testy today, she turned and marched off down the street.

Well, Bart thought morosely, apparently her 'friend' lives quite close.

He leaned against the door of Trap's, and followed her with his eyes. She turned in front of Moss' General Mercantile, and went striding northward.

And Bart followed her.

He stayed well back.

Keeping to the sides of the building.

Wanting to make sure, he told himself, that she was safe. After all, she was his employee. He had brought her to town on company business. He was responsible for her.

She turned onto another street. Then she was going up the walk to a fine, new, yellow brick house with green shutters, and lace curtains on every window. With a yellow brick carriage house to the right—and back a bit.

The instant she knocked, a hand flew out the door—and literally *dragged* her inside.

The door instantly shut, and Bart couldn't see anything.

He waited for a few minutes, to see if she came back out.

Lamps were lit. Warm yellow light spilled out the big windows. Loud rippling peals of feminine laughter came drifting out of the fine yellow brick house.

Well! Apparently she wasn't coming to any great harm!

Bart turned on his heel and strode away.

"I really didn't expect to see you back so soon!" Barbara Jo took Maggie by the arm and pulled her inside. "Get in here, before you get drenched. Is it raining yet?"

"Just beginning, that's why we didn't ride on out this afternoon. Can I— that is, would it be okay if—"

"Maggie McKinnon, stop that nonsense! Of course, you can spend the night."

"Wonderful," Maggie laughed. "It'll be like old times."

"I certainly hope not!" Barbara Jo giggled, "Not *too* much like old times. Remember the day of my birthday, when I was turning fourteen, and you set that big *rabbit* of yours loose, and it came ripping into the kitchen. 'Til my dying day, I'll never forget the look on Mama's face, when that big bowl of her best cake batter went crashing to the floor!"

"And then *you* sat down in it!"

"I did *not* sit down in it! I think you *pushed* me!"

"I did *not* push you! I wasn't even in the room when you fell. When I came in, there was Mama, with her mouth open. And there you were, and then there was the water bucket, and there was the stove pipe—and the entire room covered in cake batter and bits of broken bowl and spilt water and ashes—"

"And Papa, when he opened the door and said that—" Barbara Jo howled:

"All together now: '*When you girls throw a party, you sure do things up right!*'"

"And the time you pumped a knot up on my forehead—with your rock throwing, then kept the family on pins and needles all day long—locking yourself in the outhouse."

"Oh, Barbs! I can't *believe* you actually remember all of this!"

"Then you shoved poor Alfred Stillwell into that icy river—!"

"You knew about *that*?"

"And then that *raven of God*, of yours, that sent all the ladies' into wild shrieks, at Mama's quilting party."

"I'm surprised," Maggie howled, "you haven't yet mentioned—"

"Oh, yes! And the corn huskin' party, when I was—what—sixteen? And you were barely fourteen, claiming to be almost fifteen! Driving old Job like his tail was on fire! Down that long grade! Then hitting that creek! I don't know *why* we didn't bust a wheel! Water flew clean up to the top of our heads! And all of us in our fine party dresses! Maggie, how could you?"

"I don't know, Barbs, but it seemed like *such* a good idea, at the time."

"I'll never forget the embarrassment, the sheer *horror* I felt—standing in that big barn door, that evening, wet as a drowned rat. My hair hanging down in streams. And you, bribing me to keep quiet—"

"You still have that piece of red candy, Barbs? Or did you eat it up, just for spite?"

"I'm not about to tell you!" Barbara Jo wagged her head, "And the way you brushed off poor Alfred Stillwell, that night at the corn huskin', and went sashaying off with every other fellow in sight. I thought his poor chin would surely drag the floor!"

"Don't you go feelin' sorry for Alfred Stillwell, Barbs. I heard since getting back home to Rhyersville that Afred married himself a *rich* girl, from down in Atlanta."

"I wonder…" Barbara Jo gave a slight frown, "if she's pushed him in the river…"

They broke into bouts of giggles, and so it continued into the night.

"I trust that you found your *friend* in good spirits?" Bart drawled. His mood seemed to have mellowed, as he gallantly helped Maggie to mount the following morning.

"Oh, yes," Maggie laughed, recalling what an absolutely riotous time she and Barbs had, "I really think I should do that more often."

"Oh?"

"Everybody needs to relax, and just have a party—every now and then."

"So, you had a *party*?"

"I wouldn't say that, exactly. But we sure had ourselves a few good laughs."

"Well," Bart said brusquely, "I'm glad you had such a good time. You'll have to introduce me to your 'friend,' one of these days."

"Maybe I will." Who on earth put a burr under Mr. Logan's saddle? And she had thought that things were looking up.

Chapter 33

"Mr. Logan?" Maggie stuck her head out the door, hoping to catch Bartram Logan before he became all tied up in the mill doings, "Where are the ledgers? And the blank drafts? I planned to make some entries, and do the month's payroll—and I couldn't find a thing! Did you move them?"

"I thought it might be a good idea to…"

"Yes?"

Bart crossed the clearing in a few strides, and stood facing her, eye to eye, as she stood on the steps above him.

"I carried all the records to an accounting office. I thought they should be audited."

"Audited? What on earth for? Is something missing? Did the receipts come up short?"

He was gazing down at his boot tips, unable to meet her gaze. She had never known Bart Logan to avoid any glance, even that of the devil.

"You think—! *You think—!*" Maggie could say no more. She was petrified with rage.

He looked up, his eyes—

"It's just normal business practice, Mrs. Evans. To have the records checked by a reputable firm now and again."

"How *long* have you been in the lumber business, Mr. Logan! *How* many times during those *years* have you had the books *audited*!"

She slammed the door, and stalked inside.

Bart followed her in, demanding, "Why are you assuming this *injured* attitude? This is *my* company, and if I wish to have *my* records checked—"

"If, Mr. Logan, you wish to have your records checked, it's because you think I am a *thief*! You think I have been funneling off funds for my own—"

Maggie was so angry, so hurt, she could no longer speak. But she would not cry! She would *not* give this, "Money grubbing, skinflint, heartless, cold, mechanical, suspicious-minded—"

"*What* did you just call me, Mrs. Evans?"

"I said, Mr. Logan, you won't *ever* have to *fire* me again! I *quit!* And just as soon as I can pack my things—which, by the way, Mr. Bartram Logan, shouldn't take very long since I have so few of them. Oh! But…then…there's all your *money*, I'm going to be forced to drag along? Huh? Probably need an extra pack mule or two to cart all *that* off! And everything else I've taken from this fine place? Want to go count the tin forks and spoons? How about the *cups*? And the garbage *pails*—and the *water* buckets!"

"Have you *quite* finished, Mrs. Evans? When you have settled yourself down, I will explain to you, when you are of a rational mind to listen—"

"Oh! So! Now! Not only am I a thief, but I'm an *irrational* thief! You—! You—! You get out of here!"

"This is *my* place!"

"*I*—*don*—*'t*—*care*—*whose*—*place it is! If you don't get out of my sight*—*this minute*—*I'm going to*—"

Bart did not slam the door behind him.

Well, so much for that. She'd settle down. She always did. What on earth was she *doing* in there? Tearing the place apart?

Bart slid the door open a crack.

Good grief! She was slinging, throwing, piling every tin plate, cup, fork, spoon, pot, pan—everything she could get her hands on—along the entire length of the tables. She even threw the fire poker on top of the pile, before she slammed into her room.

The banging and slamming slowed, but it did not stop.

If the whole thing wasn't so ridiculous, he'd—

Why *had* he ordered that audit? He did find it difficult, sometimes, to believe what came out of that pretty mouth. And she was so *desperate* for money. And handling all that cash.

But deep in the deepest part of his heart, he didn't actually think she would steal from him.

Bart went on about his business. Towards mid-afternoon, a rig pulled into the logging yard.

Her *friend*!

She had sent him word—!

Bart walked over to him.

"Hello," the man said politely.

"You have...some...business...here?" Bart growled.

"It's Maggie. She sent me an urgent message. She needs to get into town. Quick. She said."

"I...see...Mr.... will you just wait out here for a moment—"

Bart yanked open the door to the cookshack. She stood just inside, glaring at him.

"Well," she said, cool as you please, "I see my ride's here. Don't bother yourself, Mr. Logan, with my trunk. Mr. Thomas Beyers will get it. Johnny, stop dawdling back there, and come along."

She walked out the door. Mr. Thomas Beyers doffed his hat at Bart, slid past him into the cookshack, and then came out, dragging the heavy trunk. Clear of the door, he hefted the heavy trunk onto one thin shoulder. Bart made no move to assist him. He made no move to walk out that door, and talk to her—or at least to attempt to talk to her—-or to even say goodbye—-

Then the door closed.

And she was gone.

The day after Mrs. Evans and Johnny left—was a total and complete nightmare for Bart.

Jacob Barnabas refused to get out of bed. He also refused to eat the terrible bowl of gruel Bart carried to him.

The men stood about, half the morning, their faces hanging out—-as if all their best friends had just died.

One of the huge draft horses was sick, maybe distemper.

The belt pulley on the big main saw blade broke. First thing tomorrow, he'd have to go into town—

Bart rode slowly down the main street of the growing town they had named Rhyersville. He pulled his mount up, at the end of Main Street, and rode slowly back down. Nothing had changed. *Where was she?*

He'd probably be forced to spend the night, to get all his—to get everything set right.

He rode over to Jonas Trap's. Dismounted, and strode inside.

"Mornin' Mr. Logan. What can I do for you?"

"The main pulley broke on the big saw, over at the mill. I was wondering if you could repair it? Or will I have to order another one?"

"I don't know, Mr. Logan. I can give it a try. But I'm afraid if the mend don't take, you might have to wait as long as a week—maybe two—before another one could be ordered in. Have to come all the way—"

"Do whatever you have to—-to get me back up and running. Still no place in this town I can get a decent bite to eat, bed down for the night?"

"Nope. We're growing like sprouting mushrooms. But we don't got a restaurant no more. Had one, few months back. It closed. Word is, though, a new one might be opening up. Any day now."

"Oh?" Bart picked up his ears.

"That Mrs. Evans—lady I thought worked for you—anyhow, word is, she's over there now, scrubbing and cleaning on that empty building used to be the only restaurant. Plans on opening next week, if she can. Gettin' a new sign painted and everythin'. *The Sparrow.* Odd name, don't you think, for a eatin' place?"

So! *That* was it! She had herself a *plan*, all this time. All this time, she was *biding* her time. Squeezing every dime and nickel she could out of him. Picking blackberries! Digging sassafras roots for tea! Stripping off slippery elm bark, for medication! Gathering ginseng, too! Picking wild greens, down in the big meadow! Perhaps he was wise, after all, to have the ledgers checked! Even *catnip*! He actually paid her for gathering *catnip*!

Bart stormed across the street. Then, having reached about the middle of the dusty, rutted thoroughfare, he halted.

Perhaps, knowing Mrs. Margaret Ann Evans the way he did, perhaps he should devise some sort of *strategy*. No, that was her game. Circle and calculate and connive and deceive—

Not for him. He was what he was. His way had always been, straight out with it. You had something to say, say it. No shilly-shallying about. Get to the point, and on with it.

And look where that had gotten him!

Where had it gotten him?

Why was he here? Standing in this dusty street, in this dusty burg—

He was crazy. *She had left. She was gone. He was rid of her.* And good riddance. How many nights had he dreamed of *just this*! Mrs. Margaret Ann

Evans had actually *quit!* And he didn't even have to haul her down off the mountain bodily, himself!

What a relief that was!

But, then, old Jacob Barnabas had taken to his cot—almost the minute that buggy drove out of the clearing and down the incline.

Bart had seen Jacob, the day she left. He'd no doubt heard the banging and the big ruckus, and, afraid to actually *enter* the cookshack, Jacob Barnabas had crept around the corner to the front, to watch the goings on.

After the 'friend' drove off with their only cook, Jacob Barnabas' shoulders drooped. He went—in less than five minutes—from looking like a sixty year old man—to a ninety year old shadow of his former self.

Bart knocked politely on the door of *The Sparrow*. He couldn't help but notice that there was a large empty space at the bottom of the brightly painted sign. Maybe Mrs. Margaret Ann Evans had grand plans to add another business venture to that one of an eatery.

A lady opened the door and stuck her head out, "We're not open yet. Be at least another week."

"I'm not looking to order food. I was looking for someone—"

"Oh?"

"Yes, a Mrs. Evans?"

"You mean Maggie? She's out back."

She was here. Now—!

Bart walked around to the back of the place. She was dashing out a bucket of water. Standing on the back step, one hand on her hip, she gazed at the sky, as if expecting some good omen to appear.

"Good Morning, Mrs. Evans," Bart said very sadly.

"Oh," she said, "it's *you*."

"Look, Mrs. Evans...I'm afraid...there's been some grave misunderstanding...here. And I just...wanted to..."

"I have no *idea* what you want, Mr. Logan. If you've come to try to claim back some of your belongings—"

"I haven't come on behalf of myself. No, not at all. It's...poor Jacob."

"What's happened to Jacob Barnabas?"

"He fell..."

"He *fell?*"

"He fell...very ill...almost the moment...your *friend's* rig left the logging yard. Very ill."

"Is that so? Just what form, Mr. Logan, does Jacob Barnabas' illness take?"

"Form?"

"What's wrong with Jacob?"

"He's not eating. He…talks in his sleep. He…"

"Jacob Barnabas was never a hearty eater. Is he drinking anything?"

"Maybe…a…bit…of coffee. Just a bit."

"Coffee? No water?"

"And…a bit…of that…too…"

"Did Jacob Barnabas send you?"

"No…he isn't able…"

"He's not even able to talk?"

"No. Not a single word. Since yesterday."

"Well, Mr. Logan, I've listened very carefully to everything you have said. If Jacob Barnabas is drinking coffee—and no water—he certainly doesn't have a fever. What I would suggest to you is, give Jacob Banabas a good hefty dose of *castor oil*—

"—And if there's still any left after that—

"—*Take it yourself*! You're not very good at this…not good at all! You think I was born in a barrel? You make a *very* poor liar! Good day to you, Mr. Logan!"

She slammed the door.

Bart went back to the wheelwright's shop.

Two days later, Maggie saw him ride out of town.

"The very nerve of that man!" Maggie grumbled to Barbara Jo.

"You surely were hard on him. I think, Maggie, that he—"

"*Hard on him!* Don't get me started, Barbara Jo. I'd like to open this place with all the windows and doors intact. Why don't you sit down and rest? Time was, as I recall, I couldn't get you to stir from off your bed until three o'clock of the afternoon. Now, you show up here, knocking on my door, at seven in the morning with your apron on, and you don't stop until dark. What's happened to you?"

"Maybe, Maggs, just maybe—I grew up."

"Well, and seeing that you're going on towards—"

"Let's not get *that* cruel. Let's not start talking about age."

"Well," Maggie surmised, squeezing out the soapy rag she was vigorously applying to the walls and windows, "Whatever the age you're approaching, it's about high time you grew up."

"Same ol' Maggs."

"Yes. Well," Maggie paused and stretched her back. "Thanks, Barbs, for everything. But the things you bought, the money for the tables and chairs. What little I had managed to scrape together, I couldn't have done nearly this much…and still had enough to…by the way, what's Fred got to say about all this—the money you're spending?"

"It's not Fred's money, Maggs, it's mine."

"Yours?"

"I made Fred start paying me a weekly salary, years ago."

"You what?"

"Well, I was doing quite a bit of work. And anytime I wanted the least little thing—here I was sticking my hand out like a beggar, and I got sick of it."

"Barbs! I'm so proud of you! When you first said you were going to marry Fred Moss, well, I thought—"

"If you will recall, Maggs, you made it quite clear to me—what you thought."

"Oh. Yes. There…was that."

"And partly, you were right. But Fred's a good man—underneath all the grubbing and groveling for every nickel and dime."

"If you say so!"

"He's been good to me, Maggie. And for the most part, I've had a pretty good life, with Fred. Better than—"

Barbara Jo broke off, afraid she would say too much. All that hurt Maggie had endured with that Len Evans—! If the man hadn't up and died, she might have been sorely tempted to shoot him herself.

"It's over and done, Barbs. I just try to put it away, and forget it. We can't put the spilt milk back into the pitcher. Remember that?"

"Mama said it a hundred times a day."

"Well, Barbs," Maggie looked at her older sister and sighed, "It's true."

Chapter 34

Things didn't see much improvement, at the logging camp. The men grumbled; the rains came. The sluiceway had to be repaired. One of the draft horses was still off his feed.

And so was Jacob Barnabas.

"Jacob!" Bart called entering the room Jacob now called home.

"I want you to sit up here, now. And eat something."

"I's not—hungry."

"You don't have to be hungry. You just have to get something inside that skinny frame of yours!"

"Just let me go, Mr. Bart. Jacob Barnabas thinks hee' final home goin' time is near."

"Nonsense! Why, Jacob, you're burning up!"

"Nosuh, I's cold."

"Hey, you, Henderson! Fetch me a pail of cold water! And some clean cloths!"

Bart began to sponge him off. Jacob's ribs were protruding almost through his shiny black skin. His face was a skull, with papery thin black skin stretched over it.

"I's sure would cotton to seein' Mizzz Maggie—and th' chil—"

"It's all right, Jacob—"

"Jacob...Barnabas. Mizzz Maggie, she don' giv' me a *free name*. That's whut it says, on my fine headstone. And Mizzz Maggie, she gwin' sing—and you, Mr. Bart, you gwin' play—"

"Maggie. There's a man at the door. It's for you."
"Coming! Oh, its you!"
No, how are you Mr. Logan. No—
"What's wrong?"
"It's Jacob. He's asking for you."
"I'll get my wrap."
"And the boy...he wants...to see Johnny."
"Johnny! Get down here! This instant!"

Maggie couldn't wait for the horses to climb the last feet up the incline. She slid down off her mount, and flew along the ground, her shawl and skirts billowing out behind her. She left Johnny for Bart to bring along.

Breathless, she entered Jacob Barnabas' room. She laid off her bonnet, and sat down beside him on the bed.

"Jacob Barnabas Logan! Now don't you look so fine! I never saw a—"
"I's all right, Mizzzz Maggie. You don' hav' to—"
"Oh, Jacob Barnabas, what can I do for you? What can I get for you?"
"Did you bring...your Scripture Book, Mizzzz Maggie?"
"As a matter of fact, yes, I did."
"Then, would you read to me that part—about the shadow of death."
"Certainly, Jacob Barnabas. Let me—"
Maggie opened the Bible, and read from the twenty-third Psalm.

> *...Yea, though I walk*
> *through the valley*
> *of the shadow of death,*
> *I will fear no evil;*
> *for Thou art with me;*
> *thy rod and thy staff*
> *they comfort me...*

Quietly, Bart left the room. He went to sit on the front steps of the small cookshack. He gazed about in the gathering gloom—at his fine sawmill, the giant draft horses, grazing in the corral, the huge pile of new timbers—all cut to perfect eight-foot lengths, all rowed up in drying stacks.

But when death comes calling—all else pales into nothingness. The bank accounts, the homes, all fade into oblivion. Death—the final river to cross.

He could hear Margaret Ann Evans' voice, clear, and sweet, and fine. There wasn't a mean or impure bone in that woman's body. He'd never encountered in all his life, a finer, more unselfish human being. Everything she touched—blossomed. Even old Jacob—although on his deathbed when she came into the camp—cheated death by almost two months. Jacob got a new name, a new sparkle in his eye. He regained the human dignity that men had stripped away from him. All because of Margaret Ann Evans. And not a man in this camp had failed to be touched by the pure *goodness*—in that one woman. She brought joy, and light, with her.

She also carried it away.

What a fool! What a *fool* he was! Why could he not have seen!?

But, now, it was too late.

She hated him with a vile passion. They still hadn't gotten the kitchen sorted out, and everything stuck away in some cupboard or shelf.

What a fool he was! Worrying about stands of timber, and board feet, and grades and sluiceways—

When death was stalking every man. And—until he met Mrs. Evans—he never gave it a second thought. As if he intended to draw up some drafts with his engineering skills, and map himself a pathway up to Glory! Instead of searching for that *certain* shore, and the lighthouse that sent out that saving beacon—

—But, lately, he had begun to search. He had taken out his Mother's Bible, and he had begun to read—

Mrs. Evans came softly out the door. "He wants to see you."

Bart hurried in. "Yes, Jacob…Barnabas," he hastened to add.

"Do you think, Mr. Bart, tha' ol' Jacob Barnabas could be buried near a real Church House, so's he could hear the singing and the mornin' preachin'?"

"I…don't think that would be possible, Jacob…Barnabas—"

"Why not?" Mrs. Evans fixed angry eyes on him. She drew him aside. "The man is dying! He has given so much to this world! Now, give him what he wants!"

"*I can't!* How can I promise him something, knowing full well I have *no hopes of delivering it? You think they're going to let me bury an ex-slave— a Negro—in a white man's cemetery?*"

"Well, I can!"

Going over and kneeling beside the dying Jacob, Maggie took his hand, smiled at him and declared:

"You have my word on it, Jacob Barnabas. You want to rest out back of the Shiloh Baptist Church, then that's where you shall lie—until the great trumpet sounds and the dead in Christ shall rise. You have *my word* on that."

Before the words were out of her mouth, Bartram Logan had snatched her to her feet, and was bodily dragging her out the door.

Once off the steps, he dragged her to the side of the building, and pinned her back against a big pine. He towered over her, one hand on one side, one hand on the other:

"Now, you listen to me, Miss Sunshine! I can't *believe* you! You can go rolling that pretty little tongue around in your mouth—setting every man in this camp skidding on his ear—and me along with them—with all your lies— but Jacob is *dying* in there! *Any* minute, *now!* And I won't have him go to his grave, believing one of your *lies!*"

Maggie gathered all the strength within her, slammed upward with both her hands, and sent his arms flying. Putting both her fists in the center of his chest, she gave him a mighty shove, rocking him back on his heels.

She stepped in close:

"And you listen to me, Mr. William Bartram Logan! Jacob Barnabas Logan will take his final rest *in* the graveyard *behind* the Shiloh Baptist Church *in* Rhyersville—and you have *my word* on *that*."

"Every good thing I ever thought about you, Mrs. Evans—I take it *all* back!"

"Well, Mr. Bartram Logan, you can *have it all back*! I wouldn't give a *rotten fig* for all your good thoughts!"

She whirled away, then spun back to confront him:

"Just see to it that you *show up*! Ready to play a *fine* fiddle! I'll be leaving at first light—to make all the arrangements. I'll send you *word*, when to bring...Jacob Barnabas...and his headstone...to the Shiloh Baptist Church!"

"Mr. Logan, message for you, from Mrs. Evans."

"Thank you, Roberts. Everything set?"

"Yes, Boss. He's been put in, and the black stroud looks...mighty fine. He looks good, peaceful like."

"Thank you, Roberts."

Bart drew on his gloves, his best hat. He stepped outside. Jacob Barnabas' hearse was waiting—his best wagon—the sides all draped in fine black stroud.

Jacob would be proud.

It was a long, sad, silent procession that pulled out of the logging camp, wending its way carefully down off the mountain. The newly-cut road was a bit easier to maneuver, with several months' traffic packing it down.

At exactly two o'clock, the little procession pulled in front of the Shiloh Baptist Church.

Out back, a piece up the side of the gentle slope, Bart could see an open wound in the earth. It was on *her* grave lot! Well, she might control that grave lot, but she certainly didn't control the *church*. Or did she?

Exactly *how* had Margaret Ann Evans pulled off this little coup?

"My friend Jacob will be buried on my plot, and that's the end of it, Fred Moss." Thomas Beyers had managed to purchase for Maggie a large lot adjoining his—so that Maggie could one day rest near Katie Ann and Nellie.

"I don't *own* the church, Maggie. For heaven's sake, I'm only Chairman of the Deacon Board."

"That fine belfry, that big iron bell, didn't come cheap. You have given more money to this church than any one single member it ever had—that's *why* you're Chairman of the Deacon Board. And what you say—goes! We're having a closed-casket funeral. Saying the remains will not be opened for viewing—for personal reasons. No one has to know—"

"We can't *deceive* the people like that!'

"Well, Fred, my fine, upstanding, pillar-of-the-community brother-in-law, if I recall correctly, *you* have been in the business of deceiving people for some years now. Do you recall, Fred—when I lived out on the river road? And you showed up, that evening, just out of the blue. And do you recall, leaving my house on the river road, yourself all *covered* with a sack of *fine flour* you had just so generously delivered? What *did* you *tell* Barbara Jo, about what had happened to you? Or anyone else you happened to meet along the road?"

"Maggie, you wouldn't. That's in the past—"

"It wasn't that long ago, Fred. And anyhow, I have a good memory. I'll *never* forget how you—"

"All right. All right. You can put your…friend there. I'll have the grave dug! Yes! Yes! At my own expense! I have to go!"

Maggie had fetched along the fiddle, for Bart to play. They stood close together, he playing so awesomely, she singing so beautifully. There was a very large attendance. And everyone present thought it was the most lovely, most moving funeral they had attended in quite a while——

And they all wagged their heads—

And wondered—

And speculated—

"Who *is* that in that casket? Some relative, I suppose, of Mr. William Bartram Logan."

"Must be. That name, Jacob Barnabas *Logan*—do you think *he* was as well off as *Mr. Bartram Logan?*"

"And—there was his *grandfather*—owned property from here to Charleston and back—"

Maggie watched the dirt cover the black-draped coffin.

She bent, picked up a handful of red clay, threw it in, and said:

"Goodbye, sweet Jacob Barnabas Logan."

Then she took Johnny by the hand, and walked away.

"What's that you said, sweetie?"

"Don't cry, Maggie. Not even a sparrow falls, but God knows about it."

Maggie gave Johnny's small hand a tight squeeze, and walked on down the slope.

———————

Barbara Jo walked to the door of the *Sparrow Restaurant*, and peered worriedly out.

"I don't know, Maggs. I can't recall ever seeing it get *this* dark, just because a storm is brewing over the mountains. What do you think?"

"I think, Barbara Jo, you might ought to head on home, unless you want to spend the night in one of the unfurnished upstairs rooms—that haven't been cleaned quite that well yet. I'll be fine, now, without you. Why don't you just go on, and see about Fred."

"Well, Fred does get a bit antsy—whenever a big storm's brewin'. I guess I will just head on home. We can—"

"Tomorrow's another day, Barbs—oh, my! You're right!" Maggie had put down her broom and now came to stand beside her sister and peer out into the gathering darkness. "It's almost black as night, out there!"

"Well, I'm gone, then," Barbara said, quickly slipping on her shawl and bonnet, "You close everything up tight. And it might not be a bad idea if you and Johnny and Liza Mae bedded down somewhere on the lower floor—just in case—"

"We'll be fine. You just go on now, and don't worry about us," Maggie assured her sister.

As Maggie attempted to close the door behind Barbara Jo, a gust of wind came whipping down the street, snatched the heavy door from her hands, and sent it banging back against the wall with a loud thud. The door then whipped out, as if it were going to bang the wall again. Maggie laid her slight weight against it, and forced the door shut, dropping the heavy bar in place. She leaned against the closed door for a moment, and whispered a prayer—that Barbara Jo reached home safely.

Then, "Johnny!" she called.

Johnny scooted out of the kitchen at a run, and Maggie ran to scoop him up in her arms.

"What's the matter? Is something wrong?" Johnny looked into her eyes, worry plain on his little face.

"Oh, no, sugar," Maggie flashed him a quick smile, gave him a tight, reassuring squeeze, "It's just that…it may be coming up a bad…rain. And I didn't want you to be outside playing, and get caught in it. Where's Liza Mae?"

"In the kitchen."

"Good. You can go on in the kitchen, then, with Liza Mae, and I'm just going to run upstairs…and see about a…few things And make sure all the windows are shut."

"Maggie?" Johnny paused and gazed at her uncertainly.

"It's okay, sweetie, just go on into the kitchen. We'll have a bite of supper in a bit. You getting' hungry?"

"Can I go upstairs…with you?"

"No, sugar, not this time. I…won't be long. Now scoot!"

Maggie flew up the stairs, flung open the big brown leather trunk, and began tossing out whatever resembled a piece of bedding of any sort. She needed enough to make the three of them a half-way decently-padded pallet for the night. As she worked, she could hear the wind outside, picking up by the moment, whistling down the tall chimney, and about the corners of the building. But she knew the restaurant was well constructed, and she hoped it would weather whatever storm was in the offing. She gave an involuntary shudder. Maggie knew the havoc a mountain storm could wreak—sometimes leveling entire farms, even entire *communities*—flat to the ground—strewing the wreckage of homes and barns and outbuildings all up and down the mountainsides—

Her arms filled with bedding, she raced to the stairs landing, and began tossing the quilts, sheets and blankets down to the first floor. Then downstairs, she gathered them up, and began laying out a thick pallet in the small alcove beneath the stairs, near what she supposed would be the sturdiest structural point of the building.

Outside, the wind gave a series of fierce, gusting shrieks. As she laid out the quilts on the floor near the supports of the stairs, she heard something hit the wall of the building. She raced into the kitchen. But found everything intact. Liza stood at the cookstove, ladling food onto three plates. She turned and gazed at Maggie with wide, terrified eyes.

"Well," Maggie announced in a strained voice as she took her chair at the table, "I see we have our supper about ready. Well, eat up, Johnny!"

"What was that awful noise?" Johnny looked up at Maggie, his blue eyes wide, "It sounded like—"

"It's nothing, sugar." Maggie said quickly, "Just the wind, picking up trash, and flinging it against the building."

"I never heard *that* before."

"Well, sugar, to be quite honest with you, I'm afraid a storm's brewing…up on the mountains. And it…seems to be kicking up quite a breeze. But, not to fear, we're shut up in a fine, stout building. We'll be okay. Now—"

KAAAABAAAAAAMMMMMMMMMMMMMMMM!!!!!

"Maggie?" Johnnie gazed at her with frightened eyes.

"It's…okay, sweetie. Just eat your supper. Then we'll bed down…down here tonight. Just in case, the wind gets worse."

"Is the wind going to blow the upstairs away?"

"I certainly hope not. No. Nothing is going to happen to us, sugar. Sleeping downstairs—it's just a precaution. We never know, Johnny, what's going to happen next…in this world. So, we just have to pray that God, in his infinite love and wisdom, will keep us safe. We just prepare the best we can, then we just…sit tight, and weather the storm. Liza Mae, would you please pass me the green beans. My! Don't these look good! Fresh from the field, aren't they? And I'll have a bite of that—"

KAAAABAMMMMMMMMMMMMMMMMMMMMMMMM!!!!!!!

"Go ahead, and just fix your plates," Maggie said above the howling of the wind, "Then we'll say Grace."

"I want some green beans, too," Johnny said calmly, "and can I have a bowl of bread pudding, if I eat all my beans and stuff?"

"You sure can, honey. And how about a big glass of cool sweet—"

KAAAABAAAAAAMMMMMMMMMMMMMMMMMMMMMM!!!

"That didn't scare me *near* as much as the first one, Maggie!" Johnny gave Maggie a nod and a brave little smile. "Can I say Grace?"

"How nice that would be!" Maggie smiled.

"God, please make th' storm not hurt me and Maggie and Liza, and thank you for th' supper. Oh, and 'specially for the bread pudding. Amen

Maggie smiled. Quietly they ate, amidst the howling of the winds that caused the sturdy oak building to shudder once or twice, and kept a loose shutter thumping frantically against a wall, somewhere down the street—as well as the occasional banging against this wall and that, of their building. Maggie tried to encourage Johnny to clean his plate, hurrying the meal along. Then she rose from the table, and motioned to Liza to put the dishes to soak, and to cover the food and store it on the stove.

"Now," Maggie announced, "I think we're going to play a little game."

Johnny gazed at Maggie, "What kind of game?"

"Well, I've fixed a little hide-out—for all three of us—to huddle up beneath the stairs. Then, we'll put out the lamp, and tell stories. Come on, now, the two of you. You've each got to come up with a *really* good story. It can be about anything…something you heard…something that happened to you, or to someone you know…"

As she spoke, Maggie was patting out the quilts and blankets, preparing a little nest for the three of them beneath the stairway.

"Now, Liza, blow out the lamp, and push it behind the stairs, so it won't get accidentally knocked over and spill lamp oil all over the floor. And would you like me to begin? Okay—

"Once upon a time, up on a *very* high mountain, there lived a little boy—"

"How little?" Johnny immediately interrupted.

"Oh," Maggie whispered, pulling Johnny close in the howling darkness, "I guess he was just about *your* age."

"What did he do?"

KAAAABAAAAAAMMMMMMMMMMMMMMMMM

"He had a great love for…. everything God had created. Every creature living—"

"What was his name?"

"I believe it was—"

KAAAAAAABAMMMMMMMMMMMMMMMMMMMMMMMMMMMMMM
"Joseph. Joseph loved animals. Very much. He kept bringing them into the little hut where his family lived, upon the high mountain."
"Like you did with the rabbits and the raven, huh?"
"Well, *something* like that. Anyhow, finally they had so many animals in the house, that one day his Mama declared, "Joseph! We can't even walk about this place anymore, for all the animals! If you keep this up, son, pretty soon, we'll just have to *abandon* the house, and go and live in the woods!"
"What did Joseph say to that?"
"Well, he—"
Her mind on the storm, Maggie finished the story, punctuated now and again by the fierce howling of the wind. At one point, she heard a distant roar, the snapping of trees—and knew that the tail of the storm had dipped into the timbers, somewhere up on the mountains. She prayed no one was hurt. That the storm stayed on the mountain, and away from the town. She prayed that Barbara Jo, and even Fred Moss, were safe—in their fine yellow house. But she bet with a storm howling over the mountains, Fred had slept on the tiny cot at the back of his store, to keep an eye on his fine stock of merchandise.

Before her story had ended, Maggie noticed a slowing, a softness of Johnny's breathing. He was fast asleep. "Good night, Liza Mae," she whispered, and tried to settle herself down in the nest of quilts.

Maggie awoke with a start.
BANG!!!!!! BANG!!!!!!! BANG!!!!!!!!!!!!!!
"I do believe there's somebody at the *do'r*, Missssus!" Liza muttered.
"Liza Mae," Maggie whispered, "you have the matches? Light the lamp!"
The lamp in one hand, Maggie reached the door and called loudly:
"Who is it?"
"*Stephen Giles*, Mrs. Evans! There's been some…trouble up at the logging camp. Mr. Logan said we should—"
By now, Maggie had flung up the heavy bar, and swung wide the door.
There stood Stephen Giles, blond hair straggling into a face that was scratched and bleeding. "Mr. Giles—!"
"It's the storm, Ma'am. Blew away about the whole camp. Nothing left on that side of th' mountain—but the sawmill and—"
"Mr. Giles! Come in!" Maggie insisted, "How…is…is…anyone hurt?"

"That's why I'm here, Mrs. Evans. The men were all huddled in the bunkhouse. The tail of the funnel lifted it…and…flung it half a mile up th' mountain. We found all the men."

"How are they? Is Mr. Logan…?"

"Everyone's alive. The Boss is all right. He's coming along. Bringing the injured, in some wagons. He just wanted the rest of us, those who were able, to ride on ahead, to see if we could find a shelter for the—you're the only person in town Mr. Logan could think of."

"Well, of course," Maggie said quickly, "I'll do anything I can to help. You have some of the men with you?"

"The ones who could walk. Mr. Logan's bringing down a couple of wagons with the rest."

"Get them inside," Maggie ordered. "Liza Mae, put on a big pot of coffee, and heat up all the leftovers, in case any of them is hungry. I'll get my wrap, and see if Dr. Ellis—"

"No," Stephen Giles spoke up, "It's still blowing out there, and there's trash in the street. I'll get the doctor, Mrs. Evans, if you would just kindly show the men where you'd like the injured placed—when they get here."

"With the weather this uncertain," Maggie said, "I think we'd better keep everyone downstairs—for now. Liza Mae, as soon as you get the cookstove going, why don't you light a fire in the fireplace? They'll all be soaked and shivering, might take a chill. I'll see what I can scare up in the way of towels, washcloths and bedding."

The building had one huge fireplace, set in the back corner, spanning one third of the eastern wall of the dining room. The red-clay-and-river-rock chimney reached to the second floor—where another fireplace opened into an upstairs room—before lifting its rocky surface safely above the rooftop. And upstairs, flanking the narrow hallway leading from the steps, four additional small rooms comprised the upper floor. But Maggie and Barbara Jo had not gotten to them yet, with their vigorous cleaning. They were all cold, and littered with dust and debris, except for the one with the fireplace, which Maggie, Johnny and Liza had taken for sleeping quarters.

Stephen Giles rushed in, with Dr. Ellis in tow.

"If we're expecting injured men, can't we find something softer than the *floor*, to place these men on?" Dr. Ellis asked as he entered the restaurant, irritation in his voice, as he gazed about him at the dining room that he expected shortly would be littered with injured loggers.

"Well, Dr. Ellis," Maggie offered lamely, "I wasn't exactly expecting…that much…. company, tonight."

"I'm sorry, Maggie. Guess I'm not in too good of a mood. What I meant is, can't some of these loggers who can walk take a wagon over to Trap's, and at least bring us a big load of dry hay?"

"Yes," Stephen Giles, hovering anxiously near the doctor's elbow immediately spoke up, "We'll do that."

"Cover it good with canvas!" Dr. Ellis ordered sternly, "We don't want these hurt men lying on any wet bedding."

"Maybe Barbs would open the store, and we could get some more blankets and—"

"I stopped by there," a familiar voice was saying at Maggie's elbow. She turned, to see Bartram Logan.

His handsome face was drained of blood. His usually neat hair lay wet, and straggling down onto his forehead. "I spoke with the proprietor, Mr. Moss. He's bringing over everything that he has, in the way of towels, cloths, clothing and bedding. I…" His voice drifted off, as his eyes met Maggie's. Then he continued in a low, strained voice, "I'm sorry to burst in on you like this—without an invitation—I know how you feel, but I didn't know what else—"

He looked exhausted. His fine clothes were soaked and clinging to his lean frame. The dark eyes clearly registered anxiety—and pain.

"It's all right," Maggie said crisply. "Think nothing of it. I would open my door to—anyone in need—in such a situation."

Not exactly a gracious welcome, Bart thought tiredly, but at least she had let his crew in, and he knew she would do her utmost to make them comfortable.

The load of hay had not yet gotten here. The men were being brought in, some sitting on nothing but the hard oak floor. Some were bleeding here and there. Some merely looked dazed and shocked, as if uncertain exactly where they were—or what had just happened. Two or three, including Tad Horton, were brought in on make-shift stretchers.

Then in a more gracious tone, Maggie said to Bart, "It's fine, Mr. Logan. I know all these men. They are more than welcome here. They are like family to me."

"Yes," Bart nodded, rather sadly, Maggie thought. "I know…*they*…are."

Struck by the look on his face, the odd catch in his voice, Maggie quickly added, "Why don't you come over, Mr. Logan, and sit down by the fire? Could we get you a hot cup of coffee? Or a bite—"

Bart gave a grave little nod, knocked the hair from his forehead with a badly bruised hand.

"Are you all right, Mr. Logan?" Maggie asked, peering up at him intently, "You hand—are you injured?"

"No. Look after the others. I'm…fine."

"Well, you certainly don't look fine!'

"He about got himself killed, by a falling tree, trying to pull the others from the—"

"That's enough, Giles," Bart cut in almost angrily. "Let them see to the others. I'll be fine. All I need is—"

"You look as if you're about to keel over. You need a good hot cup of coffee to warm you up and settle your nerves," Maggie cut in. "You need to get out of those wet clothes. You need to stop *lying* to us—and let Dr. Ellis take a *good* look at you, Mr. Logan! That's *exactly* what you need! Now, come over here—and sit down in this chair! I'll be back in a moment with the doctor!"

Almost angrily, Maggie flounced away. The nerve of that man. His eyes seemed to be accusing her of highly-suspect Christian conduct.

She returned to where Bart sat slumped in a chair, shoved a cup of hot coffee beneath his nose and found it impossible to hold her tongue.

"You may think me the worst kind of *thief*, Mr. Logan. I know we have had our differences, but I want to set you straight, here and now, on one small detail. I am not the sort of person who would turn a man from her door, and deny him the slightest of comforts, in the midst of a crisis—"

As Maggie was railing at Bartram Logan, Dr. Ellis strode over, lifted the left leg of Bart's fine trousers—displaying a gaping wound that ran from the knee down to the ankle, laying his leg open as if it had been slit with a sharp skinning knife. His left boot was filled with slowly oozing blood.

"Oh…Mr. Logan!" Maggie gasped.

"It's nothing, Mrs. Evans," Bartram Logan sighed weakly, "Even we blackguards and heathens bleed when we—"

"Be quiet, man!" Dr. Ellis ordered, giving Maggie and Bart a peculiar stare, "And be still—at least until I can get this wound cleaned and closed up."

Maggie rushed over to a corner that had not been taken, snatched up two or three of the blankets Fred Moss had hauled in, and spread them over a pile of dry hay.

"Bring him over here!" she ordered. Then, "Liza Mae! Get a fresh pan of hot water, and some clean cloths. And bring a change of those shirts and trousers they just brought in from the store! Size large!"

Against his will, Bartram Logan was hefted onto the blanket-covered straw, and two of his able-bodied men stood holding a bed sheet, as Dr. Ellis disappeared behind the make-shift screen, to strip his patient out of his wet, bloody clothing, and tend his wounds.

Daylight revealed a room littered with piles of straw along each wall—and in every corner. A low fire had been kept going all night, to drive the chill from men who had been drenched and traumatized and injured.

Johnny awoke from his pallet beneath the stairs, where he had somehow managed to sleep the entire night through, despite the bedlam around him. He came staggering out, wiping his eyes, staring about him in a daze. Then his eyes lit on Bartram Logan, propped up on a mound of hay not far from the low fire in the huge fireplace.

Johnny went dashing across the room, flung himself at Bart with such force that he knocked him against the wall, and then he squeezed the big man tightly. Johnny would never forget—how Bart had saved him from the deadly hooves of the giant horse. And then the gentle warmth of the big man's arms about him, as Bart had hugged him real hard. Johnny had liked that feeling. He recognized that feeling for what it was, and, now, he wanted it repeated.

"Johnny!" Maggie dashed over, "What on earth has gotten into you! Mr. Logan's been—"

Bart held up a silencing hand, "It's all right. It's…fine. Johnny. Here." Bart shifted the boy's slight weight safely away from his bandaged leg, "just sit down beside me, and tell me how you've been getting along—without me there to keep you out of all sorts of mischief?"

"Are you sure—?" Maggie stared at Bartram Logan with narrowed eyes, as he continued to smile at Johnny, laying one hand fondly on his head. "Johnny can be quite a handful—"

"I believe, Mrs. Evans," Bart smiled at her thinly, "that I am thoroughly capable of safely occupying the time of a small, four-year-old boy—for just a few minutes, at least."

Maggie noticed that throughout the morning Johnny kept fetching things for Mr. Logan. First came two or three cups of hot coffee from the kitchen. Then a biscuit with butter and honey. Next, Johnny lugged in his big medical journal Dr. Ellis had given him. Johnny spread it out between himself and Mr. Logan, and the two of them pored over the book for a good long while, Bartram Logan nodding his dark head solemnly now and again, as if totally concurring with his newest physician's diagnosis.

When Dr. Ellis stepped over to check Bart, he lifted his eyes quizzically at the two of them.

Then, to Johnny, he said softly, "Maybe you'd better go on and play."

"I don't want to go on and play!" Johnny announced sternly, "I want to see Mr. Logan's wound. And what it is you do to make it all better."

His face sober as he could make it, Bart said, "It's fine with me. If he's planning to become a physician, he has to see these things, sooner or later. Might as well be now." Very gingerly, he lifted his trouser leg, and permitted Johnny to watch, as Dr. Ellis removed the blood-soaked bandage, inspected the horrid wound, cleaned it and covered it afresh.

Johnny's wide blue eyes took in the long gash in the flesh—that had been stitched carefully together with catgut. He asked several penetrating questions, about the procedure of closing the wound, what was used to cleanse it and staunch the bleeding.

Bart watched Johnny's small face, so set and filled with concern, how the boy never once flinched or showed the slightest twinge of unease, how his eyes followed Dr. Ellis's every movement. His ears soaked in each word. Then Dr. Ellis was warning Bart, "You'd better stay off that leg for a while. Give that cut time to heal. Pretty deep. Don't want to tear anything loose, and invite an infection that'll be none too easy to cure." Then, "Would you care to help me, with the remainder of my rounds?" Dr. Ellis asked his new assistant, very solemnly.

"Here's your chance, young sir." Bart nodded at Johnny and gave him a reassuring pat on the back, "Just think! You'll have a head start—when you get into medical school. You'll garner first-hand knowledge, from the town's leading physician."

"The town's *only physician,*" Dr. Ellis remarked dryly, then continued, "He's a bit young for this, isn't he?" He threw Bart a questioning glance. Then to Johnny, "But, if it's okay with your Mother, and you've got the stomach for it—then come along—"

Maggie, busy getting their patients all fed and tended, watched the three of them from across the room. She made no move to intervene in Johnny's 'medical rounds.'

Well, Bart thought sarcastically, maybe she's finally letting the boy face some of life's unpleasant music. He still couldn't understand why she had not yet made it clear to the good doctor that the boy wasn't her son. And gazing at the two of them together, as Maggie joined in the medical rounds—to no doubt, Bart thought, *supervise*—he was, as always, struck by Maggie's youth. It seemed incongruous—that she had taken responsibility for the boy, and was opening a business! He was certain she had not yet reached twenty. Amazing! She must have married at—

As if she felt his gaze on her, she turned to look at him. Bart pulled a crooked smile, and lifted a hand in a guilty little wave. Then he promptly turned his gaze elsewhere.

He needed to get his mind off the boy—and his 'mother.' He needed to get his head together. His logging camp lay flattened to the ground. The tail of the twister has laid bare the entire camp, missing only the sawmill itself. He wondered how long it would take him, to replace the buildings, get up and running again. He saw Stephen Giles enter the room from the kitchen, and Bart called him over.

Stephen sat down beside his boss on the pile of straw.

"How does it look up there?" Bart asked.

"Not too good. Could be worse. At least we have the mill still up. I'd say half the men are still on their feet. We can go on up, those of us who are able. Clean up the place. See what we can salvage. Shouldn't take but a short while, I would think, to rebuild the bunkhouse, cookshack and your cabin. Some of the stacks, those behind the mill site, are fairly untouched. There's plenty of board feet, or scrap, to rebuild immediately. You want us to go on up there and—"

"Yes," Bart said quickly, "I want us to put everything back just as it was, as quickly as we possibly can. I don't intend to intrude upon Mrs. Evans' *hospitality* one moment longer than is *absolutely* necessary. Of course, I intend to pay her for any food, or services, or any untoward inconvenience."

"I don't think—if you'll permit me to express my personal opinion—Mrs. Evans appears all that hung up on worrying about money for any of this."

"I know that," Bart said quickly, "But I'm well aware of the *opinion* she holds of me. I'd just as soon get my outfit out of her hair, as soon as I possibly can. And I certainly *do not* wish to place any financial burden…"

"Whatever you think, Boss."

"We have cleaned some of the rooms upstairs, Mr. Logan," Maggie said very matter-of-factly to Bartram Logan the following morning. He was pale, but up on his feet. "If we had some temporary cots, we could move the most badly injured into more comfortable—"

"Are you sure, Mrs. Evans? Are you sure that you want *any* of *my* men here on your premises for what might be *days*—"

"Suit yourself, Mr. Logan," Maggie said, her voice low and filled with sadness, "I can't understand why you…I can only offer. I know that Tad Horton's leg is broken. And Robert—"

"Forgive me, Mrs. Evans," Bart drew a hand across his forehead, as if totally at a loss as to what to say or do. "It's just…that…this has all been so…unexpected…"

"Yes," Maggie said curtly, "Wind storms usually are. But we must pick up the pieces—"

"Yes, I know, Mrs. Evans, and I surely do expect to 'pick up the pieces,' just as soon as I possibly can, and remove all of them, including myself, from your sight."

"Mr. Logan—" Maggie stared at him. "I know that I am *far* from being your favorite person. But…still…I—"

Bartram Logan wanted to reach out and shake her—for he had learned, very rapidly, the moment she left the logging camp, that she was indeed *his favorite person*, and the boy Johnny was running a close second. The way the boy had flung himself at Bart—Now Bartram Logan knew, for the first time in a long while, what it felt like—to be loved. He felt tears stinging his eyes; he blinked them back. But she hated him—with a vile passion. What could he say to this woman! What could he offer to the boy! Why should he torture himself?

"Please accept my most humble apologies, Mrs. Evans," Bart said in a strained, distant voice. "Oftentimes, I find that I am…that is to say…I find that I cannot say…the things I would prefer to…and the things I *do* say…all come out sounding…"

Maggie stared at him uncomprehendingly. His voice sounded choked and strained, as if Mr. Bartram Logan was on the verge of tears. Had her barbs and insults really reached him?

She had not the faintest idea what she should say to him, so she said softly:

"Your kind apology is accepted, Mr. Logan. I cannot imagine what it is, that you find so impossibly difficult to say to me. If I have maliciously offended you, with my…frank and thoughtless…I want you to know I never intended to cause you hurt. And I do have a ready ear, to listen to anything—coming straight from another heart."

"Yes," Bart said in a sad choked voice, the tears pooled in his dark eyes. She was of the opinion that he was referring to the flap she made over the audit thing. There was not a glimmer of warmth or feeling in the blue-blue eyes, or on the lovely face, or in the voice, to give him the slightest inkling that any of this talk of *hearts* meant that she wanted the slightest glance into the heart of Bartram Logan. She was speaking in a very polite, highly impersonal manner, as if she feared she had offended some passing stranger—just stopped in her doorway—

"Yes," Bart sighed, "I'm sure you have a...kind...listening heart. And nothing would give me greater pleasure, than to—"

Bartram Logan batted his dark eyes a couple of times, and seemed to come to himself. He cleared his throat and continued in a much more normal voice.

"I appreciate your allowing us the use of your....facility, Mrs. Evans. I will make an accurate accounting, as soon as I can, and will repay you—"

"It always comes down to *that*, doesn't it, Mr. Logan?" It was a great wonder, Bart thought, that she didn't stamp her foot, "Where *you* are concerned, it *always* comes down to *money!*"

"I'll send Giles by, with whatever I owe you. Good *day*, to you, Mrs. Evans!"

As Bart turned to leave, the kitchen door flew open, and Johnny came racing in. He made a bee-line for Bart, expecting to be picked up and held close.

But Bart just stared down at the boy for a moment, then laid a finger alongside Johnny's little face, very lightly, just the merest touch. Then he strode past him, never looking back

Maggie had kept paying rent on the tiny one-room shack at the end of the street. The rent was dirt cheap, and it was a place to store extra staples for the restaurant. She walked down there now, to check on things. She reached to lift the latch, and at the slight touch of her hand, the plank door swung open.

"That's odd," Maggie muttered to herself, pushing the door wide, to admit enough light to see the interior of the little cabin. Something moved, in the corner back of the stove.

"Is someone there? All right, I know you're there. So you can come on out, and tell me what you're doing in my cabin!" Maggie demanded in a loud, authoritative voice.

"It's only me," a low, slow voice drawled. "It's only Ben."

"Well, Ben, come on out," Maggie ordered. "And let's have a look at you."

As Maggie spoke, she reached her right hand into the corner, and got a firm clasp on the iron poker.

A Negro man rose slowly out of the corner. He saw the iron poker, and cowered back, "Please Missus. Ben didn't mean no harm. It's jes' that it was rainin' last night—"

"Is that your entire name, just Ben?"

"Yes, Missus."

"You spent the night here?" Maggie demanded, "Why weren't you at home?"

"Ben don't got no home. No more."

"What happened to it?"

"Th' man I worked for, after I got freed, he up an died, sometime back, and th' chilluns, they sold th' place. So I took to th' road. But I didn't find no work, yet."

"How long since you ate, Ben? How long you been on the road?"

"I don't know Missus. I don' los' count. In fact, Ben can't count."

"Well, you come with me, Ben, and we'll see about getting you some food."

Maggie looked about the tiny cabin. Everything seemed to be intact. She walked out, and motioned to the tall, thin Negro that he should follow.

Maggie entered *The Sparrow*, and motioned for Ben to follow her into the kitchen. She took a plate from the cupboard, took out some cold biscuits, a slab of salt ham, and poured Ben a cold cup of coffee from the big pot on the stove.

Maggie motioned Ben to a chair.

Reluctantly, he lowered his tall frame into one of the ladder-backed chairs.

Maggie set the food before him, and shoved the cup of cold coffee across the table.

To Ben's great surprise, and intense agony, Maggie took the chair opposite him.

"Where are you headed?" Maggie asked.

"Don't rightly...know..." Ben answered between bites.

"How long you been free, now Ben? Is it Benjamin? I thought it might be. How long you been free now, Benjamin, and why is it you still haven't taken the opportunity to get yourself a proper name?"

"Several years, now, Missus, like all the rest." Ben lowered his head in embarrassment.

"First thing a Freedman needed to do was chose himself a full Christian name, Benjamin. What names are you partial to?"

"Names, Missus?"

"Yes, you know. Do you like, say. Benjamin Israel, or Benjamin Zechariah, or Benjamin James?"

"I...I always liked the story of Noah, in the Good Book," Benjamin said, stuffing his mouth full of ham and hoecake. He ate ravenously.

"All right, then. We have Benjamin Noah. What about a surname? A last name? What other fellow did you like, in the Good Book?"

"I liked Daniels, and how he lived, in spite of th' hungry beasts sent to eat him up."

"There you have it! *Benjamin Noah Daniels*, I'm Margaret Ann Evans."

"That's who I am now, Benjamin Noah Daniels? Is it that easy, to jus' get yourself a name?"

"It's that easy, Benjamin Noah. Sometimes you have to just make your mind up, that a thing is true, and suddenly, it is. It's called having *faith*. Now finish your supper. Then you take that bucket over there in the corner, see it, that big wooden one? Go on down to the town well, draw yourself up a bucket of water, take it down to that cabin. I'll get you a big cloth. There's a bar of soap already there, and you give yourself a good bath. You got any other clothes?"

"No, Missus." Benjamin Noah Daniels hung his head in shame.

"There's no shame in not having a thing, Benjamin Noah. There's only shame in making no effort to get it. You go get yourself cleaned up. And then we'll see about getting you another change, so you can draw up some water, and take those stinking rags out back to the tubs, and give them a good scrubbing. Then, they may even be decent enough to wear."

"Missus, Ben—Benjamin Noah Daniels—does not know what to say."

"You don't have to say anything, Benjamin Noah. But I must warn you— if you stay in my cabin, you must work to earn your rent, and your food. *And* that new change of clothes. Hold up your feet. And a new pair of work shoes."

"Wha's tha' Negro doin' in this kitchin?!" Liza stuck her head in the door—at which she had just been listening intently. "How you know you's kin trus' tha' Negro?"

"The same way I knew I could trust you, Liza Mae Moon," Maggie smiled at her. "It's all in the eyes, and on the face. The way a man—or a woman—looks at you. Benjamin Noah has come on hard times. Just like the rest of us do sometimes. He needs a hand up. He needs a roof over his head, food in his mouth. We can help him—and—now, maybe he can help us—we'll have somebody around here to help with choppin' and bringing in wood, and drawing up water, and such."

"Wel'," Liza Mae narrowed her eyes suspiciously, "I still says, I's don' like th' look of 'im. Ye better keep yore eyes on that Negro."

"I will, Liza Mae," Maggie winked at her, "and you can help me."

Liza Mae let out a shy giggle, hiding her face in her hands.

"If you work steady, and good, Benjamin Noah Daniels," Maggie told the tall Negro the next day, "you can earn yourself a salary, a wage, some money, each week. Not much—we're just trying to get this business off the ground."

"You don' bin kind to me, Missus…"

"You can call me Mrs. Evans."

"Missus Evans, you don' bin kind to me. Benjamin Noah never saw a whole lot of kindness in this ole world."

"Well, kindness is free, Benjamin Noah, but still it seems there's not enough of it to go 'round. But food and lodging come at a price. And the Good Book says that he that does not work—does not eat. But it also says, the workman is worthy of his hire. So if you do a decent day's work, you will receive a decent day's pay."

Benjamin Noah's eyes filled with tears, which he brusquely knocked away with a big bony hand.

"What you like me to do, Missus Evans, you jus' say th' word."

"I want fresh water drawn—for the water bucket in the kitchen here—and for the water pitchers upstairs. And we will need extra, on laundry days, and more on bath nights. I want wood cut—for the black iron washpot out back, and for the kitchen cookstove, and the two fireplaces. I want plenty of wood and water always ready. If you have more energy left after that, you just see me, Benjamin Noah, and there'll be plenty to do around here, to fill your time. And let me warn you, you get paid according to what you do. We will keep a log—a written record—of the hours you work. You work lots of hours and you earn more—than when you work few hours. Do we have an understanding?"

"Yes, Missus Evans! Tha's a fin' understandin'—and I's won't be doin' no idlin' about."

"You take a rest, whenever you need it. We're not trying to set the world on fire here, Benjamin Noah. We're only trying to make all of us a decent living."

Liza Mae made it a point to keep a sharp eye out for that fellow that called himself Benjamin Noah Daniels. He was far too tall, for her liking, and far too broad in the shoulders, too. And he was far too free with his searching eyes, and his glib tongue. If she was in the dining room, and heard the slightest commotion in the kitchen, she went flying to investigate. Oftentimes, it was only Johnny looking for a handful of parched groundnuts or a sweet baked yam from the warming oven. And Liza Mae would be a little bit disappointed—that she couldn't let loose a tirade and fly into that Benjamin Noah Daniels.

But tonight, when she flew over and flung open the kitchen door, it was *he*!

Liza Mae screwed up her face so tight the heavy black coils of hair atop her head seemed to rise by at least an inch or more:

"Whut you doin' in this kitchin, you big black Negro?"

"I might ask you th' same thing, Msss Liza Mae Moon." Benjamin Noah grinned at her a silly grin that showed fine white teeth.

"I's live here, you big overgrowed fool!"

"Well, I's work here, Msss Liza Mae Moon."

"Well," Liza Mae relaxed her face just enough to be able to talk properly, "I's not so certin how long tha' will las'—I suppose until all the forks and spoons vanish from the kitchin' drauers."

"You know, Mizzzzs Liza Mae Moon, what you remind me of? The last place I worked, they had this little bittie bantam hen. Now, that hen, she could ruffffffffle up her feathers and put up an awful squawking and flapping all around, about the nearest nothin' you ever heerd tell of—but that little bantam, I never did know her to lay the first decent egg."

"Humphhhhh," Liza Mae stuck her nose in the air and flounced out, slamming the door behind her.

Benjamin Noah went out the back door, wiping the well water from his mouth, humming a tune.

Sometimes Maggie would hear the two of them going after each other, their voices raised loud enough to wake folks half a mile off. She would stick her head in the kitchen door and ask them politely:

"Okay, you two, how about taking yourselves outside, to air your differences, if you can't keep it to a low roar. We are trying to operate a business here—and let us not scare all our customers away."

"*You* didn't bring in enough wood," Liza Mae would complain almost every morning when Benjamin Noah appeared for his breakfast.

"How much you wants me to bring in, Mizzzz Liza Mae Moon?" Benjamin Noah would ask innocently, "It don' near reached over the sides of the woodbin, clear up to the windowsill over the stove. You want I should pile it high enough to fall into the glass and break the window out?"

"No, fool! I jus' want enough to cook a decent meal for the paying customers. You do git paid to work here."

"Yes, Mizzzzs Liza Mae Moon, I sure do git paid to work here, but I don't git paid to listen to you rattle on about something so no account as me not doin' my job good and proper. Now, let me see, if I got paid for that, well, then, in no time at all, I would be a man of grand property!"

"Could we please eat our breakfast in peace?" Maggie asked, her eyes on her two employees, "Then I'm going on in the dining room to work on the ledgers. And you two can have at each other until the cows come home. All I ask is that you don't bloody up my kitchen floors, too much."

Maggie had been shocked that first day, at how the two of them talked to one another. Then as the days passed, upon closer scrutiny, she began to get the idea that they were not truly *arguing* at all. All this verbal sparring was a sort of game, of one-upmanship they played. Like two children, testing the bounds of their newly-found dignity and liberty.

Liza Mae, defending her turf—she had recently learned that she was not an old worn out woman. But she was a fairly attractive Negress just entering the prime of her life.

Benjamin Noah weighing in, pushing back, giving as good as he got, making a place for himself. Meeting one of his own, on this new ground, where he was free to not only have an opinion, but also free to express it. Maggie noted that Benjamin Noah always left with a little tune on his lips. She had an idea that Benjamin Noah had a grand singing voice.

And Liza Mae, after a verbal set-to with Benjamin Noah Daniels, strutted and stomped about as if she owned the place.

Maggie went out early that morning. She had asked Benjamin Noah to hitch Job to the wagon. She meant to ride out and look over some produce at the Benson farm.

Benjamin Noah brought the wagon around to the front of *The Sparrow*, and tied Job to the new hitching post.

"Benjamin Noah," Maggie said, cocking her head to one side. "We need to *do* something about the look of the front of the restaurant. It certainly has *nothing* to catch one's eye."

"Whut you thin' you need, Missus Evans?"

"We need some flower boxes. Something to add color and drama. But first, we need to do something about that dull gray planking. The oak-shingled roof appears to be in good shape, but the front planking looks dull and drab. It looks just like the front of every *other* building, along this part of the street."

"You wants to whitewash the building, Missus Evans?"

"No. I don't think so. Whitewash doesn't last. First hard rain of winter, and there goes your whitewash. I'd like to get some of that new paint—the kind that comes in colors, and lasts for a very long time."

"You wants I's should paint the front of the building, Missus Evans?"

"You ever do any painting, Benjamin Noah?"

"No, Missus. I never even seed any such thing as paint."

"It's like whitewash, Benjamin Noah, except it's thicker, and instead of daubing it on the planks with an old rag, you apply it with a big brush."

"Like a currying brush?"

"No, Benjamin Noah. I'll bring one of the brushes from Moss' Mercantile and let you see it. See if you think you could do us a fine job of painting."

"Whut color, do you thin' on paintin' th' place?"

"Something, like warm wood, like rich, new wood. I'll look around, and let you know. What do you have planned for today?"

"It's a surprise, Missus Evans. But I's think you will be pleased with it."

"I'm sure I will, Benjamin Noah. You have a good day, now. Oh, by the way, after we paint the storefront, we'll be wanting to put in some plants."

Maggie walked into Moss' Mercantile, perused the small stock of paint, and chose a color called *Redwood Wonder*. It looked beautiful on the sample Fred Moss painted for her on a scrap of plank.

"You're sure it will look like that on the storefront?"

"Yes, Maggie. We guarantee all our products. You take it. And try it on some place that is not in plain view, just in case you don't like the color. Then, if you're not satisfied—"

"I'll take it," Maggie cut in. She couldn't help herself, but she still found Fred Moss' presence so obnoxious as to make her want to vomit. Every time she saw the man, she saw him coming at her around her own kitchen table, that lustful gleam in his eyes—

"What's that, Fred? Oh yes, I will need a brush, too."

Maggie liked the color so well, a rich reddish brown tone, that she decided when she had the money available, she would do the sides and back of the restaurant, too. But that would have to wait. Some of the plants, she could scrounge up from the forest, and she had several of Mama's plants she had dug up and transplanted to the little sharecropper house—then to the back of the little one-room cabin. She had brought two roses, and two hydrangeas, and two camellias.

Now, what she needed, were a couple of evergreens. Cedars—they would not grow too big, too fast. Some of the small cedars from the mountainside— yes, she and Benjamin Noah could dig those up. Maybe they'd find some holly, too—pretty in winter, shiny green leaves and all laden with red berries.

She wanted her front garden—which is what Maggie began to call it—to have color both winter and summer. The camellias would bloom in winter, the hydrangea in summer. Then she could put in some lilies and some snapdragons and some—

Maybe she could trade a few *meals* for some colorful perennials for her front garden. Though in truth, the area was narrow, so she would have to be very selective. But it would be lovely, she was certain, against the redwood siding.

And it was.

The next time Bart Logan rode into town, he could not believe his eyes.

Two perfectly shaped green cedars flanked either side of the front entrance of *The Sparrow*. Next came—on either side just past the cedars—a large blooming shrub of some sort. Absolutely covered with huge blossoms as large as both his fists put together. But, upon moving closer, he saw that what looked like one blossom from a distance, was actually three or four dozen tiny, perfect flowerets.

Beyond these, stood rows of low blooming plants. Then another large shrub, which he immediately recognized as holly, covered with darkly green shining leaves that fairly glistened in the sun.

All this against a backdrop the color of California redwood, and all set off by each window in the restaurant front—glistening and gleaming clean in the afternoon sun.

Altogether, Bart thought, a stunning effect. Where, a week or so ago, there had been only dust, and weeds, and rocks—-

But when he entered *The Sparrow*, Mrs. Evans, it appeared, was not to be found anywhere in the establishment.

With the new storefront, and the extra pair of hands for the wood and water and odd jobs, Maggie had more time to devote to her choice of cuisine.

Business began to boom. Ladies began to book the restaurant for their teas and parties and meetings. Wedding receptions were held at *The Sparrow*.

Maggie counted her receipts, and decided she had enough ahead to begin work on the upstairs.

Brass beds and dressers were seen disappearing up the narrow stairway, as well as colorful cotton rugs and tufted counterpanes. There was also an assortment of washstands and matching pewter bowls and pitchers. Curtains appeared on the upstairs windows, clean shining in the sun and very visible from the street.

After a week or two of all this commotion, the sign was taken down from over the doorway of *The Sparrow*, and re-hung after several hours. It now read, in red letters on a green background, with a black border:

The Sparrow
Restaurant
&
Rooms to Let

The next time Bart Logan rode into town, he saw the new sign, and he smiled.

"I'll take a room, if you please," he told the little Negress at the front desk—they now had a front desk.

"And for how long will that be?"

"Let's say, I come to town quite often, and never know exactly when my business will bring me in this direction, so I would be interested in leasing the room with exclusive rights."

"What do that mean?"

"I would like to pay rent on the room for each and every night of each and every week."

"You wants the room *all* the time? I don't know if we rent like that. We never had *nobody* rent like that. It's always for one or two—maybe three—nights at a time. We never had nobody rent like that."

"Let's make this simple," Bart smiled at her. "How much does a room rent for—for one night?"

"Twenty-five cents."

"Then two nights would be fifty cents, three would be seventy-five cents, and so forth, until seven would be one dollar and seventy-five cents, right?"

"I guess so," Liza Mae wagged her head in great confusion, "But, I still say, we never rent to *nobody*, like that."

"What's your name?" Bart smiled at the attractive little Negress.

"Liza Mae Moon."

"Well, Liza Mae Moon," Bart smiled, plunking down the correct change, "You just did. Here's seven dollars, which should be four weeks' rent, paid in full, in advance."

"You can just sign the book."

"Liza Mae!" Maggie yelled so loud, Bart heard her all the way upstairs. He smiled.

"Mizzz Maggie? You called me?"

"Liza Mae! What *have* I ever done, to make you go and do a fool thing like this?"

"What's that, Mizzz Maggie?"

"Renting this room…to that *William Bartram Logan.*"

"That was sure a stroke of luck, weren't it, Mizzz Maggie? And us with the rooms all *just* ready to let! And here come this fine, rich gentl'man, and rents one for every night of every week. It's just like a gift from Heaven! Maybe it's true, what you said about The Almighty caring for His little sparrows."

"Yes," Maggie sighed resignedly, "I see that Mr. William Bartram Logan has paid in advance for the—*entire month!*"

"And how, Mr. Logan, are all the injured? Recovering nicely I hope. And the leg?" Maggie asked, as she filled Bart Logan's cup with fresh hot coffee the next morning. "Have you gotten everything rebuilt, and all up and running?"

"Men are doing fine. The leg's almost mended. Everything's rebuilt, good as new. Saws are humming. I just rode into town, to check on Jacob Barnabas' grave. Make sure it wasn't covered in weeds—or what not." Bart Logan took a long, appreciative sip of the deliciously hot coffee.

"Did you find any?"

"What?"

"Weeds, or what-nots."

"Not the first one. Someone told me, might have been Trap, down at the wheelwright's, that there was some talk of *a tall Negro man,* being seen, going into the graveyard, and doing some work. You wouldn't by chance, know anything about him?"

"That would be Benjamin Noah Daniels."

"Where does Benjamin Noah Daniels hail from?"

"Here and there. Not much of any place you could put your finger on. Sort of a wanderer, I suppose you'd say."

"Does he just wander in, and clean off folks' graves?"

"No. Actually, Mr. Logan, Benjamin Noah gets paid for that."

"Just like he got paid for painting the front of the building, and—"

"And digging the well out back, and whatever else I find that needs doing about *The Sparrow.* Does it not sit well with you, Mr. Logan, that I, *a woman,* can actually *hire* a person to do work for me? You think I'm paying him with *your* money, filched from *your* coffers, while I was still in *your* employ? Is *that* what you think, Mr. Logan?"

"No, Mrs. Evans," Bart lowered the deliciously hot, steaming cup of coffee carefully to its saucer, and looked Margaret Ann Evans straight in the eye.

"I actually wanted to say how much I admire what you have done with the place. It's an amazing transformation. As it is with Benjamin Noah Daniels."

"What do you know about Benjamin Noah Daniels?"

"I saw him, the first night he came into town. I was lounging in the door of Trap's, and I saw him. He came stealing along in the rain, keeping to the shadows of the buildings. So, naturally, I jerked on my slicker and hat, and I followed him, to see what he was up to. The fellow was thin as a rail, and almost bent double. He went in the little cabin down at the end of the street. I've seen thousands of misfits and vagrants in my time. So I know one, when I see one."

"And when you look at Benjamin Noah Daniels now, Mr. Logan, what do you see?"

"I see a *man*, Mrs. Evans. You have an amazing touch."

"It is not *I* who has the touch, Mr. Logan. Good day to you now. Enjoy your breakfast."

"Well, good evening, Mrs. Evans. I must say, business is certainly booming."

"Yes, Mr. Logan. We did a birthday party for one of the town's leading citizens, today."

"Cake and all?"

"And punch. Would you like a cup?"

"That sounds fine. None of the cake left, I don't suppose?"

"No cake. How about a nice slice of hot apple pie, with clotted cream?"

"And another cup of coffee?"

"As long as you have the money, Mr. Logan, we have the coffee."

"So, good morning to you, Mrs. Evans. Looks to be a fine day, out there."

"It was nice in here—until a few moments ago," Maggie smiled sweetly at him.

"Well," Bart grinned in return, "Maybe there will be a change in the air soon. I'm going back to the logging camp this afternoon."

"We won't have the pleasure, then, of your company for luncheon? And we were planning to have smoked trout on—"

Before Maggie could finish her sentence, Bartram Logan had risen quickly to his feet, planted a kiss squarely on her lips, and was saying:

"I'm afraid, Mrs. Evans, you shall have to forego the pleasure of my company at luncheon. But, it would please me greatly, if you could prepare me a lunch to go. Could you perhaps do that?"

He was standing so close, Maggie could see the dark stubble on his chin.

"Yes, Mr. Logan," she replied, "I think we could do that."

A few days later, Maggie entered the kitchen to find Liza Mae firmly clasped in the arms of Benjamin Noah. And he, apparently, quite intent upon kissing her.

"All right, you two!" Maggie shouted at them, "I don't know what sort of establishment you think I am running here! But let me let you in on a little secret— I will abide no hanky-panky in this kitchen. If I catch you in a like position one more time, I will call the minister of the Shiloh Baptist Church—and I will marry you off to one another! Now, just what do you think about that?"

"You think, Mizzzz Evans, we could get married in the Shiloh Church?" Benjamin Noah reluctantly released his grip on Liza Mae, and grinned sheepishly at Maggie.

"Maggie! You must be *out of your mind*! I know I acceded to your wishes— no, not wishes—your demands, about the graveyard thing, and the devious burial of your *friend*. But, surely you cannot—you do not expect—"

"I don't *expect* anything, Fred Moss. I am simply telling you that my two employees, Liza Mae Moon and Benjamin Noah Daniels intend to be joined in Holy Matrimony. And it is their desire that the marriage ceremony be in front of their God—and all His People.

"It is," Maggie continued firmly, "our plan that this ceremony take place Saturday afternoon next. I will supply the flowers and pay the minister, and there will be a reception party immediately following, at *The Sparrow* dining room. All will be welcome. This is the notice that will be posted in the town newspaper, and several conspicuous places about the town.

"Good day to you, Fred Moss.

"Oh, and by the way, Mr. William Bartram Logan will be providing the violin music for the ceremony."

Small article on the back page of the **Rhyersville Monthly Chronicle**:

This Saturday past, the Shiloh Baptist Church was filled to the limits of its seating capacity for the wedding of Liza Mae Moon to Benjamin Noah Daniels. Following the ceremony, refreshments were enjoyed by all, in the main dining room of The Sparrow Restaurant with Rooms to Let.

"Mr. Logan, there's a matter of a bit of business I've been meaning to discuss with you," Maggie said as she set down the plate of steak and eggs and hot biscuits—and then she sat herself down in the chair opposite Bart.

"Well, then, Mrs. Evans, why don't you—sit down, and join me?"

"I believe I just did," Maggie smiled sweetly at him.

"What is this…matter of business, if I dare ask? I feel sure it's bound to cost me money."

"No. Not at all," Maggie wagged her head in denial, "I, in fact, wish to make a purchase—from your lumber company. Seeing that it's the only lumber mill for miles about, I am forced to give you my business."

"Oh, you want lumber, Mrs. Evans? And, pray, what is this lumber for?"

"Well, now that Liza Mae and Benjamin Noah are married, and living in that little one-room cabin, I decided to buy the little thing, *very cheaply*, you understand?" Maggie was gazing at him, so innocently, with those blue-blue eyes.

"Oh, *yes*," Bart nodded, chewing his steak, "I understand."

"Well, as I was saying," squinting her blue eyes, Maggie wrinkled her smooth brows prettily, "the cabin is in dire need of a wooden floor, and is only one room, and as Liza Mae is still of child bearing age, I purpose to floor it—build at least one additional room onto the little place, and then present it to the happy couple—as a wedding gift."

"Well, Mrs. Evans, if you can be so generous as to donate the cabin, I suppose I could supply the lumber—and labor—to build on the addition and the floor."

"I wasn't asking, Mr. Logan, that you donate anything. And most certainly not—"

"I know you weren't asking, Mrs. Evans, but I would be much obliged if you would just—just this once—*graciously* accept my offer."

Maggie stared at him, momentarily taken aback.

"Yes?" Bart Logan was gazing at her quizzically.

"Well, since you put it like that, Mr. Logan, well—" Maggie shrugged.

"Yes?"

"Yes."

Bart rose from his chair, pulled Maggie to her feet, clasped her close to him and spun her crazily about the room.

When at last he came to a halt and released her, after giving her a sound kiss, Maggie stepped away from him, patted her hair and lifted her chin:

"Well," she said, cool as you please, as if speaking to a great uncle, "I suppose I'll just go get you another cup of hot coffee."

Bart had been hanging about *The Sparrow* for weeks now. Letting his business interests stew in their own juices. And seemingly he had made absolutely no headway with Margaret Ann Evans. Why did he keep battering his head against these stone walls! Why did he find himself totally unable to just forget about her, and let her go? The walls of defense were as high as ever, too high, maybe even getting higher, he thought dejectedly. And he remained totally in the dark, totally unarmed, and totally unable to scale them. He knew little more about the mysterious Mrs. Evans, than he did the first day he laid eyes on her. He sat now at a table near the front door of *The Sparrow*, turning a cold cup of coffee between his hands, attempting to make a sensible decision—concerning his future actions.

He raised one hand and felt his chin, his eyes glued to the kitchen door. She had not appeared, to bid him a good morning, and serve him his breakfast, as she usually did. She had sent Liza Mae, instead. He should go up to his room, he thought, he could really use a shave. But he was going back to the logging camp this afternoon. Why hang around here? He'd just wait, now, and clean himself up, when he got there. No use, that he could see, in hanging around *The Sparrow*, any longer. It was clear to him, that whoever Mrs. Margaret Ann Evans was—that would remain to him forever a mystery. The woman's mind was as closed against him as a steel trap.

Bart pushed back the now completely cold cup of coffee, and heaved a great sigh. He had kissed her on the face—several times. He had held her in his arms and danced her about the room, on several separate occasions, until they were both giddy. And then, just last night, he thought he had sensed a yielding, for just an instant there, to his touch. But apparently he was sadly mistaken, for this morning, she would not even bother to appear, and give him the time of day.

He had looked deep into those blue-blue eyes, countless numbers of times. With his heart, he felt, in his own. And she remained as stiff and as cold, as unresponsive to him as if he were a ninety-year-old cripple—if he were *that*, then he could, perhaps, have garnered some *crumb* of affection. Bart gave a soft, resigned snort, and started to rise.

"Mr. Bartram Logan, isn't it?"

Bart rose slowly to his feet. He found himself looking into the face of a very nicely dressed lady, in a dark blue bonnet, somewhat pretty, perhaps in her early twenties. Her face seemed vaguely familiar. He knew he had seen her somewhere about Rhyersville.

"I wonder, Mr. Logan," Bart heard her saying, "if you would care to call upon me?" She smiled up at him. "At my home? This evening? Say, at seven?"

This was not entirely foreign to Bart Logan. He was not totally unacquainted with being accosted by a young lady—but not in such a public place—and not by one so openly issuing an invitation to—?

"I'm afraid I—who are you, Ma'am?"

"Margaret Ann McKinnon's sister."

Chapter 35

He arrived at the fine yellow brick house with its green shutters and a pretty little garden out front, shortly before seven o'clock. Immediately, the moment he had turned into the street behind Moss' Mercantile, Bart had recognized the place. Her *sister* lived here—!

Barbara Jo opened the door, and ushered William Bartram Logan into her well appointed parlor.

She closed the door gently, and motioned Mr. Logan to a chair.

Barbara Jo sat down opposite him.

A sparrow gazing through the front window that night, should a sparrow have been gazing, would have seen the small, slight woman gesturing with her hands, going on and on.

Pausing from time to time, to let the incredible story of love, joy, and pathos in McKinnon Valley, sink in.

The tall, handsomely dressed, freshly shaven man, rose from his overstuffed chair now and then, to run a tanned hand through dark thick hair, and to gesture helplessly into the air. Then he would retake his seat, at the lady's urging.

And the story continued.

About a marriage that began with such promise—and ended so tragically—leaving Margaret Ann McKinnon Evans emotionally spent. Now, there was only one driving force in her life:

The need to make a home and a future for John Thomas McKinnon, Junior.

There was now no room, no emotion, nothing, for anything—or anyone— else.

It was late, when at last William Bartram Logan reached his hat down from the ornate rack near the door, said thank you and good night. He made his way slowly, thoughtfully, back towards *The Sparrow*.

"The *Sparrow!*" he muttered, and laughed softly to himself in the cool mountain air.

Maggie, fast asleep upstairs, heard the loud banging on the front door. Groggily, she rose from her bed and threw a thin robe on over her nightgown. It must be some weary traveler, seeking a room for the night. What on earth was any *sane* person doing out at this *unholy* hour? Lighting a taper, she made her way slowly down the stairs.

"*Yes? Who is it?*" Maggie called through the front door. "*We are closed!*"

"It's me! Let me in, Mrs. Evans. It's Bart Logan!"

"Mr. Logan?" Maggie called back through the door, "I thought you said you were heading back to the logging camp—this afternoon?"

"Well, something important came up. I had a meeting...could we please continue this conversation inside? Would you please let me in?"

"Well, Mr. Logan!" Maggie lifted the heavy bar, opened the door and peered up at him accusingly, as Bart stepped inside, his hat held before him in his hands.

"Well!" Maggie continued to stare at him uncomprehendingly, "I certainly don't know what could be so important—that you're out and about at this unholy hour. It must be well after midnight!"

"I suppose it is, Mrs. Evans," Bart sighed, gazing at her in an odd manner.

"Mr. Logan, have you been drinking?" Why was he staring at her in such a peculiar fashion?

"No."

"You look a little pale, a bit...upset."

"I'm just tired," Bart said, twisting his expensive hat in his hand. "And I'd just...like to go on up to my bed."

"Well," said Maggie, a bit put out. "A man comes knocking on your door in the middle of the night and offers no reasonable explanation—except to say that he had this 'meeting'—"

"Excuse me," Bart leaned in close to her. "But—we're not married—yet."

"Well!" Maggie's blue eyes flew wide in the dim light of the taper. She started to open her mouth and say something. But all the wind was apparently taken from her sails.

She clutched her lighted taper before her, and moved towards the foot of the stairs. One hand on the balustrade, she turned.

"Since you are the last one in the door, Mr. Logan, I suppose it falls your lot to lock up!"

She disappeared up the stairway, and left him standing in the dark. Bart slid the heavy bar in place, felt for the waxen taper he knew resided in a sconce by the front door, removed a pack of matches from his breast pocket, lit the taper, and slowly mounted the stairs.

"It's Sunday," Barbara Jo said sternly to Maggie, as she poured herself a second cup of tea. They were seated in the kitchen of *The Sparrow*.

"When have you *ever* been out? To a party, or *anything*? Not since Liza Mae and Benjamin Noah's wedding. Which was weeks ago, for heaven's sakes. And the reception was held *here*. Which really doesn't count at all. You never do anything but work."

"Oh, Barbs, how you do go on!"

"And it *is* Sunday afternoon. And the restaurant's closed."

"You said that, already. You're repeating yourself," Maggie smiled sweetly at her sister, whom—she still felt it hard to believe—she now admired and loved dearly.

"And look!" Barbara Jo brought out from beneath the kitchen table a large package, which she had obviously been hiding.

"What is it?" Maggie asked, cocking her head to the side, her blue eyes narrowing suspiciously.

"Well, go on, silly." Barbara Jo laughed nervously. "Open it."

"It's...lovely! Where on earth would I ever find any occasion—in Rhyersville—to wear *this*?" The dress was a stunning creation, in blue silk.

"This particular party is not in Rhyersville. We have an exclusive invitation to a party...a piece out of town."

"Barbara Jo, what is going on here? You've been acting like the—"

"Nothing is going on, Maggs. I just am bound and determined—to get you out of this place—for just one night. Look at all I've done for you! Can you deny me this *one* little favor? Fred's busy tonight. And I can't *possibly* go alone. I need you, Maggs! Tell me you won't let me down!"

"Oh, all right!" Maggie sighed, rising to remove the scraps of their lunch, and clean up the kitchen.

"Here, I'll do that," Barbara Jo rose and bustled excitedly about. "You go on up, and get dressed. We'll leave as soon as you get down."

"Why so early?" Maggie stared at her,

"It is...a way...out of town, Maggs. Go on, now, and don't ask so many questions. No wonder Nellie Sue threw her new shoe at you."

"You knew about that?"

"Of course, I knew, the same as Papa did."

Maggie went up the stairs, holding the new dress, recalling how concerned Papa was—that one of his girls would so carelessly risk the loss of a new shoe, with postwar prices through the roof.

"How much farther is it?" Maggie asked tiredly, "We've been on the road for hours! Where, exactly, is this place? This duster is getting hot."

Barbara Jo, keeping the horse at a steady gallop, humming a little tune, refused to answer.

Maggie thought she must have dozed off. She awoke to find the carriage still traveling steadily towards the east.

"Barbara Jo McKinnon Moss, this looks like the road...the road we took...that day we went *blackberry picking*...and came back with empty buckets."

The carriage topped a little rise. The road leveled out. Sure enough, there stood the grand house they called *Cottonwood*. Maggie stared at the big house in open amazement. How well she recalled the day they had walked over here.

The sun had begun to descend behind the mountains. Every window of the big house was ablaze with candlelight. There was not one single weed in the yard.

"Oh, my! Isn't it lovely!" Maggie whispered. "I thought this place would have rotted down—years ago. I heard that Mister—what's-his-name passed away. And I don't know...I never heard...whatever became of the mysterious, much talked of Hurston grandson. Oh, my! Is *he* back, Barbs?"

"I think he may be," Barbara Jo grinned at Maggie, "And I think you're about to meet him."

Barbara Jo drove her rig around the half-moon, freshly graveled drive, stopped and motioned to Maggie to get out and go to the front door. "Go on, Maggs, don't just stand there like a ninny with your mouth wide open. We're invited. They're expecting you."

"*Me?*" Maggie wagged her head, drew her new white shawl closer about her shoulders, "Aren't you coming in...with me?"

"I'll be in, a bit later. I'm just going to drive the carriage around back. I'll see you inside. Now, go on in!"

Maggie gazed after Barbara Jo, as her sister's fine rig disappeared around the corner of the grand house. Then, heaving a sigh, she walked slowly toward the front door.

Maggie reached for the knocker. To her great surprise, the huge door swung wide at her touch.

"Hello? Anyone?" Maggie called softly.

Then a bit louder, "Anyone here?"

There was no reply.

"That's odd," Maggie murmured to herself, a feeling of foreboding, something like a cold chill, creeping up her spine. Was this place still *haunted*?

With great trepidation, Maggie stepped inside, removed her shawl, and draped it over one arm.

The first thing that caught her eye, as her gaze swept from the entrance into the main downstairs parlor—

—The huge organ! *Her lovely pipe organ—!*

Maggie glanced anxiously around. Then slowly, very slowly, she moved toward the grand instrument. Oh, how lovely it looked! Still as fine as the day she first saw it—sitting on that low platform at the Mountain Fair.

Scarcely aware of what she was doing, Maggie reached for the round padded stool, ran the ornately carved seat up a wind or two, slid onto the stool—and placed her fingers on the chord of 'C'. Then one by one, she pulled out the stops.

Her feet firmly on the pedals, she began to play.

The chords to one of her favorite tunes swelled from the organ, and rose up the grand staircase, and to the second floor. How often she had heard Papa playing it on his fiddle. Then the fiddle aside, singing in his sweet, fine baritone.

> *I was seeing Nellie home*
> *I was seeing Nellie home*
> *And t'was from Aunt Diana's*
> *Quilting Party*
> *I was seeing Nellie home...*

Maggie heard a soft clapping.

She leapt up from the bench, and turned.

There stood—

"Bartram Logan—?"

!!!!!!!!!!!!!!!!!

"Oh!" Maggie gasped at him, stepping quickly away from the lovely organ. "I'm…sorry. I called…but no one answered…"

The initial shock passed. Maggie stepped toward him and demanded:

"Mr. Logan! What on *earth* are *you* doing here?"

"Me?" William Bartram Logan smiled at her, so innocently.

"I don't see anyone else in the room!"

"Well, for your information, Mrs. Evans, I *own* the place."

"But the heir was supposed to be Mr. *Hurston's*…his grandson."

"My mother was Eleanor *Hurston* Logan, William Bartram Hurston's *daughter.* But, that's a long story." Bart took Maggie by the arm, steering her away from the organ, and into the grand parlor.

"Why don't we, Mrs. Evans, seat ourselves?"

"I really don't…know…that I should," Maggie deferred, refusing to take the chair he so graciously offered. She felt confused, angry.

"I fail to see why I am here. I think I have been brought here…under false pretenses. I have obviously been horribly deceived—"

"False pretenses? Mrs. Margaret Ann McKinnon Evans? *Horribly deceived? Widows? And orphans?"*

"I...I..."

"Please, sit down. Maybe I should get you a glass of water."

Bart Logan disappeared in the direction of what Maggie could only conclude was the kitchen. In a few scant moments, he was back, holding out to her a lovely tray, with beautifully carved vines trailing along its fine maple planes.

Maggie stared at him. She reached out, lifted the glass of water, and ran a finger over the smooth planes of the maple tray.

"This…" she murmured, the glass of water beginning to tremble in her hand—

"This…is from the cupboard…in the kitchen—"

"At McKinnon Valley?" Bart smiled.

"It's Grandpa Thomas's tray! The one he carved by hand—!"

"—Upon which you served punch to all the ladies of the quilting bee, the day the raven broke up the party? The one you overlooked, when packing, and left behind when you made that dreadful move, south?" Bartram Logan was saying.

"How did *you* know any of *that*? How did *you* get this? *Where*…did you get this?"

"*That* is a long story, Mrs. Margaret Ann McKinnon Evans. But for now, let's set the lovely tray of your Grandfather's aside, and let us repair to the dining room. I think I just received the signal. That dinner is about to be served."

Bart reached for Maggie, and guided her firmly by the arm.

When they reached the high arch leading into the vast dining room, Maggie pulled up with a start.

"*Johnny!*"

"Yes," Bartram Logan smiled at her, as if this were the most ordinary day of the year. "We did have our violin lesson this afternoon, remember?"

"Well, yes. But—"

"Please do be seated. So that we gentlemen can take our chairs."

Maggie slid into the mahogany chair he was holding for her.

John Thomas McKinnon, Jr. was beaming from ear to ear.

Even *Johnny* was in on this—*whatever* it was!

Then Liza Mae came out of what Maggie knew was the kitchen door. She was bearing a huge platter, laden with little roast fowl of some sort. It smelled delicious, and Maggie suddenly realized that she was hungry.

Well, Margaret Ann, she smiled to herself. Let's just play this little game out to its conclusion—and see where it takes us—

"More buttered vegetables, Mrs. Evans?"

"Thank you, you are *too* kind, Mr. Logan. Could I have another of the delicious buttered scones?"

"Most certainly," William Bartram Logan smiled and gave a slight bow in her direction. Never, Maggie thought, had she seen him like this. So relaxed. So handsome. So charming.

"Did you have a pleasant drive out, Mrs. Evans?"

"Oh yes," Maggie smiled at him sweetly, "Encountered no difficulty at all. Came right to the place—

"—But, then, as you, no doubt, know, Mr. Logan, I've been here before."

"Oh, yes. So I've been told."

"Yes, well," Maggie smiled right back at him, her blue eyes shining. "And just who, Mr. Logan, told you?"

"Let's just say—a little *sparrow*?"

"Would that *sparrow* have a name?"

"I never divulge my confidential sources. Bad. Very bad, for business."

"Is that what *this* is, then, Mr. Logan? Business?"

"Oh, no, of course not. I'm afraid I did misspeak, in this instance. This is not at all...not at all...your...usual...business."

"Then why don't we just get right down to the point, Mr. Logan. And suppose you go ahead and tell me. Just what kind of business *is* this, that's so—*unusual*."

"Let us just say...it's a few old friends, getting together. For fine food, and good conversation...to...shall we say, clear the air.

"We are friends, aren't we, Johnny," Bart winked at the small boy sitting to his right.

"We sure are, Bart!" Johnny beamed to one and all.

"*Bart*?" Maggie's brows shot up, as she frowned at her small brother.

"Sure, Maggie," Johnny announced with a broad grin. "That's what Bart said I should call him, now that—"

"Now that—what?" Maggie asked.

"Why don't we have dessert?" Bart smiled. And dessert immediately appeared.

"I suppose you know...everything else...*everything*...about me..."

Maggie fixed William Bartram Logan with narrow, accusing eyes.

"I certainly hope I do," Bart said, almost wearily. "I hope you haven't...that is to say...I hope that from here on out, your life will be a happier one. And I'd like to be a part of that. I'd, in fact, *love* to make it just that...a happy life...for you...and for John Thomas McKinnon, Jr."

He said then, very calmly, very matter-of-factly, while he was serving up dessert. Not even looking at her.

"I love you, Margaret Ann McKinnon. I think I have since that first day you broke into my hiring line. And I would be very much obliged if you would do me the honor of becoming my wife."

Maggie dropped her silver fork with a clatter. She felt as if she was going to choke.

What was he saying?

This was impossible!

She thought of rising from the table, and fleeing from the room, but felt that something—some powerful force beyond her control—was holding her here, bound to this rich chair, in this fine mansion. Listening to this handsome, charming man. She was being drawn into something—from which she knew it would soon be impossible to extricate herself—

He bent close, setting the small plate of dessert before her. Maggie couldn't even tell what it was through the tears in her eyes. Her heart was pounding. Suddenly the whole of her life seemed to be crowding in upon her.

But Johnny sat smiling at her, as if he thought it was Christmas morning.

And Liza Mae and Benjamin Noah had just poked their heads through the kitchen door, apparently to see how things were progressing.

They had all *plotted*! They had all *ganged up* on her! *She didn't have a chance*!

Then Johnny jumped up from the table, his dessert untouched, ran from the room, and in a moment, he returned—with Papa's fiddle firmly tucked beneath his little chin.

Slowly, beautifully, John Thomas McKinnon, Jr. began to play.

William Bartram Logan was bending over Maggie, slipping a ring—it looked to be a huge diamond, set in rich gold—onto her left hand.

Then he was pulling her gently from the mahogany chair. He drew her close, her head tucked beneath his chin, the way Papa used to do with Mama.

Then to the lovely music Johnny was playing, he was whirling her around the room.

He was whispering in her ear:

"Know what I'm giving you, for a wedding gift?"

Stunned, she raised her head—and looked into his eyes.

He tucked her head back, firmly beneath his chin.

"*McKinnon Valley*," he whispered.

Then, William Bartram Logan began to sing, in tune with Johnny's playing. Maggie had never heard the man sing. He had a fine baritone. Maggie closed her eyes, and listened:

> *If a body meet a body*
> *Comin' thru th' rye*
> *If a body kiss a body*
> *Need a body cry*
> *Ev'ry lassie has her laddie*
> *Nane a one ha' I*
> *Yet a' th' lads they smile at me*
> *When comin' thru th' rye........*